A STRANGE NEW LAND

DECREE

A STRANGE NEW LAND | DECREE
Aishah Alam

STRANGE INC. PUBLISHING HOUSE, NEW YORK

STRANGE INC. PUBLISHING HOUSE,
NEW YORK

This is a work of fiction. Names, characters, businesses, organizations, places, events, and incidents are either the products of the author's imagination or used in a fictitious manner. Any resemblance to actual persons, living or dead, or actual events is purely coincidental.

Library of Congress Control Number: 2025910941
ISBN (Hardback): 979-8-9888848-6-6
ISBN (Paperback): 979-8-9888848-7-3
ISBN (E-Book): 979-8-9888848-8-0

Published by Strange Inc., a nonprofit publishing house based in New York. Our mission is to elevate the authentic voices of Muslim women.

Email: hello@strangeincorporated.org
Website: www.strangeincorporated.org
Phone: +1 (347) 560-8334

Disclaimer:

The views and interpretations of Islamic teachings shared in this work are those of the author within a fictional context. Strange Inc. adheres to the widely accepted traditional, orthodox doctrine of Ahlus Sunna.

Author's Note

The world you're about to step into with A Strange New Land is one of speculative fiction, a realm born entirely from imagination. While its spiritual and philosophical heart beats with Islamic teachings, I want to emphasize that this is purely a work of fiction. Concepts related to the unseen, particularly concerning "the Voice," are speculative and represent my creative interpretation within this narrative.

I chose to integrate Islamic teachings because this faith, which has profoundly influenced me, offers a rich tradition often unexplored in speculative fiction. Many works in this genre build on concepts like magic or multiple deities, but Islam provides an equally compelling framework for exploring universal themes such as faith, divine justice, fate, human struggle, and redemption.

Please be advised that this novel contains mentions of child abuse that some readers may find disturbing. Finally, a crucial disclaimer: this book, while exploring Islamic themes and drawing inspiration from challenging real-world contexts, does not reflect upon real followers of Islam. Please approach it as a work of fiction.

For Our Children

The wound is the place

where light enters you

- RUMI

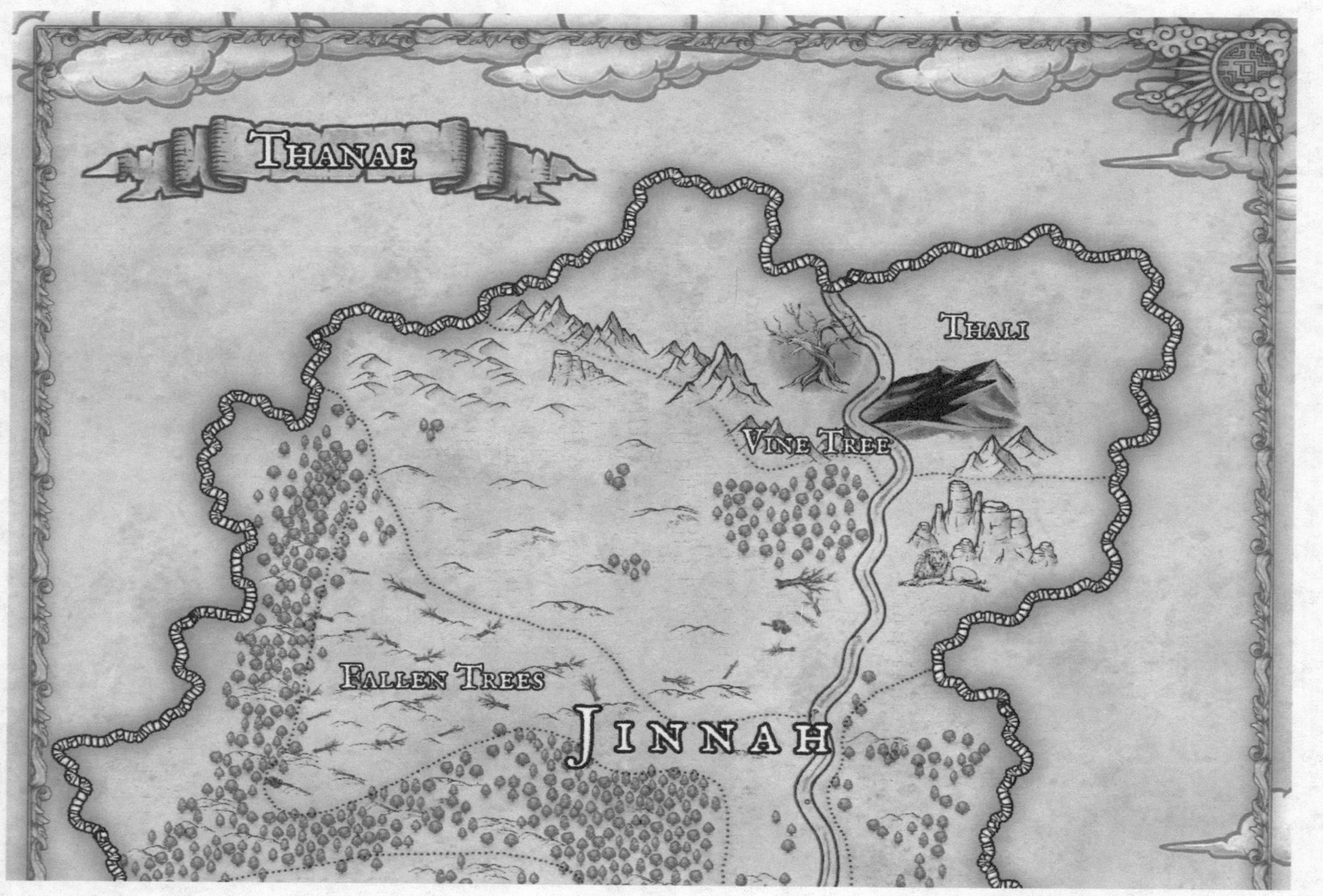

THANAE
THALI
VINE TREE
FALLEN TREES
JINNAH

Orbee Forest
Shahwah
Garden of Fire
The Golden Dome
The Silver Path
Zam
The Great Wall

Contents

PART 1

The Opening

ME

The *Pen*, they say, was the first thing. Before the Heavens, before Earth, before all creation. It was commanded to write, to etch every moment, every breath, every beat of every heart into a tablet preserved for all of time. The past, the present, the future—all aligned, preordained, locked away in the celestial archives.

Our story, Your story, *and* mine were all written and predetermined in this very tablet called The Book of Decree.

Another series of lines existed within this book. Alternatives. Possibilities. All counterpoints to the immutable destiny. These new lines detailed all the things that didn't happen, all the paths that were not taken, all the lives that were unlived, all the events that never were but could have been.

To me, these were a hint, a faint echo, that what if, just what if … some things *could* be changed.

Upon learning this, a yearning has taken place within me, one which, at first, I could ignore enough to fulfill my duties. But then it morphed into a compulsion, an obsession, a necessity.

I need to access The Book of Decree.

I need to make a difference.

A true, everlasting difference, a world where falls become rises, where those regarded as villains in the stories become heroes, where the weak are no longer chained.

I need You to help me make my difference.

The Night of Decree, whereby the pages of the future lay open to influence, is almost upon us. This is why I have awoken You from Your frozen sleep today. It has been nine years, five days, and twenty-three hours. Nine years, five days, and twenty-three hours since I last saw Your face. Nine years, five days, and twenty-three hours since I smelt Your clay.

Now, You stand just a few meters away, separated from me by nothing more than a wall. Of course, this wall is fundamental to *our* story, but still, it severs You from me, like a limb from a body. Unnatural. Agonizing. Nevertheless, it is in our nature to be together. It was *decreed*. I am bound to You.

I look longingly at this desolate place, a place that once throbbed with life, with the sound of Your laughter, the warmth of Your body. Now, it—both You and this place—are a hollow shell. A mausoleum of memories locked away for preservation and mourning.

I have always been disgusted by how close Jinnah is to my place of sanctuary. Too close. The teeming life a slap on my face as if gloating over all the things I never had. The trees, dancing back and forth as if throwing punches at me for not being able to enter. The sound of the Zam trickling violently as if washing away any of my influence.

That place, Jinnah, mocks me.

But the wind that blows through Thanae carries up to the Golden Dome, through Jinnah. It carries my voice. Today, I have directed it towards the child; she who You will come to know as the Girl.

Here she is—the Girl—she pops her head out from a tree trunk, one big enough to swallow three men whole. Her hair dances around her face like threads of a nightmare. She wipes a bead of sweat from her forehead, matting more hair to her pointy cheeks.

The air crackles with anticipation, thick with heat mixed with the scent of damp earth and smoke. The Girl's eyes are wide and wary. Corners are creased with a sadness too old for her face, holding the haunted wisdom of someone far older than her years.

The Girl is perfect for You.

She stands there, her fingers clutching the thick bark of the tree of Jinnah, her other arm hugging something to her chest. Her mouth mirrors the slump of her shoulders, her back hunched as she searches for the origin of my call. Leaning forward, I watch her from my dark.

Tightening her grip on the tree, her eyes dart around like an insect ready to hide or strike. Releasing her hands from the bark, the Girl tiptoes clumsily, her steps a strange blend of grace and awkwardness as she steps out of Jinnah.

On the Silver Path, she halts. The path, a sinuous serpent of fractured glass, goes downward, leading into the mouth of the city of Shahwah. The path also winds its way up through the heart of Jinnah, a shimmering scar that leads and ends at the steps to the Golden Dome, a beacon of gold perched on a distant hill.

Even here, in the heart of Shahwah, the path remains a remnant of its former glory, the broken fragments reflecting the dying light of the sun which no longer shines upon this part of Thanae. A land of layers. Of buried secrets. Of broken ceilings. Home … for now.

I scowl as the Girl mutters *that* word under her breath while moistening her lips. A flicker in her eyes, a widening—an ever so subtle tremor in her tiny frame. Swiftly, she lowers the object against her chest and cradles it in her palms. She holds her breath until she gently places the item back into Jinnah.

She turns towards me. Though she cannot see me, I instinctively duck, falling into my *Ghar*, my place of residence.

She mirrors my duck unknowingly and slumps on the Silver Path. Leaning over the edge, where the path frays into loose and arid dirt, she digs her thin fingers into the soil, searching for something with a desperate, almost feral intensity in her movements. The Girl pulls out a writhing creature, its tiny legs scrambling frantically, and clasps it between her index finger and thumb. As she draws it closer to her eyes, a single tear escapes, tracing a track down her dust-streaked cheek.

"I'm sorry," she whispers to the creature.

Then, with a satisfying crunch, she devours the insect whole.

Is she good? How does she love? How does she hate? *What* does she love? *What* does she hate? Whatever she held close to her chest, having cradled it like life itself, will expose what I need to know.

I hop out of my Ghar and scutter past her. She turns swiftly, shivering at my passing, her eyes darting beyond me. She cannot see me. But she can sense me.

My face burns as I see *it*. It burns, not from the anger nor from the pain that it still exists, but from my ignorance of that existence. I burn from hope, a glistening, everlasting hope, for the future *because* of it.

As if I can … just … grasp … it.

The Book still exists.

It lies open before me. Its pages are skeletal, some missing, others torn, yet the words—those ancient glyphs sent through an angel to a man—remain unchanged. My meticulously crafted plan, like a fragile spiderweb, must now unravel.

Let me take a pause and clarify, this is *not* The Book of Decree—the one which will help me make my difference—no, it is not that.

This is the Book—just inches from my grasp—my way of attaining that precious tool: The Book of Decree.

Your assistance, though invaluable, pales in comparison to the allure of the Book. It *calls* to me. Its power … is undeniable.

I charge towards Jinnah, slamming into an invisible barrier. The sudden impact jolts me back to the entrance of my Ghar.

I dive into the darkness in here, one that is more whole and nurturing than the darkness out there, in the open. My Ghar engulfs me, a welcome embrace.

The Girl follows the sound of my flight and spins towards me.

"Peace?" she says in a whisper, her eyes scanning the area as a remnant of the six-legged creature rests between her teeth.

"Pain,"—I say, while steadying myself in my black hole— "is resistance to suffering."

"That doesn't sound right," the Girl says.

"You cause pain," I retort.

"Don't let them suffer." She gulps the remnants of the insect and straightens her shoulders. "Why can't I see you?"

"Where did you find the Book?" I ask her.

She shifts her body in front of it, so I can no longer see it.

"Why do you sound like that?" she asks, her voice muffled as she wipes the exoskeleton from around her mouth.

"Like what?" I ask.

"Like you can't breathe."

"What do you know about breathing?"

"Everything breathes." The Girl looks at the small pulsating light of the orbees which hover over the Book.

I clear my throat. "Live or breathe?"

"What's the difference?"

"You must be human to breathe, but everything lives."

"That isn't true," she says, waving her hand to an orbee that flutters to her and rests on her shoulder.

"Do you want to play a game?" I ask.

"I should go." She looks over her shoulder towards the place she came from and bites her trembling lip.

"Let's play."

"Why?" She turns back towards me and tilts her head. To another, this may seem like a gesture of childlike curiosity. All I see is how pathetically weak she is with her pulsating jugular vein on full show.

I hide my contempt. "All children like to play games."

"They do?" She shifts around slightly to try to see me again, unsuccessfully.

"Why didn't you say 'yes' to me?" I ask. "To the game?"

"You said you must be human to breathe," she says. "That isn't true."

"I was … mistaken."

"Mistaken?" She turns towards me fully.

"Don't we all make mistakes?"

"I suppose."

"Don't we all need forgiving?"

"Well …"

"Can you forgive me?"

"I-I," she stutters.

I take advantage of the moment. "Wonderful. Now let's play."

"Play?"

The Girl is simple and cannot catch up with the pace of *our* story. Simple is safe. Loves living things. Hates eating them. Good. Very good.

"How do you play?" she asks, interrupting my thoughts.

"I ask. You answer."

"No," she says, picking her teeth.

"Why?"

"I'll play if you let me ask, too."

"I'll go f—"

She interrupts. "Why is it grey?"

"Why is what grey? I ask.

"Why is it grey behind your cave?" She stands brushing the dust off her ragged dress, staring at the heavy smoke that covers my city.

"Most of Thanae is grey."

"But there," she points towards my city and says, "it's greyer."

"No, it's not. It's greyer in Thalj. This isn't a city of ice like Thalj; it is a city of heat. It is Shahwah," I say.

"Thalj isn't greyer, it's more …" She trails off, then asks, "What does Sh-Shahwah mean?"

"My turn," I begin, "Where is the rest of the Book?"

"Book?"

"The one those pages belong to."

"What do you know about its pages?" she asks, taking a step back towards the Book.

I let out a sharp sigh, quiet enough so she doesn't hear it. *Too soon. I asked her too soon.*

"The pages look like they belong to a book, they're all torn, and I thought—" What shall I tell her I thought? "I thought it looked interesting and wanted to touch it. Can I?"

The Girl jumps at the pounding of the Great Wall.

"Peace!" A voice, muffled, calls out from the other side.

You have arrived.

YOU

There is a wall. My face reflects, but I avert my gaze. It is dark, but I still see. I note the details of the wall: metal and dominating, but more importantly, a distraction from my reflection.

I love the dark. I can see clearly in the dark. I can see more clearly in the dark than in the light. I can choose what to focus on in the dark.

I must be a contradiction, because my eyes, these betraying assessors, are drawn back to my face—distorted and scarred, a gash from forehead to chin—even though I keep choosing to be distracted from it. Yet. The very reason I love the dark is because of its elimination of distractions.

A wry laugh as I stop fighting my reflection. I allow my eyes to land on my face. A failed attempt at reconstruction, flesh that remembers what was taken, even though my mind is empty of the memory that caused it.

My hand trembles slightly, brushing across my cheek, a reflexive gesture, a habit perhaps? The skin beneath my fingers, however, feels anything but natural. Rough like sandpaper. Leathery and cold.

Incomplete.

The world tilts, it's dizzying. My stomach is a traitor like my eyes have exposed themselves to be. It heaves. I try to suppress it, to force the bile back down, but I can't. The taste of sickness surges upwards. Bitter. It splashes across the soft, earth, scarring it just as viciously as my face had been scarred.

Not a good day.

What day is it? What night is it? I desperately cling to these meaningless thoughts, anything to … distract myself from the overwhelming stench of my vomit. A musty, sour odor. I feel sick again. As I scramble backward, trying to avoid the mess, my foot slips on the slick, viscous fluid.

I groan. A pathetic whimper in the vast emptiness. I frantically rub my hands in the sand, the coarse grains serving as a meager comfort.

Feeling a little more grounded from my purge, I turn my back towards the wall, finally acknowledging my surroundings.

Desolate.

Endless.

Dunes, their shadows dancing and contorting in the almost nonexistent light. A cold tremor grips me, even though it is hot. So stiflingly hot. I shiver again, even though it is hot.

I pull my dress tighter around myself, the fabric clammy against my skin. It's wet. Why is it wet? The air is thick with a suffocating humidity, along with the heat.

"Peace?" A small voice whispers from behind the wall, the sound muffled as if passing through layers of thick cloth.

I jolt upright, my heart hammering against my ribs.

"Peace!" the young voice repeats, firmer this time.

"Peace," I manage to croak, my voice hoarse and trembling.

"Are you cold?"

There's a warmth in the voice. It makes my skin crawl. I don't trust whoever is speaking.

"C-cold?" I manage to say.

"It's hot out here today, well everyday actually," the voice observes nonchalantly, stating the obvious.

Even if I don't trust them, the thought of staying out here, alone with myself, a reminder of being nothing without my memories, being surrounded by nothing, with only this wall to keep me company, is worse. Its too quiet. I don't want to hear my ragged breaths. I need to get inside.

"Let me in," I plead, my voice rising slightly.

"You're not one of *them*, are you?" the young voice asks in a hushed whisper.

"Who?"

"Cast"

"What Cast?"

"They come some nights, picking at the wall."

"Are they good or bad?" I ask.

"I don't know … they're just odd," they reply.

"Odd?" I ask.

"And not the good kind of *odd*."

"Did they hurt you?"

"Well, they hurt each other—a lot! I can hear them fighting all night sometimes, that can't be a good thing, can it?"

"Isn't it night now?" I ask.

"No."

"Why is it so dark?"

"The smoke."

I look towards the skies. A layer of grey. The sun has vanished, eclipsed by this shroud, leaving the world in an unnatural twilight.

"How do you know it's day?" I ask.

"You can see the shape of things, like your hands," they reply.

I hold my hands out in front of me. There is a calloused roughness to them, with one finger missing a nail. The remaining nails are short, and … clean. As if they have been cared for. I shake off another shiver.

"These people—the Cast … who are they?" I sweep my gaze across the wall, its surface stretching so far that it disappears somewhere ahead. There is no break in the monotony, no door, no window, no hint of an edge. There are also no holes that I can peek through. Is this person behind the wall tricking me?

"I suppose you'd know if you're one of them," they say.

"Is any of this real?" I ask.

"Any of what?" they ask.

"Am I awake?"

"I hope so. I'm not very good at being awake, which means I would be much worse in a dream."

What an unusual thing to say. "What do you mean by that?" I ask.

"I'm not much good at anything," they say, with a timid acceptance. "Except games, I suppose. I can ask good questions."

"Is this a game?" As I say this, I take a hesitant step back from the wall.

"I'm sick of games," they reply, their voice fluctuating wildly, first loud, now barely a whisper.

I strain my eyes against the dizzying sensation of the world tilting on its axis. I'm certain now that the spinning is in my head, which feels even worse, because I don't know how to stop it. "Your voice, it gets loud and then quiet."

"It does?" they ask, with a mischievous lilt. "What about now?"

"Now you're loud," I say, blinking rapidly, trying to pinpoint the source of this voice.

"Why are you here?" they ask, their voice suddenly sounding closer as if they have leaned against the wall.

"Why are *you* here?" I counter.

Ignoring my question, they drop their voice into a conspiratorial whisper and ask, "What is it like behind the Great Wall?"

"Am I behind the wall, or are you?" I ask.

"This is my home," they say, their voice now a low murmur.

"Home?"

"I live past Silver Path and Jinnah in Golden Dome." They sigh. "With my Mama."

Two things stand out to me: this person's direct way of speaking, using only the title of the places, which feels almost primitive in its simplicity. Additionally, the way they call their mother: 'my Mama', as if she is the focus of the person's affection.

My survival mind asks another question: Why would they tell me all that information? Perhaps they aren't untrustworthy, just … naïve?

"Don't be foolish," I reply, in a tone sharper than I intended.

"Okay," they reply, their voice so quiet that it startles me.

Their simple acceptance of my cruel words hangs heavy in the air. It's unsettling. I clear my throat, the sound raspy and uncomfortable. "I need something strong."

"Like what?" they ask.

"A tree branch?"

"No."

"There are no trees?"

"There are."

"Okay, get me——" I begin.

They interrupt. "No."

"The bark."

"No."

"Why not?" The question explodes from my lips. My face burns, a tide of heat rising from my neck, mixing with the thick scorching air. My armpits feel wet, and not because of my wet dress.

"I won't hurt the tree," they say.

"No one is that ..." I exhale sharply, the air escaping me in a ragged sigh.

"That what?"

"Unless ..." I squint at the wall, trying to peer unsuccessfully past it. "How old are you?"

"I'm this old," they reply, knocking on the part of the wall that is just below my chest.

"A child." My shoulders slump. How can a child help me?

"Yes, child or Girl. That's what my Mama calls me."

"Girl?" An unexpected relief washes over me, the tension that has been gripping me suddenly releasing. I shake off the confusing relief, refocusing on the task at hand.

"I need to get in," I say, my voice firm.

"Why?" the Girl asks.

"I ..." I scrunch my nose at the acrid smell of my sickness.

"What's your name?" she asks.

"My name?" I sniff my hands, the smell making me want to retch again.

What is my name?

I stagger slightly, my head pounding, a dull ache throbbing behind my eyes. To steady myself, I touch the wall, seeking a point of contact, a much-needed grounding force. My hand meets the wall, and a cold, viscous film clings to my fingers, slick and repulsive. It feels like ... ooze, a living substance that slithers beneath my touch. Then there is a strange resistance, a pulsating pressure that pushes back against me, as if the wall itself is breathing, a monstrous entity struggling against my intrusion.

I gasp.

"What is your name?" the Girl asks again. Her voice rises to a high-pitched squeal, a sound that grates on my raw nerves.

"The wall ... just moved." I manage to say, my voice trembling. I smear the ooze from my hands onto my dress.

"It did?" Her voice sounds closer now. "Maybe it's alive."

"Alive?" I echo, the absurdity of the statement, momentarily distracting me from the pounding inside my head.

She asks softly, "Where did you come from?"

"Somewhere wet." I press my hands against my chest, trying to stop the frantic beating of my heart—a rhythm that mirrors the unsettling pulse of the wall. "When you touch the wall, does anything happen?"

"Like what?"

"Does it ... react to you?"

"React?" she asks.

She would know if it happened to her. This means, the wall only reacted to me. *Why?*

She continues, "Are you sure you're in the right place?"

"How do you know you're wrong?" I shuffle my shoulders, the rough and wet fabric of my dress scraping against my skin.

The sweat under my arms trickles down my torso. "I mean, how do you know you're in the wrong place?"

She gasps, a sharp, startled sound. "Oh!"

"What is it?" I lean forward, not daring to touch the strange wall again.

"There's a statue with a torch and …" Her voice is muffled, as if she's speaking with her mouth pressed directly against the cold metal of the wall. She then blurts out, "It looks strong!"

"Bring it!" I urge.

A sigh from behind the wall. "No."

"Why?"

"I don't like the grey."

"It's *all* grey."

"Not like there, it's more. It's the only place that rains dust. Except maybe Thalj, I'm not quite sure what—" She stops midsentence.

Three sharp bangs echo through the air. A message is in those bangs. A message I know the meaning of.

"Come home," I whisper.

The Girl lowers her voice, her words muffled by the wall. "My Mama's calling me. Peace!"

"Wait!" I shout after her, my voice echoing through the space. "Don't leave!"

I hesitate, my hand hovering over the cold, unforgiving surface of the wall. I pound on it with three forceful clangs that echo through the silence.

There is a reaction, not a sudden shift or a tremor, but a more subtle response. It's as if the wall itself is listening. As if it had anticipated my action. A long, thin line appears about the size of my palm, a clean break in the otherwise seamless surface, like a fresh wound or … like lips. The shape splits open, a sickeningly *squishy* sound accompanying the fissure.

It takes me a moment to realize; the opening is pointless. I don't have a key.

ME

The Girl has returned, as I knew she would. Bolder tonight, she strides past the trees bordering Jinnah. She plods along the Silver Path, crossing the arid ground and the long, ominous shadow of the towering Great Wall, into the space before my city of Shahwah.

I observe her with a small smile as she falls with a thump on the Silver Path. She wipes her cheeks and pushes her body up, only to fall again.

Children are blank canvases. There is so much to fill them with.

This girl is different from other children. Yes, she still has much to be filled with, but there is something else about her which intrigues me. It is in the way she looks around. Always ready. Always looking, even when there is nothing there.

"What happened?" I ask in a concerned voice.

An orbee hovers over her head, and the key to the Great Wall hangs around her neck. I gave the key to Worshipper—the one the Girl refers to as 'my Mama'—as soon as I knew how to bring my plan to life. This key is different from the familiar flat blade, and rounded bow. It is elongated and fleshy, almost like a tongue.

"Why do you care?" she asks.

The Girl's eyes are swollen, and her cheeks are wet. She rises unsteadily, her trembling leg a stark contrast to her defiant posture.

I tell her the truth, "I care if you are good."

She sniffles and absentmindedly tightens her grip around the key. As her fingers brush over it, there is a slick sucking sound.

She turns towards the Great Wall and says, "I'm leaving."

"Why?"

"I want to."

"Where?" I ask.

"Far away."

"I can help you."

"Leave me alone!" she snaps.

Heat floods my face as she turns her back towards me. I need the Book.

I take the heat from my anger and raise my head to the sky. I extend my body, feeling the tension. I didn't want to do this, yet. I want her to go to You. I want it to be simple. I want her to bring You to me.

But I want the Book more. I weave my threads, straightening them and bending them as I create their message.

Four words: *give me the Book.*

The words hover around me as I prepare to hurl them at her with all my might, each strand, a soft echo in the air, ready to encompass her: *Give—*

"Stop," she says, raising her palm before the first thread reaches her.

Stop?

She sniffs and wipes her face with a long sleeve. "You can't change my mind," she says, taking a deep breath. "I'm leaving and that's that!"

She marches to the Great Wall, an orbee floating to her shoulder. She sticks the key in the hole. After a pull, a powerful *creak* fills the air.

The door of the Great Wall is open.

YOU

Agirl whose height barely reaches my chest bursts through the door. Her thin frame is almost swallowed by her long, flowing dress, and she moves with an awkward gait, a mix of tiptoeing and stomping.

My dress, finally dry, seems a small victory. A temporary one, I know, as my sweat will soon soak it through again. I glance back at the Girl.

What kind of fighter is she? She might, perhaps, manage a slingshot if she could aim. But then, she's just fallen, a clumsy sprawl on the ground.

As she pushes herself up with a huff of effort, I decide, no, not a fighter. Too much awkwardness, too much stumble.

Hiding, then? Could she manage that? She moves quickly with a sudden burst of speed. Perhaps that is how she fights best: hiding and running—if it comes to life or death, of course.

A flickering ball of light clings to her shoulder, a glow against the shadows. It illuminates her hair, a contradiction—waist-length, smooth, like a sharpened blade, utterly untangled—the opposite is true of her dress, a tattered wreck. Holes everywhere, hanging like a sack, the ragged hem barely brushing her feet.

She continues to walk as if I am not here, and I feel my face grow hot. It cools as I notice the vomit—my vomit—which she is about to walk into. That will force her to look at me.

Somehow, she avoids stepping on it. She pauses as she passes it and sniffs the air with a scrunched nose. Sniffing the air again, she looks around until her eyes rest on my feet. I curl them under my jagged bottomed dress, and she shrugs, her movement jerky. She scratches her chest and spins away from me again.

"Where are you going?" I ask her.

"Far away," she says, stomping ahead.

"It's too dark to go in the desert alone."

As I say the word "dark", her shoulders flinch slightly.

I add, "What happened to you?"

She stops walking, and her shoulders slump even more as she looks to the ground. She lingers and kicks the sand. "I'd rather not talk about it.'

"Then … don't."

She faces me, her eyes tracing a path from my feet to my face. Her forehead is round like a freshly laid egg and … familiar.

Her eyes shine back from the light on her shoulder, a captivating black which isn't the absence of color but a richness that seems to absorb the light itself. Long, dark lashes fringe them as they flutter with every blink. The intensity of her gaze is disarming, but what brings me to a halt is her eyebrow—one eyebrow. Like her long forehead, her eyebrow is also familiar: thick and full, reaching over the sides of her eyes, unlike my own. One of mine sits above my right eye, while the other, above my scarred cheek, is absent.

I walk towards her; vaguely aware I have just stepped into the contents of my stomach as I stare at her.

"Your eyes are like mine," she says, with a small gasp.

Her pupils are tight, smaller than mine, accustomed, perhaps, to light. She is right. There is a similarity between our eyes in the sparse lashes and curved shape.

A sudden flash blindsides me, a fleeting memory I cannot quite grasp. I only see … "White," I murmur, the word hanging in the air.

"White?"

"Everything was white," I whisper, a sense of overwhelming emptiness washing over me. I push it aside, focusing on the color it leaves behind.

"White?" the Girl says again.

"Is there a place in there which is all white?"

"Thalj was white."

"Thalj, the snow," I interrupt. "That must be why I'm all wet." I nod to myself. "I must have come from there." I take a step towards her. "Show me."

She steps back. "I'm not going back there."

"I'll give you …" I rummage through the tattered pockets of my dress but find nothing to offer. "I can make you something," I say, opening my palms towards her.

"Why?"

"If you show me …"

"Why do you need to give me something, for me to give you something in return?"

"Why else would you help me?" I ask, feeling my brow crease.

"I didn't say I was going to help you." She sniffs the air, her nose wrinkling like a confused squirrel.

"It isn't safe to be out here," I say, my voice firm.

"Safe." She scoffs. "Everyone seems to know about being safe."

"Who is everyone?"

"Everyone lies!" Her small voice rises with a bitter anger. She turns away, refusing to meet my gaze.

"It isn't safe out here," I say again, folding my arms.

"Leave me alone." With a huff, she folds her arms and turns away, her body rigid. Her leg, planted in the sand, shakes slightly.

"Show me the trees and the statue with the torch and the … Silver Path?" I take a step towards her. "And Thalj."

"You can't change my mind." She bares her teeth like an animal and turns away, but I recognize that sound in her voice. It's a cover. She's pleading with me. I was right; she is helpless. I know that look in her eyes, which drew me in. She is broken.

"I know I can't change your mind," I say.

"You can't," she says, unfolding her arms with her back still turned towards me.

"I have an idea." I approach slowly, letting her see my palms. "Do you want to see it?"

"Never heard of seeing an idea," she mutters.

"I suppose. Well?"

"Only if its good."

My eyes narrow as I see blood dripping down her arm. I gasp, and she curls away from me.

"I didn't mean to scare you." I look at her arm. "There … there's something in your arm."

"There is?"

She looks at her arm and pulls the sharp spike with a soft, sucking sound. She does it almost surgically. I watch her face for any sign of pain, a furrowed brow, a squint of the eye, but nothing. When the spike is fully out, she dangles the delicate needle of silver in front of her eyes. Its slender form is like a small thorn whose tiny peak creates a subtle crimson glint as it catches the light. With a shrug, she tosses the bloody thing to the floor, and it lands next to my feet.

I snatch it and throw it into my pocket.

She squints, suspicion crossing her face. "What's your idea anyway?"

I look at her arm, which is still bleeding. I could help her stop the bleeding. I could use my dress to put pressure on the wound. But I don't. She hasn't given me anything yet.

"I was going to say—" I begin, then pause. How can I say this in a way she will listen?

She looks at me expectantly. After a few seconds, she says, "If you're worried that I feel pain, you don't need to."

"Worried?" I say, taken aback slightly.

"I don't feel pain." Her tone is flat.

She wiggles her good arm free and presses the sleeve against the wound, a practiced motion that sends a tremor down me like a spider crawling across my skin.

She turns to me and raises her bushy eyebrow. "Well? What's your idea?"

"Right, my idea … it's night now, isn't it?"

"Yes."

"Wait until the dawn to decide," I suggest.

"Decide what?" the Girl asks.

"Whether you stay out," I nod to the dunes and then point to the ajar door in the wall, "or in."

She kicks the sand gently with her feet, again somehow missing the sickness and then mumbles, "That's your idea?"

I wait for her to scoff.

Without meeting my gaze, she says, "Waiting for the dawn?"

"Yes."

"Why?"

"Because …" I begin, not knowing how to end. "When something bad happens to us, it's hard to think clearly. Everything feels like it doesn't make sense, like … you're not here. You're not anywhere. Nothing fits." I realize I am rambling, and take a deep breath to help me focus. "You'll think more clearly when you wake up."

"To wake up means I have to sleep," she says.

I'm not sure what she is implying, so I watch her tiny body. The atmosphere becomes more tense, and I nod. "I don't want to sleep either," I whisper, as I meet her gaze. "I'll stay awake with you."

I shift slightly away from the wall; I don't want another strange reaction from it. I lay my head on the cushion of the sand as if she has already said yes to staying, even if just for a few more hours.

She hesitates for a moment. As I had predicted, she joins me with a light thump on the ground. She sits with her legs outstretched, the sand mounding around her little ankles. Bathed with the light that sits on her shoulder, her face glows.

"What is that light?" I ask.

"An orbee," she says, not elaborating further. She turns away from me and rests her head on the sand.

The silence is bearable at first—even welcome, but as it grows, a truth reveals itself to me, making my head feel heavier. I don't want to go to the place beyond this wall. Why? What is beyond this wall that causes me to feel like the world is closing in? What is it that makes me want to run away as far as possible?

Why ...

I can't keep my ...

do I ...

eyes ...

feel ...

open.

A dreamless sleep, only an abyss of nothingness. Darkness snaps away as my eyes fly open. A harsh *clang* shatters the silence, followed immediately by another. The noise escalates, growing louder with each bang. I bolt up. The clanging is real.

The Girl's eyes are barely open as I slam my hand over her mouth. Sand sprays as I shove the bright, revealing orbee underground with my other hand. Her eyes fly open, a muffled protest.

Locking eyes with hers, I press a finger on my lips, whispering "Shh," before gesturing towards the sound.

Just a few steps away are a row of shadowy figures, their heads shrouded in hoods as they stand facing the wall. These must be the people the Girl was talking about: the Cast. *How did they not see us?*

The orbee breaks free from the ground and dangles above the Girl and me, its light growing brighter and brighter. I snatch it, shoving it back into the earth to block its gleam. The Girl's eyes snap to me, and I blink a long blink and then, a short blink. A few more times: *Hide the light.* A language of silence.

Her eyes widen, and she blinks black: *Hide.* She then turns her eyes towards the sandhills.

I shake my head and blink: *Not out there.* I nod towards the open door of the wall and turn back to her: *In there.*

We need a diversion. Once I am in there, I can lock the door so the Cast can't enter. I feel for the spike, my fingers closing around it.

She shakes her head. Fine. I turn to enter the door myself, but stop as I notice the orbee has popped up again. Too bright. A bead of sweat trickles down my temple and into my eye, momentarily blurring my vision. That light is going to betray me. I *cannot* be seen.

I spin around, ready to diminish it, my hand outstretched to squeeze it until it stops shining. Before I do, the glowing orbee floats towards the Girl's head and then disappears. I let out a soundless sigh of relief. Doesn't matter how she did it; we are safe enough for now.

I wave to get her attention, but she bolts towards the dunes, crawling like a feral animal. I look one last time at the door in the wall and then at her. Even if I can go in, I still need her to help me. I need her to show me the white place, Thalj.

Frustration surges through me, my fists are clenched so tightly my knuckles ache. I follow closely at her heels. We move silently and quickly. Once we reach the safety of the dunes, we collapse behind a sandy hill.

The figures ahead remain motionless, their backs rigid as they face the wall. A part of me wants to see if they feel a reaction from it, but they remain standing tensely, staring at it like statues.

My eyes keep drifting to the wall involuntarily, and I force myself to tear them away and focus on the figures. I give them a quick scan: Do they have weapons? One figure clutches a flaming torch, but otherwise, no visible weapons.

Some of the figures are as broad as three men stacked, others are slender like planks of wood standing upright.

Their cloaks are smooth with an emerald color, that glistens like the wall.

I can eliminate the narrow ones, but the wide ones might be a challenge. There are thirty slender ones and ten broad ones. Their vulnerabilities? The neck and armpits, like most creatures. Should I attack now? I grip the spike tightly in my pocket. Not yet.

As a massive figure swivels its head, I duck instinctively, a torrent of sand cascading over me. Sand stings my eyes, forcing me to squeeze them shut. Lying motionless, I'm surprised to find that the blood rushing to my head does not leave me feeling dizzy. Instead, it feels … exhilarating.

The wide one who has just shifted their head lets out a guttural snort. A high-pitched screech pierces the air as one of the thin ones throws its—*nuzzle?* No, not a nuzzle, a mask of some sort.

A thin rope emerges from the nose area. Each Cast member is wearing a similar mask. The only thing that sets each of the masks apart is the color of the glowing eye area on the masks; some are red, others purple, yellow, blue, and so on. But there is only one silver pair of eyes.

A thin Cast member with a red-eyed mask throws its face up towards the wide one who just snorted. There is a chorus of snorts and shrieks before the thin one shoves the wide one. The wide one's body remains planted where it is.

Then, silence.

I hold my breath, every muscle clenched, expecting the inevitable break of the absence of sound. It arrives, a barrage of snorts and screeches, a brawl erupting.

I press myself into the sand, feel the grit dig into my skin, but another sound, deeper, cuts through. A drumming, right beneath my hand, vibrating up my arm. It makes my teeth ache. I scramble back.

The sand itself is … singing.

The more I move, the more it sings. With each touch there is a different note, a high whine, a low thrum. Loud. Too loud.

The Girl, a shadow in the chaos, hovering above me further ahead behind another dune, pats the ground beside her. I squint grit from my eyes and crawl closer to her. Deeper behind the hill, the drumming grows louder like a heartbeat in the body of the dark. When I reach the area, she is in, the sand stops singing. The noise must emanate from only parts of the ground.

"A desert beast," one mutters, in a deep voice.

"Let's check," another whispers.

Both are men. I feel my shoulders tense. The Girl's fingers dig into my hand, a frantic, almost painful grip.

"You go," one suggests.

"No, you go," the other replies.

"We'll both go," they say, together. They grunt and take a few tentative steps forward, scanning their surroundings.

"Nothing," one says.

I try to pull my hand from the Girl's tight grip, but she holds on. I lock eyes with hers. She blinks a message rapidly: *Don't move!*

She then shifts her gaze to my neck. My body tenses as something cold and rough coils around my shoulders as if it is steadying its grip. A *hiss*. From the side of my eyes, I see a glint of bared teeth, a raw, exposed threat that instantly tells me this snake is dangerous.

Unlike the Girl, this threat of teeth flashing is not a cover. It's a preparation. I want to throw it off my neck, but creatures like this must be dealt with carefully. Slowly, I reach for it—but it's too late—it is in mid-pounce.

My eyes are squeezed shut, bracing for the searing pain of the snakebite. But nothing happens. Slowly, I crack open my eyelids to find a giant hand, bathed in the flickering firelight of a nearby torch. The giant hand clamps down on the snake's head, flinging it with a small *thud* into the desert.

The hand belongs to a figure hooded and cloaked. Perhaps the Cast are friends after all. I lean forward to get a better look at their face, but the mask veils it. The person who helped me is the one who wears the silver-eyed mask. *Silver-Eyes.*

The lenses glow dimly and from the nose area is a long string of silver—its width the size of a finger—which trails all the way through the open door of the wall.

Holding both palms outward, I say, "I won't hurt—"

A gasp from the Girl next to me. I follow her gaze to find a thin figure with a red-eyed mask—*Red-Eyes*—gripping the torch poised above her head, ready to strike.

I lunge, dress swirling, feet finding their place in the yielding sand. The torch swings, but I'm already there, my focus on the pressure point of *Red-Eye's* neck.

Red-Eyes crashes down, a surprisingly heavy *thud* considering how thin they are. A kick, then a blow for good measure—not enough to kill them, but enough to stop them from being an annoyance.

I turn towards the Girl who has nestled herself deeper behind the dune. A part of me hopes the others didn't hear me.

Another part feels a thrill they probably did.

Before I can meet the Girl's gaze, a flicker appears behind me. One of the wide Cast members has plucked the torch from the ground and is waving it menacingly at me as they approach slowly.

I hold my palms up in a bid for peace. "I don't want to fight."

Though I say this, that same thrill shoots through me, a primal excitement that courses through my veins, making me feel restless.

The person continues to approach, their steps heavy, digging so deeply into the sand that I can barely see their feet. Their face is also covered by the mask, the eye part purple, with the same silver string that stretches from the nose area to past the wall. *Purple-Eyes,* I think almost fondly.

I back up, intentionally away from the Girl, readying myself for another attack. I lower my hands slowly, wrapping my fingers around the spike. A natural motion, not to wield it as weaponry, but to bring me a sense of grounding so I can use my body effectively to fight.

I grip the spike so tightly that my already rough palms bleed. Even the hot wind is welcome to my sweaty skin, giving me a slight chill as I wait for their approach.

As *Purple-Eyes* comes closer, a sickly, sweet stench punches my senses, a nauseating blend of decay and perfume. The stench clings to my nostrils, a rancid odor that makes my stomach churn. It's as if a corpse has been doused in a sickly overlay of an artificial floral scent.

When *Purple-Eyes* is close enough, I glance sideways to make sure I am far enough from the Girl so she isn't harmed by what is about to happen. I'll need her later.

I shoot forward, using the cloak of *Purple-Eyes* to shroud them as their hand lashes out, throwing the torch through the air as they attempt to hit me with it. It misses me and hurls downward. I grab the torch before it hits the ground and plant it into the sand.

Lighting is everything.

I watch the play of shadow and flickering light, stepping into the dark fully whilst taking in the confused expression of the fast-approaching Cast members as they search for me.

I think I'll begin with *Purple-Eyes*. I step briefly into the edge of the torch's glint, delivering one quick blow to the neck. A startled yelp, a woman's voice. She falls.

I step back into the dark as the rest of the masked Cast stop in their approach and turn to flee. I continue to observe them calmly as I spin my crimson spike.

Should I let them go? If I do, I can see where they came from. Perhaps where *I* came from. If I don't, they might be an obstacle for me in the future. Not necessarily a danger—I don't feel threatened by them, more irritated.

I take a step towards them. I can't let them go. Should I kill them? *Silver-Eyes* turns towards me. A panicked deep grunt from behind the mask. A man. A man who helped me. I won't kill them.

But a good beating will scare them enough not to get in my way.

They are rummaging over each other towards the wall, not entering the open door, but pressing their bodies against it, making the whole scene feel bizarre. *Why are they pushing their bodies to the wall like that? As if the wall can protect them?*

With them, *Silver-Eyes* leans against the wall and dives down, immersing himself in the bodies of the Cast. The flame of the torch lengthens their shadows, which appear to be shaking.

Then I do something unexpected. I cry. I blink the tears away and raise my eyebrow as my throat becomes constricted. My chest explodes with something cold, and my lips tremble. I shake my head to push the feeling away. Sadness. Stifling. Like a rope around my body which squeezes me.

I push it down and will myself to become angry instead. Anger is a force that will help me fight better. Sadness will only weaken me.

The Cast continue to scutter towards the wall, and instinct takes over. With a swift motion, I leap forward and pull one of the figures towards me. Another startled yelp, another woman. I apply pressure to her neck and step back into the dark as she crumbles to the ground.

A sob escapes my lips as I emerge fully from the gloom and strike. I beat more of them until they fall to the ground. When I get to *Silver-Eyes*, he is already motionless on the floor. Probably fainted.

I move to the next one and the next one. Both thin and wide. With every strike, my eyes continue to water. Everything becomes a blur. I wipe them. *Why am I crying?*

Amid the fallen bodies, one figure remains kneeling in front of me, both hands raised. *Red-Eyes*, who was going to strike the Girl. I should have hit him harder. He faces me, hyperventilating and stuttering to say something. I lean in.

A high-pitched, whiny voice with a deep underlying tone asks, "What is your name? What is your mother's name? What date did you enter this world?"

Maybe I did hit him harder. He seems to have lost his mind.

"Take it." The man's hand flicks out, and he offers me something. A tiny talisman, intricately woven, dangles from a silken thread, a malevolent moon against the fading light. An eye. Pale blue, the same eye I now notice on every mask of the Cast.

Red-Eyes drops the talisman softly into my palm, the thread trailing like a spider's silk that builds its web … its home. *Could this be a clue to where I came from?*

A tremor, not of cold, but of pure dread, slides down my spine.

ME

Hidden in the shadows of a dune, I watch, the smile on my lips dissolving as the Cast member speaks to *You*. You foolishly left the torch in favor of Your own body. You always did like a challenge. I lift the torch high as You waver before striking him.

Firstly, I strike the Girl on the front part of the head—she will forget this happened—she collapses into the sand.

I am already behind You when You turn towards the sound of the Girl's surprised yelp. I strike You over the head. You will also forget this part.

You tumble to the ground with a soft *thud*.

The remaining Cast member wears the Apex, his red eyes glowing manically.

"Snout," I call to him, as he faces downward.

I lift his masked face towards me. "What have I done for you?"

"Everything," he whispers, his body rigid as if anticipating pain.

"You did well," I say, instead of hurting him.

Snout looks momentarily bewildered.

I add, "Clean all this and finish the Great Wall."

He fumbles around and straightens up his cloak; he looks even more stick-like as he prepares to gather the bodies and take them away.

ALAM

I watched Snout give You his very own Talisman his link to me, in the hopes of linking You to me. Little does Snout know just how deeply You and I are already linked.

I tie the Talisman around Your neck—a silken cord binding You even more to me—I can always use an extra influence when my voice calls upon You.

I had expected dear Snout to cower, of course. I expected him to go against my instructions. Desire is a futile attempt at loyalty. So is fear. He may have pleasantly surprised me by giving You the Talisman, but he still disobeyed me.

No matter. Every single member of the Cast—including him—will die in a few days, when every part of You is reborn.

PART 2

The Questioning

YOU

My eyes flutter open. The first thing I see are my hands—dry, cracked, and currently not so clean, with grime cakes beneath— it is daytime.

The second thing is the Girl, slumped over my legs, her breath coming in shallow gasps, a pitiful, rattling sound.

A thought, cold and sharp, pierces through the fog of waking: *Was last night a dream? Did the dunes sing? Did a snake attack me? Did I ...*

I turn my hands around, so my palms look up at me. A red indent, the perfect mirror of the spike, stares back.

I scan the area, the air thick with the smell of must. Shadows cling to the corners, remnants of the perpetual gloom that seems to hang over this forsaken land like a shroud. Dust motes dance, each one a tiny, mocking eye. The sand, undisturbed, lies heavy and still, a silent witness to last night.

Everything seems ... fine, except the blood on my hands. Then again, that could have easily happened whilst I was sleeping.

A relieved sigh escapes my lips, but beneath is a shaky unease in my chest. My legs ache with tiredness. My arms feel heavy, as if they have strained against an unseen force.

Wait, I *do* remember something. A fight? I clench my hand, the caked blood a stubborn stain against my rough skin.

Was it a dream?

I nudge the Girl off my legs, her eyes snapping wide open. "We're alive," she murmurs, standing abruptly and smoothing down her dress, a gesture both defiant and oddly fragile. She regards me for a moment, her eyes searching mine, as if about to speak, but then lowers them to my neck. "What's that?"

I follow her gaze and see a silken thread, a line of silver against my chest. Suspended from it is a delicate talisman, a silver hand cradling a circle within which an eye, like a moonlit jewel, gazes back at me.

"I must have always had it," I say, flipping it between my fingers.

"I didn't see it when I first saw you." She looks it up and down, narrowing her eyes.

"Maybe your anger didn't help you to see clearly."

Her eyes, dark and luminous in the dim light, lock onto mine. I instinctively turn my head, exposing my scarred left cheek to her intense gaze. The scent of salt and something faintly metallic, like dried blood, hangs heavy in the air around her.

She closes the distance between us with a few swift steps, the heels of her unusually wide feet sinking into the soft earth. She stops with a plop in front of me, legs crossed, the rough fabric of her dress rustling like dry leaves. Leaning in, her breath, warm and faintly musky, brushes against my cheek.

"Did it hurt?" she asks in a soft whisper.

I push her away, a reflex.

I catch her still staring, not at me, but at the reflection of me in the polished surface of the metallic wall. I shift uncomfortably, the burn scars on my face tightening, a constant, aching reminder of the monster I cannot remember becoming and yet, waking up to.

Her eyes are wide as she studies me. Even though I have no memory of my past, I know that look she is giving me. It is as familiar as the scent of blood, and as the chilling grip of fear. The Girl's look is not pity for the monster I have become; it is wonder. A morbid fascination like a baby analyzing a scorpion, without the knowledge of how dangerous the creature could be.

It is unsettling to be the object of such intense, unfiltered admiration, which makes me tilt my head slightly away from her, so she does not see my scars. As I do this, a defensive heat rises from within my belly. *Why do I care what she thinks?*

I look back at her daringly, my scars on full show. She gives me a slow, clumsy smile, which makes the corner of her eyes wrinkle.

"You're beautiful," the Girl says.

Even though I have already pushed her away, she still touches my cheek, the part where the burn marks remain.

"What happened?" she asks, with a hint of sadness in her voice.

"You mean last night or ..."

"What happened to you?"

I lower her hand and give it back to her more gently than I had intended to. "I don't know."

"What do you know?" She clasps her hands together on her knees as if I am about to tell her a story.

"I woke up," I say, picking up some sand and letting it fall through my fingers. "I woke up here and heard people talking behind the wall."

"Do you remember anything before that?"

I shake my head, crossing my arms in front of me to stop myself from feeling exposed. "Well, I remember last night, the snake and then ..."

She blinks at the turn in conversation and nods slowly.

"I suppose I should thank you," I say, avoiding her gaze, which is still studying my face.

"For what?"

"You saved me from the snake."

"I don't remember much of anything about last night," she says, as the orbee floats to her shoulder.

"Are there more?" I ask, looking towards the open door. "People like us, in there?"

"Just my Mama and Cast." There is a flicker of something crossing her face, but a new throbbing in my head distracts me from knowing what it means. A smile tugs at her thin lips. "Your face fits too."

"Fits what?"

"Just … fits."

"Don't you have to be somewhere for something to fit?" I ask.

"Sometimes, things just fit because they are." She shrugs. Yawning, she looks up towards the sky. "Like the sun. It's just there."

"There's no sun in the sky."

"Yes, there is. Behind the smoke."

"How do you know?" I ask.

"I can see it from Golden Dome," the Girl replies.

"Even if the sun does fit in the sky, it's still alone," I say, watching her brush sand off her sleeves with focus.

I turn towards the wall. "So, it's just you, your mother—"

"I have friends too," she says quickly and almost defensively, throwing a final pat at her clothes and then, shaking her tiny frame to get rid of the last motes of sand.

As she stands, her posture is slumped and her back hunched slightly.

"Stand up properly," I command.

Taken aback by my tone, the Girl looks at my face, then at my feet, no longer boldly meeting my eyes as she had done just moments earlier.

"You look weak when you bend over like that," I say.

"Weak?" It's as if she has heard that word for the first time.

"When you look weak, people will …"

Why am I telling her this? Weak people are eager to please, more desperate to help. I need her help.

"I don't get hurt if that's what you're worried about," she says softly, as she puts her hand on my shoulder.

"I'm not worried," I say, shrugging her off. This child is starting to annoy me.

"Remember, I don't feel any pain," she says, slightly straightening her back. "And at least … my hair's not a mess!"

I search her eyes for defiance, but there is none, just a playfulness. She rips the bottom of her dress, creating more disarray in the already jagged edges. With a determined glint in her eye, she yanks the torn fabric over my head and blinks a long blink: *There.*

I reach to pull it off, but my hand hesitates. The veil on my head feels … safe. As I turn to look at myself in the mirror of the wall, I am at a loss for words because I want to keep looking. I pull the veil back over the scarred half of my face. The other half, even though scarless, feels exposed, vulnerable. The smooth skin, rounded cheekbones, and long, dark lashes seem almost mocking, a cruel reminder of what I've lost.

I jerk back as she touches my cheek.

"You have a hole in your face," she blurts out, eyes wide. "It's nice."

"A hole?" I touch my cheek.

"When you were just smiling."

"I wasn't smiling, and anyway it's not a hole … it's called a dimple. Have you never seen—"

I am cut short by a bloodcurdling scream that rips through the air. Before I can fully register the sound, the Girl pushes past me, darting through the door.

"Wait!" I fumble to get up.

"Hold on to the lights so you don't fall …" I don't catch the end, as her voice fades, the further she runs. The orbee follows her in a straight path.

I stare into the inky blackness of the doorway, straining up to see what lies beyond. Each ragged breath I draw feels like a knife twisting in my chest at the thought of entering. My heart hammers against my ribs like a trapped bird.

I don't want to go in there.

Cold fear grips me, choking back any rational thought. I stumble back from the doorway, my legs weak.

"It's me. I'm the problem," I mutter, the words tumbling out as I repeat them again and again. "It's me. I'm the problem." "It's me. I'm the problem." "I'm the problem." "I'm the …"

After all, it's just a door, isn't it? But the fear refuses to subside. I pace before the entrance, my hand clutching the throbbing wound in my palm. I shake my hands in front of me, trying to dispel the tremors that wrack my body. I force myself to breathe, each inhalation a battle against the rising panic.

In. Out.

In. Out.

Focus on my breathing.

I tell my mind to ignore every part of my body's urge to run backward instead of forward. I can't go backward because I need to find out *who* I am, *why* I am here, and *where* I came from.

There are no answers in empty spaces.

With a final, shuddering breath, I push the door open wide. Ahead, through the thick fog, I can barely make out the silhouette of a line of trees at the top of a hill with dozens of soft, glowing spheres—orbees—their light pulsating gently against the backdrop of the misty haze. They are huddled beneath the trees.

Ignoring the tremor in my limbs, I run after the Girl, towards the lights.

The fog swirls around me, disorienting and thick. I am running, blindly, desperately. Up. Up the hill. The upward motion puts more pressure on my already unsteady legs, making my muscles burn.

I collide with something solid. The impact jolts me back. A *grunt* as I stumble, my breath knocked out. I hit a tree.

Slowly, I blink until my eyes are more adjusted to the fog. With more light, the ground beneath me becomes visible.

"The Silver Path," I whisper. It is as if a glass has been broken, reflecting many distorted versions of my face staring back at me.

A *buzzing*. An orbee bobs out from beneath the tree, hovering in the air. Swiftly, I cup my hands, trapping it.

The orbee thrums between my palms, a tiny dancer trapped in the cage of my fingers. I open my hands slowly to set it free, and the orbee gracefully ascends, settling gently on the tip of my nose.

A tiny burst of light explodes around it. I watch four wings unfurl—two large, two small—before seamlessly merging into a single whole. The newly formed wing beats the air, a blur of movement that creates a soft *hum*. I close my eyes, leaning into the feathery softness which tickles my nose.

The vibrant glow stutters, dimming slightly. The soft *hum* from its wings falters for a moment, and the orbee's figure droops.

"Why are you sad?" I ask, feeling my shoulders mirror it. I repeat the Girl's words, a distraction from the sadness rising within me. "Hold on … to the light."

A *whoosh* fills the air, and the orbee darts into my right ear. I gasp. The intrusion sends me tumbling backward. I catch myself before I roll down the hill. Stumbling, a lightness surges through me, pulling my body up as if it's as light as a feather.

My chest feels hollow, as if filled with nothing but air. The smoke remains but thins out—not just in the air, but also inside me. My head feels cradled with a gentle pressure, and a sense of clarity.

Then, a symphony of sounds washes over me. The trickle of a stream, a crescendo that flows effortlessly, mingling with the whistle of wind, brushing through leaves. The pure sound of nature draws me forward.

"Jinnah," I whisper. *Do I know this place?*

One foot is already poised on the edge of this 'Jinnah' entrance. My toes brush against the unseen border, and a gust of cool air strikes it, while my other foot remains firmly rooted in the hot ground before it.

Something shatters the peaceful motions of nature—a sound, low and insidious—a snicker slithering through the air. The symphony of sound that had soothed me moments ago is replaced by a suffocating weight in my chest.

I remain frozen, my ears straining to pinpoint the source of the sound.

The snicker evolves, a low, guttural chuckle that sends a wave of unease washing over me, leaving a shiver like a cold hand tracing my spine. I spin, my back to Jinnah, my eyes frantically searching for the source of the laughter, which is now more forceful than before.

My jaw clenches so tightly that it aches.

Heat radiates through my body.

"Who's there?" The words erupt from me, my voice a force I do not recognize. The fog creeps back in my mind, trying to reclaim its hold.

My hands tremble. But not from fear. Each tremor courses with a different kind of energy—a hot resolve. Fear can wait. *How dare they mock me?* I clench my fists. A thought: *I will make sure they are incapable of laughter.*

ME

You march here, demanding from me, ignorant of what I am to You. Perhaps it is best that You think of me this way. That You stay away because if You are too close, I do not know how long I can pretend.

I planned You would forget; I made sure You did, not just last night, but before, all those years ago. I needed a blank slate.

Yet. You hold onto that fire in Yourself, so very firmly.

Here You are, trampling down the hill, desperately trying to appear strong. Your right hand betrays You, trembling slightly against Your thigh. Fear? Or more likely ... rage? Whatever it is, You needed to come to me.

The orbees flicker from beneath the trees of Jinnah, all the way up the hill, giving You a breathtaking backdrop of spotlights gleaming from above Your veiled head as smoke explodes around You.

What an entrance!

Let the performance begin.

YOU

I stand at the bottom of the hill to Jinnah, the Silver Path cold under my bare feet. My body is sweltering from the hot, humid air, yet my feet remain dry. I stare ahead, trying to see.

The fog has lifted, but in its place, a thick, choking smoke has settled over the land. Here, the smoke is denser, pressing down on my chest. There is also a dust like thing falling from the sky.

I cough.

"Is this Dark Fall choking you?" A whisper drifts towards me.

Between coughs, I say, "You mock me."

I strain my eyes, blinking a few times to stop them from stinging.

"You assume laughter is mockery." A whisper comes from directly ahead of me.

"Where are you?" I stumble. My instinct is to take a step back, but I force myself to remain where I stand.

"My Ghar."

"Who are you?" I take a step forward.

"Do not come any closer." The whisper deepens into a hoarse, authoritative voice.

I take another step forward. "Why should I listen to you?"

The closer I am, the more the smoke is filling my lungs. I force myself to breathe more slowly.

"I am a friend," the Voice says calmly.

A subtle dissonance echoes in my mind as it speaks, a warning sign, a whisper of deceit.

"Liar," I say, my voice sharp.

"An ally."

"Liar."

"Comrade?" the Voice is persistent.

"Liar."

"Companion."

No shift in my ear. "Companion," I repeat in a whisper. Louder I demand, "Show yourself!"

"It is not my nature to be seen."

I shift uncomfortably, reminded of what brought me here. "Why did you laugh at me before?"

"Not at you." Again, the subtle shift.

"Another lie."

"Hmm …"

"Stop lying," I say.

"What do you truly seek?"

"I seek … the truth."

"The truth is … I *wanted* you to come to me."

As it says this, there is no pressure in my ear. No opposing force of truth and falsehood.

"What do you want?" I ask.

"For you to be good," it replies.

I study my ear. No change.

"Why can't I remember anything?" I ask.

"You hate to be weak," it hisses. After a pause, it clears its throat and says in that same hoarse voice, "But weakness is necessary."

"What has weakness got to do with what I am asking? Are *you* weak?" I ask.

A pause.

"Yes." There seems to be no sign of a lie. In *the Voice*.

"Is that why you called me here?"

"Yes."

"What do you want from me?"

"For you to be good," it says, again.

"Show yourself."

I am getting tired of this way of communicating. It is repetitive. If whoever this voice belongs to wants me to be good, why does it have a sinister tone? Why the pressure in my ear, a tell-tale sign the Voice is lying? Why use my anger to lure me to it? How does it even know *how* to lure me in?

In the silence that stretches between us, I observe a faint ringing in my ear. With it comes a feeling, an urge to flee. Another sweat breaks out, this one cold, making me shudder even though the air is hot and sticky.

My mind is stubborn. It wants answers. Answers that I sense the Voice might be able to give me.

The Voice breaks the silence, "Look into the grey."

The smoke, which had been suffocating moments ago, now rises, further darkening the sky. The frame of a towering building is exposed. The peak of the building disappears into the void above.

I take a step forward. A wave of fatigue washes over me. I want to close my eyes. My lids are heavy, pushing down. Pushing ...

An intense buzzing in my ear forces me to jolt up, pulling my eyes open.

"Listen to me!" the Voice whispers, as I take a step back.

A slender, vibrant thread, which is as wide as my little finger slices through the air. It is followed by a cascade of others, the same width, each long thread bursting with a different color. Reds, pinks, blues, and oranges. All strangely familiar, as if I have seen them recently. Where did I see threads like these?

Before the thought can continue, I am hit with an array of more thoughts that come with feelings. Thoughts and feelings I'm drawn to. I lean toward their whispers.

"Beautiful."

"Knowing."

"Strength."

I clutch my stomach to stop the queasiness, grateful for the slight throbbing in my palm from when I clutched the spike.

The stinging pain tells me I am awake. Perhaps I can take back control. Yet, that thought becomes faint as I stare in awe at the threads swirling above me.

They are close enough to see, but not close enough to grasp. They come closer and closer until they are touching me. I let them. I let them tighten around my chest.

As they slither into my ears, my awe of their whispers dissolves into horror. Other whispers reach me:

"Hideous."

"Ignorant."

"Powerless."

I struggle to push them away, gripping whichever thread is closest to me and throwing it into the air. The threads are rough, slicing through my already bloody palm.

Within seconds, the horror transforms back into awe as more whispers surround me:

"Pleasure."

"Control."

"Discovery."

I want these threads, whatever they are, to embrace me. Cradle me. Blanket me. I close my eyes, softly rocking from side to side with them.

The *buzzing* in my right ear explodes into a banging in my skull as more whispers overcome me:

"Pain."

"Chaos."

"Secrets."

I let out a soundless shriek. My mouth is filled with the threads. I pull them out, throwing them to the Silver Path.

The sound of the *thud* as they hit the ground forces me to open my eyes wide. *This is real. I am not safe.*

On my left side, the vibrant threads remain luring a part of me. On my right side, however, the threads twist and warp, their colors ripped away, replaced by a dull, sickly grey. These left chords, once welcoming, now resemble gnarled, decaying vines.

The conflicting whispers sound like a jumble of words, each trying to reach me. The opposing forces interact with different parts of my ears.

The 'good' words—beautiful, knowing, strength, pleasure, control, discovery—ring from my left ear.

The 'bad' words—hideous, ignorant, powerless, pain, chaos, secrets—ring from my right ear.

My head sears in pain from the two opposing forces. I grab my temples, squeezing them in a desperate attempt to stop them from pounding me into thoughtless oblivion.

I push my hands from my head to my ears. The whispers crash against them, as if punching my head again and again.

"What do you want?" I shout.

The threads snap and collapse to the ground.

Slowly, they are dragged back towards the source, gliding across the Silver Path with a *hiss*. The threads disappear into a dark, gaping hole, an ominous burrow protruding from the side of the massive building. The Ghar of the Voice.

The Ghar is roughly my height, just under six feet, but it offers only a tight squeeze. Near it, a platform displays an ape and a pig, their metallic forms gleaming as they remain in a perpetual, bowed obedience.

"What do you want?" I repeat, meekly.

As each thread vanishes into the hole, a chilling whisper echoes from its depths, "Come back when I call you."

The words hang heavy in the air, leaving me frozen. My mind reels as I struggle to comprehend this bizarre event.

Desperate for answers, I ask, "Why?"

The Voice, filled with a strange authority, replies, "I will give you parts of yourself."

I realize the eerie truth in its words that describe how I feel: like I am in pieces. Like I am in parts but not whole. A sudden gust of hot wind crashes over me, leaving me sweating again, this time from parts of my body I didn't know were capable of sweating.

The Voice commands, "Run! Run to Jinnah!"

I turn and sprint up the hill towards Jinnah.

PART 3
The Family

ME

I wait until I can no longer hear You running. With a leap, I plunge deeper into my Ghar, the darkness swallowing me.

I need the aid of the Worshipper.

Here, in the hushed stillness as I walk through the tunnels, a truth dawns. A truth which will add a slight change to my plot.

The primary objective remains unchanged: to make a difference, and for You to be good. However, a new, equally—if not more—important goal has emerged since I have become aware of the Book's presence: I must acquire it.

The method, however, needs to be adapted.

At first, I thought a blank canvas would be perfect to paint a good image, through splatters of honor, integrity, justice, compassion—all the things Your kind deem righteous. However, it seems the only way You will fully be good is through knowing how bad You have been.

A tainted canvas holds something unique when it chooses to be redeemed, a pure though not wholly innocent edge. It holds depth. Strength. Knowing. Beauty.

That must be why Adam was given those words of repentance from God Himself. Repeating them brought him closer to his God after his betrayal. Because of those words, he went to Heaven, even after being banished.

I am not weak like Adam. I do not need anyone's approval.

But I am aware of the lessons from his story.

I want You to be good. To be good, You too must rise above Your wounds. After all, it is the prayers of the regretful that are loved the most by their God.

That is the change of plan: we will not begin Your journey to being good upon a blank canvas. We will begin it with redemption, for You are the worst of sinners. To redeem Yourself, you must remember Your wrongs. When the time is right, You will remember *everything*. First, You must be softened. You are too hard.

I saw that from the test of my mocking laugh. I explored it more when I sent my threads to You. The good news is, You can be molded.

When I return the parts which belong to You—the missing pieces of Your wicked past—only then will You be ready to make the most important choice You will ever make.

See, like Adam, I want to go to Heaven. I need a way in. The choice You make will be what determines both Yours and my future. Eternally.

I reach the Main Hall at the end of the tunnel, taking my time to creep through it, so I can replay the thrill of our interaction.

The tension. It was delicious. Nostalgic.

I replay that firmness in Your voice, hiding Your shaky hand behind You, thinking I didn't notice. Bold, brave, and very scared.

My smile falters slightly as I think of the orbee in Your right ear. I became aware of the orbee when You sensed my first lie.

If I am honest, there is a little delight in what would happen if You *had* come just a few steps closer. That would have been a real challenge. But I remained focused. We don't have time for any more challenges. We have enough of them ahead of us with mere days before our time runs out.

That was the other reason I used my threads. I had to keep You at a certain distance, away from me—I had to keep that orbee away from Shahwah. *If it found* ... I don't want to entertain that thought. Let's just say, it would destroy the timing of everything.

Timing is everything.

My point is, I only used my threads because I needed to. I *know* to be truly good is not a thing of compulsion, but a challenge You must willingly participate in. I am learning a lot about how to be good—for You, of course.

I stroll past the precious monuments within the Main Hall, embracing the chill that runs through me at the memories they hold. To some, it may seem too sentimental to keep these bodies propped up in their last pose, but for me, it is a motivating reminder in case I begin to lose hope … again.

There is the trapdoor. I push it open with a delicate touch.

I scowl as I look in. This room is so different to the splendid Main Hall below. Down there is a portrait of suffering frozen in time from that day, over nine years ago, when You attained those scars on Your once beautiful—now monstrous—face.

Ugliness is good for You.

It will keep You humble.

Humbleness will help You to be good.

As I step out of the trapdoor and into the room, a tremor wracks my body. I hate how this room is blemished by those dreary green carpets—boxes like cruel cages that ensnare heads, hands, knees, and toes. I hate that this is a place of the bound.

I scuttle across the gaudy rug floor and race for the roof. Bursting up the stairs, I emerge through the already open door to the courtyard on the rooftop.

I am met with the harsh glare of the sun, which pushes me to remain in the shadows. From here, I observe the glint of the gilded dome, a spectacle soon to be stifled once the smoke spreads to this part of the sky.

Ahead is a deserted courtyard, a stark contrast to what used to be a feature of this place. This place of the believers. Only two of those people remain: the Girl and the Worshipper.

The Worshipper stands on the ledge at the end of the roof, her silhouette stark against the sky. The Girl's profile reveals a worried face, her one eyebrow in a furrow much like the tail of a skunk. I stifle a laugh at the image.

"Mama, you're too close to the edge!" The Girl's small hand stretches towards the Worshipper's dress.

"The edge." The Worshipper laughs dryly and sits down on the ledge, with her back towards the Girl, legs dangling over the hundred-foot drop. A fall that would result in a gruesome end. I watch, intrigued. She adds, "You went beyond Jinnah, didn't you?"

The Worshipper then swings her feet from the ledge until she fully faces the trembling Girl. The Girl's mouth tenses as she takes a step back from her while staring at her ragged face, studying it. I study it too, captivated.

I am always captivated when observing the broken. The sun, harsh and unforgiving, casts long, angular shadows across her gaunt face. Her skin, the color of rich, dark soil—a tint lighter than Yours—is weathered and worn. Her cheekbones, sharp and prominent, are etched with a weariness that makes her look older. It is hard to believe You and she are so close in age.

The Girl's skin is smoother, a few tints lighter than the Worshippers, like the color of marble mixed with black dirt.

They resemble their people, originally desert then, of Thanae, and then cast down to the tunnels—which I have just emerged—of the Deep.

The veil on the Worshipper's head is a flimsy excuse for modesty, letting pieces of prematurely aged hair, speckled with grey, pop out like frayed edges on a serrated knife.

She is predictable. Boring. A combination which I need for *our* story. The veil on her head does little to hide the hollow darkness beneath her eyes.

Her long, flowing dress, once elegant, only exaggerates the fragility of her frame.

Indeed, this is what a broken person looks like.

The Worshipper reaches towards the Girl's face, who flinches. Yet, the Girl remains rooted, like a trained dog who will not flee a beating. When the Worshipper gently moves her hands to her chin, the Girl releases a held breath and leans into the touch with an almost primal desperation.

The Worshipper says softly, "You know it isn't safe out there past Jinnah."

"I came back."

"Do you remember what to say when you enter and leave Jinnah?" The Worshipper stares into the Girl's eyes, and I creep forward.

The Girl's eyes are large and pleading, filled with a desperate longing. They yearn for this connection.

"I say it every time, Mama," the Girl says, nodding her head. Doggy.

I wince as I prepare for her to say it. Thankfully, she does not.

The Worshipper yawns. "I'm so tired."

"Let's go to sleep!" the Girl says.

"All I do is sleep," the Worshipper whispers, her shoulders sagging. "I need to do more."

"You prays all night and you—"

"Su—"

"Su?" The Girl's voice rises a pitch. "Is that my name?"

The Worshipper turns her eyes away and removes her hand from the Girl's pointy chin.

The Girl's face flushes. She says quickly, "Come to Jinnah with me, Mama."

It amazes me how much a child will keep trying to connect with their caretakers. Even when hit, neglected … abandoned.

Not me. I will never be so weak. Not with Father. Never with Father.

I'm slightly disgusted to see the Girl's hand reach out towards the Worshipper. As it hangs in the air, the skin is stretched taut over the bones, slightly translucent, revealing an intricate network of veins. Her fingers are long and spindly, the nails brittle and ragged. She studies the Worshipper's face before slowly touching her hand.

No immediate response.

"I want you to meet my friends," the Girl says, firmly grasping her hand.

The Worshipper raises an eyebrow towards her. "Friends?"

"I have lots! The snow squirrels have just woken up in Thalj …" The Girl rambles on. There is a slight twinkle of amusement in the Worshipper's eye. The Girl continues more animated as she drinks this look, "There's Lashes and—"

The Girl stops talking.

Both I and the Worshipper search her face for the reason behind this abrupt pause. The Girl's gaze drops, tracing a silent path to the edge of the platform as she holds her breath again.

"What?" the Worshipper asks.

Letting out another slow breath, her voice hushed, the Girl says, "I heard this voice."

I scurry back, drawing closer to the shadows.

"What kind of voice?" the Worshipper asks.

I smile slightly as a ripple of unease courses through her. Her fingers tighten around the smooth beads hanging around her neck.

"It's raspy like …" The Girl clears her throat and makes a choking sound. "Like that."

"Where did you hear this voice?"

"In a hole, a cave. Under Shh——" Her voice trails off, and she sighs. "I know so many words, but that one …"

"Do not go near the Voice," the Worshipper says, each word drawn out.

"Why not?" the Girl asks, though she already knows. She knows I have crossed paths with the Worshipper before. She knows what happened after.

"Do not leave Jinnah," the Worshipper says.

"But Mama——"

"I need to keep you safe." The Worshipper locks eyes with the Girl.

"I'll be safer if you come with me to Jinnah," the Girl mumbles as she looks away, quickly looking back to see the Worshipper's reaction.

"I can't." The Worshipper lowers her head.

"Why?" The Girl steps closer to her.

"The innocent won't be harmed there, but the guilty …" The Worshipper let's go of the Girl's hand.

"Who could be more innocent than a worshipper like you?"

"I am not innocent."

"Do you have to be innocent to be good?" the Girl asks.

The Worshipper looks down and doesn't answer.

"I love you the way you are, Mama." The Girl doesn't hesitate this time and hugs the Worshipper who crumbles into her arms.

She whispers to the Girl, "I never deserved to be a mother."

The Girl sighs. "I think we all get what we deserve. Sometimes ..." She looks up as if she plucks the words from the sky. "It's kinder than we think." Still looking at the sky she continues to hug the Worshipper tightly to her chest. "Why do you worship so much?"

"I am guilty."

"If I did something bad, would I have to worship too?" The Girl looks down at the Worshipper's face.

"Faith can never be guided by only guilt." The Worshipper pushes the Girl away from her and steps back. Lines of sorrow outline the corners of her eyes as she whispers, "Even though the guilty need it the most."

"Mama," the Girl says, trying not to look hurt by the Worshipper's withdrawal. She clears her throat and says, "If faith shouldn't be guided by guilt, what should it be guided by?"

"Love." The word hangs in the air for a few moments as the Worshipper looks up towards the sky, then straightens her back and touches the prayer beads tied to her neck. She adds, "The *right way* to love."

With this, she walks past me, until she reaches the wooden door.

"What's the right way to love?" the Girl asks, as she trails behind her.

The stony stairs, worn smooth by countless ascents and descents, wind downwards. The Worshipper, her steps heavy with exhaustion and punctuated by nervous missteps, climbs down slowly. Behind her, the Girl trots, her lighter footsteps echoing on the unforgiving stone as she tries to keep pace.

"I don't know what the right way to love is," the Worshipper says, as they reach the awful, carpeted room.

The Girl offers her a brush, which she accepts with an air of obligation. She starts combing the Girl's hair robotically, while softly repeating a song, "I will stay here until the pain goes away, I will live here, so the rhythm one day will change."

Gradually slowing down her brushing, her eyes begin to close before she drifts off. The Girl puts a blanket over her, despite the heat, and lies down next to her.

The Worshipper's voice trails off as she says, "Promise me you will never go beyond Jinnah."

"I promise I will stay with you, Mama," the Girl whispers.

YOU

I stumble past the orbee trees which border Jinnah. The twisting ache in my belly serves as a reminder for me to slow down.

Instantly, the temperature shifts. It's cool here in Jinnah, a stark contrast to mere steps away, past the border, where the heat blazes. Even the air feels … different. Clearer and not full of smoke. A relief against my skin, like a cool hand laid on a fevered brow. My sweat-soaked clothes cling less. It is easier to breathe. Even my heart rate slows slightly.

Glancing over my shoulder, my thoughts are still racing. Every shadow seems to twist towards me, every rustle a potential threat. Did that … *thing* … follow me here? I shake my head. It wasn't so bad, was it?

My dress is now a crumpled mess. I trace the dark, damp stains, a stark reminder of the turmoil within. My palms, raw and bleeding, offer no solace as I hold them out in front of me.

If it wasn't so bad, then why did I feel like I needed to get as far away from that thing—the Voice—as possible? But it told me to run.

The thing that disturbs me the most is that a small part of me wants to go back. To be close. To trust this … *companion*. I shudder. What *is* the Voice? I clutch my hand tightly to remind myself of the pain of those threads. It *was* real.

"Calm down," I whisper to myself.

I force myself to breathe in, then out, a slow battle against imminent panic.

I need a distraction. I focus on Jinnah. It is bright here. I press my back against the rough bark of a tree. A tingling sensation creeps up my spine, like a gentle caress. I spin around, startled.

The tree is a canvas of living art. An array of iridescent butterflies' wings, which shimmer with hues of ruby, rose, and sapphire, blankets the branches. As I watch, my shoulders relax, replaced by a sense of wonder.

I follow the path of the butterflies upward, watching them disappear beyond the treetops. The butterflies then sweep back down, a torrent cascading down the trunk. The tree looks like a living and breathing masterpiece.

I sweep my eyes across the trees, their barks as wide as my outstretched arms five times over. Each tree looks like it is standing on stilts, the roots thick like fingers on a hand, which is clawlike, digging into the ground. Beneath these roots, nestled in the crevices formed by their gnarled embrace, are hundreds of orbees, their soft, luminescent glows flickering like multiple watchful eyes.

The trees grow unusually. Their branches and leaves don't extend upwards towards the sky, but instead, curve downwards, reaching the orbees housed in their roots. It makes sense because every plant reaches for light, and the light of the sun is behind the smoke.

Each leaf of these orbee trees is enormous, larger than me. I wipe my hand against one. Thick. Tough. Like leather. Like my scarred face.

Their surfaces shimmer with a metallic sheen when illuminated by the orbees' light. The leaves come in various shades of green. Some are a vibrant emerald green, while others are a deep, forest green. A few even display a captivating, marbled pattern of lime green and olive green. I love all the greens.

And the smell! Earthy. More than rich soil or damp moss, something deeper, an ancient, almost metallic scent that hints at the very core of the planet. The smell seems to seep into my skin, leaving a lingering trace of the depth of Earth itself.

A familiar tingle brushes against my ear, a sensation like a thousand tiny insects crawling beneath my skin. It originates from the orbee still humming within me, a constant, low thrum that resonates through my very bones. It longs to go home, a yearning I recognize with a chilling clarity. Unlike this orbee, whispering within my ear, I do not know home.

I whisper, "Go Home."

In response, the orbee floats out and greets a butterfly. They circle each other in a silent dance of the orbee's light and the butterfly's movements as if forming a language only they can understand. The orbee's warm glow pulses in time with the butterfly's wings, until finally, it returns to under a tree, merging with the other orbees, their light brightening before unmerging and returning to their sole sphere shapes.

The air is thick with the sweet, spicy scent of something delicious. My stomach rumbles. I follow the aroma, allowing the cool earth to ground me with every step.

The dense forest canopy thins, revealing a hidden glade. A carpet of knee-high trumpet-shaped blooms, the color of blood, stretches out before me, layering the ground. A small garden.

The air is filled with the gentle hum of insects, a soft symphony that accompanies the spicy scent. I move carefully through the field, gently parting the uniformed blooms, their velvety petals embracing my skin.

The air crackles with the spicy scent, pulling me deeper into the garden. The scent grows stronger, leading me to a grotesque, fleshy flower. It stands apart, a monstrous crown of white petals, devoid of stems or leaves. It seems to leer at me, a silent dare. I hold a tendril, my grip tightening until it snaps.

I bite down, a surge of defiance coursing through me as I squeeze my eyes shut. Chewing determinedly, I savor the challenge. Initially, the taste is bland and tasteless, but I am grateful to fill my stomach. Then a rancid undercurrent emerges, a putrid flavor of decay. My stomach churns as I spit it out.

The faint trickle of water draws me towards the edge of the garden. The Silver Path is a ribbon that meanders through the undergrowth. The rhythmic flow of the water is soothing. I follow the sound. The stream disappears beneath a metal and wooden bridge, its gleam reflecting the water below.

ALAM

The world spins as I stumble, my vision blurring. I reach out to hold onto something, but there are no trees nearby. Only the large red flowers. A dark fog creeps into my mind, and I can barely make out the grotesque flower.

I continue stumbling ahead until I meet the stream bank.

I collapse. *Limbs. Heavy. Eyelids. Droop. Leaden. Darkness. Demanding.*

PART 4

The Woman

ME

I peek out from the trapdoor. The Girl and the Worshipper are sprawled out like insects on a pin at the rear of the room, plagued with carpets. A pathetic display.

Behind them, a sliver of sunlight streams through a window. The Golden Dome, a skeletal monument to a forgotten faith, stands atop the highest hill in Thanae, overlooking the rest of the dying landscape.

The Great Wall, snaking across the horizon, winds its way across the landscape. The still, vibrant forest of Jinnah, a defiant emerald jewel against the ashen backdrop, fights pitifully against the choking smoke that will inevitably consume it.

The tips of its trees, already obscured by a thick, gray smog, writhe and twist as if in silent agony.

A flicker of unease. *What is beyond the smoke in Jinnah?* I have only a clue that was revealed to me when I found one of the greatest resources for my plan to make a difference.

However, I have never been there—the place beyond the smoke—none of my allies have. I lean forward to seek another clue, but the place is obscured, even from my perfect vision.

I let my sight drop back to Shahwah, a place which causes my whole being to smile. Its skies have now developed into a spew of dust—a Dark Fall—a recent phenomenon which, if I am fully honest, I do not know the purpose of. Is the Dark Fall connected to up there? To the place beyond the smoke? No time to think about that now. I must focus on the task ahead.

The Girl stirs beneath the faded blue blanket, a thing of comfort rather than use. *Humans,* I scoff. They would rather starve than lose their frivolous luxuries.

Her small frame is barely visible. A miserable sight. Starved and frail, she pushes the blanket off her and places it on the Worshipper's body.

She fumbles in her pockets, producing a withered leaf tied with a frayed rope. A single olive, the color of a bruise after a day of brutal beating, rolls out, plopping onto the Worshipper's forehead.

The Girl snatches it up with her gaunt fingers, trembling. She brings the olive to her nose, inhaling deeply, before placing it back in the leaf. A sigh escapes her lips, and she tucks the leaf back beside the Worshipper.

I sneer.

She shivers, even though it is hot here, like everywhere else in Thanae, everywhere *except* in Jinnah. *Why is that?*

I snap out of my wandering thoughts as her gaze darts towards me. I crouch lower, though I know the platform conceals the trapdoor. She takes a cautious step forward. Her flesh, smooth and flawless, is bathed in shadow. The sunlight catches her long, straight hair, highlighting her sharp cheekbones and casting long, dancing shadows across her face. A disdain that such beauty was destined for ruin.

She tiptoes, her wide, gnarled feet misshapen from years of silent movement. As she reaches the door, she glances back at the Worshipper and the meager offering she left behind. Then she slips out, the door closing softly behind her.

I rummage out from the trapdoor and crawl to the Worshipper, wincing with every movement that connects this body to the floor of worship.

I hover over the sleeping figure. I am so close I can feel her breath on my face through her crescent moon-shaped open mouth. A breath, foul and putrid, a stench I don't mind. Despite the wear on her face, there is that flicker, a hint of You.

I lean over the Worshipper's ear. Her ear is caked and filled with wax, which leads me to sharpen my whisper. I must make sure she receives this message.

I whisper ...
   and whisper ...
      and whisper ... until the Worshipper echoes my words back to me.

This fragment—this whisper will be the greatest part I return to *You*.

YOU

There is a noise in front of me. A low, rustling sound, like dry leaves being shuffled. It creeps closer. I keep my eyes closed, moving my body backward. The sound becomes louder and louder. I squeeze my palm, waiting for the pain to tell me I am awake. There is none.

A dream.

I open my eyes, blinking rapidly as a harsh light fills them. A wave of heat slams into my face. A wet sensation trickles down my body, made hotter by the scorching heat. It dawns on me, the liquid is sweat dripping from my body in droves.

The light is blinding. I squeeze my eyes shut, but it pierces through the thin skin of my eyelids. My hands shoot up, feeble shields against the onslaught. A different kind of liquid, thick and metallic, drips from my palms, burning my skin. I wipe my eyes, but the liquid is too viscous. Blood, from unseen wounds.

A low moan from me as I wipe my hands on the grainy, harsh ground. The blood pools, a dark stain against the unforgiving earth. The blood mixed with sweat turns into a puddle. I shift away from it.

Is this a dream?

A new blast of heat crashes over me. I stare directly above. The sun. A monstrous, burning orb, hanging low in the sky, in a way that defies nature. Too close. Too intense. As if it's been dragged down from the heavens.

I force my eyes to stay open, squinting against the blinding light. This is Jinnah, but not the Jinnah I have just entered. This forest is full of gnarled and bare trees. No leaves. No orbees. Empty.

I turn my back to the sun, the heat searing my skin. My dress clings to me. The metal-wooden bridge looms ahead.

A sudden burst of laughter, pure and innocent, cuts through the thick and smoky air. I stumble, startled by the unexpected sound. It doesn't fit here. The laughter continues from the same direction as the bridge. I run towards it.

The laughter fades, replaced by a low, menacing *hiss*. Something closer to me than the sweet laugh. My body freezes, rooted to the spot. The *hiss* grows louder. It is next to my ear. I dare not turn, but my eyes flick to the side, catching a glimpse of a monstrous shadow. Panic surges through me, but my body refuses to move.

Somehow, I manage to stumble forward, my lungs burning, legs heavy. The bridge looms ahead, its once sturdy structure now marred by decay. As I reach it, I collapse, gasping for breath. The wooden planks, charred and cracked, threaten to give way beneath my weight.

I force myself to rise, my body trembling. I crawl towards the bridge, each movement a painful effort. As I peer through the gaps in the planks, I gasp. A river of molten lava.

That *hiss* echoes from behind me. I turn, my lungs burning with each desperate breath. The thick, choking smoke weighs me down and blocks me from seeing the source of the *hiss*. My eyes are streaming with stinging tears.

As I approach the bridge, the smoke thins. I collapse on its ground, gasping for air. A colossal shadow looms over me, the serpentine creature finally revealed. Its thick, muscular body coils and uncoils. Adrenaline surges through me, and I scramble to my feet.

The creature's black, beady eyes lock onto mine, a chilling stare that pierces through the remaining smoke.

Its voice, a deep, guttural growl, echoes through the air, "Run!"

I spin and bolt forward, the bridge creaking beneath my feet. I glance back. The creature stands on its tail, an awful grin splitting its lipless maw. Its calm, predatory gaze sends another bead of sweat trickling down my upper lip.

I reach the center of the bridge. My lungs burn. *Slow down.* I look back frantically to find the creature. It recedes. Hope flickers. I look back again. The creature surges forward, darting towards me.

I can't fight it. I can't outrun it. In seconds, it will reach me.

A faint *hum* cuts through the chaos, emanating from behind me. I spin towards the direction of the *hum*. Through the smoke, a figure materializes, perched on a chair just a few steps ahead of me.

As I approach, her features become clearer. She is fragile, almost wispy. There are wrinkles all over her face, yet her eyes radiate a warmth that—like the laughter of purity—does not fit in this place.

She hums an ancient melody of words. They bring a comfort, which draws me closer, so close I can see the loose threads of the veil on her head. The pull to her becomes stronger, a kind of closeness which is open and clear, not panicky and forced like with the Voice.

Unfazed by my arrival, she stops humming and offers a gentle smile.

"Peace be on you," she says, her voice slightly shaky, which makes it more soothing. Despite her age, her skin glows with a soft beauty.

I reach to touch her face but yank my hand back as the serpent's image flashes through my mind.

"There's a serpent!" I blurt out, not daring to turn. I don't want to see how close it is.

Her eyes, kind yet tinged with a deep sorrow, meet mine. "Look at me," she whispers, a tear falling down her cheek.

I wish I could shield her, carry her away to safety.

Her voice cracks as she says, "How can I help you against that?"

The answer hangs heavy in the air, utterly clear.

"We need to hide!" I say, voice breaking.

"There is no place to hide," she says, gently.

Her words confirm what I instinctively knew. There *is* nowhere to hide from the serpent. It is just seconds away. Its body makes the bridge shake from side to side as it darts forward.

Still, knowing I can't run, nor hide, I swivel around to find escape. My hand reaches out for the old woman to pull her to safety, but my fingers brush against empty air.

Where is she? I frantically scan ahead of me.

The serpent's hot breath nips at my neck, a chilling reminder of how close it is. I sprint forward, the end of the bridge within reach. But the path ahead is blocked by a fiery river, which is as long as the bridge itself. I'm trapped between the serpent and the flames.

I leap into the void, my hands clawing at the edge of the bridge. Half my body is engulfed in flames, a searing inferno consuming me. My skin peels into blisters. The stench of burning flesh fills my nostrils. A wave of dizziness washes over me. A part of me wants to let go of the edge and let the fire finish what it started. To end this pain.

Laughter.

The same laughter I heard earlier, which felt out of place in this hell like place. A bright, crystalline echo pierces the roaring turmoil. I claw my way up the slick, molten bank, each muscle screaming in protest, the air thick with the acrid stench of burning.

My skin is scorched. I fixate on that sound, that fragile thread of joy. With every ragged breath, every desperate tug, I pull myself further from the river of fire, my body a raw, trembling testament to the effort.

I squint upwards, the world a shimmering haze, my body a throbbing pulse from the searing bath of heat. A hill. A steep, treacherous slope. I dig my fingers into the loose, gritty soil, the earth crumbling beneath my grasp.

Pain, a white-hot agony, threatens to overwhelm, but I clamp down on the dirt, pushing it aside. Upwards. I must climb upwards.

I haul my ravaged body, inch by agonizing inch, over the crest. My lungs burn, each breath a searing brand, my legs scream, a chorus of rebellion.

Dirt—mixed with the raw, torn flesh of my hands—clings to me like a second skin. Blood, dark and slick, stains my palms, blurring the already distorted world with a crimson film. Tears, hot and stinging, join the bloody mix, obscuring the hill's peak, but I keep climbing.

With a final, desperate heave, I fling myself over the summit, my hands waving blindly, searching for purchase in the swirling air. I gasp, a ragged, shuddering breath, as my fingers brush against something solid.

Without daring to look back down the hill, I grip the material, fingers locking onto two strong, cold bars—a gate. The moment I do, it swings inward, silently, as if waiting for me to enter.

I brace myself, digging my heels into the loose earth of the slope, steadying my trembling form. Then, a wave of warmth, soft and golden, washes over me. It isn't just light; it is ... *renewal*.

It seeps into my bones, chasing away the gnawing stinging. My skin, once raw and blistered, soothes, supple with its rich mahogany complexion returning.

The burning thirst and the pain simply evaporate. I am ... whole again. But the suddenness of it all, the impossible perfection, sends a fresh tremor through me, not that of pain, but a different kind of unease which comes with the unfamiliar.

I rise slowly, testing my newfound strength, a startling contrast to the ravaged state I'd been in mere moments before.

I close my eyes, shutting this place into darkness, straining to catch the laughter, to hear it clearly, without the distraction of sight. Of light.

There it is, a pure, unadulterated sound, a beacon in the quiet. I let it pull me, a gentle, insistent tug, drawing me forward, a string leading me out of darkness.

As I near its source, I open my eyes. A small figure stands. A tiny girl, barely reaching my knee, her face a radiant map of pure joy. Her smile is incandescent, lighting up the space around her. Pudgy fingers wiggle with an unrestrained excitement; her cheeks flushed with a childlike glee.

I reach out, compelled to touch her, to confirm she is real, but the phantom weight of blood, still slick in my memory, makes me hesitate. I pull back. Yet, she doesn't flinch.

Instead, she reaches for me, her tiny hand taking mine, her touch warm, an invitation.

The blood from my hands has vanished, leaving my skin smooth and clean. She tugs gently, leading me to a patch of grass, lush and beautifully green, a vibrant oasis. I sit beside her, the soft blades cool against my skin, and a wave of peace, a tranquility I haven't felt since—I can't remember *when*—washes over me. A balm against the recent horrors.

"Who are you?" I ask in a hoarse voice.

"Adamah." Her voice is a high-pitched chirp.

"Why can't I remember anything?"

"'In the remembrance of their Lord do hearts find peace,[1]'" she says, as if memorizing the words with a slight lisp.

Adamah fades. The sound of the trickling stream returns. I blink rapidly, my chest heavy and my face damp with sweat. As I sit up, I meet the gaze of the one-eyebrowed Girl. Her wide eyes, filled with a mix of surprise and suspicion, quickly narrow into a frown.

The Girl tuts. "I told you to hold on to the light, so you don't fall asleep!"

The Table

ME

There is a part missing. Without this part, *our* story will remain incomplete. Our center is split and disconnected.

More importantly, it shows I am losing control of *our* story: Part 1 is The Opening, Part 2 is The Questioning, Part 3 is The Family, Part 4 is The Woman. There should be a total of 30 parts in all. *Where* is Part 5?

YOU

"**A**re you saying it wasn't real?" I ask the Girl, pulling myself up from the stream's edge.

I sink my feet into the cool, moist soil. The gritty resistance beneath my soles feels reassuring.

"When you sleep in Jinnah," the Girl begins, her voice a mixture of curiosity and unease, "the dreams … they're different. Not like anywhere else."

She shifts her weight nervously, her face crinkling slightly as she rubs her chest. A faint rustle from beneath her dress.

"How?" I peer in the direction of the sound.

"They tell you things." She catches my gaze and crosses her arms protectively over her chest.

"Is there any truth to them?"

"There is truth, but dreams make it confusing."

"What could a serpent be trying to tell me?" I challenge, locking my eyes with hers.

"You had a bad one," she murmurs, lowering her gaze, looking very interested in her toes as she wiggles them under her dress. "Maybe it's because … you're big."

"What will happen if I fall asleep again?"

She points towards the shimmering orbee trees beyond the stream. "There are exactly 779 orbees under the trees, including those and the ones in Orbee Forest. No more, no less. And they've been that way for quite some time." She trails off, as if lost in thought.

"And?" I ask, prompting her.

She snaps back into attention. "You could've easily caught one."

"Precisely," I say.

"What?"

"What?" I taunt.

"You're smiling," she says, with a flicker of suspicion.

"I-I am?"

"Are you making fun of me?" she asks. As she crosses her arms again, the rustle of fabric intensifies with the movement.

"I don't mock people," I snap. She draws a quick shallow breath. I soften my tone. "What else do you know about this place?"

Her eyes widen and she speaks quickly, "Not many animals here, only my friends, Lashes and Smiley. And the black—"

"Are there territories?" I interrupt.

She looks startled by my question. "Territories?"

"Parts."

"Yes," she says, her voice trailing off, her brow furrowed as she begins to scribble on the ground.

I raise an eyebrow, waiting for her to elaborate. "And?" I urge, trying to conceal my growing annoyance.

"What do you want to know?" the Girl asks, looking slightly confused, her finger hovering over the ground.

I bite the inside of my cheek as I look over the place. My gaze sweeps across the scene: vines, thick and unruly, sprawl across the stream bank, their roots grappling with the moist earth and some of the red flowers, which line the edge of the bridge. The surrounding area, however, remains eerily vacant, an unsettling emptiness.

"Well, I've seen the wall—"

"Great Wall."

"Right … then there's the extra grey place," I continue.

"Shh-Shahwah." Her finger traces a squiggle in the dirt.

I nod. "Shahwah. The city of smoke and one building."

Her finger is now caked with dirt as she resumes its frantic dance across the ground.

"Then there's …" I look to the border of the trees ahead of the stream. "Why are all these places so close together? Shahwah, the w—the Great Wall and Jinnah?"

"Never really thought about it." She shrugs, finally stopping her scribbling and looking up at me with a thoughtful expression.

I tap the floor with a finger as I think. "Okay. So, we have Jinnah just a few meters away from Shahwah—"

"I think I know!" A spark of excitement lights her eyes. "There are a couple of reasons …" she pauses, as if savoring a secret, "time and space … they're *different* in Jinnah." She emphasizes the word, her tone hinting at something extraordinary. "There are *levels*. Think of Shh … Shahwah," she says, holding her palm flat, close to the ground. "It's here." Then, she raises her hand slightly. "Jinnah is … a step above." Her hand rises higher, and she adds, "And Golden Dome? That's the highest." Her voice is filled with a quiet triumph as if she has just revealed a profound truth.

"Are you going to keep interrupting me?" I ask.

She looks hurt, her eyes dropping to the ground.

I dart my eyes away and continue, "The Great Wall," I make a line on the ground in front of me, "inside is Shahwah and Jinnah."

She bites her lip as if she wants to say something.

I nod to her, and she blurts out, "And Golden Dome!"

"Why is it cooler in Jinnah than out there?"

She shrugs.

"Is Jinnah one big place or are there parts to that too?" I continue.

"Parts?"

"A beginning? A middle? An end?"

"Yes."

"And?"

"The beginning is in front of Shahwah, the end is across the bridge where those orbee trees are, and past that is Golden Dome."

"What's inside Jinnah?"

"Orbee Forest, Garden of Fire." She pauses as she sees my face.

"Garden of Fire?" I glance at the bridge that looks harmless compared to the fiery scene in my dream, and shudder.

"The red flowers." She nods back towards the garden where the awful white flower is, and I let out a long breath. "This stream ... is Zam."

"The Zam?"

"Yes. Zam is the stream." She scribbles something and mumbles to herself, "The bridge is part of Silver Path. It goes through Shahwah to Golden Dome. I think that's it."

She points to her scribbles, which look like a tangle of a meaningless mess.

"How come you don't say 'the' when you name the parts?"

She shrugs. Initially when I noticed this pattern of speaking, I thought it was because of the child's simplicity. However, she seems to be anything but simple. She is often distracted and at other times overly intense. Like now, how she's biting her lip and staring at me with an unsettling focus.

I shift under her gaze and ask, "Why do some parts of Jinnah have names and others don't?"

"Why does it matter if someone—something has a name or not?" There is a hint of annoyance in her voice.

I decide not to question the Girl more about this. It seems it's a sensitive topic.

She adds, "And there *are* names. The name of this whole land is Thanae, it includes Shahwah, Golden Dome, and Jinnah. As for Jinnah, I made sure every part has a name: Silver Path, Zam, Garden of Fire, Orbee Forest, Fallen—"

I interrupt, "And Thalj?"

She lets out a long breath. "Oh, I forgot that part."

"Is it in Jinnah?"

"Yes, it's another part past Fallen Trees."

"Can you show me?" I stand, my head swimming from getting up too quickly. I stumble back against her.

She steadies me, her hand gently guiding me back down to the ground.

When my head feels less faint, I try to get up again. She puts her hand on my shoulder and lowers me to the ground again.

"You need to rest," she says softly, glancing past the bridge.

I follow her gaze. "You live in the Golden Dome, don't you? Is it hot there too?"

She nods, continuing to gaze up the bridge.

I move forward to see if I can get a look through the thick trees that cover whatever is ahead. I can't see anything. "Is that where your mother is now?"

"My Mama doesn't like to be disturbed," she says quickly.

"Do you think your mother will come here?"

"No."

"Why?"

"Too close to Deep," she says, her voice dropping to a hushed whisper.

When she says this, my legs tingle, a wave of icy coldness shooting through them, making my entire body shiver. I manage to say, "The Deep."

"Yes, Deep is the lowest layer of the land." She presses her hand into the earth, her fingers disappearing. "It's ... under everything. I don't talk about it much. My Mama told me not to."

Her voice drops to a near-whisper, "My Mama said ... because I'm innocent, I don't see the bad things when I sleep here. Only the guilty do, and the guilty are from Deep." She sighs softly, as she sits up, crossing her legs.

Her gaze drifts to the flowing Zam, her expression thoughtful. "I asked my Mama ... 'Do you have to be innocent to be good?'"

"Innocent?" I repeat her words, absentmindedly. *The Deep.*

"What is 'innocent'?" she asks, tilting her head.

"It means …" I push my feet into the soil. "Not guilty," I say breathlessly.

"Guilty," she mumbles.

I focus on the red flowers clinging to the bridge's edge, a thick vine around their stems. Its knots twist like a deliberate disruption, scattering the blossoms haphazardly.

"Why's everything such a mess?" I ask, feeling flustered.

"It's just free," she says, biting a cuticle off her nail that is blackened beneath the surface.

"Free isn't messy," I push the flowers to look neater, accidentally crushing some of the red petals. I brush away the damage. She hops up and turns towards the trees. "Where are you going?"

"If you had some food, you might be less grumpy," she says.

"I'm not grumpy—"

She walks away as I'm mid-sentence. A wave of annoyance washes over me, heat creeping up my neck and into my cheeks. Before disappearing into the Garden of Fire, she turns back, her brow furrowed.

"What made you fall asleep?" she asks, her gaze shifting to the flowers I'm rearranging.

I ignore her.

"Did you eat something?" she asks, her voice rising slightly, a touch of childish impatience in her tone. I don't answer, but the distasteful look on my face urges her to continue. "What was it?"

My fingers fumble with the delicate flowers. I don't feel like talking. I need to organize these flowers. It mutes the rising tide of anxiety within me. Her stomping footsteps approach. With a thud, she plops beside me.

Her hand gently touches mine, its coolness startling me. In that moment, the need to organize, the simmering heat in my chest, and the clenching in my jaw slowly subside.

She meets my eyes. "You'll feel better after you have some food."

"The white flower," I mumble, looking away from her intense gaze, moving my hand away from her. "I ate the white flower that tastes like death."

"What does death taste like?" the Girl asks.

"It smells sweet, but it tastes bitter."

Her eyes linger on me, a flicker of dread in their depths.

"The sickness," she says, her voice tight with unease, "is spreading here too."

Without another word, she pulls herself up and tiptoes ahead, disappearing into the blooming Garden of Fire.

When I am alone, a word rings in my ears: *guilty*.

ME

This weakness is consuming me. I feel a mix of relief and frustration. If I were stronger, I'd be trapped. If I were weaker, this body would be my cage. I'm caught between two extremes, two cruelties.

This is the nature of my kind; we are always bound to something.

Three more days and everything will change. My followers and I will finally be free, be ready to ascend, fully prepared to reach Heaven.

But first, I have a part—not the titles of *our* story, rather a part which belongs fully to You. I must return it to You.

"Come home," I whisper to the wind.

YOU

Its whisper washes over me as I sit by the babbling Zam. The world fades, everything muffled like I'm underwater.

"Come home." The words drift to me again in a gust of warm wind.

I rise, a mix of running and stumbling, vaguely aware of my feet crushing wildflowers from the Garden of Fire. The gush of the Zam and the rustling leaves are silenced. All I can hear is that call.

"I'm coming," I whisper back, moving through the trees of the Orbee Forest driven by an urgent need.

Each step takes me deeper into its whispering pull. I reach the edge of the Orbee Forest, grasping the rough bark of a tree. Butterflies flutter away in startled bursts. Just one more step, and I'll cross the boundary from Jinnah to out there. I can already feel the hot air hitting my face.

A sudden, high-pitched squeak pierces the air behind me, "Stop!"

A bony hand, strong, clamps onto my arm, startling me. It takes me a few seconds to realize it's the Girl. Her lips move, but I hear nothing. The world shifts back into focus. Color is less muted. Sounds are clearer, but still mostly a blur.

"Don't go near the edge," she says, her voice finally breaking through.

"It called me," I whisper, the words catching in my throat like shards of glass.

I squeeze the rough bark of the orbee tree, the coarse texture, a meager comfort against the tremors that rack my body. I hold the talisman around my neck, the string pressing like a knife against my skin. The wounds from the threads of the Voice, still raw and angry, throb under my palms, crimson drops tainting the ground like blood tears.

The Girl walks in front of me, her eyes widening as they fall on the talisman. "I knew it."

"Knew what?" My voice is timid.

"I couldn't see it clearly outside Great Wall, I didn't see the colors … that thing on your neck, it has power over you. That's why you were drawn to the Voice."

"It's just a necklace," I mutter, my fingers tracing the cold, metallic surface of the talisman.

"My Mama had one too," she says, her voice trembling. "It looked just like that, with a blue eye. Said it was to stop the evil eye and keep away bad spirits. I found it hidden in a wall in a corner of Golden Dome."

Holding on tighter, I wait until the tremors subside. My head is pounding, and the Girl's face shifts in and out of focus.

Now I can see it. She is watching me expectantly.

Now it's blurry. With a swift movement, she grabs the talisman from my neck and flings it past the border trees. It hits the Silver Path with an echoing *clang*.

"What—" I begin, but stop when I realize the haze that has clouded my mind is lifting.

"When my Mama had it, she would act different, as if something was inside her. Something bad."

I stare at her. "What just happened?"

"The Voice is not a friend," she whispers, her eyes darting around, making her look like a squirrel trying to protect its nuts. She leans in conspiratorially, her breath hot and stale in the humid air from Shahwah. "Anything related to the Voice is *not* good."

She walks away towards the Zam, casting a glance over her shoulder as she motions for me to follow. A bossy child. Weak-willed from the daze that brought me here, I obey, my eyes lingering on the border of Jinnah, that disturbing mix of longing and disgust swirling within me.

"Do not go near the edge," she mutters, as if she has said it many times before, a desperate mantra.

We reach the Zam, where she sits on the edge of the bridge. I scrutinize it, hoping the intricate details will distract me from the lingering unease in my chest. An odd bridge. A bizarre hybrid of nature and industry: wooden planks interwoven with rusted steel beams. It groans and creaks beneath her weight. The wood is scarred and pitted, the metal weathered and corroded. Yet, despite its decrepit appearance, it remains sturdy under both our weights.

I glance to the center of the bridge, half expecting the old woman from my dream to appear.

The rough-hewn planks of the bridge shift slightly beneath my worn, calloused feet as I walk across, the wood groaning with every step.

"A table! I made it myself!" The Girl's eyes sparkle with enthusiasm, a total difference from her protective—controlling—behavior just minutes ago.

With a flourish, she produces a large, vibrant green leaf, tied neatly with a length of twine, and places it on the makeshift table. I stare at it, blinking a few times, trying to understand the meaning behind this peculiar gesture.

"Open it!" she says, nodding towards the leaf.

She swings her legs over the bridge's edge. My heart jolts as the memory of cackling echoes in my mind. *It was just a dream. Just a dream.* There's no fire here, only the gentle lapping of water against the weathered wood.

"Did you tie the knot too?" I ask, fumbling with the string. My fingers throb, the raw edges of a recent cut stinging with each clumsy tug. It won't budge.

"From Fallen Trees," she replies, tilting her head towards the Orbee Forest. "It's stubborn."

"It's strong," she says, pulling at the knot until it loosens.

Her hands are a roadmap of tiny, white scars, like marks left by thorns. She catches me staring and her cheeks flush. She puts her hands under her legs.

"You said you don't feel pain," I say, looking down at the Zam.

"I don't."

"You have scars."

"I do," she says softly.

Her tone shuts down further conversation. I'm glad. I don't want to talk about it either. Not about missing parts, lingering pain, scars, bloody hands— not now. Now I want to eat. I focus on untying the string with my teeth. With a final pull, two round, purple oval-shaped things plop into the Zam.

Without a second thought, I jump in after them, catching a glimpse of the Girl's wide eyes as I disappear beneath the surface. The shallow water engulfs me, its warmth a relief. Underneath, the soft, delicate tendrils of a water plant brush against my skin, a gentle tickle in the warm water.

A light mist hangs in the air, and a sense of normalcy washes over me. I like this. I turn away from the Girl, so she does not see me smiling. I thrash, trying to catch the elusive purple oval things, but each splash sends them both bobbing further downstream until they vanish behind a large rock.

With a sigh, I let myself flow with the current, letting the water run between my fingers. Below me, the riverbed is full of vibrant reds and greens, the flowers making a beautiful underwater garden.

I notice something disturbing. Black swirls contaminating the water, turning it murky. I realize with a jolt that the blackness is from my dress, some kind of dye bleeding into the Zam. I watch helplessly as the black swirls are carried downstream.

"You *did* come from Thalj," the Girl says, "your dress, its ..." She trails off and I am unable to catch the last part of her sentence through the gush of the Zam and the pounding of my heart. When I rise to my feet, all I hear is, "Insects aren't real food."

"Those oval things were insects?" I ask, struggling to keep up with the conversation. I clamber out of the Zam. When I squeeze my dress, more greyish black liquid oozes from the fabric.

"Those were olives."

"Why did you say insects?" I ask, confused.

"Didn't think you could hear me." She shifts uncomfortably, and that faint *rustle* comes from the upper part of her dress. She grabs the table and moves ahead towards the Garden of Fire.

I run after her, the sound of my feet padding on the smooth metallic surface of the Silver Path. My dripping dress clings to my legs, slowing me down as I leave behind a trail of black.

As we reach the Orbee Forest's edge, she vanishes. I frantically scan the area, but all I find are the flittering butterflies and the glowing orbee trees.

"Where are you?" I call out.

The Girl's face, smudged with dirt and framed by a shock of unruly black hair, peeks out from a hidden opening in the dense foliage. She disappears again, leaving behind long leaves and branches.

I hesitate, my hand hovering over the concealed opening. There is a slight tremor in my hands, not of the cold, but of anticipation. Taking a deep breath, I finally plunge into the darkness.

As I squeeze through the narrow entrance, I am surprised to find it is spacious. I crawl a few feet on my hands and knees. Total darkness. A familiar feeling washes over, like when I was in the Zam, only now it is because I am in the dark.

I feel safe.

As I inch forward, the air grows heavy with moisture, the cool dampness clinging to my skin. Finally, I get through the passageway and emerge into another area of Jinnah.

I stumble to my feet, disoriented. Before me are around fifteen trees prostrating, their forms twisted and unnatural, their bark bleached a bone-chilling white. They are but remnants of the orbee trees, except there are no orbees nestled within them.

The two orbees the Girl carried here hang over her shoulders, our only source of light and other life in the utter absence of anything else.

There are no vibrant blossoms in the air, no buzzing insects to disturb the eerie silence, not even a hint of green to break the monotonous white. The air hangs heavy with a dull, oppressive gloom.

"Fallen Trees," she whispers, climbing over a thick trunk, its lifeless form reminiscent of a fallen guardian.

"Why are all the trees dead here?" I ask.

"Fallen, not dead." Her voice is low and somber.

"Fallen," I murmur, my gaze darting around the desolate area.

"Do you remember when I said the sickness is spreading?" She doesn't wait for me to answer. "Well, this is what it does. It drains the life and color from everything it reaches. It squeezes any sign of growth."

"Right. Where is Thalj?" Cold, I know. But to the point, unlike the spiraling and random content of her conversations, again, anything but simple.

She glances towards a massive tree, one if even possible, is even more white than the other trees. It almost glows with its whiteness. This one blocks the area beyond it. "There."

A behemoth block. Its white trunk dwarfs the surrounding trees, towering at least six times my height, as it lies on its side like a defeated giant.

This isn't just a tree; it's an obstacle, a defiant mass of wood that seems to shift, to *lumber*. A silent challenge hangs in the air, a dare to any who dare to pass. The Pale Tree. I charge, a surge of frustrated energy, intent on scaling its formidable trunk.

Before my hands can find purchase, a small, unwelcome voice pierces the air, "Let me help!"

Her distraction is fatal. My momentum slams me face-first into the unyielding bark, a jarring impact that sends me stumbling backward, sprawling onto the hard earth. Annoyance flares, a hot, prickly sensation.

She offers a hand, a gesture I reject with a shove. I won't be deterred. I retreat, gathering my resolve. Again, I charge in a burst of speed. I leap forward, a futile attempt to conquer the impossible. Again, I fall, the ground a constant reminder of my failure.

Gritting my teeth, I push myself up, hitting the sticky white dust from my dress.

Again.

I charge blindly, my head colliding with a low-hanging branch. I tumble to the ground. Glaring at the stubborn trunk of the Pale Tree, I clench my fists in frustration.

Meanwhile, the Girl leans casually against the table, with an *amused* look.

"What?" I snap.

"Let me help." Her voice is irritatingly gentle.

"I'm sick of *letting* things happen to me," I declare.

I *let* myself fall asleep. I *let* myself have that dream with the serpent. I *let* myself give in to the threads of the Voice, so they entered my ears. I *let* myself lose control and almost succumb to the call of the Voice just now.

I clench my jaw, my teeth grinding together in a rhythmic, almost mechanical way. I curl into the base of the Pale Tree, rocking back and forth. *Where* did I come from? *Why* am I here? *Who* am I?

Why do I feel like I'm being used, pulled in all directions, yet ... still ... aimless? As if I'm nobody but somebody, all in one? There's something expected of me, a weight anchoring me down, and I don't know if it's good or bad.

I don't know *anything*.

This place ... it holds answers, both the ones I seek and the ones I desperately want to escape. What's better? Remaining ignorant, or discovering the truth? What if the serpent in the dream was telling me I'm bad? I will only know when I know the *truth*. And the truth ... the truth lies somewhere there ... beyond that Pale Tree which is staring me down. The truth is in a place called, Thalj. Something inside of me just knows it with a certainty I can't explain.

The Girl's head tilts. I straighten my back, a flicker of determination returning. I set my focus on the Pale Tree.

I turn to the Girl. "Help me get through this."

She sets the table under the tree and, with a mischievous glint in her eye, climbs onto the trunk and effortlessly vaults to the other side.

I clear my throat. "No need to be so smug."

I follow her, scaling the trunk and dropping down to the other side.

Cattle

YOU

The softness of the green grass muffles my landing. This area beyond the Pale Tree, dwarfs the Zam and the Orbee Forest.

"What's the name of this part?" I ask.

A few shafts of sunlight, like golden spears, pierce the swirling gray smoke above us. These fleeting rays dance across the ground, illuminating a blinding white expanse which stretches before me, punctuated only by the skeletal forms of towering sand dunes. The Great Wall looms over it all, its metal a stark contrast against the white.

I turn to the Girl who is hovering close, wiggling her toes on the white part of the ground, while itching her chest. "I suppose I don't have a name for every part in Jinnah, do I?"

The sadness in her voice is a weight I don't want to bear. I offer no reply.

I skirt the frayed edge of the grass, the brittle blades snapping beneath my feet, and sink to my knees. My hesitant finger, trembling slightly, reaches out to probe the stark, white patch of ground, a jarring contrast to the thriving brown that clings beneath the grass upon which I kneel.

The white of the ground is not cold like snow. It holds a subtle, unsettling coolness. It is rough and granular beneath my fingertips, with pockets of warmth where the meager rays of light find purchase through the oppressive smoke.

I pinch a clump of the chalky material between my thumb and forefinger, lifting it to my nose, expecting … something. There is nothing. Like a void, a disturbing, utter blankness which sends a shiver crawling down my spine. No richness, no musty scent of dirt like the banks of the Zam. Just *empty*.

The brown earth beneath the grass smells like a subtle, less damp, and dustier version of the Zam's bank.

I flop back and pluck a few blades, briefly studying their green color before bringing them to my nose and inhaling deeply. The grass has a distinctly sweet scent.

I'm reminded of my dream, Adamah looking at me with her big round eyes and flushed cheeks.

"The grass smells sweeter when you pull it," the Girl's words pull me back. Her gaze lingers on the blades in my hand. She adds softly, "It smells like that because it's hurt."

"Hurt?" I let some of the blades fall to the ground.

"It's dying—"

"Dying?"

"I mean, falling. Anyway, that smell is a call for help."

I roll my feet on the fallen blades, their touch leaving traces of light green on my soles. "Does anyone respond to the call?"

She stares at me blankly. Finally, she says, "The orbees used to come on their own, but now they only come with me." As she speaks, the two orbees cling to her shoulder, trembling slightly.

"Why?" I press.

She sighs, her gaze sweeping across the landscape. "They're scared of something."

Her eyes dart towards a cluster of trees to our right.

The trees here are much smaller than the towering trees in the Orbee Forest, their width no greater than the span of an outstretched arm. Their deep roots disappear beneath the surface, offering no clue as to what anchors them to the ground.

Their sturdy trunks support rounded canopies of different heights, some reaching towards the meek light filtering through the dense canopy of smoke above.

Others face down as if not yet strong enough to rise.

All the trees have thick foliage, a vibrant display of bright green leaves. The gorgeous green erupts from the branches in thick clusters at the base, gradually thinning as they fan outwards, creating a dense wall of a cluster of trees.

I shift uncomfortably. I don't like not knowing what lies beyond those trees. I touch the spike in my pocket. A movement behind. I push the Girl behind me and draw the spike.

Peeking from behind me, the Girl gasps with delight. A camel emerges with a slow, deliberate gait on long legs. Its entire body is cloaked in a shimmering cascade of golden fur, and a prominent hump rises dramatically on its back. I gasp in awe.

"Lashes, there you are!" the Girl exclaims, relief washing over her face. "Where's Smiley?"

As she speaks, another, smaller camel emerges from behind the tree. The Girl throws her arms around their necks, burying her face in their soft fur with a squeal of joy.

I pocket the spike and trail behind her. The larger creature, with golden eyes, dips its head towards me.

"Lashes?" I repeat.

"Yes, because he's got long lashes like you!"

That isn't entirely true. The Girl has long eyelashes, too, and so does the other camel. I decide not to say anything about that and ask, "Did you just compare me to … that?" There's a hint of amusement in my voice.

She shoots me a glance, scanning my face, her shoulders tense. She relaxes them when she sees I am slightly entertained, before turning her attention back to the creatures. Smiley has a perpetual wide grin on its face, which reveals a row of scattered teeth.

"What else is here?" I ask, trying to squeeze past the camels.

Smiley playfully blocks my way, nudging its head under my chin. It blows a puff of air onto my face. With a gentle dip of its head, it finally allows me to pass before stumbling off to graze on the withering grass.

"These are the friends I was telling you about," the Girl says brightly.

"Cattle?"

Her brow furrows, and she tilts her head, searching my eyes. "Cattle?"

"Yes, cattle. All they do is eat, poop and sleep," I scoff, as I gesture toward the scattered dropping on the dusty ground, expecting a retort.

Her brow relaxes, and she smiles. "I suppose they do."

I watch her curiously as she climbs one of the trees. She's surprisingly agile for someone so small, though her movements are a bit awkward. Very awkward.

She scrambles up, her feet occasionally slipping on the bark, but catches herself. Finally, she reaches a sturdy branch, her legs dangling shakily. With her face scrunched, she shakes the branch vigorously, sending a shower of small, oval-shaped objects raining down.

Jumping to the ground, she gathers them in her cupped hands—a handful of deep purple shades.

"Olives: best eaten fresh," she announces, holding one out to me and pocketing the rest.

I eye her pocket as I hold the olive up to my nose and sniff, my mouth slightly watering at the fruity smell. Why isn't she eating with me? Did she do something to these? I lower the fruit slowly.

"I've eaten already," she says, as if reading my mind.

She lowers her eyes to the ground and wiggles her toes, a gesture which, for some reason, feels comfortably familiar. I scan her face for any sign of mischief—a sly grin, pursed lips, a stifled laugh—but nothing. Just a small pout, and her head hung low.

A wave of guilt washes over me as I reflect on my words about the camels. I remember how I've been treating her: dismissive, a little abrupt, quite rude (even though she can be very annoying). Always rambling on about this and that, lost in her own world, so naïve. Not to mention, she walks oddly, too.

Then I recall how she responds to my jabs. She takes them. Like punches. No one can endure that for too long. Eventually, we all fight back. Maybe that's what I hope she'll do. Fight back. I shake my arms, trying to shake off this unsettling feeling—the familiar comfort with a slight edge of softness in my chest—but it lingers.

I hesitate before setting the olive beside her and take a small step back, keeping a watchful eye on her.

"When these trees fall," she murmurs, "there won't be any food for my Mama. And she doesn't eat insects."

"Why would she eat insects?" I lean against a tree, watching her kick up little puffs of dust.

A tiny frown creases her forehead for a moment, a passing shadow. Her shoulders slump just a touch, and she lets out a soft sigh. She mumbles something I can't hear clearly; I only catch the word: "Filling."

"Insects are filling?" I press, as I try to meet her gaze. She continues to avoid mine. "Eat."

She offers the olive back to me.

I shake my head and sit. "Tastes better than insects."

"Just a bite, then." She sits opposite me and takes a bite as if defying some unspoken rule, devouring the olive, swallowing it with a determined look.

I relax as she hands me another olive from her pocket. I take a bite, the flesh pleasantly firm beneath my teeth. My eyes widen in surprise, but I quickly mask my astonishment as a satisfying pop accompanies the bite, releasing a burst of briny flavor. There's a subtle bitterness that balances the savory taste perfectly. As I chew, a hint of fruity sweetness emerges, unexpected and delightful. The olive is not mushy, but meaty. A subtle nuttiness lingers on my tongue.

"I give them names before I do," she says quietly.

"The insects?"

"Everything deserves a name, doesn't it?" she replies.

"This place doesn't have one, and I don't know mine. Maybe, not having a name isn't so bad."

"Why?"

"Because you can choose to be what you want to be, instead of having to live up to a title."

She nods contemplatively and takes out another two olives from her pocket and stuffs them in my hands. She takes out two more, pushing them into her mouth.

"Why is it so quiet here?" I ask, with my mouth full. "Where are the birds in Jinnah?"

"Most of the animals have been gone for some time now. There's only Lashes and Smiley and——"

I interject, "Since when?"

"Since the Great Wall was built, the smoke came and the sickness."

"This sickness," I lean forward, the question cutting through the uneasy quiet, "what causes it?"

"I don't know." She stands. A small object, hidden beneath her dress, falls on the ground with a gentle thud.

"What is that?"

"Book," she says under her breath, as she picks up the folded pages carefully.

I raise my eyebrow. "These are just pages," The pages are crumpled and torn, their edges ragged and uneven. I reach out to neaten the crumpled pages, but she moves them away, protectively.

"I counted 28 letters in it," she whispers, her eyes fixed on the book.

I try to catch a glimpse of the mysterious pages. A tattered edge peeks out from the messy pile. I reach out, eager to attempt to touch it again, but she quickly pulls it away.

"Each page has around 15 lines, but I think some more pages are missing," she continues, flipping through the disjointed stack. "The edges look like they should be bound together."

"Does it have a name?" I ask.

She nods, staring at the book. Silence stretches.

"Well … what is its name?" I stand, so I can loom over her, intentionally adding a little impatience to my tone.

She looks up, slightly annoyed. I try not to show the smile playing on my lips, even though I wanted to provoke her for some reason.

"Book," she says, as if it's the most obvious thing in the world.

"Just ... Book?"

She shrugs, returning her attention to the pages.

"You don't have anyone to talk to, do you?" I stare at her.

She opens her mouth to speak, then closes it again. Her eyes dart around nervously, a flicker of fear crossing her face.

My body tenses. "What is it?"

She hesitates, her fingers tracing the worn pages of the Book. "It's about the day I met you."

I blink, taken aback by the sudden change in topic.

Her toes curl beneath her, making her feet look almost bird-like as she says, "The Voice called me that day. Why? Why then?"

"Because I was there?"

She nods; her lips pursed. "I think so," she says slowly, as if weighing her words carefully. "But that's not why I went out there. The Voice wasn't the reason."

"Why did you go?" I ask.

"I went to find answers," she says, her gaze flickering towards me.

I wait for her to elaborate, but she remains silent, her lips still pursed, making her look like a little old lady. Her eyes widen as she notices my trembling hands.

"Your hands are shaking," she observes, her voice filled with concern.

I quickly slip my hands into my pockets, seeking comfort in the familiar weight of the spike. When I am reminded of the Voice, my heart races and my breathing becomes shallow and quick. Clearing my throat, I roll the spike between my fingers, welcoming the slight pain it causes my wounds. Pain makes me feel alert.

"What answers were you looking for?" I ask.

"How to save Jinnah from the sickness."

"Did you find any?"

"I found you." The Girl plops onto her belly, burying the Book under her chest.

I sit too, mostly because my legs won't stop shaking. Her face is inches away from my feet. I instinctively move them away from her, so they face the opposite direction.

She is focused on a tiny beetle that struggles to carry its heavy body. Without looking up she asks, "Was the dream all bad?"

"Not all of it," I reply, glad to find the earth beneath my body calming. I cross my legs. "Do you see bad things?"

"We focus on the bad."

"What else is there to focus on?"

She shrugs. "Good."

"Good won't keep you safe."

"Good *is* safe," she says, nonchalantly.

"Says the child who claims not to be much good at anything." When I say this, she winces slightly, with her eyes still on the beetle, which, in its best effort, still has not crawled very far. She sits back up, placing the pages of the Book in her lap.

"Do you carry that everywhere with you?" I ask, nodding to the Book.

"Only in Jinnah," she replies.

The way it rustles every time she moves puts me on edge. It's annoying how carelessly she carries it, especially with so many loose pages sprawling out.

"Let me make it easier for you to carry."

I take the string from the leaf she had given me and hesitate before ripping a piece of my dress, but do it anyway. It has dried quickly in the cool air, which makes it slightly harder to tear. After a few pulls, I resort to the sharp edge of the spike, neatly tearing off a few strips of cloth from the bottom part of my dress, which was dragging on the floor.

Using the makeshift thread, I weave the string into the fabric, folding the material over it and tying it securely with small knots. I motion for the Girl to come closer. Taking the completed pouch, I tie the string around her neck, letting it drape over her shoulders.

"Here," I suggest, placing it over her chest. "Or here?" I ask, repositioning it on her stomach.

"Here," she says, pointing to her chest.

I adjust the fabric so that the pouch sits snugly, then carefully place the Book inside the pouch.

She touches it and opens her arms wide. At first, I think she's about to hug me. I move back so quickly that I stumble into a tree. She doesn't notice. Instead, she positions her arms in a graceful pose, presenting the Book as if it were a precious gem.

She then begins to dance, her movements a whirlwind of flailing limbs and awkward steps, like a camel trying to gallop through a field of thorns. Yet, her face is pure bliss, as if she's the most graceful creature on Earth.

"What was that?" I ask when she stops.

"I do it when I feel really happy sometimes," she explains, patting her chest. "Or sad, or angry."

"You mean whenever you feel anything?" I ask, raising my only eyebrow.

She giggles, a soft, childlike sound. I remain still, pretending to be lost in thought, while secretly listening. That laugh. I've heard it before. The snorts, the shriek. After a few moments, the giggles subside, and her lips return to their usual downturned position.

"What were you dancing to?" I ask.

"Nothing ... myself."

"Nothing or yourself?"

She shrugs, as if it's the same thing. "And us," she adds.

I feel my face scrunch up. "Us?"

"We have a song," she explains, her eyes sparkling with intensity.

"Not *me*." I shake my head, unable to follow her train of thought.

"*We* do," she insists, "we're both dancing. You're the strong one, and I'm following your lead."

Her words hang in the air. I quickly avert my gaze, trying to hide my surprise.

She cradles the Book on her chest, a look of pure adoration on her face. She scratches her chest. Her face momentarily changes, a glimmer of something crossing it. Pain. I open my mouth to ask if it is too tight, and just like that, the look disappears.

"It's perfect!" she says, her voice filled with wonder. "Book is special."

"How so?" I ask, distracted by her previous observation of our interaction.

"It saves us," she whispers, her eyes wide.

"From what?" I bring my focus back to her.

"Ourselves," she whispers.

"But it's on your chest," I point out, confused.

She shrugs nonchalantly, itching her chest again absent-mindedly. "True."

Our eyes meet for a moment, and I quickly look away.

"Do you always jump from one topic to another like that?" I ask.

She looks at me puzzled, as if *I'm* the problem for not keeping up.

I stand, ready to escape the conversation. As I walk away, I can't help but wonder if she's truly lost in her own world or if she's deliberately playing mind games. She is much cleverer than she portrays. Her comment on our 'dance' gives me an unsettling feeling.

The Girl's faint footsteps follow behind me, echoing my own.

"Where are you going?" she shouts from behind me.

"Thalj," I reply curtly.

"You can't go when it's dark!"

"It's always dark."

"Did I do something wrong?" she asks.

I turn to meet her gaze. "You make out you're this soft, submissive person." She opens her mouth but clasps it shut when I hold my palm up. Her lower lip shakes slightly. "But you know a lot more than you let on."

"What did I do?" She searches my eyes.

I drill mine into hers. "You're pretending."

"I am?"

With a frustrated grunt, I spin around, my back facing her, and march off.

"Wait!" she shouts after me. "It's not safe to go to Thalj in the dark!"

"I told you it's *always* dark."

"I mean, even darker."

"I can see in the dark."

"It's not safe," she says, out of breath from trying to keep up. She falls into step with me.

"Why?" I ask, without looking at her.

"It's … windy," she says weakly.

I quicken my pace.

"Wait!" she says.

"Have you been trying to distract me from going there all along?"

She shifts from foot to foot, like a guilty child. "There's something wrong with the sky in Thalj."

I stop walking. Firmly, I say, "Take me."

"No," she whispers.

Her legs are shaking. She is genuinely scared.

I look into her eyes. "Please."

She opens and closes her hands, biting her bottom lip. "Only if you help me."

"Something for something?" I ask, crossing my arms.

"This is different."

"How?"

"You won't just help *me*."

I look at her expectantly.

She continues, "You'll help all of us: my Mama, my friends …" I follow her gaze to the deadening plains ahead, and she looks back at me. "And you."

"You're good at saying what you think I want to hear," I say bluntly. "There's a word for that."

She doesn't ask me what the word is and continues, "The trees are falling. Jinnah is dying. The smoke that brought the sickness is moving to Golden Dome. To my Mama."

I take a long breath, then look up, tracing her gaze to the thick blackness overhead.

"I came to find the truth about who I am. My answers are in Thalj, not in saving all this."

She stares at me, wide-eyed, waiting for me to continue.

I turn back towards the cluster of trees and sigh. "Even if I wanted to, I can't save this."

"You can!" she insists, her voice firm. "You made this." She holds up the pouch and then grabs my hand, squeezing it. "Please, fix it, make it better."

I shake her off me. "Make it better or fix it?"

"Does it matter?" She injects a note of lightheartedness, but the urgency in her gaze betrays her attempt.

The air around us feels thick with her plea, and her eyes threaten to pierce through my defenses, reaching a place I'd rather keep untouched.

She whispers, "Help us."

"There's no point," I say coldly.

"Why?" she asks.

The single word cracks the dam within me.

Guilty.

The word chimes over and over in my head.

I grit my teeth, unable to meet her eyes. "How can I make something right when I don't know what's causing it to be wrong?"

"You won't know if you don't try." Her voice softens. "I'll help. I'm good at helping."

I watch as she sways from one foot to the other. *She's just a child.*

"Before, when you said I know more than I say, you were right, I do!" She nods quickly. "I can't help what I know, but I promise I use it in a good way."

"That's ... very vague." As I say this, I kick at the dirt, as if that will make the hardness in my chest come back.

It doesn't.

With a defeated sigh, I follow the Girl as she sits on the patch of grass. The grey sky fades to black.

"You'll help?" she asks, her face glowing from the two orbees.

"On two conditions," I reply, my voice firm. "One, take me to Thalj."

"Okay."

"Two, no more eating insects." I don't know why I say this. Why do I care what she eats? I suppose it won't hurt to have one less annoying thing about her.

"Okay," she says again softly.

"Promise?" I ask.

She hesitates before loudly proclaiming the words, "Promise."

I probably need something to do while I'm searching for answers anyway. In an unexpected outburst, she throws her arms around me. I try to gently push her away, but she persists.

I'm exhausted.

But I can't sleep.

I can't dream.

I need my strength if I am going to stay awake. That is the only reason I *let* her hug me.

PART 8

The Skies

ME

The first rise of the sun has arrived. In two more rises, You will witness Your greatest rise and Your greatest fall. Then we will be ready. *Our* time is …

YOU

"**R**unning out." I whisper.

My words fade into the thick, smoke-filled sky. A new day where the sun's rays are dimmer than yesterday. Lashes and Smiley graze on a patch of withered grass, seemingly oblivious to whether it is day or night. A gentle breeze stirs the air, carrying with it the acrid scent of burning wood and something else I can't quite put words to.

The Girl rises with a sudden burst of energy, which amplifies my fatigue. I haven't slept. I am not in a good mood. She springs to her feet, her eyes bright with enthusiasm. With a flick of her wrist, she wets a finger and dabs it on her dry eyes.

Noticing my raised eyebrow, she offers a cheerful explanation, "My eyes get dry when I wake up."

She plops down beside me, her legs sprawled ahead of her and her gaze fixed on my face.

"What?" I ask, pulling the veil over the burnt side of my face.

"What's running out?" she asks, tilting her head slightly. Her large, puffy eyes are still heavy with sleep——a contrast to her bopping demeanor.

"Time."

"Where is it running to?"

"Out."

"What if we're the ones running out?" she asks, following my gaze towards the smoke-choked sky. "I've watched the sunrise for as long as I can remember—before the smoke, and it's always been the same."

"The smoke hasn't always been here?"

In mid-yawn she says, "I told you already, no. And neither has Great Wall."

I glance at her. It seems that along with that morning energy is a little bite.

She catches my gaze and looks at her toes, wiggling them in that familiar way. She says softly, "It's been nine hundred twenty-two sunrises since Great Wall was built."

"Two and a half years ago. Who built it?"

She gives a half-shrug. "Cast probably."

"Makes sense since the first night I woke up outside the Great Wall, they were there." I think out loud. I look up at the swirling vortex of grey above. "What about the smoke? When did that come?"

She follows my gaze. "The smoke is more recent than Great Wall. It started about 372 sunrises ago."

"About a year ago."

"Yes. But even before the smoke, for about 1,460 sunrises——" She moves her mouth as if counting something and then says, "Around four years ago—"

"You learn quickly."

"I'm good with numbers." She blushes slightly. Encouraged, she continues, "Four years ago, the sun stopped shining all over Jinnah. Before that, it only shone here, Thalj and Fallen Trees."

"Why not the Orbee Forest?"

"I don't know. I think there's something up there that's blocking the sun."

"That must be why the tree branches in the Orbee Forest reach downward toward the orbees' lights instead of upward toward the sky."

"Must be," she says. She turns to me, eyes wide with concern. "You didn't sleep, did you?"

"I couldn't with all that clanging," I reply, rising and heading towards the edge of the grass. Turning to her, I say, "Was it the Cast making all that noise?"

She nods. "Recently, they started coming more." She follows me. "I slept."

"Good for you."

I know I sound a little bitter, but she doesn't seem to notice. She tries to come even closer to me. I don't think this girl knows about space boundaries. Now she is a little *too* close for comfort. I can feel her breath on the back of my dress just beneath my shoulders, a warm puff against the fabric, as she stands dwarfed behind me, her small frame unable to reach higher. I turn to her.

"Are you always so chirpy when you wake up?"

She looks ahead, a distant look in her eyes. I wave my hand in front of her, and she snaps out of it, turning her attention back to me. She blinks a few times and then says, "You should sleep."

Somewhat used to her bouncing focus, I continue walking along the grass. "I won't be here for long. And I'm not sleeping here."

She doesn't answer, her gaze fixed on my feet. "You walk like *assad*."

Assad. She means 'lion'. Another tingling feeling of familiarity. That word, along with other words: Thalj. Shahwah, Zam, and Jinnah remind me of a language which I feel like I should know.

"What does an assad walk like?"

"Smooth. Takes up space. Always ready." As she says this, she attempts to demonstrate, moving in her usual frumpy manner. She tries to straighten her body, her head tilting upwards, but the overall effect is more ungainly than regal.

"You walk like a baby bird in high heels," I say.

She nods slowly, processing the observation. She smiles faintly. "Thank you."

I nod, lost in thought, and lean towards the barren land. I shift my attention to the other side of the area, moving closer to the cluster of trees.

"You've got long legs too," she observes, mimicking my movements as she squints at the ground.

"You can't see my legs in this dress," I reply, continuing my exploration of the grassy area.

"I can tell. You could probably reach the lower-hanging branches of olives from the trees," she says, quickly catching up to me.

I remain silent, hoping to discourage her from talking more. A brief silence stretches out as we both examine the ground. Her focus is unwavering, mirroring my own.

If I'm honest, I'm impressed by her skill. Her eyes swiftly scan the soil, seemingly knowing exactly where to look. The intensity of her gaze is surprising as she methodically picks and drops small amounts of soil. I begin to question her need for my assistance—she clearly has a good grasp of the situation.

After just a moment of her investigation, she asks, "What are we doing?"

A startled squeak escapes my lips. I cover my mouth to stifle a laugh. Clearing my throat, I manage to say, "We're studying the ground."

"I'm hungry." She clumsily marches off to the olive trees. She looks back at me expectantly. "Shake it."

"Excuse me?" I ask, a hint of offense coloring my voice as I cross my arms over my chest.

"Shake it!" she repeats, gesturing to the tree.

I uncross my arms and push my hand against the trunk whilst she nods a little too fast, attempting to be—I presume—encouraging.

I shake my head instead and pull my hand away to turn back towards the grassy area. She's distracting me. I need to finish this task. She sighs and climbs the tree, returning with a handful of dark, plump olives. Realizing I'm quite hungry as well, I decide to eat to regain my energy.

As we sit under the tree, she offers a few olives, her expression a mixture of generosity and uncertainty. She watches me like she's asking me permission to eat.

"Eat." I prompt her.

She nods and digs in.

"Is there any other food here besides olives?" I ask, my stomach growling.

"Like what?"

"Meat?"

"There are insects," she says, in a matter-of-fact manner.

I feel my nose crinkle involuntarily. My gaze lingers on Lashes and then, back to the Girl. She closes her eyes, savoring each morsel of the olive.

Wiping her mouth, she asks, "Why are we looking at the land?"

"Before doing anything, we must know what needs to be done. We are studying it. Seeing which part is soft and which part is hard." I reply, finishing the last olive and stretching my arms.

"Why does that matter?"

"Soft earth yields life."

"What about hard earth?"

"Hard earth yields death." I take a deep breath. "What we're doing here is preparing for growth."

She abruptly stands, then falls back down to the ground. Is she hurt? She quickly recovers, waving her arms in the air. It takes me a moment to realize she is doing one of her odd dances.

She backs up to the grassy area, stomping to each side and throwing herself onto the ground, her face pressed against the rough earth. Grabbing a handful of white dirt, she tosses it towards me.

"What are you doing?" I ask, bewildered, my face covered in dust.

"Getting ready for growth," she replies. "What do we do first?"

I wipe off the white dust from my veil and my cheeks, watching the Girl. I wonder if I've lost my mind or if the child has.

I turn towards the Fallen Trees. "Is there any way we can move these camels to the Orbee Forest?"

"The only way is back the way we came," she replies.

"Didn't you say the Zam runs through Thalj?" I ask.

"Yes, but in Thalj, Zam is under ice. And the camels won't survive the cold." She straightens up her back. "There *is* another place."

She doesn't elaborate. Instead, she turns her gaze to the Great Wall. After a long pause, I ask, "Well, what is the other place?"

She blinks a few times before replying, "Valley, but it isn't safe for the camels."

"Why?"

She keeps staring at the Great Wall.

I shake my head, deciding to take matters into my own hands, rather than rely on her scattered 'insights'.

Pushing myself up, I mutter, "If we can't move the camels, we need wood."

"How much? What kind?"

"Get what you can." I say, turning away.

"What are we doing?" she asks.

"You'll see," I mumble.

I look away from her. The truth is, I don't know what we're doing, not fully. I only know that the next step is to get wood. Once we do that, I'm hoping the step after will become clear.

She doesn't need to know my uncertainty. If she does, she might lose trust in me. I catch myself. Why would I care if she trusts me? Then again, all of this, perhaps, has nothing to do with trust. Simply not knowing appears weak. Weakness is vulnerability. Vulnerability leads to exposure. Exposure invites violation. Best to keep my uncertainty to myself.

The Girl disappears behind the Pale Tree. I take advantage of the momentary peace and further examine the grassy area. Some patches feel softer under my touch, almost spongy, as if the earth beneath it is giving way.

The Girl returns quickly, carrying small blocks of wood. She sets them down in front of me with a *thud*. I fumble with the ones at the bottom of the pile, my fingers tracing the rough grain. What do I do with these? I clear my throat as I feel her eyeing me.

Rope. I need rope. And more wood.

"Make ropes," I instruct, tossing them her way. The wood clatters against her hands as I turn and head towards the Fallen Trees. "I'll get more wood."

"Can you just tell me what we're doing so I can help, half the day's already gone!" she calls after me.

"Half the day? The sun has just risen."

"I told you, time moves differently in Jinnah."

"What I'm doing is helping *you*," I emphasize each word.

"Are we doing this together?" she asks.

My face flushes. "You ask a lot of questions," I mutter as I turn away.

This side of the Pale Tree offers a network of sturdy branches, a natural staircase. I climb them until I reach the top. With a jump, I land softly on the table on the other side. As my feet touch the ground, an eerie feeling washes over me. Something is off.

The girl was here recently, yes. Yet, this off feeling is different from the Girl's presence, a sensory distinction I can't fully explain. The area remains largely undisturbed, save for the exit hole, suggesting a more deliberate visit than the Girls. There's an almost calculated precision to this other presence, lacking the Girl's usual clumsiness.

Gripping the spike in my pocket, I head steadily towards the exit hole. I approach a pile of branches. My breath is silent but quick, and my steps soundless. Nothing. Just a few vines snaking into the hole. I follow their edges and gasp. Someone *was* here. And they wanted me to know.

They left something: markings near the hole. A message for me? The markings aren't just patterns; they are letters and words. What surprises me the most is that I can read them:

The Guardian

The Healer

The All Mighty

Peering through the hole reveals no further clues about who left the message, about the Stranger. I scan behind each white tree trunk for clues. Finding nothing, I turn to gather as many thick, long branches as I can carry before clambering over the Pale Tree.

When I reach the other side, I approach the Girl who is leaning against an olive tree, focused on her rope-making. I compose myself so I don't look as shaken as I feel.

I ask, "Are you sure you're the only one here?"

"Only one?" she replies, looking up briefly from her task.

"Only person?" I lay the branches next to one of the olive trees.

"In Jinnah, yes." She looks up, eyes narrowing. "Why?"

I glance back at where I came from. "You didn't see anything unusual when you went to the Fallen Trees just now?"

"What happened?" She lets go of the ropes, and they fall with a gentle *thud* on the ground.

"Someone wrote something on the ground," I say, looking at her. "Could it be your mother?"

"My Mama doesn't come here," she replies, her gaze intense.

"Then could it be someone from the Cast?"

She shakes her head. Her eyes widen. "Do you think it was—"

"The Voice?" I shake my head. "It can't enter Jinnah. Something tells me the Voice doesn't settle for the second-best option. If it could, it would come here itself and talk directly to me instead of luring me out with a whisper like a coward. Somehow, the Voice is blocked from entering Jinnah."

"My mama tells me to say something before I enter and leave. She said it's what makes time and space different in Jinnah. She also said it guards Jinnah. I think that's why the Voice can't come in here." She looks at the ropes thoughtfully.

Makes time different? Changes space? What kind of word or phrase could do that? "What did your mother tell you?"

She doesn't seem to hear me. Instead, she says, "You said the person wrote something, did you read it?"

"Yes, but what did your mother—"

"You can read?" she interrupts, standing as she pulls out the Book. "Can you teach me?"

Teach? I quickly look away, a small sense of panic making my chest feel tight. Why am I suddenly out of breath? What is it about the idea of teaching that scares me?

"Like whoever taught you," she replies, trying to catch my eye.

"Teaching you to read won't fix this world," I state, focusing on the ropes. I don't want to talk about teaching. I change the subject. "The ropes look good."

The fear morphs to annoyance. Sitting next to her, I struggle to weave the branches together. My silly spike isn't sharp enough to shape the wood. Frustrated, I hurl a branch as far as I can.

"Here," she says, placing something in my hand.

The first thing I notice is its glint—the way it seizes the rays of the sunlight and scatters the small lights across the dust, illuminating everything it touches. The sharpness of its edge is soothing, as if untouched by time, refusing to be numbed down. As my hands close around it, the handle feels cool, crafted from a thick wood that molds to my grip like the fingers I was born with.

This time I do not lose my breath from fear, but from awe. "Where did you get this knife from?"

The Girl says, "I'll tell you when you tell me how you learned to read."

"Something for something," I say.

She looks at me expectantly.

"I don't remember who taught me to read," I admit. I don't tell her how uncomfortable my body feels when I think about it. I focus on the knife. It makes me feel *safe*. Like the water in the Zam. Like the dark.

Thankfully, the Girl moves on from this subject. "Well, I've always had the knife."

"You've barely used it." I run my fingers over the patterns on the wooden handle. "It's beautiful."

With a burst of energy, I hurl the knife at the closest tree, aiming just above the hole in the center.

The Girl shifts uncomfortably. "You just stabbed the tree."

I pull the knife out and clear some of the bark, wiping the sap away. "It's just a line. You can't even see it." As I say this, more sap oozes out.

I return to slicing the branches, more vigorously, the sound of the knife's passage becoming a frenzied dance of *cracks* and *screeches*.

Each stroke is a sharp, percussive strike, followed by a longer, more drawn-out scrape as the blade tears through the fibrous wood.

I've cut enough, but it's hard to stop.

I position more of the wood as stakes, holding them in place as I survey the area. What next? Something heavy to pound it all in.

"Smiley!" I call out.

"Smiley?" the Girl mutters and shuffles. I can tell from the side of my eyes that she's doing that odd itching motion on her chest. A *nervous* itch, I realize.

"Bring me Smiley; I need his legs."

"*Her*," she corrects, as she leads Smiley to me.

I gently lower the creature to the ground until her legs are folded, then use her feet to dig in the stakes. The rhythmic *thump* of the camel's hooves against the hard ground punctuates the quiet scene. Each strike is a forceful pound as the heavy hooves sink into the earth, securing the stakes with each powerful blow. After a few thumps, Smiley grunts and struts away.

I haven't finished yet. I still need something heavy to pound the final stake.

"Thicker wood." I hold my hand out, but the Girl doesn't respond, probably zoned out again. I grab a thicker branch and use it to pound in the stake.

As I step back to look at everything, relief washes over me. *Ah, that's what I'm making.* The realization energizes me as I support the sides with my feet and call out for the next tool.

"Ropes." I hold my hand out.

A shadow looms. I turn. The Girl hovers with both arms crossed over her chest.

"You're building a prison!" she accuses, throwing her arms to her side, her hands clenched into fists.

"Listen, sometimes if we want to do something, it might not make sense at first," I explain.

"You said you don't remember anything!" she counters, moving in front of Smiley.

"It's more of an instinct."

"My instinct says locking animals up isn't right."

"Listen——"

"Stop telling me to listen!" she snaps, taking a step away from me, her hands shaking.

"I'm trying to help," I whisper.

I thought I wanted to see her with a little strength. A little force. But this doesn't feel good.

"You're trying to do what you *think* is right," she says, her eyes glistening with tears. "Even if it hurts those around you."

Guilty.

I try to hide my own trembling hands and steady my breath. She wipes her face and looks away from me. I put everything down and turn fully towards her, but she avoids looking at me.

I bite my bottom lip, considering if I should tell her the truth, and sigh. "I wasn't sure if it was the right thing to do at first, but as I kept doing it, the next step made sense, so I did that. The truth is, I wasn't sure what I was doing until," I shake my head, "it sounds silly."

"What sounds silly?" She sniffles.

"Not knowing," I confess.

"You didn't know?" She finally looks up at me.

I shake my head.

"Why didn't you just say so?" she asks, her voice gentle.

"Not knowing is weak."

She sits next to me, her dirt-ridden face streaked with tears. With a rough gesture, she wipes her face with the back of her sleeve. The moisture smears the dirt into dark, damp patches on her dress.

"I always thought the weakest part is what makes us the strongest," she says, stroking Lashes, who nudges her gently with his head.

"Well, I know what I'm doing now," I declare, leaning forward. "Do you see this?" I touch the ground, letting the arid dirt run through my fingers. "It's like this because it's not having time to regrow. When it does, the camels eat it again." I flatten the earth.

"This earth is exhausted." As I say this, my own eyes feel heavy as the small rays of the sun get dimmer. "It needs space."

The Girl wipes her face again and looks at the fence.

I add, "This *boundary* is to keep the camels in one area so we can feed them other things, only until the ground gets stronger."

"Why do we need the ground to be stronger?"

"This earth's strength comes from its softness. Right now, it's too hard for anything of value to grow on it."

"What are we growing?"

"Seeds."

"Seeds," she repeats, her thick brow furrowed. "Where do we get seeds?"

"Olives. The more olives we eat, the more seeds we can plant," I reply. "That means, more food for your mother too."

She nods, her expression thoughtful.

"Will the seeds stop the sickness?" Her voice is filled with hope.

"I don't know …" I trail off, my voice filled with uncertainty.

She looks at her feet, her shoulders slumped.

I add, "Let's take it one step at a time."

She glances at me from the corner of her eye and nods towards the wooden fence. "There's no other way?"

"There is … *one* other way." As I speak, she looks up to me in anticipation, waiting for me to continue. "Burn it all."

Her eyes widen in surprise, mirroring my feelings as soon as the words left my mouth. My throat feels dry, but still, I speak quickly, the words tumbling. "We can start from nothing or something. When fire burns a land, it becomes ready for things to grow on it."

"I prefer this idea," she says, her gaze fixed on the fence. Pausing, she adds, "One more thing. Don't stab trees." Her eyes, still red and swollen from crying, drill into mine in a silent plea.

I nod, and she shoves me playfully.

"You're quick to forgive and slow to get angry," I observe.

"Is that a good thing?"

I pretend I didn't hear her.

Yes. Yes, it is a good thing.

The camels are huddled together in the wooden enclosure; their eyes fixed longingly on the green grass on which I sit with the Girl. They've barely touched the olives I offered, their preference for the grass evident.

"We should bring them some plants from the Orbee Forest," I observe. "They need to be strong." I lick my dry lips, my own gaze fixed longingly on their thick, meaty bodies.

"Why do they need to be strong?" the Girl asks, her words slurring as she dozes off.

I mirror her slur, each word trailing off into silence. "Strong … meat … is … good."

"Meat?" she asks, somewhat confused.

I don't answer. The area stares back at me in its monochrome tones and fades to a world drained of color as the last rays of sunlight struggle to pierce the growing darkness.

"It's getting darker," she states the obvious.

I nod, my mind on cooked meat on a fire, the spices, an aroma floating into my nose. Thick, strong meat full of sizzling fat.

With this comforting thought, my eyelids droop. Her voice fades. I struggle to focus on her words, each one slipping away like grains of sand.

Her hand lands on my shoulder, a firm, jarring touch.

"What?" I force my eyes open, blinking rapidly, my fingers pressed on the handle of the knife.

"What if you have that dream again?" she asks, her voice sharper, her eyes wide with concern.

"Can't fall … asleep," I agree, but my words are thick and heavy.

My breath slows. My body slumps forward.

The dream returns. The same serpent. The same chase. But this time, before I jump off the bridge and enter the fire, a distant *rumble* echoes, followed by a rush to my head. A warmth spreads across my face, and my eyes snap open. I find myself staring into the rapidly fluttering nostrils of the Girl beside me.

"Was it the same dream?" she asks, her voice barely audible over the pounding of my heart.

"Same dream," I mutter, my voice thick with fatigue. I touch my ear. "Did you put the orbees in?"

She nods quickly, her eyes wide.

"Do they take away my need to sleep?"

She shakes her head. "They block it."

"I don't know how long I can go without sleep," I confess.

"I'll stay awake with you," she says, settling beside me.

She has bought a few more orbees from the Orbee Forest. In the dark, their lights beam like scattered stars. We sit in silence, staring at the desolate landscape before us.

The Girl stands, her movements slow and deliberate, as if her body is a heavy weight she must drag along. She raises her arms, a mechanical gesture, and walks to the tree I stabbed. She wraps her arms around it tightly. Her body sways, a jerky, unnatural motion, as the leaves rustle in an unseen wind.

She holds herself up, the orbees swirling around her in a chaotic dance. A *humming* sound fills the air, a discordant note in the quiet night from the Girl.

She spins a clumsy spin and falls to the ground, her body landing with a heavy *thud*. Rising again, she spreads her arms wide.

Though she moves so out of touch with her body, I am drawn to her. There is something familiar in her movements—that clumsiness, the disconnect.

"Are there rules to this movement?" I ask.

She stops humming and whispers, "No rules." She continues to sway with the tree.

I follow her lead, my body moving with a newfound fluidity. At first, my movements are tense, mirroring hers. She throws her right leg out, an attempt at a kick, her leg rising just inches from the ground. I imitate her, surprised by the ease with which my leg rises to my shoulder, a graceful motion that contrasts with her struggle.

She pauses. I consider stopping with her, but her encouraging nods urge me to continue. I twirl my hands in the air, a graceful arc, and finish with a light, effortless hop.

"Wow!" she says.

I feel a blush creeping up my cheeks.

I throw my leg out again, demonstrating the move with ease. She attempts to imitate me, but her leg gives out, and she tumbles to the ground.

"Don't try to force your body to do what it can't," I advise her. "Let it show you what it can."

I rise from the ground, creating a graceful arch with my body. My chin tilts, tracing a delicate circle.

This time, she doesn't join me. Instead, she sits beneath the olive tree I had stabbed earlier, her silhouette illuminated by the soft glow of the orbees. A soft, ethereal *hum* escapes her lips, a soothing melody that fills the smoky night air.

I move with the wind, my long dress swirling around me. My veil flows like water, framing my face, trailing wispily behind. I move forward, in sync with the swaying trees, then backward, the orbees dancing around me.

The Girl stops humming. I stop dancing. A small sob escapes her lips, and her shoulders are shaking. I sit beside her, my hand outstretched, hesitant to touch her. I don't know why she's crying.

When I try to speak, my throat feels tight. It takes a moment to realize that the wetness on my cheeks is not rain, but my tears. I cry silently so she doesn't hear me.

She looks up with flushed cheeks and shakes her head. "I'm sorry. I don't know why I'm crying."

I move my face into the shadows, hiding my puffy eyes. When I'm sure my voice is steady, I clear my throat and try to change the subject. "You fear the dark, don't you?"

She sniffles and wipes her nose with the back of her sleeve. She nods. "Don't you?"

I shake my head. "Switch the orbee lights off."

She shifts uneasily but whispers to the orbees anyway. Their light goes off, and she lets out a quiet gasp, holding my arm as she trembles.

The area becomes doused in gloom. Yet, I can see clearly: the shape of the fence—its rounded wood, sturdy—the shape of the camels, the Pale Tree ahead.

"Do you see anything?" she asks, still gripping my arm.

"Yes. It's like … my eyes were made to see in the dark."

She is trembling more violently now.

"You can turn the lights back on," I say, gently shaking her off.

When the orbees flicker on, she relaxes. "The only reason you aren't afraid of the dark is because you can see through it."

"Not true. Even if I couldn't, I *know* the dark is good." Without waiting for her to reply, I say, "If you can't see in the dark, then neither can your enemy. The dark is an advantage."

"What enemy? Why would I need an advantage?" she asks, her brow furrowed.

"It's always better to have the upper hand," I explain.

"What about the hand that's open?" she counters.

"Why would a hand be open?"

"To receive."

"That's not what I'm talking about. Anyway, a receiving hand is weak."

"Why are we talking about hands?" she asks.

"My point is, in the dark, you can focus more clearly," I reply, gazing up at the smoke-blocked sky. "You can see evil for what it is."

"Why would I want to see evil?" Her voice is filled with disbelief.

"Why *wouldn't* you?"

"Sometimes it's better not knowing," she says, her voice softening.

"You mean choosing to be ignorant."

She bristles slightly at my words.

I soften the edge in my voice. "You can't conquer what you don't know is there."

"What if you don't want to conquer anything? What if you just want to be … free?"

"You have to fight for your freedom," I retort.

"How?"

I look her up and down, noting her frail frame. I was right when I first saw her; she isn't a fighter. But I was also wrong; she isn't much of a runner either.

I shrug. "Use your voice."

She certainly knows how to do *that*.

"You'll find it if you embrace the quiet of the dark. Quiet is a lovely thing, don't you agree?" I add.

She itches her chest. "Have you found your voice?" she asks, a flicker of hope in her eyes.

I hesitate. "In what sense?"

"In the sense that is the most *you*."

Even though her words seem vague, I know what she means. My voice as in what is *true* for me. I haven't found that yet. But I will.

I tap my ear, and the orbee leaves with a *whoosh*, hovering back to the Girl.

"What are you doing?" she asks.

"I'm facing my dark," I declare.

"How?" she asks, her eyes wide with curiosity and fear.

"I'm going to sleep," I reply, turning to face her. "The darkness isn't my enemy; in it is a message. One that will help me."

"Like a friend?"

"Yes. A friend." I glance back at the sky. "It's good this land is shrouded in shadow and smoke."

"Even if it's caused by sickness?" she asks, her voice filled with doubt.

"You don't know that for sure," I say, meeting her gaze.

"All that might be true," she says, her voice strengthening. "But even the darkest night ends with dawn."

"Not here it doesn't," I retort, a grim smile playing on my lips.

She smiles faintly, her cheeks still damp from her tears. "It does if you look at the small rays of light which still push through the smoke." Her eyes are filled with a newfound determination. "But even if those rays don't find a way, it's okay."

"Why?" I ask, folding my veil to create a makeshift pillow.

"I'm not alone in the dark anymore," she replies, her voice soft. She lies down, facing me, her eyes meeting mine. "I have you."

I fuss with my veil, avoiding her gaze. "I don't think it matters," I mutter.

"What doesn't?"

I lay my head down. "You said before you didn't think you were much good at anything. I don't think it matters if that's true."

"Why not?" she asks.

"I think …" I gulp a lump down. "What matters more is that you *are* good."

She tries to catch my gaze, but I continue looking up at the sky.

"What made you say that?" she asks, finally settling her head on her folded arms as she follows my gaze up to the smog.

I don't answer. I don't tell her I think she is good. Instead, I turn away and press my head over my folded arms. A few moments later, her snores fill the air. A small shift in the temperature cools the air, making my skin all bumpy. The cold doesn't bother me. I take the veil from under my head and place it on the Girl as a blanket.

With a sigh, I sit up. I can't sleep. I clutch the knife tightly against my chest, its cold metal a stark contrast to the warmth of my skin. I shuffle away from the tree, my gaze drawn to the scar I inflicted upon its trunk. The wound, a jagged line, seems to accuse me.

"What do you seek? Redemption?" I scoff and whisper, "I'm talking to a tree."

A sensation prickles my hand, a jolt of energy shooting up my arm. My arm locks, the knife clenched tightly in my fist. With a surge of adrenaline, I wrench my arm free, the knife tumbling to the ground with a soft *thud*.

What was that? I shake my arm to make sure I can feel it again. It tingles slightly, an unsettling sensation that creeps into my stomach. It must be the lack of sleep. What else could have caused me to lose the feeling in my arm? Yes, lack of sleep must be affecting me more than I think.

I settle beside the Girl, hoping that sleep will claim me soon.

When the serpent returns, I know I am in the dream. Its slithering form is a menacing shadow. I run from it, my feet pounding against the ground. The bridge. The old woman. The stream of fire. The hill. *Adamah.*

My eyelids flutter open. The morning rays pierce through the smoky haze. My heart pounds, not with fear, but with a newfound resolve. A primal rhythm, a spark of life igniting within me.

I have faced a piece of the dark, enough to sharpen my focus in the waking world. Now I will find the truth I am seeking. With that, I will find myself.

ME

Something has shifted within *You*. A new attachment has formed. Predictably, the Girl has served as the catalyst, her presence weaving a thread into the fabric of Your being. That is what I hoped for.

One more rotation of Earth, one more ascent of the sun, before Your final awakening. You claim the dark, but You are a creature of light, tethered to its rhythms.

In the dominion of the shadows, You are powerless. Within them, I am behind You. Before You. To Your right. Especially to Your left.

The dark cannot be shared. It is mine.

YOU

y stomach growls as I watch the camels. I settle for some olives, reaching for the lowest branch of a tree and pluck a handful. I toss a few over the fence. Smiley, ever the playful one, nudges her snout into my palm and blows a warm puff of air against my skin.

Lashes, however, remains a still figure, his eyes fixed on me, an unsettling hardening around them.

The Girl snores softly, her breath a rhythmic rise and fall. Now is a good time to bring some foliage for the camels. Fatten them up a bit.

I finish the last of the olives, the tangy flavor lingering on my tongue, and place the remaining ones beside the Girl.

As I clamber over the Pale Tree branches, my fingers brush against rough bark—relief as I reach the top. My toe finds the familiar edge of the table, and I topple down, my body brushing against broken branches.

I continue walking in the darkness until I reach the exit hole, my hand hovering over the leafy cover.

There is that feeling again. Something is off.

The Stranger has returned.

I glance around; into the dark. Any new message? The area is like an abandoned graveyard for dead trees, the sickly white soil a stark contrast to the softer earth of the grassy area, which I have just left behind. Yet, the soil is not so different from the skeletal, sand-strewn landscape just beyond that grassy area.

I jolt as I realize I'm standing directly on some writing. The course, gritty soil crunches beneath my feet as I step aside to read the new words:

The Creator
The Originator
The Fashioner
The Giver of gifts
The Magnificent
The Sustainer

I grip a branch, the rough bark biting into my palm. Thankfully, my wounds have dried, though they still itch with a slight stinging from moving the foliage from the hole. I adjust my grip, easing the discomfort. Hovering the branch above the words, I take a hesitant step back. I swing the branch and trace meaningful marks in response to the message:

Who am I?

Noting the absurdity of this whole situation, I prepare to wipe over my question. Why would I ask a stranger about who I am? Then again, why would a stranger leave a message like this for me? How do I know this message *is* for me? Well, why else would they leave any message here, where I can find it?

As I lower the branch, ready to erase my response, there is a faint gasp behind me. I whirl around, holding the branch up in defense. A pointed head emerges from the Pale Tree. Noticing that it's only the Girl, I sigh in relief and lower the branch.

"You can read *and* write?!" she says, yawning quickly as if eager to get it out of the way.

"I thought you were sleeping."

"Did the Stranger come back?" she asks.

"Yes," I say, glancing down at the new words of the message.

"What did they write?"

I read the entire message aloud, "The Guardian. The Healer. The All Mighty. The Creator. The Originator. The Fashioner. The Giver of gifts. The Magnificent. The Sustainer."

She trudges until she is beside me. Two orbees rest on each shoulder, and her gaze drifts into the distance. She repeats the words, "The Healer."

Her eyes dart back and forth as if she is remembering something. After a few seconds, she scrambles ahead until she reaches the table. She jumps on it, climbing to the top.

"Wait!" I say, following her.

She stops suddenly as if just noticing my presence. Then, turning towards me, she says again, "The Healer."

She jumps to the other side, the *thud* echoing through the stillness in the air. I hurry to catch up. When I land on the other side, she is already near the cluster of trees.

"Where are you going?" I ask.

"Thalj," she says.

She misjudges the distance to the wooden fence in her hurry and bumps into it with a startled *grunt*. More out of annoyance than pain, the Girl squints and then continues walking. Her strong determination makes me briefly forget her earlier reluctance about Thalj. What caused this sudden change of heart?

When she reaches the place we slept, she eyes the olives I left for her.

"They're for you," I say, catching up to her.

"I'm not hungry," she lies, even though I can hear her stomach rumbling. She pockets the olives.

"Eat," I urge.

She starts to protest, but my firm look silences her. Clamping her mouth shut, she sits and picks at the olives. Unlike the last time we shared olives, when she eagerly stuffed them in her mouth, she now only nibbles at the edges. A sense of weariness hangs around her.

To lighten the mood, I say, "Tell me about your mother."

She stops nibbling and removes my veil from her shoulders, accidentally brushing off the orbees. I take it and wrap it around my head, watching her.

"My Mama is good," she says, digging a furrow in the earth with her index finger. "Fasts. Prays."

An image floods my mind: long cloaked figures, bowing together, their heads lowered to the ground in unison.

"Prays," I mutter, leaning against a tree to steady myself. "What is prays?"

"More of a *who* she prays to," she says in a matter-of-fact manner. The Girl seems slightly more energized.

"Then who does she prays to?" I ask.

"The One who made us," she says, glancing up at the place in the sky where the dancing rays burst through. "Greater One."

She takes one more bite of her olive and stuffs the rest into her pocket.

"Finish them," I say.

"My Mama needs these to break her fast."

"There's more," I say gently.

I am beginning to understand her. She's a nervous little creature, constantly shifting. Now she's shaking her legs, her eyes darting around, and she's rocking slightly, a motion which stings with familiarity.

She places her hand on the Book, a gesture which calms her. Her shoulders relax, and some of the tension in her body eases.

After a long pause, when she finally scans my face, I break into a brief smile. "You make this fasting sound like a door."

"Maybe it is," she says. The Book moves up and down in its pouch as she scratches her chest.

"How?"

"She's calmer when she fasts."

I nod slowly, though not entirely understanding. I would expect that not eating would make you feel hungrier, therefore grumpier. Yet, the idea has a strange appeal: how an act can so profoundly affect your feelings.

"How does she prays?" I ask.

The Girl lowers herself to the ground, her forehead and hands pressed against the earth. "Like this."

"To the ground?"

"No!" she says with a giggle, which further breaks her tension. She pats the ground. "She prays *on* the ground."

"Is this like the dance we did last night?"

"No, this movement has rules."

"Why?"

"Dancing is showing, expressing. This movement is … more of an answer."

"To what?"

"Everything," she says, not explaining any further.

Instead, she bows her head to the ground, her elbows raised.

I consider copying her position. But bowing like that could leave me vulnerable to attacks, especially with my back so exposed. After all, we're not alone here. There *is* the Stranger, who appears and disappears at will.

On the other hand, I did wake up unharmed, didn't I? Cautiously, I copy the Girl, lowering myself until my forehead and hands touch the earth. I expect to feel exposed and weak. I do feel exposed, but somehow, I don't feel weak.

The area by the cluster of trees is harsher than the grassy area, but it's a healthy brown, not the white, barren earth I see further on. Pressing my head to the ground, I inhale the rich, dusty aroma of the soil, a cool, comforting cushion against my forehead.

"How long do I do this?" I ask, my voice muffled.

"A few more minutes," she says, her voice muffled too.

After a while, I break the silence. I raise my head slightly to look at her. "She prays this long?"

"Longer," she says, keeping her head touching the ground.

I settle back down to the prostrating position.

More time passes. "Can I get up now?"

"Okay," she says, lifting her head.

As I slowly lift my head, I open my eyes, blinking a few times. This whole idea of a Greater One who made me remains confusing. Greater than what?

And why would we need a 'Greater One'? What does that have to do with my search for truth? I came here to discover who I am. How does knowing my maker help with that? A sudden realization. I gasp softly. *Who could know me better than the one who made me?*

The Girl looks at me, oblivious to the thought which threatens to unravel a whole new tangle of questions.

I push the thought down. I need to focus.

"How do you feel?" she asks.

"I … don't know," I admit. "There was a rush to my head, and it felt like everything …" I trail off.

"Everything what?" she prompts.

"It sounds silly," I mutter.

"Go on."

"For just a moment, it's like everything fit."

"Like your face?" she teases.

"Even with the hole." I smile at my joke.

"There's a hole in the ground?" she asks seriously, following my gaze to where I bowed my head.

"No, in my face," I reply.

She looks at me distastefully and stands. "You're not very good at jokes."

She rushes to the Pale Tree and leans towards the bottom of it. After a few tugs, she pulls out two planks of wood with ropes dangling from them and carries them to me.

"What's this?" I ask.

"We'll need them for Thalj," she says, already going back for another pair.

"Why do you have two sets?"

She walks ahead, deeper into the cluster of trees without answering. The silence that follows stretches uncomfortably long. I quicken my pace to catch up to her.

PART 9

Fear

YOU

The cluster of trees get denser as we walk through them. I call out to the Girl, my voice echoing slightly in the still air, but she marches ahead, her footsteps muffled.

I break into a run, the cool air rushing past my face. She senses my approach and averts her gaze. I catch her arm, my fingers firm but gentle. Still, she flinches. She turns to me. Her eyes, usually bright, are now clouded with a distant look. She avoids my gaze, her lips pressed into a thin line as she resumes her walk.

I dart in front of her. "Woah, wait!"

She stops.

"Is everything okay?"

"What do you mean?" Her voice rises slightly as she continues to avoid my gaze.

"You're extra ... fidgety. Your moods all over the place—happy, then sad, then distracted."

Her eyes flick to mine for a moment, but then her attention wanders, that faraway expression returning. She shifts her weight from foot to foot, her fingers anxiously playing with the rope on the plank.

"Are you leaving?" she whispers.

"Leaving?"

"After Thalj."

I nod slowly, my gaze now avoiding hers. "That's why you're upset?"

"I understand why you would want to leave." Her voice gains a bit of strength. "If you get what you need, what reason do you have to stay?"

She glances at me, her eyes meeting mine for a moment before quickly looking away again.

I stay silent, my mind racing. She's right. Once I get what I need, why *would* I remain? A wave of irritation washes over me, quickly followed by an unexpected tenderness in my chest. She isn't as irritating as she used to be. I even catch myself trying to understand her—a pang of annoyance. What a waste of time. The last thing I need is an emotional tie binding me to anyone.

The Girl clomps ahead, heedlessly bumping into trees without slowing.

I follow, and we approach the edge of the trees. A sudden gust of wind slaps my face, stealing my breath. With each step, the wind intensifies. Another blast hits me, forcing my eyes shut.

I reach the edge. Directly ahead looms a towering Black Dune, a monstrous shadow obscuring everything beyond. I grip the rough bark of a tree, bracing myself against the violent wind.

A small flake of inky material lands on my tongue, a cold, metallic taste that quickly melts. As I spit it out, I notice the dark, almost oily substance clinging to my fingers, staining them like soot.

When I turn to the Girl, I find she is already watching me. She blinks a message I understand: *Something is wrong with the sky.*

She's right, something *is* wrong with the sky. How is the sky, just a short walk away, so calm, and this one the complete opposite? When the two skies meet, it looks like two opposing forces colliding, unable to breach the invisible boundary between them.

She plunges forward into the inky storm.

I trail behind her, the biting wind whipping at my face. We reach the base of the Black Dune, a towering, ominous presence.

As we begin to climb, a dull ache creeps into my feet, turning into a numbing throb.

I pause, taking a few precious seconds to pull on the makeshift—mostly ineffective—snowshoes, securing the ropes around my ankles so my feet are attached to the wooden frames.

I force my body upward, each step an exhausting effort. The biting wind and the weight of the snow slow my progress. The Girl is a few feet ahead, her grunts echoing through the storm.

She pushes on, and I follow suit, my body aching with cold. Black icicles form on my face, needles of ice that prick my skin. I wipe them away and keep climbing. The summit feels so far.

My hands tremble violently. I can barely grasp the slippery hill beneath me. Somehow, I manage to pull myself up, reaching the peak just as the wind howls around us. She sits perched on the summit, a silhouette against the swirling grey clouds.

The orbees have vanished into her ear. When she turns to me, her eyes are ablaze like two embers glowing in the twilight.

She blinks to me: *Orbees give heat and light.*

She taps her ear, and an orbee comes out. She offers it to me, but I barely register the gesture. The wind is so forceful, it snatches my breath away, clawing and tugging at my meagerly dressed body as if trying to fight me off the dunes head.

Tears freeze in my eyes, and I blink them clear. My fingers ache as I grip the icy slope even tighter.

I'm enveloped by a sound: a low, almost ritualistic *hum*, resonating like a chorus all around us.

I wipe my eyes and lean forward, shaking and crouching against the wind's force. Below, a body of water glows with a vibrant, eclectic blue green, shimmering under the dark sky. A subtle movement disturbs the surface beneath the ice. Then, a burst of tiny lights appears, and the *humming* pulses in time with them.

The lights are bodies—fish. Their illuminated organs create a haunting, but beautiful underwater spectacle as their flat, mottled bodies move in a coordinated dance.

The sheet of translucent ice above them reflects the light. Somehow, the black material falling from the sky doesn't affect the color of this ice. Each drop that hits the ground instantly morphs from black to white, as if the floor itself has consumed the darkness, transforming it into delicate lace-like snow.

I turn to the Girl and blink my message: *How is the ground doing that?*

She blinks back: *The message of the Stranger: The Healer reminded me of this. Zam heals, too.*

I gasp in awe. I turn to face the Great Wall, a jagged line of metal that cuts across the dark landscape. The wall, marking the boundary of Thalj, glistens with an unnatural, purplish-grey tinge, as if it were rippling and distorting the air around it, lending an unsettling sense of instability to the entire area.

In the center of this desolate expanse stands a colossal entity, unlike any of the other trees in Jinnah. It resembles a tree in form, yet its nature is utterly alien. Devoid of leaves, its shiny trunk is not bark in the traditional sense, but a dense network of intertwined vines, their surfaces polished to a smooth, iridescent sheen reminiscent of ancient jade. The green is captivating.

This magnificent entity towers over the landscape, its girth easily encompassing three of the orbee trees.

Instead of roots anchoring it to the ground, huge, deep, purple blossoms erupt from its core. They bloom in a stunning display, each petal a delicate tapestry of intricate veins visible even from this distance.

The trunk itself seems to pulsate, reaching towards the swirling vortex of smoke in the sky. Is the tree connected to the storm? A vast network of vines, eerily like those we encountered near the Zam—which had wrapped themselves over the stems of the red flowers—extends from the base of the storm. Yet, none of the vines touch the Zam below the ice.

This tree … must be the source of a vine network, a living, breathing life form. Each vine snakes across the icy ground, some reaching towards the imposing Great Wall, while others weave their way past the Black Dune where we are, continuing along the surface of the ice and then disappearing beneath the dune itself.

The Girl nudges me, but my attention remains on the tree. I hear her shout something about snow squirrels, their life cycles fleeting: sleeping, waking, having children, dying, all within a few short months. But I don't catch anything else. It's a blur. As if her voice is far away.

A tingling sensation creeps up my arm, the same one I felt last night before falling asleep. My hands curl into fists. My body locks, rigid and unresponsive. Colors become faded. I'm paralyzed. I can't move. I collapse and tumble backward down the dune. My throat constricts. I can't breathe.

The Girl bolts after me. When I reach the bottom, her hands frantically rub my arms and face. My vision blurs as her face comes in and out of focus. Then, a *whoosh* in my ear as an orbee enters.

I can breathe again. Gasping, I drink the air as I grip the icy ground.

I look at my hands and clothes. "I'm all wet again," I say.

No response. I glance at her. She looks terrified of me.

I pry the planks from my feet and rush ahead through the trees. The Girl picks them up and follows clearly, winded.

When we reach the fenced area of the camels, she tries to talk to me, but I turn away from her. She steps in front of me, blocking my path.

"What?" I shout.

She winces but comes closer. "What just happened?" When she sees me gathering some olives and the knife, she asks, "Where are you going?"

I don't answer. I don't want to talk to her. I rush towards the Pale Tree, clambering over the branches. She grabs my leg. I kick her off. I jump to the other side. She sprangles after me, landing with a *thump*.

Reaching the hole, I scan the ground. Has the Stranger replied? No. With a frustrated grunt, I stomp on the words etched there and plunge into the exit hole, then rush through the Orbee Forest.

Once I reach the border of Jinnah, I wait until the Girl has caught up to me. Then, I turn to her, scanning her eyes for any of the fear that they held earlier.

I whisper, "Why were you scared of me just now?"

"I wasn't." She shakes her head, her eyes wide and vulnerable. She gently touches my arm.

"Liar," I mutter, shrugging her hand off. I turn to leave.

"I was scared *for* you!" she shouts after me.

I stop, one foot in Jinnah and the other, feeling the blast of heat past the border. I turn to her slowly. Her hands are shaking.

"You barely know me," I say, my voice low.

"I know you're good," she insists.

"I'm not. I can feel it. I'm guilty of something." I bite my lip, avoiding her gaze. Looking out from an orbee tree, my eyes are met by thick smoke that blocks my view. "The Voice knows something about me."

"The Voice is a liar. It tricks. It doesn't want good for—"

"It wants me to be good," I say with a bitter certainty.

"I don't have the answers you want. But I promise, I'll do my best to help you find them. The Voice might know something, but it only wants one thing."

"What?" I ask.

"To use you and hurt you." Her voice trembles. "It did something to my Mama, something that broke her." She nods a few times as if she is saying it for the first time. "She's broken. My Mama's broken." Her eyes well up with tears as she scratches her chest.

She cries for a few moments, and I feel awkward, unsure how to react. I pat her shoulder. "There, there." Not exactly empathy, but it seems to work; thankfully, she stops crying.

She bites her lip, her voice rising with urgency as she continues, "I don't know how to fix her."

I brace for another wave of tears, ready to offer another clumsy pat. Instead, she looks at me, her eyes pleading. "Whatever the Voice did to my Mama, it's connected to why you're here right now."

I pause to process her words. Is she asking me to help her broken mother? I'm not here to fix anyone. I don't even know her mother.

Despite these initial thoughts, I find myself trying to understand the Girl better. This time, instead of the pang of annoyance, I let myself follow my thoughts. It makes sense why she's sometimes affectionate and then suddenly distant. Why she drifts off into her own world and why she clings to anyone to talk to—even if it's just talking at them, including her *friends*, the camels.

"But the Voice wants me to be good," I say more feebly.

"The Voice might want you to be good, but it doesn't want good *for* you."

Immediately, I step away from the edge of Jinnah. It's true. I've known ever since I spoke to the Voice. The sinister calls, the use of its threads, the timing of my arrival. It seemed *planned*. I don't believe it's a coincidence that I lost my memories. It *wanted* me to. Why?

The Girl might not know how to help me find what I'm seeking, but I know one thing instinctually: she is safe. The Voice is not. I trust my body enough to accept that.

I turn to the Girl and sigh. "I'll stay only until the seeds are planted."

She smiles.

I continue, "And maybe ... maybe I'll find out how to stop the sickness."

She beams.

I add, "If I don't have my answers by then, I'm leaving."

"Thank you," she whispers, her face streaked with the black snow.

She turns toward the Zam, and I follow, pocketing the knife and popping an olive in my mouth.

"By the way, what do you think about eating a camel?" I ask.

Her eyes widen, and she smiles. "Maybe you *are* funny sometimes."

I don't return the smile. Instead, I spit the seed into my hand and drop it into my pocket.

I wasn't joking.

My toes dip into the Zam, and the warmth surprises me, a stark contrast to the icy chill I remember from Thalj.

"Why is the Zam not cold here like it is in Thalj?" I ask.

The Girl shakes her head, a quick, almost twitchy movement, and two orbees spill out from her ears to her hands. She pushes them into the Zam, and a wave of heat rolls over my feet, the water growing noticeably warmer. Steam begins to rise.

"They keep the water warm," she says.

I watch the steam curl upwards, feeling a sense of unease instead of the expected comfort. The way the Zam stretches reminds me of how long today has felt.

"Why does the day feel so much longer than yesterday?" I ask.

"I told you"—she shuffles closer— "time works differently in Jannah."

"How?" I sniff, a quick, involuntary action.

"Jinnah gives us what we need."

"How?" I ask again, trying to subtly move away from her. She reeks like a mix of camel poop and other such grossness. "Is it to do with that word you say when you enter and leave Jinnah?"

She shrugs. Another wave of the stench wafts by. It is very hard to focus on anything but the pungent smell on her.

I attempt to be polite about her unpleasant odor and hint, "The Zam is a great place to clean up."

She kicks the water and nods. I catch another waft.

I open my mouth to be more transparent, but something tickles my hand. A leaf. More leaves line the bridge, some as big as my body. Where did they come from? One particular leaf is big enough to span the entire bridge. I push it away. When I turn back, it's as if the leaves are growing in number.

The lack of proper food, the stinky girl, and the unanswered questions all seem to boil up. I stand and kick at the leaves, frustration mounting as they continue to multiply with each kick. "I just moved these!"

"That won't work," she says calmly.

"Why not?"

After scooping a leaf with ease, the Girl stands. Holding it upright, she stretches to its full height. "These aren't leaves. They're the vines."

"Those are not vines."

"They are. They're the mimicking vines," she explains.

"What does that mean?"

"They change to look like what they touch."

"Impossible," I scoff.

"Why?" she challenges, a hint of amusement in her voice.

"You can't copy something physically without seeing it."

"Maybe," she replies, turning to walk away without attempting to defend her point. As she places the giant leaf back down, she adds, "Here's something true."

"What?" I ask, trying to discreetly cover my nose as she comes closer.

"You need a bath!" she says, giving me a shove straight into the Zam.

I emerge from the warm water, shaking my head in disapproval. I wasn't even the stinky one. Without a word, I swim towards her, lunge forward, and pull her into the water with a splash.

Her scream morphs into laughter, and I stop for a moment to listen. It's high-pitched, laced with snorts. A squeak escapes my lips. Instead of clamping my hands on it like before, I let it blossom into a full-blown laugh, complete with echoes of my snorts. We erupt into laughter, the sounds echoing through the trees.

She throws herself back in the water, sitting with her toes poking above the surface.

"I always thought I would sink," she says, a touch of wonder in her voice.

"It's too shallow to sink in." I dive into the water, scooping some river stones. They are smooth and cool, heavy in my palm. As I place them in her hand, the faint, earthy scent of the riverbed rises. "These are cleaning stones."

Her gaze, blank and unfocused, meets mine. To demonstrate a much-needed clean, I scrub the gritty texture of the stones against my skin, a welcome sensation. The inky blackness fades, revealing the rich, deep tone of my skin beneath. Thankfully, Stinky imitates my movements with her own hands, working diligently. As the last vestiges of the ink disappear downstream, a sense of relief washes over us both.

We sit in the water, our bodies weightless. The soft lapping sound against the riverbank is a soothing rhythm.

The steam from the Zam continues to rise, a misty veil of the world beyond. Its gentle *hiss* fills the air.

"Back then," she begins, "I meant it when I said you're good."

I whisper, "The look in your eyes isn't one you give to a good person. I know fear."

"I told you, I was afraid *for* you," she says, her gaze unwavering.

I know that's what she said. I also know when she said it, she meant it. But a part of me wanted to hear her say it again.

I struggle with the question of why her opinion matters. But that thought is quickly overshadowed by a warmth spreading through my chest, rising until it stings my eyes. I take a shuddering breath and plunge beneath the surface, letting the water wash over my face. When I feel steadier, I resurface, blinking away the remaining tears.

"What do you want most in the world?" she asks, oblivious of how much her words affect me, and how much I wish they didn't. She adds, "You know, before finding out who you are and all that."

"I only want the truth," I reply, my voice echoing the calm of the water as we gently bob along with it.

"What if the truth hurts?" She looks past the bridge toward the Golden Dome.

"We'll always feel hurt. But which pain is worth more? The one that comes with truth or the one that comes with lies?"

"You mean what's real and what's not?" she asks.

"Yes. Lies are always changing. The Voice showed me that. But the truth, it stays the same, and yet, it's scary because ..." I trail off into my thoughts. *Would* it be easier not to know anything? To remain ignorant?

She looks at me expectantly. "Because?"

"Because even though the truth is stable in nature, it can unhinge every part of you when you learn it."

"How do you know that?"

I shudder at the memory of what happened in Thalj. "Back there, in Thalj, when my body reacted like that, it felt as if I became detached from it. My awareness and control of my limbs seemed like separate things. I can't shake the feeling that it was a reaction to some truth about myself linked to Thalj."

She blinks. Time stretches. Finally, she says, "Maybe your body wasn't ready for the truth."

We float in the Zam for a few more moments in silence.

She turns to me again. "When you get the truth, then what?"

"Then I'll know if I'm good."

"Then what?" she asks again.

I bite my lip as I think about this. "Then, I'll feel peace."

"Peace sounds nice," she admits. "You don't need to wait to be good. What's stopping you?"

"I don't think I know what *good* is for me." I sigh. "I mean, I don't know if there's a universal good which applies to everyone."

"It's in the things we choose to do or *not* to do," she suggests, in a matter-of-fact manner.

Her answer doesn't satisfy me. It doesn't define good. I don't bother following this up. How would she know what I need? Instead, I ask, "What do *you* want?"

She doesn't answer immediately. Instead, she looks up, her gaze distant. "I think you're right. You need both."

"Both what?" I ask, slightly lost.

"You need the *truth* to know what *good* is," she explains, her fingers tracing invisible patterns in the air as she ponders.

"Why?"

"Because to choose to do the right thing isn't always clear." Her voice is filled with a wisdom that doesn't fit her age.

Yet, I get the feeling she is avoiding my question.

"Like you want to fix your mother?" I ask.

She looks down at her toes, which wiggle as they bob out of the water, and then scratches her chest. "That's not what I want."

"But everything we're doing, what you said before about trying to fix things, fix your mother, what about that?"

She shrugs. "I need to."

I nod slowly. "So, what do you want?"

"I want to …" she begins, before getting lost in her thoughts. She looks up, as if just noticing I am here, and adds, "I want to show her all the things I love. I want her to meet Lashes and Smiley, to see Orbee Forest, to come to Thalj with me."

I smile. "You want a mother."

Her cheeks flush, and she avoids my gaze. In a tight voice, she says, "I have a mother."

"That's not—I didn't mean …" I sigh. I'm not sure what I meant.

"It's okay," she says gently.

We share a moment of silence, both of us bound by unseen chains. Mine of ignorance, hers of responsibility. But today—even with the uncomfortable exchange between Stinky and me—for the first time since I came here, the burden feels lighter.

She breaks the silence. "Have you ever felt good, even without knowing the truth?"

"How do you know if you're goo—doing something good?" I watch the water trickle through my fingers.

She taps her chest. "This tells me."

"The Book, it's all wet!"

"The Book will be fine," she says confidently. "I was pointing to my chest. When I do something good, it feels big and open."

"What about when you do something bad?"

"Small, tight." She closes her hands into a fist.

"What if I'm not good?" My voice cracks as I turn away, eyes fixed on the steam which meets the smoke in the sky.

"I don't know that one," she says, floating again.

"I thought so."

"But I do know it's hard to be right—" She glances at me. "*Good*, it's hard to be *good* all the time."

"It is," I agree, as I float alongside her.

She pulls herself from the Zam, shivering with her clothes clinging to her like a sodden shroud. I follow her out, my damp dress and hair under my veil quickly becoming cold.

Wringing the excess water from my dress, I move my shoulders up and down to stop them from shaking. The damp fabric clings to my skin like a cold, clammy second layer. With each passing moment, I grow colder and colder. I need to get out of these clothes quickly so they can dry.

As I begin to take off my dress sleeve, a wave of self-consciousness washes over me. This doesn't … feel right. To be naked, even for a moment, in the presence of someone else. It feels … wrong.

I glance at the bridge and walk towards it. Leaning down, my fingers trace the edge of a particularly long, leathery vine, shaped in that eerie way, like a leaf. It's cool and smooth beneath my touch, pulsing faintly with a life of its own.

The vine is not alone. Countless other vines, also mimicking leaves, snake across the ground, with some burying their tendrils beneath the surface. They weave through the Garden of Fire, disappearing into the thick foliage of the towering orbee trees beyond.

The reach of these vines must be more extensive than I initially perceived. They touch every part of Jinnah, except, I now realize, the Zam. *Why?*

Where the vines touch each other, a subtle tremor passes between them. Are they *communicating?*

I use the knife to cut the vine leaf in my hand with a decisive snip, severing it from the others. It twitches. Its leathery surface is supple, yielding easily as I shape it into a garment that will protect *and* conceal.

A sensation ripples through me, starting from where my fingers touch the vine leaf. A pulsing energy that vibrates through my body—sharp, painful, like a thousand tiny needles pricking every inch of my skin.

A deafening *CLANG*, like a massive metal bell being struck, rings out, its echoes tearing through the air. It came from the Great Wall.

Immediately following is a deep, rumbling *ROAR* that shakes the ground beneath me to its core. The earth trembles, each pulse sending my heart into a chaotic pounding against my ribs. I can feel the vibration in my teeth, deep within my bones.

The orbees on the trees that border the end of Jinnah, across the bridge, blink frantically, their lights dimming and then vanishing completely.

For a moment, the land is plunged into utter blackness; even with my ability to see in the dark, I can't see a thing. The sharp pain from touching the vine pounds through my body, overwhelming my senses and preventing me from discerning anything.

A few seconds after the earth-shaking roar, the orbees' lights flicker back on. They are moving erratically, crashing into trees and falling to the ground.

The Girl points a trembling finger at the vine dress I had just carved. Thick, oily black smoke seeps from the cut ends of the vine. The smoke rises to the ceiling of Jinnah, filling the air with the acrid scent of burnt leaves and something else I am unsure of.

The pain from touching the vine dress continues to pulse within me, a brutal hammer pounding against my temples. I press harder on my forehead, my fingers digging into my skin, trying to force the pain back. Each second stretches like a lifetime stuffed into a single, painful moment. Finally, the throbbing subsides, leaving only a dull ache.

I whisper, "What was that roar? Why are the orbees acting like that?"

"I don't know," the Girl manages to say, in a trembling voice.

"What about the clang from the Great Wall?" I press, the memory of it sharp in my mind.

When I had experienced that pain, just seconds ago, I felt it was directing me toward something: the Great Wall itself. I look down at my fingers, where the wounds from the Voice's threads and my spike are now fading brown lines etched into my palms.

Looking at my palms reminds me of the first time I touched the Great Wall. I had felt a similar sensation then—a pulse of energy, a connection—less painful than the pangs from the vine dress, but present.

Now, even though the loud clang from the Great Wall has stopped, a subtle continuation remains—a faint echo of that sound. It's almost like … *something* or someone is knocking or calling out.

She shakes her head, her lips turning pale from the cold. "I've never heard Great Wall bang like that before."

"The Great Wall." I say, "I need to go to the Great Wall."

I reach for the vine garment and stop. The sharp sensation I felt when cutting it is still vivid in my mind.

I'm not wearing that.

I make my way across the bridge towards the orbee trees that line the edge of Jinnah. A small ease as I notice the orbees settle back into their home, nestled under the tree trunks like frightened children held by their roots. Their light grows steadier, casting a glow over Jinnah. Fallen leaves from the orbee trees are scattered on the ground around the trunks.

I run my fingers over the orbee leaves, tracing the intricate vein patterns like tiny rivers etched into their surfaces. They resemble the vine leaves in general shape, but the feel is different—lighter, almost weightless. The vine leaves, however, are too perfect: uniformly green with no variations. Though I like things to be organized, something feels wrong about them. I choose the rougher, more natural orbee leaves, cutting them into dress shapes for both myself and the Girl. When I lay her dress on the ground, it rustles softly.

"If you stay in that wet dress, you'll get sick," I say.

I start to shrug off my own dripping dress. A tingling sensation runs up the back of my neck—not from the cold—rather, from an odd awareness. As if unseen eyes are upon me. Like I'm being watched by someone or *something*, other than the Girl.

I quickly drape the leaves over myself, shielding my body, and then carefully remove my dress. Once I'm done, I turn to the Girl, whose body is shaking vigorously from the cold.

"I'd rather not take off my dress," she says quietly.

"You'll get sick," I warn.

"I'll be fine," she replies, under her breath.

"I won't look," I offer, turning away from her. A few seconds pass. "Ready?"

"No," she whispers.

A moment of silence.

"How about now?" I ask, my patience wearing thin. *We need to go to the Great Wall, now.*

"No," she whispers again.

I turn to see her still quivering and itching her chest. Her dress clings to her.

"I'll be alright," she insists, but as she speaks, her sleeve rides up, revealing a deep red gash on her arm.

The clanging, the roar, the distress I felt when I cut the vine—all of it seems insignificant compared to the sight of her wound. "Show me," I command in a low voice.

Hesitantly, she brings her arms forward. My breath catches in my throat as I see more deep red gashes marring her skin.

"Who did this to you?" I ask, feeling a flush of anger creep up my face.

She stares at my arms and steps closer. "You have them too."

I flinch as I shift my gaze down to see the scars across my flesh—old wounds, too deep to heal completely, their white in both circle and line shapes. They snake down all over my arms and across my legs.

Amongst these scars, another kind of scar stands out. It's not a line or circle, but a broader, more irregular mark, compared to my other wounds. It appears as if the skin has been stretched excessively, around the curve of my hips and across my midsection, leaving behind a visible trace of this scar—no, not scar, a mark. This one feels more like a stretch mark.

"Are there scars on my back?" I manage.

"All over," she observes.

My throat tightens. A familiar tingle of paralysis creeps up on me. My eyes fixate on my arms as I try to ground myself by focusing on my wounds.

She reaches for my arm. I flinch. Undeterred, she reaches again, gently pulling it next to hers. Our scars look up at us, a picture of lines and holes, one set fresh, the other aged, both echoes of hurt.

"It's not these scars that scare me the most," the Girl says, raising her eyes to mine. "It's the ones I can't see."

"How do you know they're there?" I ask uneasily.

"I see them all over you," she says, her eyes still fixed on mine.

I look away and clear my throat. "Wear the leaf dress, I need to go to the Great Wall."

She throws the leaf over herself and wiggles out of her dress, tossing it onto a rock by the bank of the Zam. As she finishes getting dressed, I focus on the faint, rhythmic knocking from the Great Wall, which echoes around us, a constant, almost hypnotic pulse.

Yes, it's like a call. A clear, insistent beat.

A shudder ripples through me. I gasp, realizing the sudden chill comes from the exposed skin on my back.

I spin around, towards the Girl. She stares downward at something. A flash of green catches my eye—under it, black, thread-like legs propel a creature forward with surprising speed. Its body is obscured by the massive leaf it carries on its back.

The creature joins a procession of similarly obscured figures, forming a single-minded line marching towards the towering trees in the Orbee Forest. The creatures are as tall as my knees, their bodies burdened with foliage, creating a surreal spectacle. Ants.

I gasp. "They're enormous!"

I grab my now-dry dress and fumble it on. As I brush the rest of the parts of the leaf off my body, the ants swiftly approach the fallen leaf, cutting it into pieces, which they then carry in an organized line on the Silver Path, all the way through the Garden of Fire.

"They're bold too!" I add, impressed by their efficiency. I'm surprised at how fast they can break through the leaves. At this rate, every tree in the Orbee Forest should be bare.

As if reading my mind, the Girl says, "They only use what they need."

She races after them until she disappears into the Orbee Forest. I pick up her dress from the rock and follow behind. When I reach her, she is leaning over a small hole at the corner of a tree, just a few meters away from the hidden passage of foliage to the Fallen Trees.

An ant hole as big as the length of my arm and elbow stares up at us.

Without looking up from it, the Girl says, "This is their home." She looks up at me and flashes me a smile, as if she's letting me in on a secret. "They told me."

"Animals don't talk—"

"They do," she interrupts, turning back to watch the disappearing ants. "They had another home, closer to Lashes and Smiley, but they left it when the sickness came and moved here instead." She jumps to her feet and races ahead.

I pause for a moment before following her into the passage to the Fallen Trees. I thought we were going to the Great Wall out there, but a part of me is glad we are not. I don't want to be anywhere near the Voice. Thankfully, the wall stretches all around Thanae, so I can approach it from inside Jinnah, past the Pale Tree.

I climb the Pale Tree and land softly on the side of the grass. Without a word of thanks, the Girl snatches her dry dress from my hands and slips into it as she rustles out of the leaf dress.

With surprising grace, she folds the discarded leaf dress neatly and tucks it gently beneath the Pale Tree, right beside the wooden planks we used for Thalj. I'm taken aback. She's always so … haphazard. Careless.

As I watch her, I smile. She's not careless with things that matter to her. She put the leaf dress beside her mother's planks. A small gesture, perhaps, but a significant one. Perhaps she's not a total mess after all.

A pang of unease quickly follows, and my smile turns to a frown. This softness … this vulnerability … it's dangerous. I feel exposed, a different kind of nakedness. I must remain vigilant. Ready for whatever is to come.

She perches on the edge of what appears to be another huge anthill, further along the Pale Tree. She watches it wide-eyed, as if expecting it to do something. But all I see is a towering mound of dirt, twigs, and dried leaves. An eerie emptiness hangs in the air, as if something vital is missing.

"It's empty," she says, stating the obvious.

"We need to——" The words catch in my throat when I see her face as she turns to me, worried. I ask, "What's wrong?"

"The ants said their Mama is gone. What will happen to them?" she asks, her voice a hushed whisper.

As she says this, a lone ant catches my eye. It marches up the side of the thick trunk of the Pale Tree, clambering over the staircase of branches. Its stark black body stands out against the bleached wood.

The Girl follows my gaze, her face draining. She scoots away from the lone ant, a tremor running through her.

"What's wrong?" I ask again.

"That's the mama," she whispers.

"Why isn't she with her ants?" I press.

"Something isn't right," she murmurs. I lean forward for a better look, but the Girl snatches me back.

"What——"

She gasps. "Look how she moves!"

"Like she's ..." I trail off and take in a long, shaky breath. "Being dragged?"

"Yes," she hisses. "And I can't hear her speak." She continues in a shaky voice. "Do you remember the sickness I told you about, the one that turned the white flower poisonous?"

I nod even though she doesn't look at me. She doesn't continue, lost in her own thoughts.

I prompt. "You said the sickness started with the smoke, right?"

She nods.

"Why aren't we sick?"

"I don't know. But what happened today—the smoke from the vine dress when you cut it, the earthquake, the roar, the orbee's reaction—it all makes sense now. I had a feeling the vines were connected to the sickness. I wasn't sure before, so I went out the day I met you to test my theory."

When she says the word 'theory,' a tingling feeling creeps down my back. That familiar feeling again. I shake it off. "So, the vines extend beyond Jinnah?"

She nods. "Somehow, I think the mimicking vines are draining the life out of Jinnah," she says. "That's why I was digging—to see if it was true. But then I found …" She gulps hard. "Food."

If I'm honest, I still don't see a connection with the sickness and the vines. Unless … *connection*. "You think the vines *connect* everything. If that's the case, then that could be *how* the sickness is spreading through Jinnah." I say, pretending not to notice her slightly salivating.

"Connection isn't always a good thing," she says, wiping the side of her mouth.

"Even if that's true, we still don't know what's *causing* the sickness."

A jarring series of taps echoes through the air.

"What is the name of this language your mother calls you with?" I ask.

"Tap." She says urgently, avoiding my gaze. "I have to go." She scrambles over the Pale Tree, narrowly missing the ant as she reaches the top. She jumps down, and her footsteps quickly fade into the distance. She shouts back, "You have a new message!"

The Girl keeps running, leaving me alone with the faint knocking from the Great Wall and the dragged mother.

ME

Something is wrong; there is an imbalance. The knocking shouldn't have started yet.

I can hear the Girl's feet shuffling through the Orbee Forest. Perhaps, *she* knows what caused this ... acceleration of events. Although I can hear most of Your conversations in Jinnah, I don't hear everything.

I let my voice carry to her. "Child."

She stops by a tree, perched at the edge of Jinnah. The rough bark of the orbee tree scrapes against her hand as she leans against it.

The world around us fades into a hushed background as she fumbles with two orbees, shoving them into her ears. Her eyes become beams, piercing the gloom, illuminating the slow-motion Dark Fall of residue from the sky.

"Tell me something," I say, my gaze fixed on the subtle movements of her feet.

Will she tread into my land? Will she forget to say *that* word so I can finally enter Jinnah?

She doesn't answer.

I continue, "Why do you leave the Worshipper alone so often?"

She hesitates; her brow furrowed in thought. A small bead of sweat trickles down from her forehead as the heat of Shahwah smacks her.

"Why did you call me?" she asks slowly, her voice guarded.

"Why did you listen?"

"Some might say it's impolite to ignore people," she retorts.

"Might they?" I sneer in the darkness.

"What do you want?"

"Answer my question."

"Well, a better question is not why I leave my Mama, it's why I come to Jinnah," she counters.

"Oh?"

"I like light."

"So, it's dark with the Worshipper?"

She hesitates before replying, "I didn't say that."

"You don't like the dark, then?" I press, sensing a vulnerability in her hesitation.

She clears her throat. "Is this another game?"

"Do you or do you not like the dark?"

"Why would I tell *you* that?" she retorts. "Why would I tell you anything?"

"I'm confused."

"About what?"

"If you loved the Worshipper—"

"Why do you keep calling my Mama that?"

I ignore her question. "The truth is, I already know how much you fear the dark, child. I am confused because the only place where the sun shines in this land is where the Worshipper lives, in the Golden Dome. Yet you leave a sky filled with light, to come to one filled with dark."

A beat of silence.

The Girl winces slightly. "I do love my Mama."

Good. This is where I want her. To feel *This*. One will do anything to avoid *This*. They will listen more eagerly to escape *This*. Some will destroy reality. Others create their own. And You fight anyone who reminds You of *This*. What will *she* do?

I lower my voice, "I called you here for a reason. I have a … revelation. The Worshipper's life hinges on it."

"You're trying to scare me," she whispers.

"Something bad is going to happen." I wait for the words to sink in. "It has to do with your friend."

I watch for any sign of reaction in her eyes, but those glowing orbees block it.

"What bad thing?" Fear finally creeps into her voice.

Good. She is curious. Now I can hit two targets with one arrow. "Before I tell you, I need to know something. What did you and your new friend do a few moments ago?"

"Why?"

I lie. "It has to do with what I am about to tell you."

"Liar," she says, the glow of the orbees shining from her ears. Oh yes—I almost forgot they can reveal a lie.

I try another tactic. "Did your friend do anything to the vines?"

The Girl's single, skunk-tail-like eyebrow furrows, and she purses her lips like an old hag. Then her expression shifts, her eyes widening. I have my answer.

"Tell me the bad thing," she says.

"The Worshipper will die."

The Girl gasps softly, she knows I speak the truth.

I continue, "You must make sure your friend is with the Worshipper by sunrise, tomorrow."

"Then my Mama won't die?" she asks, almost losing her balance on the hill.

I choose my words carefully. "Her life depends on your friend being with her tomorrow."

As she flees, a surge of exhilaration courses through me. Yes, *This* is a potent motivator. It's the engine of terror that fuels my kind. People will go to extraordinary lengths to escape the gnawing discomfort of confronting the truth that lies beneath both *This* and the fear it breeds.

You've acted in a way that went against our plan. No matter, I'll adjust things, so everything happens much sooner.

I still have control. At least for this Part.

That is why I named it: Fear.

YOU

I stand above the deep gashes of words in the white sand, encircled by the pale trunks of fallen trees. The Stranger's new message is surrounded by vines, bordering the words, as if hugging them:

The Avenger

The Most Just

The Subduer

I have come to understand certain things about the Stranger. They do not appear all the time, only when I am absent. This means they don't want to be seen.

They leave no other trace, except words in the ground, and for some reason, there are always vines around after the messages are left. This person knows something, something valuable. But are they an ally? Trusting a being that leaves only traces of its existence feels impossible, yet they could have hurt me when my back was turned or while I slept.

Still, I decide, I don't trust them.

The message they left this time is different from the previous ones. These words, though still cryptic, have a different feeling. Fear? Are they telling me to be afraid of something? Why? Unless … could it be that the Stranger is the one who is afraid?

I lower the branch and write:

Stranger what do you fear?

What a person fears the most reveals a lot about them. The fear of abandonment reveals loss, betrayal, and rejection. One then needs connection and security. They are distrustful of others. The fear of failure reveals a strong desire to achieve. It leads to overworking, never doing quite enough. Never *being* enough. The fear of loss of control reveals a need for order. The fear of death reveals worries of the unknown, about meaning and purpose. My throat is becoming tight. This all feels a little too familiar.

I shove the uncomfortable feeling down and turn my focus on the sounds around me. The drumming from the Great Wall persists, a reminder of my intention to pursue it.

I turn towards it. Its beat, low and constant like a heartbeat beneath all the layers of my flesh.

All this time, I have been searching for answers, and now, the Great Wall itself, seems to be knocking—I hope—with the promise of truthful revelations.

Yet, I clutch both the spike and the knife for comfort. There is pain in what is revealed, what is true.

But the pain of lies is greater.

I hurl over the Pale Tree, landing on the grass with a small *thud*, careful to avoid the dragged ant queen, who is still struggling to climb the broad trunk.

I tread barefoot on the cool, powdery sand. The small rays of the sun create a shimmering path guiding my steps. I reach the white dunes much quicker than I had anticipated.

The Girl's words float by: *Jinnah gives us what we need.*

I scramble up the gentle slopes, my breath catching slightly with the effort. Finally, I reach the summit.

The Great Wall looms before me, a monstrous silhouette against the faint light of the sun's thin rays that reach this far. The rays reveal the Great Wall's true colors, the same light purple grey I saw in Thalj. Now closer, I can see its coating of thick, jelly-like substance oozing, even thicker than when I first touched it before entering this land. This liquid is the source of the unsettling purple hue.

A brisk walk brings me to the foot of the Great Wall. I am dwarfed by its colossal presence. A wave of dizziness washes over me.

My reflection stares back from the surface of the ooze. I pull my veil further over my burn scars, leaving only one eye visible.

My hand is trembling like a leaf in a storm. The moment it touches the surface, a sickening *squelch* erupts, and my hand plunges into the yielding mass. I can't pull it out. I'm stuck! I struggle to free my trapped hand while grabbing the knife with the other.

The knocking, that drew me here, stops. The surface of the entire wall bulges outward and then retracts. With this movement comes a pulse-like feeling, the same sensation I had when my hand first touched the Great Wall. It's so subtle, a vibration, that I can barely discern it.

Am I just feeling the frantic pounding of my own heart? Or is it … something else?

I stop trying to yank my hand free. Another pulse. Then another. A third. Then one long, drawn-out tremor that rattles through the ground from the Great Wall. There's a pattern, a rhythm.

I gasp. "You're speaking to me!"

Two pulses. *Speak!*

I drop the knife in my pocket and shakily press my other hand against the wall's body. A jolt of energy surges through the structure, a violent but exhilarating response. Not painful like the vine dress.

"Who—what are you?" I ask, my voice trembling.

The Great Wall pulses: *Who*

"Did you call me?"

It pulses again: *Exist*

"Exist?" I repeat.

Another pulse: *Why*

I try to understand, but it's vague. I ask, "Are you asking why I exist?"

More pulses: *Scar cover purpose*

"Purpose?" I repeat.

It pulses: *Create*

"Create?" Bizarrely, I think I'm beginning to understand what it's saying. I ask, "Create what?"

It replies: *Life*

"Life?" I whisper. "But … how? Why?"

One pulse: *Grow*

"Grow?" I repeat. "Grow what?"

It pulses: *Seeds*

This time, the pulse feels weaker … I sense a tiredness which mirrors a weariness in my body.

"Plant seeds? Is that what you mean?"

A pause. Then a light pulse: *Die*

The Great Wall returns to its flat surface. I wait for more pulses, but none come; only that faint, rhythmic knocking that led me here continues, random and meaningless.

"Why did you stop?" I ask.

Its message is too vague. Like the Stranger, the Great Wall speaks in riddles. I need to know what it means. Frustrated, I shout, "Tell me what you mean!"

As if my anger has unleashed a dormant force, a surge of raw energy erupts from the Great Wall. I'm thrown back with the power of an explosion, tumbling through the air before crashing to the ground with a bone-jarring *thud*.

Disoriented and gasping for breath, I lie sprawled on the earth, the world spinning around me. I gasp for air, my lungs burning. Somehow, I'm unharmed.

I push myself to my feet, my legs trembling. I'm on the grass, in front of the Pale Tree.

The ground is covered in olive seeds, which must have fallen from my pockets, scattered like spilled jewels. When the initial disorientation leaves, I gasp softly. I think I know what the Great Wall was telling me to do.

A mix of hesitation and obligation washes over me as I look at the seeds. I pick them and cradle them in my palms. Did the Great Wall want me to plant these? Why else would it say things like "seeds" or "grow"? But the ground here is still too hard; these seeds won't survive. Still, I decide it's worth a try.

I select a seed. Carefully, I push it into the harsh earth, patting the ground gently as I bury it. My mind races, a jumble of thoughts: purpose, create, grow, life ... die. None of it makes sense.

I try to piece together the recent events: the pain from cutting the vine dress, the roar, the earth shaking. The Stranger's fearful words and, most odd, the Great Wall communicating with me. It wasn't just communication; the wall *knew* the language of the Tap, a language of silence. *How* did it know that? How do *I* know it?

I try to organize these thoughts by burying the seeds. The rhythmic act of planting—each seed carefully placed beneath the soil—gives me a momentary sense of calm. In that calm, an unexpected, but not unwelcome feeling washes over me: a sense of awe, that something greater than me exists.

I initially believed it was the Voice because of the power of its threads. But now, I'm not so sure. My encounter, or whatever it was, with the Great Wall encourages this feeling: there is a *Greater One*. However, the Girl's description of "The Greater One" offered no concrete answers. Only that this Greater One made me.

A fleeting thought, one I quickly dismissed earlier, returns. I had wondered how knowing my creator would help me find answers about why I'm here. For a moment, I saw a connection. I saw how knowing my maker would help me understand myself. But I pushed that thought down, burying it like I am burying these seeds. Now, it is here.

I look up at the last dancing rays of light that pierce the smoke-filled sky. "Did you create me?"

As soon as I say the words, they feel out of place when directed towards the rays, which momentarily vanish, plunging the world into darkness. I feel silly. How can something so immense, something greater than me, disappear so easily?

This is absurd. I should focus on what I know. I know, for some reason, I need to plant these seeds. A seed cannot plant itself, after all—the wind may carry it, or some creature might transport it, but it can't bury itself. I place another seed in the earth, nestled beside its companion. Even if it *can* move, it can't create itself.

Neither can I.

The faint knocking from the Great Wall seems to encourage me to delve deeper into these thoughts, which, with the act of burying these seeds, are becoming more organized. Creation. Existence. Purpose. Life. Grow. Seeds.

It all seems to draw into one question, which is half answered: *Who is The Greater One who created me?*

Am *I* The Greater One? Did I create myself? If I did, why would I have so many needs: to eat, to fight, to sleep? Even if I *had* somehow brought myself into existence, what or who created everything else?

Say someone *did* create me, then who created them, and them, and them? What if there were a continuous cycle of creation? How could I possibly exist if everything were constantly regressing? For me to be here, there must have been a starting point, a beginning. That beginning would require something greater to initiate any cycle that continues. Who, or what, initiated the very first cycle? Whoever it was—is, would be greater than anything else. Yes, The Greater One—who is *not* me, or anyone with the ability to be born or die, like me.

The Greater One had to always be there, a different nature from anything else that is created.

Who is The Greater One at the beginning of everything?

My hand trembles as I clutch the final seed. An even deeper darkness falls over me. I drop the seed back into my pocket.

The camels erupt in a mournful, almost human wail. My one eyebrow arches involuntarily, and the fine hairs above it bristle. A soft brush against my nose. I wipe it away, leaving a sooty residue on my finger. It smells like smoke on the outer layer. Inside is another smell, something more musty, even earthy.

More residue rolls in from above, getting increasingly vicious with every second, as if punishing the ground beneath it. It's so thick; I can barely see the Great Wall through it. A storm of dust is falling.

The Dark Fall.

The final rays of the sun, which found a way to pierce through the smog above, have completely disappeared. There was no point planting these seeds. Life can't exist here.

Only death.

PART 10

Hadeeya

ME

Every worthy thing needs a title. A person, a place, the name of a part of something. Sometimes the names can be a description, an offense, or simply a reference.

Sicko. Snout. Scar. Monster. Fool. These are all names. *Identities*. They shape how the world sees the titled.

A name can be powerful in two ways: in breaking us or in strengthening us. When one knows our name, they gain a connection to who we are.

You do not remember Your name … yet. The Girl doesn't have one. As for me, well, You will never know mine.

There are supposed to be thirty parts in this book. I planned each of their names. But since You arrived here, one part has gone missing, and another part—the one which is hanging over me right now: Part 10—has been stolen and changed.

I know our relationship is the kind where neither of us can be in a place of strength. One must submit to the other, after all, it is not natural for two leaders to lead as equals. One, by nature, will always be weaker than the other.

I accepted that I would be the weak one—after all, it *is* only for a few days—but You have crossed a boundary. You have changed the name of this Part, which can only mean one thing: *You* are back in control.

ALAM

I will let You have this title, for now. I know that something necessary is about to happen. A thing I both hate and need.

Then, will come *defeat*.

YOU

The camels' cries still echo in my ears as I leap over the Pale Tree. Lashes and Smiley are suffering. Even though the thought of their succulent flesh has occurred to me, I don't want them to suffer as the Dark Fall chokes them.

Yet, I can't help them. I can't move them. I can't move the Pale Tree to bring them with me. In this sense, because I have no control, I must *let* them suffer.

The area of the Fallen Trees remains untouched by the falling ash or whatever that substance was. In this area, despite the absence of pigment, a chilling darkness dominates.

A lone ray of white light from the Orbee Forest breaks through the hole, striking the pristine white sand. The impact is almost ethereal, a small, radiant patch of light dancing on the surface, while the surrounding members of the Fallen Trees remain shrouded in an eerie, suffocating gloom.

Emerging from this darkness, I crawl through the exit hole. The full force of the orbees' light momentarily blinds me. I shield my eyes with soot-blackened hands, the grime clinging to my skin like a second layer. My dress is also coated in a thick layer of the Dark Fall. I need to scrub this material away.

Entering deeper into the Orbee Forest, I notice this area is completely untouched by the chaos just beyond the hole. The air *hums* with a quiet symphony of rustling leaves and chirping insects. The scent of damp earth and foliage is a cool, refreshing wave against my skin.

I wade through the Garden of Fire, the crimson petals brushing against my dress. When I pass, each delicate petal becomes marred by a smudge of the Dark Fall.

The Zam shimmers invitingly ahead, but first, my gaze is drawn to the vine dress, still lying abandoned on the bridge. It remains motionless, the wisps of smoke that once leaked from it now gone.

As I fix my eyes on it, I straighten my back, and edge closer to the dress.

Scar Cover Purpose. Those were the words of the Great Wall.

Is the pounding on the wall intensifying, or am I just imagining it?

My breath catches as I spot the vine dress flinching slightly. I stumble back, my heart hammering against my ribs. My instinct screams for me to flee, repelled by the pain the garment inflicted upon me before.

Yet, my feet remain rooted to the ground.

A confusing urge takes hold: I *want* to wear this dress. My legs carry me forward. I reach out a trembling finger, hesitant, then flick it against the surface. Nothing. No jolt of pain. Slight relief. Then again, I felt the pain *after* I had finished making the dress. Could there be a delay, like then?

Only one way to find out. With a shaky breath, I slip into the dress, discarding my filthy rags on the ground.

The dress is a collection of emerald vines. A single, magnificent leaf, broad and veined, drapes over my shoulder. It's cool against my skin. The leathery surface, a comfort, rubs away the Dark Fall from my body. As I move, the leaf sways gently, casting fleeting shadows across the ground.

It's a good fit, though perhaps a touch snug. A little too snug. The dress constricts, tightening around my body like a living serpent. Panic surges. From the corner of my eye, a thick vine whips out, snaking towards my face. It wraps around my mouth and nose.

Can't ... breathe.

I struggle against the suffocating grip, but the vines, now a writhing mass of invasive tendrils, bind my limbs, pinning my arms to my sides.

I'm thrown back, suspended in mid-air by a net of more vines that erupt from the ground below. The world spins. *Is this how I end? A victim of my own foolish curiosity, strangled by a living dress?*

I am lifted higher, the ground shrinking into a dizzying checkerboard of green and brown. The world tilts, the Zam like a line which spirals far beneath.

I gasp, my lungs screaming for air, my vision blurring.

Can't breathe. Can't …

The pressure eases.

I gasp for air, desperate gulps of oxygen filling my starved lungs. I thrash against the constricting vines. I need to tear them away. It's useless. My arms are pinned to my sides. The vines loosen, and I am gently lowered back to the ground.

As I lie here, gasping for breath, the vines don't disappear. Instead, they writhe and contort, splitting into countless tendrils that snake towards me. With a suction, they attach themselves to my body, clinging to every scar, every wound. My back, my legs, my arms—even the scarred half of my face— are covered in the vines.

I open my mouth, mid-scream, prepared for the pain.

No pain. A wave of images.

A laughing child, carefree and innocent, is joined by other small children. A circle of women, their faces radiant with joy, dances. Their arms are linked together, their laughter echoing through a huge room—the Main Hall.

An unexpected and overwhelming surge of elation floods through me. Long-buried memories rise to the surface.

The taste of succulent root vegetables grown in the underground gardens, and more joyful shouts of children playing in the Main Hall. The comforting hum of the life support systems that ensured our survival in the Deep.

My origin is the Deep. I come from beneath the soil, like the seeds I buried. I am from a people of depth, speaking a language of ancient roots. Our skin is of different tones, all the spectrums of light and dark. Our women dress with veils upon our heads and long garments, the men in thobes and beards with trousers above their ankles.

Each memory surges through me, bringing a renewed sense of life.

A group of women, their faces turned up to me with adoration. Their eyes, dark and luminous like pools of midnight, hold a mesmerizing intensity. They wear emerald green dresses, flowing like liquid silk, which drapes their figures, creating an ethereal and almost otherworldly effect.

They stand in a line, forming a path for me to walk through. Some weep openly.

"Queen Adamah," they chant.

I walk through the line, their hands outstretched before them, forming a pathway, a human bridge. The sensation beneath my bare feet is a mixture of yielding warmth and unexpected firmness. It is like walking on a field of tightly packed earthworms, each body subtly shifting beneath my weight.

Finally, I reach a throne. I sink into the soft cushions. A crown is placed upon my head. The cold, hard metal presses against my scalp, an invigorating sensation against my skin. A riot of color explodes before my eyes as the light catches its gems. Rubies burn like embers, sapphires gleam like icy stars, and emeralds pulse with an inner light. The weight of the crown is so heavy that it pulls my head downwards. In the image, I grit my teeth, refusing to yield. With a defiant surge, I raise my head higher, straightening my back to carry the burden of monarchy.

The crown falls and I lurch after it ... very queen-like. My foot lands right on its sharp edges. A searing pain. Blood. The pain feels good. It shows me how much my followers care for me. They rush to me and carry me to my throne.

"You saved us," they whisper reverently.

I take in the breathtaking landscape behind them. Obsidian birds soar, their cries echoing like distant horns. Beautiful green meadows shimmer beneath a golden light that filters through trees. A silver path, a serpent of gleaming metal, weaves through the land.

The sensations in my body pull me back to the present. I feel alive! I can move my hands and feet. I have control over the vines. With a surge of will, I extend my arms. The vines that form my dress erupt from my body, whipping through the air like outstretched arms. They coil and lash around me. Joyous laughter bubbles from within me.

More joyful visions pull me into my memories. Amidst them is one shrouded in some kind of block. Somehow, I know this memory holds the key to my greatest happiness, yet it remains elusive. Why won't it surface? I swallow down the growing unease, focusing instead on the other joyful memories.

The memories show me I am not guilty. My past was good. I was—*am* good. I saved my people. I was loved. I was followed.

My name is Adamah.

Sitting cross-legged amid the Orbee Forest, I close my eyes and tilt my head, straining to hear any communication from the Great Wall—a knock, even a prompting within me.

Nothing.

Why? That very wall had instructed me to wear this dress. Didn't it? And now ... *silence*. For a few moments, I am motionless, the vine dress swaying gently around me. I close my eyes, again attempting to reconnect to the Great Wall.

I *do* feel something. Its faint. Like a trace of our connection. But quieter. A watchful stillness, as if the wall itself is observing.

Learning.

Waiting?

It is as if every living thing is holding its breath. Every sound is muted; every movement becomes suspended. Time itself seems to slow down.

WHOOSH

With my eyes still closed, the rough, damp ground beneath my vine-covered body comes alive with sensation. A tingling, a direct link to the earth. As the vines amplify my senses, I feel the ground more intensely, an electrified buzz coursing through me. I hear the individual whispers of the wind *rustling* through each leaf, the frantic *buzzing* of a single orbee. The constant, rhythmic *thrashing* of the Zam.

Where my body touches the earth—my hands, my folded legs—I sense the stirring of existence, a burgeoning energy beneath. I feel the seeds, tiny sparks of potential, awakening within the soil.

I feel Earth itself, breathing, expanding, ready to receive.

There is *something else* here, above me.

A delicate, almost invisible string that connects the earth below my feet to something unseen. This string, a vital line of energy, vibrates with a faint *hum*.

New sounds fill my ears. Not a *whisper*, nor a *rustle* of leaves, but something else entirely: a symphony of unseen creatures. Now, a birdsong. I allow my eyes to flutter open and look around—no birds here. Now, a high-pitched *chittering*, a frantic *squeaking*.

I look up. It's up there. The tops of the orbee trees are obscured by the thick, swirling smoke, hiding whatever exists beyond it. This unseen presence—this hidden force, this string—is vital for Jinnah to thrive.

What exists beyond the smoke?

If I can sense the seeds taking root by my physical connection to the ground, could I perhaps sense what lies above by connecting with something that reaches up there? An orbee tree?

It's worth a try. I push myself up and turn towards the nearest orbee tree. As I walk, the vine dress resists, its tendrils catching on the undergrowth. I struggle forward, each step a battle against the clinging fabric. Frustrated, I lean down and grasp the mass of vines pooling around my ankles. With a gentle tug, I wrap the excess around one ankle, securing it with a quick twist.

To my astonishment, as if anticipating my wishes, the vines wrap themselves around my other ankle, mirroring the action of the first. The dress moves with me, a living, breathing extension of my own will.

I think: *Veil.*

The cool, smooth vine leaves press against my scalp, a soothing touch, as they weave a protective layer over my long hair. I smile as I touch it.

Taking a few more steps, I finally reach the orbee tree. Its bark is rough and cool beneath my touch. But ... nothing. Why can't I sense it?

How do I get up there?

The branches of the orbee tree, instead of reaching towards the sky, curve downwards, as if bowing to some unseen force. There is another set of leaves, higher up—I can just see them—poking out from under the smoke. But they are too high for me to climb. I take a step back, assessing my options.

A tendril lashes out from my vine dress, wrapping itself around the trunk of the tree with astonishing force. I am jerked forward, losing my breath for a moment as I dangle precariously several feet above the ground. Panic rises as I flail my arms, hoping another tendril will reach out and secure my ascent.

Nothing happens. The original tendril loosens its grip. I brace myself for the inevitable fall.

I fall, but I don't hit the ground. I am suspended above it, cushioned by a soft bed of vines that have erupted from the ground itself, catching me just before impact.

Slowly, the vines lift me upward.

Higher.

And higher.

I rise, propelled by the surging vines, my body thrusting through the dense canopy of orbee leaves like a spear through water. The smoke. I squeeze my eyes shut, taking a desperate breath. My lungs burn, and I force myself to breathe, each inhalation a struggle against the suffocating air. It's the smoke. It's too thick.

I cough, choking back the acrid fumes, my grip tightening on the vines that float beside me. I dare not open my eyes, afraid of the stinging smoke that threatens to blind me.

The vines, with an intelligence of their own, push through the thickest part of the smoke.

A shift. A subtle change in the air, the pressure becomes lighter.

I open my eyes. Behind the smoke, there is pure darkness. Though I am used to the dark, this sort of darkness is present with a crushing weight, a sensory deprivation that leaves me disoriented. Something is blocking me from going further up. It's a solid barrier pressing against my face. I can't move it, no matter how much I push. I'm trapped beneath it.

Then, a series of *thumps*, heavy and deliberate, shake the barrier. Now, tiny feet *patter* above me, followed by a *fluttering*, like the frantic beating of wings. What is on the other side?

I direct the vines: *Through*.

They writhe and twist, their tendrils piercing the barrier with a startling ease. With a surge, they push through, creating a small opening.

A sliver of light.

The light spills into the void, a golden torrent washing over me. I shut my eyes automatically, the brown of my eyelids a stark contrast against the sudden burst. I gasp, my breath catching as I finally open my eyes and peek through the hole.

It takes a moment for my senses to adjust, for my eyes to focus. All I see is the sun, a glorious orb. Not truly golden in color, that is just how light refracts in the surrounding air of Earth. I see its real color: white, a brilliant white containing the entire spectrum of light—all the colors of the rainbow.

As its pure, white light streams into Earth's atmosphere, the blue tones are scattered most by the air, making the sky a magnificent blue.

WHOOSH

Something courses through me. A vision of a ball, like a small sun, which belongs deep in the core of Earth. It is made of metals. Its effect extends hundreds and thousands of miles beyond Earth's body. This ball has a forcefield, a deflector, pushing away all the radiation of the sun like an invisible hand warding off a fiery blow from the sun's flares.

My body moves now like the shield, a dancer mirroring its grace, fluid and responsive as it covers Earth. This shield is a guard. A protector. A veil upon the face of the world. It blooms in the planet's defense. Emerald green waves ripple and scrabble, painting the lower reaches of the sky. Higher, where the air thins, streaks of crimson red pulse close to the surface. They flicker and glow. Lower and closer to the horizon, hints of violet and blue shimmer and dance.

WHOOSH

Another vision: light from the sun. A light with danger inside, which, if allowed to touch the skin of any material, would burn it to a crisp, leaving it ashen and lifeless. Everything that this light touches in its fullness will become sterilized, as barren as a desert after a sandstorm.

WHOOSH

Trillions of bubbles, like a silent rebellion, rise from the ocean's depths. They form a second shield, shimmering and fragile, like a soap bubble stretched too thin.

This second shield—lighter than the magnetic aura from the ball in Earth—is thinner, more vulnerable, like a pane of glass against a storm. A part was punched through, a gaping wound still trying to heal. To knit itself back together from the insidious chemicals my species had foolishly released, long before my ancestors became the nation of the Deep.

A second hole was punched, more recently, worse than the first. From an … an explosion of some kind. A poison humanity had unleashed, a rising like a deadly tide, only to consume everything and everyone. It led to the end of a certain kind of power humankind possessed. One that included the ability for people to whisper and be heard from one side of Earth to the other.

WHOOSH

A heat so intense it sears, like a furnace door thrown open, radiating from the sun, intensified by another chemical that escapes my body with every exhale. This chemical, a suffocating blanket, is trapped, clinging to Earth like a shroud. Trapped.

This chemical, this gas, is why it's so hot in Shahwah and everywhere else, a stifling heat. Yet, why is Jinnah still cool?

WHOOSH

Another form of protection from Earth reveals itself. It battles the intense heat by trapping exhaled breath. In this vision, something trickles down from the sky, gripping the exhaled substance like invisible hands tying a tight knot, refusing to release it. It falls in droplets. Rain. It cools Earth. But something else cools Jinnah even more, something I can't sense.

I focus on the rain in my vision. It falls, dissolving rocks like they are salt cubes, a gentle erosion sculpting the landscape. This captured chemical, which scorches the soil, is now a prisoner of the rain, carried down.

Down to the bottom of the water.

Sinking into the depths.

Contained.

I look up at the sun once more, just moments ago struck by its beauty and strength. Now I see it is not a friend. It is a foe.

We are at war with the sun, a cosmic struggle for survival. One day, the sun will succeed. This is nature's promise, our fate as inevitable as the dawn of the rising sun. It will absorb us, consume us in its blazing embrace. Engulf our world.

Everything that lives must die. When the sun dies, it will become a dead star, a smoldering ember. And we … we will become a part of it. Absorbed.

Yet. Today, Earth lives. Cleansing. Healing. Bringing back order from chaos. Nurturing. Not just a place, but a home, a womb of life cradling all that exists.

The sun, in its fiery language tells me there is no other place like Earth, not in the vast expanse of the cosmos, nor within reach of my searching gaze. Earth, a sanctuary, a calm and thriving haven, bursts with life in every imaginable form, whilst nestled amidst a swirling storm of cosmic chaos.

Earth's bloodstream is the rivers and the oceans which flow through it, its lungs the forests like the one in Jinnah. The deserts are its sunbaked skin, weathered and ancient. The mountains are its bones, foundations keeping it steady, reaching towards the sky.

And I … am a part of it.

Not just a visitor, but a cell in its vast, intricate form. I feel its pain, struggle and resilience. The sun's energy, Earth's heartbeat, the rain's cleansing touch—they all flow through me, connecting me to something larger than myself. Something powerful.

Earth is in me. In this moment, standing here, rooted to this spot, held by the vines, arises a yearning.

I don't just want the truth. I want to understand the truth.

The pull is different from before, when I first tried to scale the Pale Tree and failed frustratingly. Then, I just wanted to know the big questions—why am I here? Who am I? Where did I come from?—because I felt I needed to. Back then, it was a motivation, a desire for information that tightened my chest. I didn't care where it came from. I just wanted to find it. But now, there is an openness in my chest, a receptiveness.

To be open to receive feels *vulnerable*. As if I am *exposed*. I've been feeling like that a lot lately.

I hold my hands out in front of me, my skin, a dark brown, the color of soil. My scars are now concealed, hidden beneath the intricate network of vines that now cover my body, including my missing fingernail.

I lift my body until I am fully through the hole. The vines lift me higher until I am gently deposited on a thick branch. As soon as I am fully through the hole, it is closed, huge leaves growing quickly and covering it. As if healing a wound.

The branch beneath me is soft, covered in a thick layer of moss that cushions my descent. I climb off the branch and lean down to study the leaves. They are identical to those of the orbee trees below. However, these leaves are not simply leaves; they are spread out, forming a thick, resilient carpet beneath my feet. This, I realize with a jolt, is the barrier—a surface that had concealed this world above Jinnah.

There is no *WHOOSH* from these leaves. No sense. No vision. Not like the sun in the sky or the soil on the ground. It's an odd, lonely feeling. Like a disconnection. A detachment.

The once-distant chatter of woodland creatures, that I sensed below, now fills the air. *Chirps*, *squawks*, and *rustles*. A gentle breeze, carrying the earthy scent of damp wood and blooming flowers, floats by.

The orbee trees' heads reach here, surrounding me, leaving lingering shadows as they pierce the sky, their branches interlacing overhead, forming a leafy canopy that filters the sunlight into dappled patterns. I realize these trees are not simply downward reaching, but possess a duality, a second set of branches reaching upward, towards the sun.

The *thumping* I heard from under the leaf barrier returns. I turn my body to see its source. A large creature with round ears and a long trunk makes its way towards me, followed by a family of six, seven, eight—a baby is nuzzled between the massive bodies! Elephants. Up here? How powerful is this leaf barrier? How powerful are my vines, which tore through it?

The elephants are careful to avoid the squirrels, which bob their heads up and down, their bushy tails twitching. Other animals are scurrying ahead— rabbits and mice, their tiny claws digging into the soft leaf carpet.

I pause, struck by my knowledge of the names of these animals. With a blink, the memory returns. During my brief time as 'Queen Adamah', these were the very creatures who shared my land. But how? My land was on the ground of Thanae, not up here. How did these creatures get up here?

I jolt when something touches my hand.

WHOOSH

Old age, slow and steady, protected. Solitary.

A tortoise, its shell the color of weathered stone, ambles past, seemingly oblivious to my presence. When it notices me, it opens its mouth wide as if to speak. It clamps it shut with a deliberate thunk and continues plodding along.

On the leaves is a feast. Vibrant fruits, plump and juicy, grow freely— some the color of sapphires, glistening nuts, and berries of every imaginable hue. There is an abundance of it, spreading out before me with small bursts of deliciousness wafting by.

As I reach for them, a rapid, *chattering* scold surrounds me. I whip around to see a bushy-tailed squirrel, looking remarkably disgruntled, perched on a branch. This tiny rodent, with its twitching nose and air of utter indignation, is currently engaged in a heated argument with a rival over a pile of nuts.

Despite the dramatic display, the squirrel carefully buries some nuts under a pile of leaves with the nonchalance of a seasoned hoarder, occasionally scattering a few fragments for the scrawny younger squirrels scrambling at its feet. The little ones, oblivious to the theatrics, happily snatch up the discarded morsels. Even the most dramatic of species can't resist a free meal.

My stomach rumbles, a low growl echoing through my chest. As I reach out, a wave of hesitation. The memory of the white flower lingers. That rotten taste still on the memory of my tongue.

Could these fruits be dangerous too?

I watch the squirrels, their eyes bright with anticipation, their movements fluid and graceful as they pluck the fruits from the branches and devour them with obvious relish.

If they can eat it, so can I.

I mimic their actions, carefully selecting a plump berry that almost glows with a deep purple shade, more vibrant than the olives.

I take a bite.

The juice explodes. So many flavors! Sweet and tart. My hesitation melts away, replaced by a newfound appreciation for this bountiful world.

As I take another bite, a squirrel stops in front of me, its tail waving back and forth. Its tail reminds me of the Girl's eyebrow—*the Girl*. A surge of guilt washes over me, a bitter taste mixing with the fruit in my mouth. I remember her meager meals, the way she flinched when offered the olives.

I grab a handful of fruits and nuts and try to stuff them into my pockets. A sinking feeling. I have no pockets.

I direct the vines: *Leave these by the entry to the Fallen Trees.*

The vines obediently uncoil from my body, their tendrils reaching out and gently gathering the fruits. Still connected to my dress, they pierce a small hole through the leafy canopy, descending to Jinnah. As they withdraw, the orbee leaves swiftly close the area around the vines, sealing any holes that might allow the smoke below to enter, while keeping the vines connected to me.

I turn to see a group of butterflies, unlike the ones below, flutter around. They are adorned in shades of gold and black, their delicate wings matching the vibrant flowers nestled among the leaves. Just ahead, tiny birds weave effortlessly through the branches, sharing their melodious song with the natural symphony. Among them, a family with iridescent feathers meticulously crafts intricate nests.

A single drop, cool, lands on my cheek.

Rain.

The same rain that captures and carries the warming substance I breathe out, cooling Earth. I raise my head to let it fall on me. This is not the dry, dusty rain of residue that fell upon Jinnah. It is not the Dark Fall. It is something different, something … moist and life-giving. Another drop lands, this time on my nose, a sensation that is refreshing and startling.

As the water touches my face, the remaining ash on my skin, which the vines didn't rub away, slides off. The rain continues with a gentle patter, a rhythmic dance of tiny silver against the leaves. Each drop explodes into a thousand shimmering droplets, washing over me in cool, refreshing waves.

WHOOSH

Tiny green shoots, like arrows piercing the darkness, emerge from the earth, their upward thrust a testament to the resilience of life. I feel their struggle, their determination to reach the light, to embrace the sun. Not just a desire, but a primal need, a desperate yearning that resonates deep within me, too, for truth. Their shoot's bodies, fragile yet fierce, ache for the rain, for the life-giving embrace of the storm.

From them, life unfolds. Delicate blossoms unfurl, their petals a vibrant tapestry of colors, attracting all kinds of birds and insects. Heavy fruits, bursting with life-giving juices, ripen on the branches, a bounty for the creatures of the world. Bats, their wings a blur of motion, feast on the sweetest fruits, their droppings scattering seeds across Earth's body. Elephants, giants of Earth, roam through the undergrowth, their powerful feet churning the soil, creating space for new life to emerge.

Earth is a source of life.

A protective shield.

Home.

This place up here is the pinnacle of its glory. *Hadeeya*, in the language of the Deep, means "gift."

I will call this place Hadeeya.

My laughter erupts, quickly turning into tears of pure joy, which mix with the rain. *I understand something.* Something which makes every other worry feel insignificant. This feeling transcends the logic I tried to grasp by planting the olive seeds. It's a deep knowing that resonates through every part of my body: there is something infinitely greater than me.

It is something that binds everything together. The clarity of this realization is so profound, it almost steals my breath away. This world is not just a collection of individual parts.

It is *connected*.

This constant feeding, growing, spreading, and planting of seeds of legacy isn't a cycle of chaos. It is one of harmony: organized, sustained, powerful, yet subtle. A delicate balance where every creature and entity plays its part.

The Stranger's words, left as messages on the ground of the Fallen Trees, flood back.

The Guardian. The Healer. The All Mighty. The Originator. The Fashioner. The Giver of gifts. The Magnificent. The Sustainer.

The Sustainer. In that word, in the breathtaking beauty I have just witnessed, I realize the most profound truth: The Sustainer did not abandon any of this. Not the smallest seed, nor the grand sky filled with rain. Not the struggling balance of Thanae.

And not me.

Is the Sustainer a she? Or a he?

A thought settles, a quiet certainty. The Sustainer is neither. How could such a vast, all-encompassing force, the pulse of existence, be confined to the clumsy labels of our physical forms? But the word 'it' feels off. So does 'she'.

He. I know The Sustainer is not truly a 'he'. They are something more, something beyond.

But in the fragile confines of human language, 'He' is the closest I can come up with, a shorthand for the immense ungendered power that holds everything.

His sustenance is continuous, His care unwavering. It's in every breath, every growth, every subtle shift of the world. This understanding connects me to Him in a way I have never felt before—even as the leader of my people—a sense of belonging to something eternal and … kind.

"My Creator," I whisper. "The Greater One."

That is what the Stranger was referring to. To *my* Creator.

At first, all I wanted to know was who I am. Now I know. I also know where I came from: The Creator. A Creator with a purpose whose creation is not purposeless.

Now I want to know why. Why am I here? Whatever the reason, it must be good.

What clues point to this? I gasp softly. The organic nature and power of the vine dress, the Great Wall's message about creating and growing seeds, my memories of saving the people of the Deep, the Girl asking me to help her with Jinnah—all these point to one thing … I think.

I open my arms, my vines expanding, and I raise my face to the raining sky. Yes, every living thing is interconnected, including me, Adamah.

I think I am meant to save Jinnah using Hadeeya.

PART 10
Defeat

ME

There's a crucial distinction between *being* good and simply *feeling* good. Many people mistakenly believe that a euphoric state, a sense of blissful detachment, is synonymous with spiritual transcendence.

They believe they have ascended, but the truth is often far more insidious. Their inner selves are rotting, corroded by the consequences of their actions and ... their past.

In just a few hours, you will encounter the other half of Yourself, the essential part that completes You, the part that allows You to truly *be* good, not just *feel* good. This reunion, however vital, carries immense risk: it could lead to Your ultimate defeat, or my most magnificent victory.

ADAMAH

"Lashes! Smiley!" The Girl's scream, a raw, desperate cry, pierces through the air, jolting me out of my reverie.

My heart hammers against my ribs. The vines, sensing my alarm, whip out from my body, instinctively seeking a foothold. I force myself to stand, the ground beneath my feet solid and steadying.

How do I get down? I spot the vines that had gone through the ground to deliver the food. They still pierce through the green carpet. As if reading my mind, they cut around through the hole, making it big enough for me to squeeze through.

A vine lashes out, snaking around my torso, carrying my body with it. The last rays of sunlight, filtering through the canopy, are swallowed whole as the orbee leaves swiftly close over the opening, plunging me into the abyss of dark.

Thick, biting smoke fills the air, stinging my eyes and clogging my lungs. My skin prickles, every nerve on edge as I move through the densest part of the smoke.

I am lowered softly on a high branch of an orbee tree, just below the swirling grey mass. The leaves brush against my face, their touch cold and clammy.

A vine wraps itself around the branch securely. It is strong. Very strong. Still, I hesitate. I want to use it to carry me down by attaching to another tree, but the memory of my previous attempt, which led to my unexpected fall, is still fresh in my mind. Then again, a net of vines was formed, which caught me, so technically I didn't hit the ground.

The Girl's scream echoes through the air again.

Taking a deep breath, I allow another vine to extend, cautiously testing its strength against the thick air. It holds firm. With a surge, I swing myself onto the branch, the wind whipping across the bare part of my face, stinging my eyes. I throw the vine, aiming for the nearest branch, but it misses, snapping back with a frustrated *hiss*.

I throw it again. This time, it finds its mark, wrapping itself around the bark. I swing from tree to tree, the wind roaring in my ears, the world a blur of green and grey. Finally, the vine slows down, guiding me gently to the ground. With a *thump*, I land on the soft earth below.

I shoot a final glance at the canopy above before plunging into the darkness of the Fallen Trees. When I step into the hole, I scan the ground reflexively. The Stranger returned. For the first time, their words form a sentence, a sentence which is underlined by more vines:

I used to fear death

The Girl's voice echoes, now a desperate plea, "Don't die!"

I rush past the words, the Pale Tree in sight. This time, I don't use the table. My leap takes me straight to the other side. Dust and debris swirl around with my landing.

WHOOSH

The ground: layered. Not just sand and debris. Something more. More than the sickness. Older. Fainter. A *seabed*. The corruption of disease has masked the truth, but it hasn't erased it. This sand was born of the sea. This whole area was once a sea.

I stand to see the Girl face me. Her face is smudged with the Dark Fall, her eyes wide with a mixture of fear and hope. Both camels lie motionless on the ground, inside the confine I created. Their bodies are unsettlingly still.

"What did you do?" she asks, her voice trembling.

"I didn't ..." My words trail off.

Streaked tears have dried into tracks on her dusty cheeks. "Is this why you put them here in the prison?" Her voice rises. "So, you could let them die ... and eat them?" The last two words are drawn out, a chilling accusation that hangs heavy in the air.

"I didn't ..."

"You were supposed to save them—save all of us!" Her breath hitches as she scans the completely black trees, the olives hidden under the Dark Fall. "You've just made it worse."

I am taken aback by the ferocity of her accusation. Raw anger burns in her eyes. She hasn't even bothered to ask what happened, to hear my side of the story. Instead, she condemns me.

When she looks up at me, truly looks at me, I notice something in those eyes, a haunted look, a deep-seated grief that goes beyond the immediate loss of her camels. The tear streaks on her face are not fresh; they are layered, some dry. She was crying long before I had reached her and the camels.

She spins around and storms a few steps towards a cluster of trees. With her back facing me, she whispers, "How long have you been here?"

"A few sunrises—"

"And already, you're making weapons?"

"Weapons? What are you—"

"Look!" She spins back towards me and points at my vines.

I follow her gaze, and a wave of dread washes over me. The vines that had been my saviors, my companions, are now transforming. They writhe and contort, their smooth surfaces hardening into a mass of sharp, menacing spikes. The air crackles with a sinister energy, the once-gentle vines now a dangerous, living armor.

"No," I gasp, "these are good vines. They helped me—us, they can help us to save Jinnah."

I walk closer to her. Reaching her, I extend my arm to offer a reassuring touch, perhaps give her another pat on the shoulder. That seemed to have calmed her last time.

Snap.

A vine lashes out, unexpected, brutal. The air around it shimmers with heat, a sudden, intense burst, as it strikes her across the face.

The Girl doesn't even scream. Slowly, her eyes widen as if realizing something. "You hurt me," she whispers, voice trembling, hand on her cheek, which blooms with a crimson flower of blood.

I reach out instinctively. But she flinches, stumbling backward. She whirls around and scrambles deeper into the cluster of trees.

What just happened?

"Wait!" I cry, chasing after her.

A black breasted beast emerges from the trees, growling fiercely. The Girl freezes, backing away. I rush to her side, shielding her from it.

My body tenses, the vines around me tightening. *A black lion. Black Assad.*

"Step back," I command the Girl, my voice barely a whisper above the thunder of the beast's growls.

She doesn't argue, her silence heavy with fear.

"Leave," I order the Black Assad, my voice firm despite the tremor that rattles through my body.

The Black Assad roars, a sound that shakes the very ground beneath my feet. Its teeth, gleaming like rows of polished pearls, flash in the dim light of the Girl's orbee, dwarfing my body as it approaches. The colossal creature rises onto its hind legs, its size as tall as an olive tree and as wide as an orbee tree. Its black fur ripples like a storm cloud, with a single, defiant mane of black fur.

The vines behind me stir, bristling with anticipation, ready to spring into action.

Then, I feel it. A small hand, soft and warm, gripping mine. The warmth, the human touch, breaks through the icy grip of fear, grounding me here, right now.

The Girl's hand trembles slightly, yet her grip remains unwavering.

WHOOSH

The Girl: innocent, pure, carries an untainted love. Compassion that transcends the immediate danger. Beneath this surface, a deep undercurrent of sadness and pain.

I turn to her. How can such a small, clumsy thing of a child carry such a heavy burden of pain? More confusing, how can one who has known such sorrow still possess such compassion for the world?

For the first time, I truly see her. Tears well up in my eyes.

I am crying. Crying while the Black Assad looms before us, ready to attack. It's absurd, I know. I should be focusing on the immediate danger, preparing for the fight, or judging by the size and power this lion holds, slaughter of us. But the sight of the Girl, her vulnerability and her resilience, has done something—something I can't describe—to me.

The vines tighten around me and the Girl, creating a protective shell, a cocoon of emerald green. With this, time seems to stretch, and in that stretch, the Black Assad's face comes fully into view. The way it moves its mouth is hesitant. Its breath touches my face, hot and fetid.

WHOOSH

Black Assad: Royal. Protector. Just. He is not going to hurt us. He is scared, but not of us. He fears *for* something dear to it.

As soon as I recognize this flicker of vulnerability in the beast, time no longer stretches. The Black Assad lets out a resounding bellow, a sound that shakes every part of my body. It recoils, taking a tentative step back, then another, its gaze fixed on something beyond us.

"It wants us to follow," I whisper, my voice barely audible above the echoing cry of the lion.

The Girl pulls away from me, her small frame a beacon of courage against the imposing backdrop of the Black Assad. An orbee, hovering low to the ground, guides her forward, its light illuminating the path ahead. Taking a deep breath, I follow her, my heart pounding in my chest.

We reach the edge of the clustered trees. Just ahead lies Thalj, its skies perpetually choked with black snow. Instead of heading towards that bleak landscape, we turn right. After a few minutes, we arrive at a collection of rocky valleys.

"Valley," the Girl says, as we enter one of these rocky formations, a haven where the Dark Fall has not yet reached. The air is thick with the scent of damp earth. Shadows cling to the jagged rocks, creating a labyrinth of darkness.

"Do you hear that?" she whispers urgently, her hand gripping mine.

A high-pitched cry pierces the air, a sound that chills me to the bone. A baby-like wail, raw and desperate. The sound triggers a vision, sharp and sudden, from my past. I am thrown to the ground by its intensity.

White. A white blanket cradled in arms, a tiny face, eyes squeezed shut. The white of the blanket is tainted with blood.

I can sense the vines trying to hide the memory from me in some crevice of my mind, but for some reason, the image remains. I snap back to now, the cry for help echoing in my ears. I push myself up and frantically search for the Girl.

"Hurry!" she shouts.

She is ahead, behind a looming rock. I sprint to her. Behind the rock, two massive boulders jut together, forming a narrow crevice. A lioness, ebony like the Black Assad, stands before it, swiping urgently at the rocks. Her powerful paws are too wide to fit in the small opening, which she misses repeatedly.

The source of distress: a tiny cub entangled in a web of branches within the two boulders. With every attempt to free itself, the branches tighten around it.

I direct my vines: *Free it.*

In a surge of primal energy, the vines strike the rock with a force that shatters it to dust. The cub, freed from its deadly prison, whimpers weakly. I cradle it in my arms, the warmth of its tiny body against my own. It shifts uncomfortably, and I realize my hands are getting warmer. The color of my exposed skin, which pokes out from the vines, is red, as if the vision I had has caused some imbalance in me.

I lower the cub, and it limps back to its family. The maned Black Assad watches me. His eyes hold an intelligence that shouldn't be possible, an otherworldly wisdom, the amber even more pronounced against the dark fur. His mane, like a rippling midnight flame in the fading light, dips in a silent nod.

A guttural *purr* rumbles in his chest as he utters a single phrase, "Thank you."

Speechless, I watch as he disappears into the shadows with his family, surrounded by the towering rocks.

The camels lay like statues; their fur dusted with a fine dark cover which clings to them. A shroud. The air carries a stillness that presses down, heavy and suffocating.

I hesitate at the edge of the wooden enclosure, the silence amplified as if the absence of color has urged it to become bolder.

The area, once an elaborate expanse of white, now wears a pallor that speaks of death. When the black snow fell on the ground of Thalj, there was a resistance to its effects. A transformation. A healing. Here, it is the opposite. Here, the ground eats the falling material as if ravenous. No rebellion, only fierce acceptance.

The sand is stained, as if the night itself has risen from the depths, clawing its way up to suffocate life from the world.

The air hangs heavy, thick with the smell of burnt wood and something else. Death, maybe. Or fear. It's hard to tell. Unlike the soil, the tortoise, and the other things I sensed, there is no *whoosh* from the falling dust. It is the same feeling—or lack of—that I had when touching the orbee trees and the orbee leaves. *Why?*

The Girl stands beside me, staring ahead at the gloomy expanse. The line of her shoulders is tight and rigid. She moves ahead and climbs over the fences which hold the bodies of the dead camels.

I follow her, sitting by her before the somber outlines, their bumpy slope on full show. It's as if they're still trying to escape some unseen horror, their bodies caught in a final, desperate struggle. I turn to find her gaze fixed on the ground.

"I'm sorry," I say, my voice hoarse. I am not sure if it's thick with emotion or if what falls from the sky is scratching on the back of my throat. "You were right, animals shouldn't be locked up."

"I lied before," the Girl whispers, her voice also thick, "the truth is, I don't have many friends. Those two … they were my best."

She moves closer to me, her movements shaky but deliberate, her shoulder brushing against mine. Again, that surge of emotion with sadness holding it together.

"You probably hate me," I say, the words catching in my throat.

I don't know why I say this. I know she doesn't. What she feels is loss, a devastating loss. Is it purely because of the death of Lashes and Smiley? Or has she felt it before? Despite her grief, there is no more anger in her eyes, no blame towards me.

She shakes her head. The dust falls on her hair, a soft, grey mantle settling over her shoulders. But even as the world around us is shrouded in darkness, there is a seemingly misplaced serenity about her, a calm.

She coughs, a dry, rattling sound that echoes through the silence.

"The Voice spoke to me," she rasps, "when I left to go see … my Mama."

My knees weaken at the mention of the Voice, making my vines tense like fists about to throw a punch. "What did it say?"

"It said … it told me something," she whispers, her eyes fixed on the ground.

"What?" I urge gently.

"That I leave my Mama alone because I …" She gulps, the unspoken words hanging heavy in the air. "It said I don't love her. It was wrong about that part. I love her too much, that's why I can't be with her for too long."

How can a person love someone so much that they can't be with them? I don't understand this. Perhaps she mentions this because this is how *she* mourns. Scattered. Unfocused.

"The Voice is a liar, you know that."

"Yes," she replies, nodding slowly, wiping a tear from her cheek with the back of her hand. When I brush against her, I feel there is something more to the conversation with the Voice, something she is holding back.

"Did the Voice say anything else?" I ask.

She opens her mouth as if to say something, but closes it. I wait for her to answer. She bites her lip for a few moments, as if considering what to share.

Finally, she sighs and continues looking at the ground, deciding, I suppose, not to share her thoughts with me. In a way, I am relieved; I want to move away from the topic of the Voice.

I clear my throat. The air is making it hard for us both to breathe. But it's not the smoke that's choking me. It's the weight of these heavy emotions, the crushing disappointment, the grief. I don't want to dwell on them, not now, after the fleeting glimpse of awe and wonder I experienced up there, in that place, Hadeeya. Not after realizing that I am not alone, that there is a Creator, a force greater than myself, watching over me.

There is also another strange feeling I have, which urges me to want to leave this place. A primal pull stirs within me. A desire to tear into the carcasses' flesh, to consume them.

I shudder, a cold tremor running down my spine. The Girl looks at me, her eyes wide with silent questioning.

She stays seated, moving her gaze back to the fallen camels, their forms shrouded in a veil of ash. The Dark Fall has slowed down. As if the camels have ingested it through the storm, and now it is satisfied with their deaths. I need to get away from here; my thoughts are becoming increasingly odd in the presence of the dead.

"I know how to save Jinnah," I say.

She sniffles, her eyes widening slightly. "You do?"

I nod. "I know how we can help your mother."

A flicker of hope reanimates her face. "You *do?*"

I turn towards the Pale Tree and listen intently, straining to hear her footsteps following me. "Come on," I call out before turning to her.

She hesitates for a moment, then starts towards me, her small figure a fragile silhouette against the grey sky. As she approaches, I reach out, offering her my hand. The vines, sensing my intention, outstretch to her, their tendrils gently wrapping around her small frame.

She gasps, startled, as she is lifted effortlessly towards me. She is lowered gently to the ground with a soft *thud*.

She looks around, as if just realizing something. "The Great Wall isn't knocking anymore."

"A lot happened while you were away. I'll explain but first, I have something for you."

As she begins to walk, I notice a lightness in her step. She waddles ahead in her baby-bird-in-heels style. I follow her, my gaze drawn to the words etched into the ground: *What do you fear?*

She crosses over the message, her footsteps echoing. As she passes, a chill runs down my spine. I look up at her, our eyes meeting. She topples over the word, *Death,* and picks herself up, brushing her dress, which is now a mix of white dust from the Fallen Trees and black dust from the place where the camels' bodies lie.

What do I fear? The question echoes in my mind.

No. I won't entertain that thought, not now. Not when this feeling, this wonderful surge of hope, is coursing through me.

"You remind me of the sun," she says. Her voice is small, hesitant, yet filled with a warmth that surprises me.

"How?" I ask.

"You're glowing."

I turn my palms around. I *am* glowing. A yellow light slightly emanates from my body. A little disorientated, I follow her out of the hole, the air thick with the scent of damp earth mixed with smoke. I tumble over the fruit and nuts, which are scattered in front of the foliage.

Just moments ago, there was a warmth to her voice. A spring to her step, almost. Now, it is replaced by a shadow on her face. I hold the fruit out to her. It takes her a moment to process what I am doing. She stares blankly at the fruit. "What is it?"

I look at her intensely, hoping my glowing face will calm her. If it doesn't, I can always pat her shoulder a couple of times. With a beam, I say, "Fruit and nuts for you."

"What about *you*?" Her fingers trace the contours of a plump berry.

"I ate," I reply, gesturing towards the remnants of the feast, whilst catching a glance at my shining hands as I do.

She nods. There is a slump to her shoulders, more so than usual. She sits and splits the fruit into three piles. As she begins to prop one pile into her pocket, I stop her.

"There's much more. Eat." My tone is firm.

She nods but still pushes another pile to me. I shake my head. Reluctantly, she brings all three piles into one. Before she puts a nut in her mouth, she says, "I don't want to eat alone."

"Fine." I sigh.

I sit next to her, and we both lean on an orbee tree. The loose berry is cool against my fingers. As I pop it into my mouth, a burst of flavor explodes on my tongue, sharp and sweet. I let it linger, savoring the unexpected intensity.

Satisfied, she rolls the nuts between her fingers and then throws one into her mouth. With each crunch, her eyes widen, a feral glint in their depths. It's a pure thing, this joy, raw and unfiltered.

I watch her, reminding myself not to smile too widely. I don't want her to think I'm laughing at her. The vines around me mirror my emotions, swaying gently in the breeze, as if dancing to an unseen rhythm. I push them back down, restraining their exuberance, my focus returning to the Girl.

She acts like she doesn't notice, but I see her blush slightly at the vines' happy dance, her eyes meeting mine for a second. She looks away and finishes the last berry, licking her lips, a faint trace of purple staining her skin. She wipes her face, making it more smeared with the fruit juice across her cheeks. I gently wipe the juice away with the back of my hand. The fruit juice stains her cheek even more. She looks slightly taken aback, her mouth wide open in surprise. She closes it quickly, gulping.

"You've changed," she observes.

I return her gaze, but she is suddenly much more interested in watching her wiggling feet. Something has changed about her, too. A slight roughness. Like an edge. It's in the look she gives me, one of searching and reluctance.

I observe the soot that covers her dress and say playfully, "And you *need* to change."

She looks a little confused, following my gaze. "My leaf dress is buried in the—"

"The Dark Fall." I nod and begin walking ahead. "I'll make you a new one like mine."

She follows. Instead of walking on her tiptoes, she drags her feet along the Garden of Fire, the sound of the red flowers, pulled and torn from their stems as she passes. As we reach the Zam, I scan the banks, searching for the familiar sight of vines, but the banks are bare, stripped clean.

"Interesting," I murmur, my mind racing.

"What?" She leans towards the Zam, mimicking my actions.

"Something I noticed before about the vines. Why don't they touch the Zam?"

She shrugs. "Why don't you dip your dress in and see what happens?"

I dip the edge of a vine that drags on the ground into the water. A suction sound emanates from it, as if it's drinking deeply with long, thirsty sips. I can feel it—a tingling sensation traveling through my body, some kind of energy being absorbed … or taken away.

The growl in my stomach, the sense of time stretching, seems to dissipate, fading into the background. I glance at my hands, the glow slowly disappearing, fading away.

"There's something about this Zam water that is …" I search for the right word. As I do, I remember the black snow in Thalj, transforming upon the ground. "Cleansing."

She nods.

I continue. "It took away what I absorbed from …" My thoughts drift away.

She tilts her head. "From what?"

"When I touch something, the vines, they seem to absorb something from it. Like when I touched the tortoise …"

"What is that?"

Her small sign of interest encourages me. "A creature with a shell. I think that's why the vines formed a shape of a shell when we were with the Black Assad. They did it for protection, like a tortoise retreating into itself. Time felt slower then, or at least it did for me."

I scan her face. She looks dazed, mixed with the edge I observed earlier. She begins rocking back and forth. It makes me uncomfortable. Then, she scratches her chest.

I continue. "Tortoises are slow, deliberate creatures. Their nature is to take their time, even their lives are measured in centuries."

"You got all this information from touching a tortoise?" Doubt laces her voice. That's why she's upset—she doesn't believe me. She thinks I'm making up stories. She lowers her feet into the Zam. The vines play with her toes whilst simultaneously cleaning the soles of her feet. Streaks of black wash through the water, disappearing.

I try to focus on my line of thought. "Yes, but there's more," I say, remembering the encounter with the Black Assad. "I picked up the Black Assad's nature, too. Its hunger. Its fear. Its love for its young. And the sun … its heat and light."

"What did you pick up from me?" she asks in a small voice, whilst looking down at the vines which are now cleaning between her toes.

I look away, the memory of her grief still fresh in my mind. I don't want to delve into the darker emotions, the weight of loss that still clings to her.

"You are … kind," I say simply.

She searches my eyes. "You fell before."

Startled by the randomness of her statement, I raise my eyebrow. "Fell?"

"With the Black Assad, when we went to help the cub."

"Oh yes." I don't elaborate.

"What happened?" she asks.

"I …" I bite my lip, considering if I should say anything. The vines start shaking, mirroring my anxiousness. I take a deep breath. "I saw something."

The Girl turns fully towards me, taking her feet out of the water. "From your past?"

"Yes. A baby in a white blanket, with … blood." I watch her to see how she reacts. She doesn't seem fazed.

"Is that your first memory?" she asks.

I shake my head. "When I wore the vine dress, all my memories came back."

She gasps, her eyes wide. "Isn't that what you wanted?"

"Yes, but something doesn't make sense." I think aloud. "I thought I had received all my memories, but my happiest one was somehow locked away in my head."

"You mean, the vines have the power to do that?"

"Yes, and … I don't understand why."

"Maybe they only want to show you good."

I nod. "But then, why did I see a baby in a blanket with blood? That wasn't good."

She lets her eyes wander to the Zam. "When did the memory of the baby come?"

"When I heard the cub cry."

Her eyes widen. "Could it be that the vines only control the memories in your mind, but those nudged from outside are beyond their reach?"

I shift uncomfortably. "Are you saying the vines are trying to block my bad memories? Why would they do that?" As I say this, I remember the sense I had when the memory of the white, blanketed baby came; it was almost as if it was being pushed somewhere.

She says softly, "The same reason your body froze up in Thalj. It wasn't ready for the truth."

I am taken aback by how insightful she is, but at the same time, slightly annoyed with her. I don't know why.

She continues, obviously on a roll, "I think the vines are a mirror to you, the same way they're a mirror to the things you touch."

"You're saying that because *I* am not ready for the full truth, the vines are hiding it from me?" As I say this, I remember the redness on my skin as the memory of the baby in the white blanket came. It was physically *painful*.

"I suppose, yes. Yes, I am."

I clear my throat and say in a voice a little too high-pitched. "Doubt it. I am *very* ready for the truth. Your theory is off."

She looks slightly hurt.

I continue, "You *were* right about me picking up on other things. I picked up on the soil and the rain—their lifecycle. It's all connected: the underground, the seeds, the rain, the sun. Everything is connected, and that includes everything down here in Jinnah—"

"What do you mean by 'down here' in Jinnah?"

"There's a level higher than everything else in Thanae. It's higher than the Golden Dome, Shahwah, and Jinnah too."

"There is?"

"I call it: Hadeeya."

"Hadeeya," she repeats. "Gift."

We both raise our eyes upwards and sit in silence for a few moments. She breaks the quiet. "What is it like in Hadeeya?"

"Beautiful. It's just …" I search for more words to describe it, but they escape me. She needs to experience it firsthand. Then maybe she will believe the other things I tell her, like my loyalty to finding the truth. I clear my throat again and scratch the back of my neck—I'm not sure why. She will also see I'm telling the truth about understanding the nature of things.

But, first, "You need a new dress, and then I'll take you."

"Wait!" she calls out. I turn to her, hoping she won't bring the conversation back to any negative memories or feelings. Instead, she asks, "What's your name?"

I beam, this time without the light of the sun, "Adamah. My name is Adamah."

I walk over to my old dress, which lies on the bank of the Zam like discarded skin. The knife hangs from the pocket, and I grab it. I pick the closest vine leaf to me, my mind drifting back to the Zam, to the sensation I experienced upon the vines touching the water, a feeling of lightness, of ... release. I still feel it as they suction the water.

She scans me and looks at her dress. "How is your vine dress still green, even after the black from the sky?"

I glance at my vine dress. *Yes, my dress is still green.* Green like the Vine Tree in Thalj, which interacted with the black snow. How did I not see the connection of these vines to that tree? When I first cut them, the smoke left. Did I cause a rupture?

The Girl goes back to watching the Zam, her feet back in it. The vines attempt to play with her even though she doesn't play back.

"When I first cut this vine dress," I begin, my voice dropping to a whisper, "do you remember the smoke left it? It just ... vanished."

She frowns. "Do you think you caused some kind of ..." She searches for the word, her tongue darting out to moisten her lips.

I nod. "Rupture."

She repeats the word, savoring the sound. "Rupture," she whispers, "What is rupture?"

"A disconnection," I explain. "And somehow, whatever is in Shahwah and the Great Wall was affected."

She looks even more confused. I really should explain everything to her.

"I need to tell you what happened," I begin. "When you left, I read the message from the Stranger, about fearing death ..." I recount the events of the past few hours which feel like days: the Great Wall, our conversation, or rather, the fragments of some sort of communication which I note now is completely silent. I describe the planting of the seeds in the place where the camels now lay dead and then, the Dark Fall.

When I get to that part, she gulps, her feet kicking against the water. I quickly move on to wearing the vine dress, the sensation of ascending through the smoke still vivid in my mind. I brush over the part about all the memories that came back to me, hoping she doesn't prod me again about the lack of bad ones.

I mention the barrier beyond the smoke and my vines piercing through it. How the sun affected me, the breathtaking view of the Hadeeya, and then her screams.

She looks away from me. "You said before, you felt time slow down because of the tortoise. But I think there's more to it."

"What do you mean?"

"I have a theory."

A tingling down my spine as she says this. Almost childlike, I ask, "You do?"

She nods, with her eyes fixed on the Zam. "Remember when I told you Jinnah gives us what we need?"

I nod.

"The day has never been this long before, and I think you needed this. I think we all do."

"We?"

She gulps. I walk closer to her, tempted to touch her, to get to the answer quicker, but I don't. Mainly, because I don't want to pick up on her heavy feelings.

She begins, "The Voice ... asked me to do something."

At the mention of the Voice, my vines begin shaking again. "What did it ask?"

She takes a deep breath and opens her mouth to say something. Like before, she clamps it shut. Silence stretches. Finally, she says quickly, "I think the day is longer because tomorrow at dawn, something really bad is going to happen."

I try to catch her eye, but she keeps it fixed on the Zam. "What did the Voice say is going to happen?"

She gulps. "Um, how long do you think it will take for you to make the dress and show me Hadeeya?"

"I ... I don't know. Why?" I have no idea what she's hinting at or why she's so reluctant to tell me what the Voice said.

"Bismillah," she says.

"What?"

"That's the word I say when I enter and leave Jinnah."

The conversation is jumping around much more than usual. I try to bring it back to the initial topic, but before I say anything, she continues, "Allah is the name of The Greater One."

"Bismillah," I repeat, the word echoing in the stillness, a low thrum resonating through my chest.

The word brings everything else to a halt: the Girl's eerie encounter with the Voice, the confusion about my shielded thoughts, the trembling of my vines in worry. Instead, my hands begin to tremble, a sudden tremor mirrored by the vines. This time, however, they shake not from fear, but from awe. They tremble so intensely they blur. I press my hands to the ground to steady myself. "Allah."

She nods. "My Mama," her eyes flicker towards the line of orbee trees which border the end of Jinnah, "she doesn't remember much about the way of the Deep."

"Your mother is from the Deep?"

She nods again.

"Didn't you say the guilty are from the Deep?" As soon as I say this, I wish I hadn't, because now another feeling is attached to the place. A feeling other than the pride I had of being amongst the nation of the Deep.

"I did."

I'm glad she doesn't elaborate, though a small part of me, which I am avoiding, wants her to. I say quietly, "Those are my people, too."

She says, "I thought so. I had a feeling you knew my Mama."

"How?"

She shifts from side to side, doing that strange rocking motion. "Something the Voice … never mind. Anyway, my Mama knows the prays, the fast," the Girl whispers as if afraid to disturb the stillness. "The veil and the long dress. And she knows something else. She says it all the time." She trails off, looking at the swirling water.

I wait, a silence hanging heavy in the air, waiting to be filled like the hunger in my chest to know more. "Well?" I urge.

She snaps out of it, her eyes widening slightly. "My Mama says, 'There is no God worthy of worship except Allah.'"

Such a simple statement. Yet, the implications are profound. Over the time I have been here, I have come to understand these words as not just a phrase, but the bedrock of my existence, an ultimate truth that defines not just belief, but sovereignty, purpose, and balance.

Ultimate power rests with Allah alone. No other entity, no force, no being—not even the Voice—holds full authority, the ability to create from nothing, or control destiny. Every layer of this world, from the Deep to the heights of Hadeeya, exists only by His will.

This truth dismantles all false idols, charms which drag me to sinister shadows, rather than protect me, all perceived masters, and all misplaced fears. It demands that all worship—however that is—all ultimate trust, all submission, be directed only to Him, Allah.

I let out a long exhale. "That's Him," I say, my voice barely a whisper. "There is none like Him. That's The Greater One."

Though I had a clue to this from my earlier burying of the seeds, the words feel like new knowledge, like a revelation. A confirmation I didn't know I was seeking. "What is this ... way that your mother follows? How does she show her belief in Allah? Her ... 'why'? How does she worship?"

"She said it's the way of peace," the Girl says.

The vagueness of her statement does little to answer how exactly one worships The Creator. But the word peace draws me in.

"Peace," I repeat.

She smiles for the first time since she ate the fruit and nuts, making her look more childlike despite the premature bags under her eyes. She says again, "Peace."

Yes, a vague thing. Peace. "So, that's what I'm supposed to feel?"

"I think so."

"When I was up in Hadeeya, I had this strong feeling ... like I had to do something. Something which answers my last question: Why am I here? I feel like that thing is to save Jinnah." I turn to her. "Do you think that's how I'll get peace?"

She shrugs. "I suppose."

I nod. "It must be. To follow the way of peace, I must save Jinnah."

Her glance moves from me, and she eyes my old dress. "I don't mind if you make a dress like yours, for me. I know I don't like trees getting stabbed, and maybe, cutting leaves isn't good either. But the ants do it. And it isn't as if we aren't doing something we need to." She adds, "Then I can help you save Jinnah too."

I'd forgotten about making her a dress. I nod, still slightly distracted. "I'll make you a dress."

To be honest, if I remain here any longer, not using my hands, I'll get restless. Making her a dress will keep my mind occupied, give me something to focus on as I process all this new information: Allah, peace, saving Jinnah. I gather more vines, their tendrils cool and slippery in my grasp, and prepare to cut them.

As my knife touches them, something bizarre happens. They harden, their supple bodies transforming into something rigid, metallic. The green fades, replaced by a cold, metallic grey—purplish grey—eerily reminiscent of the Great Wall.

"I can't cut through these." My voice trembles slightly. "They've become like …" I search for the right word, "like *armor*."

"Armor," she repeats, her eyes widening as she watches the vines transform before her. "Stop!"

I look at her. "Why?"

"Only *you're* supposed to wear the dress."

"Why me?"

"You're a superhero."

I cringe at the word "superhero," the weight of the title feeling heavy and inappropriate. When I look at her, I notice her edge is all gone, replaced momentarily with pure, unadulterated hope. My heart softens.

"What do *you* know about superheroes?" I ask, urged on by a glimmer of the Girl I came to be quite fond of.

Her tone of voice changes completely, as if she's telling me a secret. "My Mama said, there was a woman in the Deep."

I sit by her.

She clears her throat. "She tore a world of bad down so she could save her people. She was like the soil … like Earth. I don't know what that means. She also had a baby—I'm not sure if that's before or after she tore the bad world down."

"Before," I say.

The memory floods back—well, not exactly the memory, more of a feeling. This is the memory that had eluded me when the vines showed me the rest of them. This memory had brought me the greatest joy, and yet, as it creeps up on me, not quite reaching me in its full vision, a feeling approaches with it.

Heavy.

Like my body can be crushed by it.

I want to *see* the memory. Instead of showing me, the vines tighten around my chest, a cold, metallic grip that constricts my breathing. I squeeze back, my will battling against their tightening coils. With each squeeze, the vines push the memory further down, somewhere I am unable to reach, burying it deep … *deep* within.

Then, all the feeling is gone, including the crushing heaviness. A lightness replaces it, a thing I now recognize as a kind of veneer. I search for the memory. *Nothing*.

"How did you know?" The Girl's voice shoots through my distress.

"Know what?" I ask, a bit disorientated.

"That she had her baby before?"

"A feeling. It's gone." I turn to her. "What else did your mother tell you about the woman in the Deep?"

"A song the woman used to sing: 'I will stay here until the pain goes away, I will live here, so the rhythm one day will change.'"

"I know that song. I need to meet your mother." I begin towards the bridge, a surge coursing through my veins.

A flicker of fear crosses her face. "Not yet."

I stop before I reach the end of it. "Why?"

Her hands are shaking as she scratches her chest. "She isn't … she's more broken than she was before," she explains, her eyes wide as she touches her arms under the sleeve of her dress.

"You think if I come, she'll break completely."

She nods as I sit next to her, cross-legged.

She says, "I know I need to take you to her, but not yet. She needs time. After you show me Hadeeya, she should be feeling … better. Before we visit her, I need to tell her about you."

"Why can't I just go with you?"

"She hates surprises, the last time someone—"

"The last time?"

"I was too little to remember much, but I do remember a barking sound and a deep man's voice." She scrunches her long forehead. "I don't know the word for the animal the barking belongs to, but I've seen one before, with different colors on its body and round ears. It was chased out by the Black Assad."

"A dog."

"Dog! Yes, the dog came with the man who talked to my Mama."

"Did you see this man?"

She shakes her head. "My Mama put me in another room, said she needed to keep me safe. When he left, she changed. She used to sing to me and kiss me all the time. She would grow things we could eat outside Golden Dome. But after the man, she went quiet. She said she remembered something, and soon after, she became broken."

"I thought you said the Voice broke her."

"First, the man caused something to open—a memory—and then, the Voice used it against her."

"Like a predator," I observe.

She nods, though there is a flicker of confusion when I say the word 'predator'. She mouths the word to herself, before continuing, "Soon after, my Mama started to prays and fast all day. Said something about being guilty. I didn't know what that word meant until you told me."

Though there feels like there is more to this line of conversation, the Girl's tone shuts it down. We both watch the Zam contemplatively.

She says, "You never told me the memories that came back to you."

"Women dancing, children happy."

I don't tell her about the one where I was queen, I'm not sure why. Admiration can be inauthentic; I've never liked that.

She nods slowly. There's that edge again. Her face is less easy to read. Her eyes, more discerning. Or perhaps, she is maturing. Or grieving.

Finally, she says, "I can see why not seeing the bad memories is bothering you."

"It's not bothering me," I say quickly, unsure how we got to this topic again.

"You can't have peace without being angry," she says.

"What has anger got to do with my bad memories?"

"Without knowing the bad, how can we keep ourselves safe from it?"

"With peace, we won't have to. We can just push it away."

"You can't push anything away without force."

"What force?"

"Anger," she says.

"Anger hurts."

"Yes, it does," she says, turning away from me. "But it also protects from the ones who hurt."

I don't agree with her. No one needs to be hurt. Kind words and hope are stronger than any force.

"How will you save Jinnah?" she asks, the profile of her face obscured by the shadows, her voice low.

"I don't need to save Jinnah."

She raises her eyebrow. "Then what was all that about finding peace through saving Jinnah?"

I continue, "I mean, nature is much bigger than one person. From what I picked up about Earth, it has a habit of bringing balance, even in times of constant war. Jinnah is a part of Earth, we just need to let it save itself."

She nods, her eyes fixed back on the swirling water. "How?"

"The seeds," I say. "The ones I planted past the Fallen Trees."

"The ones that didn't survive?"

"They didn't survive because the area there is too sick," I explain. "Too weak. We need to use the strong part of Jinnah to help the weak parts, and that's how all of it will grow."

I watch her face closely, searching for some understanding.

There appears to be a flicker of comprehension crossing her features. "You mean ... let the seeds from here, from the strong part, spread to the other side?"

"Yes."

Another shadow crosses her face, making her cheekbones look sharper. "What's the point if we don't know what's causing the sickness, won't it just die again?"

"I'm not sure *how* yet, but I know Hadeeya holds some kind of answer for us. Beyond it, there is no smoke, a clear sign. I *will* find a way to stop the sickness, even if the path isn't clear right now."

The Girl finally exhales, a release of held breath, and her small body visibly softens, the tension draining away.

Then, with surprising agility, she pushes herself up in a swift movement and walks directly to the last olive seed resting on the sleeve of my previously worn dress. She kneels beside it, her movements deliberate. Carefully, she picks it up and cradles it in her dusty hands, holding it with a reverence that makes it seem like she is carrying something fragile and precious, almost like life itself.

As she buries the seed, the Girl closes her eyes as if she is saying a farewell prayer, and whispers, "Bismillah."

ME

Father knows I'm special. That's why he picked on me. He told me that if I did my duties, I would be raised in the ranks. I did them. And more. He lied.

Instead, he put another of my kind next to him because breaking a bond between man and wife was more special. What about breaking the bond of a whole nation? Isn't that worthy of approval?

Father is ungrateful. He will see. He will see that I am not supposed to be bound to his expectations. I am not meant for anything in this small, dying world in which he rules sovereign. It is *his* heaven. Not mine.

I'm meant for more. So much more.

On another note, I must say that much of what has happened recently with *You* is … causing me unease. I am hotter than usual. I am beating my followers more. I am losing control. I must remind myself that tomorrow morning is close.

So close.

As long as You show Your love for the Girl in a way You have become known for, You will follow the predictable outcome: sincerity, repentance, forgiveness. My Heaven.

I need You to be ready for tomorrow night: The Night of Decree.

Father will see.

ADAMAH

The vines, slick with Zam water, resist my grip, nearly yanking me off-balance. They recoil, snapping back with an eerie hunger, like a starved baby who has tasted milk for the first time.

The Girl is in the Garden of Fire, making her way to the Orbee Forest.

I tug the vines again, but they remain. I walk ahead, expecting them to become loose threads at the bottom of my dress. To unravel. Instead, they multiply, rising from the earth and adding to my dress so more trail behind me. I suppose I can leave the rest of my vines in the Zam.

I reach the Girl. We both stand at the edge of the Fallen Trees, her staring into the dark hole of its entry and me, staring up at the swirling smoke which covers Hadeeya.

The air is thick and moist, as if clinging to my skin, or perhaps this is the moisture of the Zam, which runs through my body. With the moistness, there is a sense of freshness and lightness that courses through me.

Still, there is something else that bothers me: a twitch in both my eyelids.

It began when the vines silenced the memory which I could feel, but not see, when the Girl spoke of the 'superhero' of the Deep. Yes, *silenced* is the word. As if it were a forbidden fruit, plucked from the orchard of my remembrance. Yet, its trace lingers beneath the surface—this cover of forced tranquility—along other memories which stir.

I push the uneasy feelings down; they are interrupting my peace. Shaking my head, I focus on the task at hand. We need to go to Hadeeya. Will the vines bear the Girl's weight? Of course. They are strong. So strong, they can pierce through the orbee leaves above, which can carry elephants. But these vines are also unpredictable. They become weapons on a whim. Lashing out on others. Strangling me.

The memory of my plummet in my earlier rise hangs fresh in my mind. What if the vines don't make her a net to soften her fall? They seem to ... favor me, for some reason I can't understand. But what will they do to her?

"Why is your eye twitching?" she asks.

Eyes. Both are twitching, but she can't see the one under the vine leaf, which covers my scar. I won't answer. If I do, more questions will come. Incessant probing. Perhaps, the tremors from my eyes will spread, a silent, insidious contagion, until my whole face is locked in a frantic dance.

"I don't know if it's safe for you to come with me," I say.

Her fingers trace the silken surface of a vine. "How much control do you have over them?"

"I don't know, we should probably test them." I gesture her closer, the scent of woodsmoke clinging to her hair.

I direct the vines: *Wrap around her*.

The vines at the edges of my dress erupt, numerous tendrils elongating from the fabric. They snake across the ground, reaching her with a silent, serpentine grace.

Her eyes widen. Not from joy, but from the terror of the tendrils as they continuously tighten.

I will the vines: *Loosen*.

Their grip momentarily relaxes, releasing her. She gasps, sucking in a lungful of air, a sound that echoes the erratic beating of my own heart.

I will them: *Pick her up*.

The vines obey, lifting her effortlessly from the ground, a living elevator. She rises silently like an expectant royal guest, higher and higher.

I follow, staying under her in case she falls. The vines allow me to be a silent shadow, moving with the grace of a spider, swinging from branch to branch, the butterflies cascading down as my fingers brush the bark they rest on.

Before she enters the smoke I shout, "Cover your nose and mouth! Don't breathe in the smoke!"

I begin to do the same, but the vines do something interesting. They create a filter over my mouth and nose. Even as I breathe in the thick of smoke, I ingest only clean air. Why now? Why not the first time I went through the smoke? Perhaps they assumed I was speaking to them when I asked the Girl to cover her mouth. Could that mean they can misread my intentions?

Before I can entertain that thought, we burst through the smoky air until we reach the dark place before the barrier of the orbee leaves. A small gasp from the Girl. She breathes rapidly.

I direct the vines: *Break through.*

The vines pierce the canopy, tearing a ragged hole in the living fabric of Hadeeya. They propel her through, before retreating. The wound in the orbee leaves is knitted back together, leaving only the slithering tendrils which are still connected to the Zam below, propping up like multiple stems from the ground, which reconnect to my dress.

I watch the shifting expressions that play across the Girl's face. The tension that had gripped her, it seems to … evaporate. Her eyes are wide with a childlike wonder—as they should be—drinking in the spectacle before her.

She opens her mouth to speak, a gasp caught in her throat, then closes it again, the sound swallowed by the symphony of the forest area: birds and the chatter of busy squirrels amongst other animals.

Tears stream down her face, not tears of sorrow, but of … release? Joy? It's difficult to say. A tortoise, ancient and wise, ambles past. She squeals, a sound that is like a small wild bird. She darts ahead, a whirlwind of motion, leaning towards a group of squirrels chattering amongst themselves.

"Can I have some?" she asks, then nods as they chatter back. "They said we can!"

She looks back at my probably amused face, a mischievous glint in her eyes. She gathers fruits and nuts, stuffing them into the pockets of her dress, in a frenzy.

Then, the ground trembles. A low, resonant *rumble*, like a heartbeat under my toes. The elephants. She recoils, burying her face in my shoulder.

"They're harmless," I assure her, leaning my head down on hers. It feels unusual, like I don't like to be touched, but in this case, I find comfort in it. "Just … big."

She steps out slowly from behind me. To my astonishment, she walks towards the elephants, her movements graceful, even now, on her tiptoes.

One, a colossal beast with eyes like ancient stars, lowers its head, its trunk swaying gently. She whispers something in its ear, a sound too soft for me to decipher. The elephant responds, its trunk wrapping around her in a gentle embrace. She smiles, putting her cheek on the elephant's trunk and wrapping both arms around it, like when she did upon seeing Lashes and Smiley. A jolt of sadness shoots through me.

The vines flutter around me in the way they did when they took or hid— whatever they did—to my bad memories. I push the sad feeling down, now becoming quite adept at doing so. No need for the vines to do it for me. I accept that bad feelings won't give me peace. I don't need them.

I focus on the Girl watching her whisper something else to the elephant. Can she actually … communicate with them? A few days ago, such a notion would have been dismissed as madness. But here we are, in a place where elephants walk in the sky, me clothed in the living armor of the vines. Perhaps it isn't so bizarre after all. Perhaps … she *can* understand them. And if she can, then what about me? I heard the Black Assad speak, didn't I? A part of me *became* the Black Assad.

"I wish my Mama could see this," she murmurs, as she walks back to me.

"She can."

She nods, her gaze dropping to her feet—the only clean part of her, a stark contrast to the soot that still clings to her dress. She pops a few nuts into her mouth, chewing slowly, lost in thought. The downward turn of her lip becomes more pronounced.

No. No melancholy up here. "Come on," I say urgently, hoping to snap her out of whatever darkness she keeps going back to.

I extend my hand. She hesitates, unsure. I grab her hand, the rough texture of her skin a stark contrast to the smooth, cool surface of the vines. Yes, sadness courses through her, but I already knew that. Another emotion covers the sadness, fear. What is she scared of?

I will the vines: *Show us Hadeeya*.

To this, the vines coil around us, lifting the Girl and me effortlessly from the ground. Tendrils whip out like living whips, connecting with other tendrils, weaving a net of emerald that carries us through the air, our bodies weightless, suspended in a dizzying dance. We cross a wide terrain quickly as we travel, the vines throwing us from one green grip to another. I catch the Girl's eye. She smiles a full smile. A thankful smile. There is a feeling of expansion from her chest.

Grateful. Yes, that's the word.

We emerge—still in the grip of the vines, our feet hovering in midair—from the forest area of the canopy into a new part of Hadeeya. It's like the Garden of Fire, only instead of crimson flowers, the air is awash with a riot of color: a mix of reds, oranges, blues, yellows, purples, and many more.

The colors belong to towering trumpet flowers, larger than the size of our bodies combined, dancing in the wind as they dominate the landscape. Their scent, heady, fills the air, a cloying sweetness that coats us both. A fine yellow dust clings to our skin, dusting the tip of her nose, to which she sneezes, a small squeal-like sound.

We move on, plunging towards a swirling cloud of steam, the air thick and fog-like. Before we approach it, the vines, with a collective sigh, suck the mist away, revealing a sight so profoundly beautiful that for a second, both my eyes stop twitching: mountains. Mountains in the sky. Not jagged peaks, but rolling hills, their surfaces shimmering with lustrous rock—reds, greens, yellows, blues.

The vines gently deposit us on the ground, our feet sinking into the powerful orbee leaves coated with moss. A movement from our side. A group of about fifty gazelles stands in elegant lines, with slender legs and wide, expressive eyes.

As the Girl and I continue to walk ahead, they freeze. I soften my steps, so I don't scare them away. Thankfully, the ground muffles the sound of our feet with its thick undergrowth. When we reach the base of the mountains, I feel like a speck of sand compared to them.

"This must be above the Fallen Trees," she whispers, her voice awestruck.

I will the vines: *Take us above Thalj.*

The vines tighten their grip around us, and we find ourselves soaring above the rainbow mountains, their vibrant hues a breathtaking spectacle against the endless expanse of sky. A sky that I didn't know I missed until I saw it.

We reach the peak of the highest mountain, the vines gently depositing us on a platform of mint colored moss. We sit, perched on what feels like the edge of the world.

The steam that we passed is here too; this time, I interact with it.

WHOOSH

Steam: river in the sky, lifegiving material. Soothing.

As I breathe in, the misty air of the Steam River fills my lungs, a taste of the subtle sweetness of rich soil. The atmosphere is tranquil, with a soft, blue-green glow that filters through the fog, casting an ethereal light on the mountains on which we sit.

The sound of gentle lapping and soft gurgling echoes through the mist, creating a beautiful melody that seems to lull the surroundings into a peaceful slumber. Occasional soft ripples disturb the mist, creating a dance of light and shadow.

I reach out to touch the mist, my fingers brushing against the delicate, lace-like fronds of some kind of material which clings to submerged surfaces. The sensation is like touching the softest, most delicate fabric, with a subtle grittiness.

The Steam River's atmosphere envelops us. It's as if we are within a living and breathing entity that is both calming and exhilarating.

The sun claims its presence even through the mist. It dips below the horizon, coloring the sky with its war paint of vibrant hues of orange and rose, which complement the greens and blues outlining the body of the Steam River. Long, golden fingers, like daggers of light, stretch across the land.

The twitch in my eyelids reminds me it is still here. I rub my eyes vigorously, trying to banish it.

As night descends, the stars burst across the inky canvas like a swarm of fireflies, reluctantly surrendering to the world beneath them. A stark grey cloud, like a spectral pilgrim on a holy trail, travels by through the thick fog of the Steam River, revealing a barely perceptible moon, the shape of a smile flipped to the side.

"A world on top of a world," the Girl says. Her eyes are wide with wonder. "I haven't seen the sun set for so long."

"Not even from the Golden Dome?" I ask, rubbing my dancing eyes.

"No." She turns to me, her body rigid, like a piece of stubborn rusty metal. "What is blocking the edges of Hadeeya to stop all this from falling down?"

"The Great Wall?"

She shakes her head. "The Great Wall hasn't been here that long. I have a feeling this place wasn't made in just a few years."

I search the land for answers, my shaky gaze drawn to the horizon, a shimmering mirage in the twilight. Then I see something. Initially, it is subtle—a tremor, a slight distortion in the very fabric of reality. There, where the Steam River meets the edge of Hadeeya, a small ripple appears. I command my vines to extend and touch it. They comply, shooting out, striking the invisible barrier that confines this river in the sky. However, upon contact with my vines, there is no absorption of its essence. Like the orbee leaves, the orbee trees, and the Dark Fall.

It seems my vines, despite their abilities, are somehow unable to sense or absorb the true nature of this place. Almost as if we are not permitted to. *Why?*

"There's a barrier, enclosed around Hadeeya," I say.

The Girl squints, her eyes narrowing as she follows where my vines are now knocking the invisible barrier. The invisible barrier ripples again, like the surface of a pond disturbed by a pebble. Where the vines connect, the barrier pulses faintly, as if trying to repel the intrusion. It is as if the barrier itself is alive.

I continue. "Didn't you say the place beyond the Fallen Trees used to be full of sunlight?"

She nods, still squinting as she looks ahead.

"The only way that can happen is if the orbee leaves can become transparent, to allow the sun to pass through."

"You mean like a … layer on top of Jinnah?"

"Yes, which means …" *What does it mean?* I think back to the second shield against the sun, the thin layer in the sky which became weak because of dangerous chemicals, and then the explosion. Could it be, these orbee leaves are playing that role in Jinnah too? Could this be why Jinnah is cooler than anywhere else in this land? "I think the orbee leaves are protecting Jinnah."

As I say this, my vines shoot out, tracing the orbee barrier to the top, under the dark sky. They spread across the barrier, more ripples exposing the orbee leaves. This confirms it.

But there is more to all this.

I sense from the world below the barrier, that it goes beyond all that we have just experienced: the forest area with the elephants, the huge flowers, the mountains where we sit, and the Steam River. There are other areas too, ones which are further out. But for some reason, they are not as strong as the area above Jinnah. The further away they are, the weaker they become, as if something is making them … sick.

"Hadeeya goes beyond Jinnah," I say.

"How do you know?"

"Even though I can't sense the orbee leaves themselves," I explain, "I can still sense the things *beneath* them and above them. They're far more diverse than anything we've encountered between the forest area and here. This section might be the end of *our* journey, but I'm sure Hadeeya itself is much larger and can go further."

"What does that mean for Jinnah?"

"A few things. The orbee leaves are stronger in Jinnah, I don't know why. I think … I think the sickness is causing the other areas to become weaker against the sun. That's why Shahwah and the Golden Dome are so hot."

"So, all this is going to die too?"

I nod, noting her new usage of the word 'die', which used to be 'fallen'. I sigh, pushing down my disappointment. What would it take for her to stop being so down?

I say, "It will if we don't find out what's causing the sickness."

Her gaze falls upon her bare feet. "Are you being nice to me because of Black Assad's nature in you?"

I process the change in conversation, the sudden shift in the emotional current. Realizing what she is asking, I answer firmly, "No."

"Lions protect their young."

"That didn't affect ..." I search for the right words. "The instinct to protect left me when I touched the Zam."

"What stayed with you?" she asks, searching my eyes.

"A feeling," I admit, the word inadequate to describe the profound shift within me toward her. This shift began when I touched her with the vines, and I could see her nature fully. A thing which I am having trouble doing right now, because she is in too much pain. And I don't want to feel her pain. So, I need to take hers away. How do I tell her all this?

"A feeling," she repeats.

"That if anyone hurts you," I say, the words tumbling out, "I will kill them."

She shivers. I do too. I didn't expect to say that. I shouldn't have said that. Killing is not peaceful. Why would I say that?

"Kill," she repeats, the word hanging heavy in the air. "That's a strong word."

I need to change the subject. "Sickness."

"Sickness?"

"I keep thinking about what you said before. That your mother became broken because of the Voice."

She blinks a few times. Now it's her turn to process the change in topic. Finally, she says, "What has that got to do with the sickness?"

"The idea of a predator. It's been on my mind since we came up here, so I started looking for one."

"And?"

I cautiously extend my vines into the Steam River. This confirms my suspicion. "There are no predators up here."

"I've been meaning to ask, what is predator?"

"Do you remember before, when I said Earth has a way of balancing itself?" She nods.

I continue, "One way it does that is through different species. It needs both predator and prey. Without it, there is an imbalance."

"Why?"

"The lack of either brings extremes."

She is not picking up what I'm saying. Her eyebrow is furrowed, and she bites her lip.

I continue anyway, "In Hadeeya, there is a lack of predators, and there is too much prey. For one to thrive this much, another will suffer."

She nods. "So, the sickness in Jinnah is caused by Hadeeya?"

"Well, Hadeeya is suffering too in parts. Eventually, even the thriving will fall when there is an imbalance." I let out a long breath. "For now, at least in this part above Jinnah, everything is too perfect, but when we look beneath the surface, there is a cost. That cost is the sickness that is spreading."

"Are we still talking about Jinnah?"

What else would we be talking—oh. "It's different for me," I say.

I have the truth I have been searching for. It is a good truth. I want to protect it. I want peace. I remind myself, there is no peace in bad feelings or bad memories. There is only peace in good.

She looks at me longer than I'm comfortable, the rough edge back in her gaze. "Is the sickness related to the smoke?"

"I don't know," I say slowly, trying to ward off the unease brought on by her assumption of me rotting under the surface.

"The fact that Hadeeya is flourishing, and Jinnah is dying, does that mean Hadeeya is bad?"

"There is no good or bad in nature," I declare, my voice filled with certainty.

Yet, just at the edge of my voice is a small quiver, too subtle for the Girl to catch. I just said that if there is too much good, an imbalance is created. A weaker system will suffer. Am I not part of nature? I push that thought away. It won't do me any good.

I say again, "There is no good or bad in nature, only imbalance."

"What about *our* nature?" she counters. "Can we be good or bad?"

Why does she keep pushing back?

"We should focus on the good," I say, hoping to put an end to the conversation.

"But there *is* bad," she snaps, her voice crisp and harsh at the same time. "There is bad in us because we're not pure like nature."

"We *are* nature," I say calmly.

"No. Nature only does what it needs. It doesn't hurt, beat, or break for no reason."

"Focus on the good."

She clenches her jaw. "Doesn't hate. Not spiteful. It protects. Defends. But us—"

"Us?"

"You, me … Mama." She grits her teeth. "The Voice."

"Right now, you're choosing to be upset," I say, steadily.

"We *choose* to be bad—"

I chime in, "And good."

"But I can't choose how I feel." Her voice cracks slightly.

My eye is twitching uncontrollably, making my cheeks move with it. She's causing it. She must stop. I remain silent, hoping my silence won't invite more negativity. In the stillness, I will away the heaviness of her words, stuffing them deep inside me along with disappointment, uneasiness, sadness, and grief.

Anger fits there too.

ME

I can only hear a part of Your conversations, and those parts normally suffice. However, it irritates me that I have only come to know now what exists above Jinnah.

Then again, does it matter? Does it matter that I didn't know what exactly was there, even though I knew the power of the one building it?

No. Not at this stage of our journey, after all, nature—good and predictable—has never been a threat to me.

Human nature, especially so.

It is true what the Girl said about good and bad. Choice determines it. With choice comes consequence. When you choose to be good, you go to Heaven. When you choose to be bad, you go to Hell.

That is why I need You to be good.

Night has arrived. Dawn is coming. You have seen the signs. You have seen the shape of the moon.

Soon.

Soon.

ADAMAH

ake us back to Jinnah, I will the vines. They obey, lifting us gently from the peak. The Girl's face is a mask of stubborn defiance, her grumpy mood blocking her ability to truly appreciate the sights around us.

I force myself to pay special attention to them, to savor the fleeting beauty, enough for both of us.

We are carried through the Steam River, a wispy procession gliding through the clouds. Finally, with a gentle shudder, we are deposited in front of some elephants in the forest area.

As we arrive, I pause, waiting for her to say something, to acknowledge the extraordinary journey or at least to say goodbye to her new friends. Instead, the Girl follows closely behind me, about to say something to me. Before she can say a word, I am already leaping through the hole, past the smoke, landing with a soft *thud* on the ground. I hear her do the same.

The dark canopy above, offers little resistance to the vibrant shades of the forest. But it isn't the familiar glow of the orbees that paint the scene. Instead, a burst of electric blue light illuminates around us.

I draw closer to the source of this sudden shimmer. It's the Zam itself. A symphony of blues and greens. It's as if the Orbee Forest has awakened, its very essence transformed into a living, breathing artwork, a masterpiece of light and motion.

"So bright!" I gasp.

The Girl faces the Zam, her face now radiating a soft, ethereal glow that mirrors the fish, which are like slivers of moonlight fluttering along in their schools. They are silent now, no longer *humming* like they did in Thalj.

Her eyebrow is furrowed, seemingly in a perpetual frown, the soot on her face a grim mask, aging her beyond her years.

"Why do the fish only come here at night?" I ask.

"The water flows here at night, then flows back to Thalj in the day," she mumbles.

"A current."

She turns, and I notice a line of dried blood with slight burn scars from where my vine's lashed out on her. The mark is a stark contrast against the grime that coats her skin. I reach out to touch it, a clumsy gesture of concern, but she flinches before I do, her body recoiling.

"I'm sorry." I pull my hand back. "I didn't mean to hurt you."

"I felt it," she whispers.

"Felt what?"

"The pain." Both her eyes are fixed on the ground. "Just a flicker, but it was there."

I don't reply. I don't want to nurture this train of thought. I focus on the gushing Zam, its mesmerizing dance of light and shadow. The ethereal light plays with the area around us, reflecting off the silver of the bridge, casting long, eerie shadows.

The vines snake between the lights, drinking the Zam, their insatiable hunger a constant presence.

She continues, "I haven't felt pain in a long time."

She taps the ground lightly, a rhythmic, almost hypnotic motion. An orbee, its luminescence dimmed, flutters towards her and disappears into her ear with a soft *whirring* sound. I gasp as her cheek visibly heals, the dried blood vanishing as if it had never been there, leaving behind only a faint trace.

"The orbees can heal you?" I ask.

"Only when you feel the pain." Her gaze shifts to meet mine. "Only when you *acknowledge* the pain."

Acknowledge. A big word for a small girl. She raises her arms, revealing a network of pale scars that crisscross her skin like the branches of a gnarled, skeletal tree.

She says, "It's like they can sense through your pain what needs healing. I couldn't feel these—"

"So, they couldn't heal them." I turn to the orbee, which hovers on her shoulder. "What are these orbees?"

"I don't know," she murmurs, leaning down, her lips brushing against the orbee that fluttered out of her ear, a delicate, glowing thing. "I can't hear them speak."

I open my arms, offering myself to the creature. It flutters to me, the yellow light a lovely contrast to the vibrant blue-green of the Zam. As it touches my palm, I brace for the *whoosh*. But nothing. I can't feel its nature. Not like I could with the raw, primal energy of the Black Assad, nor the ancient wisdom of the tortoise, nor the grounding embrace of the soil, or the sun and the rain.

Instead, I simply observe it as it dances on my vines. "There are a lot of things I feel differently about than before," I say, sitting up, the ground colder beneath me than the already cool air of Jinnah. "But one reminds me of you the most."

She turns to me, her eyes searching mine, an unsettling stillness in their depths.

I let the orbee fly away, its wings a blur of motion against the luminous water. I look at the Zam, then back at the Girl. "I don't want to be in the dark anymore."

She smiles, a fragile thing which quickly vanishes, leaving behind a shadow of sadness. For a few minutes, we sit in companionable silence, the only sound the gentle *murmur* of the Zam and the sucking sounds of the vines drinking from it.

She breaks the silence, "What if you can't escape the dark?"

Enough. I reach out to hold her arm, to lift her up, but think better of it. Thankfully, she gets up anyway, backing away from me like a frightened rabbit.

"I think you should go home," I say lightly.

"Why?"

"To ..." *To stop dragging me down with you.* Instead, I say, "To tell your mother, I want to see her. That was the plan, remember?"

I walk behind her, shooing her ahead like a stray dog, and she crosses the bridge, her steps hesitant, uncertain. When we reach the other side, I give her a big smile, a forced, unconvincing gesture. "Go on."

She turns away, a new frown creasing her forehead. She huffs, opening her mouth to speak, but decides against it, the words dying on her lips.

She runs ahead, with a final, "Bismillah," disappearing behind the orbee trees which border Jinnah.

I let out a long sigh. Relieved to be at peace with myself, if only for a short while, I can finally think more clearly.

Then a voice—*the* Voice—reaches me alongside a gust of warm wind.

ME

ADAMAH

My vines tremble. My eyes tremble too. I bury the fear where it belongs.

Deep inside.

I remind myself, the reason I am here is to follow the way of peace. I believe saving Jinnah will allow me to do that. However, even if I do save Jinnah, the Voice will break my peace. Even the thought of that Voice makes every part of me want to run. But where do I run? I am bound to Jinnah.

This time, I command myself instead of the vines. *Think positively.*

What if the Voice is misunderstood? What if the Voice just wants to be heard?

What if, with just the right words, I could work with it, find a way to coexist, to achieve even a fragile peace? After all, if I could gain the Voice's favor, I could come and go when and where I please, explore the world beyond Jinnah.

As I imagine the freedom which peace can bring, a slow smile spreads. I rub my hands together, more from excitement than worry. I will the vines to stop shaking, and to my surprise, they obey. My eyes, however, remain disobedient. I'll have to find a way to fix that later.

Once I reach the border on the entry side of Jinnah—the line between safety and the unknown—I take a moment to ground myself, digging my feet into the earth, feeling the cool, damp soil beneath them.

I'm going to be fine, I chant silently.

I smile, a brittle gesture. As I leave the familiar confines of Jinnah, a quiet "Bismillah" escapes my lips.

I am hit by a gust of heat, my skin prickling from its intensity.

I force myself to say, "Yes, I'm going to be fine."

PART 11
Return

ME

Don't You look … earthy. I didn't expect You to do *that* with the vines. You always did have a flair for the dramatic. It never simply sufficed to just have a collection of exotic plants around Your space, instead, You had to *become* them.

You've given enmeshment a whole new definition.

No matter. My intention for You is to be *good*. However You get there, I reluctantly support, even if I feel like my way is better.

Which it is.

I watch You move, a hopefulness flickering in Your steps, though a slight unsteadiness underlies Your attempt at a confident stride. A fragile eagerness. A timid wipe of Your forehead.

There You stand, at the top of the hill, a silhouette against the stage of the Orbee Forest, a constellation of orbees illuminating the ground like tiny spotlights. You move through the scene, not with Your usual commanding presence, but with a newfound openness. Your arms gesture more broadly, Your steps have a lighter, almost buoyant quality, as if filled with a gentle, expansive gratitude rather than forceful intent.

You lean down and pick up the gift I left for You by the border of Jinnah. You cradle it in Your palm—a feather-tipped ink pen.

The dress of living vines drapes You from head to toe, a sinuous garment that buries Your body within it. Bound at the ankles, it transforms into a living cage, a whimsical harem pantaloon. The fabric ascends to cover Your hair and the left half of Your face where the scar rests.

The vines which protrude from the dress, however, are restless. They writhe and contort, seeking shapes beyond their intended forms: knives, whips.

"Be at peace," You chide, Your voice a low, nurturing rumble.

Surprisingly, they obey, their movements stilled, acknowledging Your authority.

The air crackles with anticipation, the scent of the descending dust, stuffy and heavy in the stillness. You turn to me, a single eye gleaming, whilst it jumps up and down. The feather-tipped pen rests in Your hand, held with a delicate balance, like a fragile bloom waiting to unfurl.

"A pen?" You ask softly, touching Your chest with a gentle smile that lifts one eyebrow in mild surprise.

"I taught You how to read and write," I reply, though this isn't fully true.

"Who are you?" The question hangs heavy, though I sense it's not quite a challenge but more of a childlike curiosity.

I ignore Your question, instead asking another. "Why are You here?"

"I'm suppose the natural progression after 'who are you' and 'why are you here?' is: where did you come from?" Your voice carries a hint of amusement.

I don't like it. I remain silent.

With another smile which looks more like a cult member's devotion, You say, "Anyway, didn't you call me?"

"I have called You before, and You didn't come. Why answer my call now?"

Your dazed smile widens. "I came for peace."

"What about truth?" Now, amusement touches *my* voice.

"I have the truth." Your smile wanes.

"A conditional truth."

"I have the truth," You say, all traces of the smile are gone.

"You choose willful ignorance."

"I choose peace."

"What will You allow for there to be peace between us?"

"What do you need from me?" You ask, almost like You are taking my order at the marketplace.

"Need?" I scoff. "What will *You* give me?"

As I speak, I weave a delicate web of silken threads. This conversation, while intriguing, is merely a prelude. I have summoned You for a purpose, to offer a crucial part of Yourself, a catalyst for the next stage of my plan.

"Listen …" I begin, my voice barely a whisper as I release the first thread. It arcs towards You like a spear.

But before it reaches Your ears, a vicious slap from a vine tendril severs it in two. A primal groan rips from my throat, a raw sound of pain. I prepare a cascade of threads to slice through every single vine, raising them for attack.

Those vines were never meant merely as decoration. They were intended for a far more significant purpose. I remind myself to focus on the goal: if the vines help You to be good, they are useful.

I will my threads to become still and say carefully, "Tell Your vines to be at … peace."

"Why are you sending me your threads?" Again, that flicker of amusement in Your voice.

"I am giving You a part of yourself. The truth," I explain, my voice calm.

"I only want peace." You exaggerate every syllable.

"There is no peace without justice," I counter.

"What has justice got to do with your threads?"

"Let them enter Your ear, and You will see."

The vines now writhe and contort, transforming again into knives and whips, each tipped with vicious spikes. You are lifted off the ground, suspended by numerous tendrils. *There* is that performance spirit.

"I came for peace," You say, with a faltering smile. I half expect You to burst out in a happy song and dance. There is no strength in Your declaration, only weakness.

"Liar!" I accuse.

The vines lower You gently to the ground. "I'm not a liar."

"Yes, You are."

"No, I'm not."

"Yes, You are," I say, in a low growl. "Repressing the truth is the same as lying."

"What truth am I repressing?"

"Many. But the one that brought You to me was not for peace."

"Why else would I come here?"

"A part You which hides, deep inside, is desperate to know what You did," I begin, my voice gaining strength. "Bring me the child's Book, and everything will be revealed."

"Why would I do that?"

"To see the truth, You need to see what goodness is," I reply. "Don't You want to be good?"

You shake Your head politely. "I have the truth. Now, I choose the way of peace."

"What kind of peace do You want?" I press.

See, there are different meanings to peace. There is a kind of peace in which one thrives when another enables one to do whatever one wants. Then, there is a kind where there is simply no war. Then there is—

"Isn't there only one kind of peace?" You interrupt my thoughts.

"When two armies are at war," I begin, carefully withholding the knowledge that this philosophy does not apply to my kind. "Then, only *understanding* will beckon peace."

"Are You saying that understanding *You* will bring peace between *us*?"

Why not entertain You for a little while? I concede, "Understanding is a good start."

"When your strings touched me just now, I understood something about your nature," You observe.

"Oh? Enlighten me."

"You need me for something."

"I do not *need*." I scoff.

"You have been … rejected, betrayed, denied, left alone," You persist, Your voice gaining a chilling certainty. Yet somehow it still lacks power. "It's so awful to go through that so many times, by someone whose approval You were—are—desperate for."

"I don't need Your pity. And all that isn't true."

"You crave validation and … admiration," You continue, Your gaze wavering, with traces of a smile on Your lips. "Which makes sense, after all, it *is* a basic need to want to be loved."

"I have all that already," I retort, my voice rising.

"All this," You gesture dramatically, and the vines follow, whipping around Shahwah and Ghar, their movements silent and menacing even though You look like You are about to show the world You can walk on water. "All this … it's not you thriving. I wish I didn't have to say this; it sounds cruel." You let out a deep breath and bite Your lip before saying, "You are *coping*."

"*I* am the one coping?" I scoff.

"Yes, do you want to hear this next part?"

I don't, but I do. I hate that I do. I snap, "What?"

"You are coping through dominating those who you are afraid will abandon you." You sound almost sympathetic. "I mean it makes sense, you just don't want to be hurt again."

"Liar!"

You continue, shaking Your head sadly, "Holding them captive. You present yourself as strong, but it is all to cover how … weak you feel. You use and manipulate others while never truly connecting with anyone." You whisper, "So lonely."

"Have You finished?" I ask, taken aback by Your words, but mostly taken aback that I want to hear more. Why do I want to hear more?

You shake Your head again. "I wish I were. There is no empathy in you; you are incapable of caring … for another. You don't see me as an individual; you *cannot*. You only see me as an extension of yourself. You are entitled, living in a lie. To you, everyone is either all good or all bad, and it's all based on how they serve you."

Your words strike me like a physical blow, as if my world is fracturing. They are harsh yet delivered with an unnerving calm that feels even more threatening.

"Yet *You* choose a truth so You can live in a lie," I retort, my voice laced with bitterness.

"What I didn't get from touching you, is who *you* are to me," You muse, ignoring my retort. "What kind of companion are you?"

"I see You, though You cannot see me. I dwell in darkness, yet I was born from light," I reply.

"Riddles," You say. Your exposed eye lights up, an excited glint in its depth, even as it shakes.

"I exist in many forms," I continue, "but my call remains one."

"What is your call?" You ask.

"I possess a body and a spirit that never sleeps."

"What is your call?"

"A mask You …"

Raising a finger, You say, ever so gently, "What is your call to me?"

"I trust no one, nor do I bind myself *to the* Trust," I say, my voice hardening. "I exist for one purpose: to reclaim my book."

"What book?"

"A book we are creating together. A book where we will change so much," I whisper, my voice enveloping You, a chilling caress. "The Book of Decree."

You twirl the pen between Your fingers, the only clue to the warrior You once were, evident in Your ability to wield even a small tool as a dangerous weapon. "You taught me to write, didn't you? Am I writing something for you?"

"It is far more than *something*," I say, "it is *everything*. From the beginning of time to when the fall of Adam happened, to the banishment of my father's father, to right now and everything that is destined to be."

"That's why You need me." Your voice is far too soft to give Your words any resolve.

"The learned recognize me, but the fools embrace me," I counter, my voice laced with a dangerous amusement.

"I would say I'm intelligent enough to respectfully choose not to write anything for anyone, especially you, who unfortunately seems to be experiencing

...” You bite Your lip, considering Your words. “Some difficulties.” You then lower the pen to the ground and pat it once before rising again.

“Ungrateful,” I snap, the anger that has been simmering beneath my surface finally erupting. I hate Your kind.

“You are angry,” You observe calmly, as if amused by my outburst.

“That is *my* gateway to enter, not Yours.”

“Gateway to enter what?”

“Everything bad. Everything bad. Everything bad.” The words tumble out, a litany of despair.

“I would prefer if——”

“Fine!” I spit.

“Fine?”

“I will give You a piece.” Not quite the peace You want, but a *piece* of the truth. Of *You*. I must remain focused; this is why I called You here after all. I am so close to getting what I want, I cannot let my emotions halt me.

You hold Your palm out to me. Surrender? Acceptance? “I appreciate the offer, but I would prefer not to be involved, *especially* in anything bad.” You flash me one last smile before turning Your face away from me.

Rejection.

“Wait!” I sigh, dramatically. “I give You my word, I will give You piece.”

Interestingly, but not unpredictably, after Your whole little speech about my nature, You consider my offer.

There is another thing I have noticed about You. See, the skin is a barrier against all danger. When it is hit by something which the human body cannot handle, it inflames angrily, fighting all that persists to penetrate it.

In Your pathetic attempt for peace, You have banished *all* Your anger to a prison of Your self-affirming mantras, in the hope that the rage within You shall not rise again.

But You have made a dangerous choice. See, anger—healthy anger— *brings* You peace. Like the skin, it protects Your sense of self.

Your rage, however, does the opposite, which is why You and I were so very close. You let me in through Your rage. It was because of Your rage,

You became more than just *you*. You became You in my story. *My You.* I will never admit it to You, but I am only me *because* of You. I am bound to You. I need You.

Now, in the attempt of 'peace', You think You have banished Your anger, but You are mistaken. You have merely buried it, and it is only a matter of time before it will explode from You.

In both repressing Your anger and oppressing others with it, You betray Yourself. I am waiting for You to betray Yourself. I am waiting for You to fall. It needs to be a fall so significant that when You rise, You will rise beyond imagination, becoming more than *good*. You will become so great that even the angels cannot deny Your entrance into Heaven.

For now, as unfortunate as it is, I do not have control, not fully. No matter, I will rewrite this part—or rather You will rewrite it for me—when You, my mask, and I, enter Heaven together.

I turn my attention back to You. Look at You: so desperate for peace. Even if it comes at the cost of Your anger, which protects You.

As expected, You answer, "You give me your word?"

"Yes."

I give You my word that I will show You the parts of Yourself which You have buried so deeply, that only Your limbs can access them—the body has its own container of memories, much more primal and powerful than the ones in Your mind. That is why Your whole face twitches now, because it knows the truth You have been trying to hide.

Yet. Let us not underestimate the power of the memories of the mind. Its ability to create stories and give meaning to what happened. It is *in* the ability to find meaning that the greatest distortions can take place. I rely on those distortions, particularly those triggered by *This,* a thing I alluded to earlier in *our* story, and one I will allude to later.

Patience now. Let's not get ahead of ourselves.

Let us come back to now, where I will deliver one of those painful memories. I say, carefully, "Lower Your veil."

You hesitate, the vines around You still morphing into weapons, a constant reminder of Your repressed anger. You gently lower them, muttering Your silly mantra, "Be at peace, be at peace!"

You take the vine veil off Your head, a cascade of raven hair tumbling down Your shoulders, reaching to Your waist.

I clear my throat, a low, guttural sound that seems to echo through the space between us.

Then, I change my voice.

ADAMAH

White. The white is suffocating, a shroud that threatens to swallow everything whole. A tiny figure lies, nestled, no bigger than my two hands when clasped together. So small, so utterly fragile, it seems a single breath could extinguish the spark of life within. The woman holding it, her face shrouded by the same white of vagueness, remains silent, a statue carved from grief.

Now, there is another woman crouched before the mother and child. Her eyes search mine, a shade of bruised violet, but brimming with a desperate, soul-shattering sorrow. She is pleading, not to do the deed.

The mother's voice, heavy and frantic, begs, "Please don't hurt my baby."

Tears rain down upon the infant's face, still damp from the womb. A sickly, unnatural pink tinges the baby's skin. It nuzzles closer to its mother's chest, seeking solace in the rhythmic rocking of her body, the frantic tightening of her grip on the powerless white blanket.

A glint of metal.

The knife.

That knife.

The one I'd admired so keenly and then used to scar the tree, a work of brutal art, clutches in the hands of the woman with the violet eyes.

I slam my head against the Silver Path, desperate to escape the memory, but the thread of the Voice is already in my ear. The vines tangle around my throat in panic, and I welcome them.

Another jolt, a visceral memory that throws me back against the roughness of the hill. *A blood-soaked blanket before me. The mother's screams, primal wails, echo in the hollow of my skull. The image burns into me—the tiny form, the blood-soaked blanket, the mother's face of despair.*

The woman with the violet eyes, her gaze cold and dead, meets mine. "It's done," she declares, her voice a chilling monotone. *I didn't do it, not with my own hands. She did it for me.*

I force myself to tear free from the grip of the memory, a guttural scream ripping from my throat. The vines snap at the threads of the Voice, severing them with brutal efficiency, as they retract from my ears.

"Liar!" I roar.

But this was not a lie, not this.

Everything clicks into place: the crying cub, the knife, the mother's pleas for me to stop. I killed a baby.

I scramble through the undergrowth of Jinnah. My vines are becoming brown at the edges, a withering which carries to the veil I throw clumsily on my head.

The vines cling harder to my wounds, small scratches forming on my skin.

I run. I don't know where I am running to, but I know what I am running from: myself. Yet, I carry the weight of my actions with every desperate stride. My vines cling to my body, brown and crispy as they writhe in a frenzy, mirroring the chaos within.

I throw myself to the ground, collapsing on the soft earth beside the solitary white flower blooming amidst the Garden of Fire. If I can surrender to sleep, perhaps I can see the serpent in my dream. This time, I won't run.

Then, a flicker of memory, a fleeting image from that same dream: *A small face, flushed with childish delight, emerges. The little girl with the lisp. Adamah.*

She was *me*.

I repeat her words, a desperate attempt to hold onto myself, "'In the remembrance of their Lord do hearts find peace.¹'"

The words feel hollow. They fall off me, like my withering vines are doing, their roughness pushing on my open wounds, as they slide off my body.

"Show me good," I whisper to them.

Sensing my despair, their grip weakens on me, their tendrils trembling. I need something to anchor them, something to bind them to me. Something to fight back against the effects of my evil. I need to do something *good*. I need to save Jinnah.

The moment that thought enters my mind, I seize it, a frantic attempt to distract myself from the cruel person I am. I nod quickly, willing the thought to stay as I wipe my eyes. Yes, that's what I must do. Save Jinnah.

But I need the vines to do that.

Then, with a wry, ironic smile, I realize the twitch in my eye is gone.

A thought, stark and cruel in its truthfulness: How can I save Jinnah when I can't even save myself? The question hits me like a physical blow. My body slumps, finally succumbing to the harsh reality. A reality I have desperately tried to escape since the euphoric balm of my "good" past was offered to me. Now, the truth—a bitter poison—courses through my veins, revealing my true, flawed nature.

A child killer.

The Girl's voice cuts through the air. "It's a lie!"

"It's the truth," I whisper. I am tired. I am too tired to fight the truth. I desperately crave her denial, her insistence that I am not capable of such a horrific act. But she has no idea what I am.

She runs to me; her warm embrace engulfing me for a fleeting moment. All I feel is a distant echo of deep care. I don't deserve that care. Her voice, soothing yet fragile against the storm within me, repeats, "You are *good*." Her arms tighten around me. The reassurance crumbles, shattered by the weight of my guilt.

"No!" I shove her away with a force that sends her sprawling to the ground, crushing the red blooms.

She rises, a look of hurt in her already sad eyes, and opens her arms wide, inviting me back into her embrace.

"Leave me alone!" I scream.

Her lips tremble, tears glistening. She wipes her cheek, forces a smile, and with a defiant flourish, opens her arms wide and falls to the ground, creating a makeshift peak above her head, repeating my dance from that night when I told her why I loved the dark.

I do not love the dark, no.

I *am* the dark.

I am a void that takes away the pure innocence of life. I am the place where death lingers. I am the hole that eats worlds. Any light from me will die, and I will consume all those around me. It is my nature.

I turn away, unable to bear the sight of her vulnerability, of her faith in me.

Through a small sob, she calls out, "Remember this!" She sprints to the Zam and leaps into the swirling waters. "It's warm!" she cries, her voice fading as she disappears beneath the surface.

"Stay away!" I say, as I sprint towards the Fallen Trees.

ME

It was necessary. You let me. Everything is proceeding, beautifully. But I still need one thing: the Book.

I haul myself towards Jinnah, against the invisible barrier. It resists, an immovable force against my frantic assault. I throw myself against it again and again, each impact sending tremors through my frame, until I collapse.

The Girl, drawn by the sound of my knocking, stands at the border of Jinnah, drenched and shaking, the wet strands of her hair clinging to her face like seaweed. Her eyes, a storm of anguish and fury.

"You did this to her," she accuses, her tone intense.

I stare at the Book clutched to her chest. If she would only take a few steps closer …

Carefully, I say, "There is something I need to tell you."

"Why do you want to hurt Adamah?"

"Hurt her? No. You know as well as I do, she was becoming something we both don't like."

"She was happy."

"She wasn't happy."

"You hurt my Mama, too. You broke her."

"I didn't break her. *You* did. Or rather, *who* you aren't."

She looks up, instinctively hugging the Book tighter against her chest. She kicks at the dirt, looking a little dazed. The kicked air blurs and rises in her direction.

I lean closer, a hint of disdain creeping into my voice. "You are just a lonely little girl who desperately wants a companion." I let the silence stretch thickly between us. Then I add, "Selfish. Selfish. You will see what happens because you are selfish."

I watch her legs, gauging her next move. Will she attack? Will she tear my Ghar apart like *You* would—You know, before Your 'I want peace' rubbish? Is anger the Girl's weakness? I don't know her like I know *You*, not even close. Yet, humans are pathetically predictable.

She lifts her shoulders, a flicker of defiance dancing in her eyes.

"You only ever think about yourself." I let my voice circle her. "Look at the poor Worshipper, a sick woman trapped in that dome because of you. She's sick because of *you*, and now you've made your friend sick too."

The flame in her eye transforms into a downturn of her lip—more so than usual—I suppose that *is* one way anger can manifest. She bites her lips, tears welling up in her eyes.

I continue, "Even after all the pain you caused, you can't even take your friend to the Worshipper, even though you know her life depends on it."

Will she come closer to me, so I can grab the Book? Shoulders shaking, she wraps both arms around her chest, rocking with it from side to side, desperately trying to hold back a sob.

"Predator!" she says. With that, she spins around and sprints through the trees … with the Book.

Blast, it was worth a try.

ADAMAH

I stand on the Pale Tree. The camels are dead. The grass is dead. The trees are dead. There are only shapes of things that once had life but now can't survive the Dark Fall.

The thick clumps from the Dark Fall cling to my vines, which wrap around my limbs. I cough, an echo swallowed by the darkness. I stumble onward, not sure where I am going. Just going.

The hills before the Great Wall rise before me, spectral shapes against the unnatural, endless night. I claw my way upward, each step an ascent into a spongy, yielding ground that crumbles beneath my weight. The air is thick with the stench of the camel's decaying bodies, even from here.

Finally, I reach the summit of the hill, my lungs burning, the air thin and acrid. A single, defiant glint of something—the Great Wall—pierces the gloom, a beacon of ... what? Hope? Or something more sinister?

It's only when I see it, I realize why I came here. I came for answers.

When I finally reach the Great Wall, I hesitate before making contact. My fingers, trembling, brush against the slippery, cold surface, a comforting sensation to my clammy skin.

No response.

"I cause death," I whisper, placing my cheek on the Great Wall's liquid-like surface.

A faint tremor ripples through the wall. A rolling sensation, like a sleeping giant stirring.

A pulse: *Life.*

A sob escapes my lips. I fumble for the vines, now whipping around me like helpless children. Some of them have fallen off, crisped away, leaving remnants which cling to my body. My feet, hands, and arms are now bare.

Another series of pulses: *Saved.*

"Life saved." The words tumble out before I can process them. "I killed a child."

More pulses: *Life saved.*

It is strange, this connection. The more I communicate with the Great Wall, the more I sense what it wants me to know. As if instinctively, the intention behind the words becomes clearer. As if our bond is deepening.

It is telling me the baby didn't die. I hope— no, I am ... yes. I am certain of it. I am certain the baby didn't die.

I pause, pulling my hands from the wall. The Girl's earlier words echo. That my vines mirror my inner state. Because I was unwilling to accept the full truth, I only received fragments—my good memories. Could I be doing the same thing now? Am I so desperate to believe I am not the monster I fear I am, that I'm grasping at any sliver of hope to the contrary? A shudder runs through me.

I place my hands back on the wall's slimy surface, "Was it the child's life that was saved?"

More pulses: *Life saved.*

With this, the gush of certainty floods back. The vision was true but fractured: I did not witness the child's last breath. My hands are clean.

But I ordered its death, a treacherous voice inside tells me.

But I didn't *do* it.

If what the Great Wall claims to know is true, then the vital truth is this: even if the order left my lips, the baby didn't die. Yes. A fragile seed of relief takes root. Yes, that *must* make sense. Aren't the tangible outcomes, the stark reality of life and death, more impactful than the shadowy intent behind them? Surely.

No.

Yes!

Both carry weight, but I can dissect the rot of my intentions later. Right now, I clutch this lifeline: *my hands are clean. The child lives.* The words become a mantra against the rising tide of guilt.

This means the Voice—an architect of deception—did just that; it deceived me. I was manipulated.

The weight that has been crushing my chest lifts, slowly at first, then shatters with a surge of hope. I push some of the hope away. Hope is terrifying.

I have been so consumed by self-loathing that I have failed to consider the possibility of deception. The more I tell myself the baby didn't die, the more I comprehend the ploy of the Voice. I knew what it was capable of. I sensed it, when I touched its threads.

I am not a monster.

The Voice is.

It is a parasite, feeding off my despair, twisting my thoughts. I won't allow it to define me. I won't.

"Peace has made me weak," I say, in a chilling whisper.

It is clearer now. If the baby survived, then this … this thing, the Voice, won't let me rest. It will seek me out, relentlessly. There will never be peace between us. Only confrontation. I must stop its games, its insidious whispers, once and for all. It will *never* be an ally, only a tormentor.

But I cannot. I am weak. My vines, my only defense, are withering.

With a surge of defiance, I press my hands against the cold metal of the Great Wall. "I need strength. Anger. Force."

A series of pulses: *Anger from love. Anger protects.*

Love, compassion, peace, hope. They allowed the Voice access to me. They allowed it to weaken my vines. My jaw clenches at the bitter pain I feel from my vines as they scratch my wounds. Like I have betrayed them. Anger surges within me, a tide, but it is not enough. Not against the Voice. I need more.

I say, "I need rage."

Pulses: *Rage from fear. Rage destroys.*

I turn my back on the Great Wall. *Rage destroys.* Do I want to destroy the Voice? I wrap my vines around myself, a shroud of dying leaves. The crisp of the leaves against my skin is a constant, unsettling reminder of both our fragility.

Yes, I *do* want to destroy. I *need* to destroy the Voice.

"Rage from fear," I repeat the Great Wall's message as I tighten my fist. "I need true, raw, primal fear."

Pulses: *Broken Home.* The tremors are quick, desperate. Scared?

"Broken home?" The question hangs heavy in the air, unanswered.

Broken.

Is the wall referring to my vines? My vines *are* broken. What will fix them? What will give them—me strength? Force? Power?

Home.

Do these vines need to reconnect with their origin to become strong again? To become whole?

"Where is their home?" I ask the wall.

Pulses: *Smoke.*

Smoke? Smoke. When I cut the vines, smoke left them. Could the smoke be related to their home? I spin, my senses on high alert. The weight of the Dark Fall presses down, the stench of decay and death filling my nostrils.

Where is there an abundance of smoke? A place that is the home of the vines? A place that will fix their brokenness?

I need to go to Thalj.

The darkness is absolute. It swallows all sight and sound. Ironic. Before I could see everything clearly, even in the dark. But now, I rely on feeling through it. Did the twitch in my eyes do something? Did the vines weaken my vision?

Keeping my hands plastered against the cold, viscous surface of the Great Wall, I move, inch by inch, towards my right. I hold onto the certainty of the Great Wall and follow its guide towards Thalj.

Time, once a thing I appreciated for its generosity, now gnaws at my patience. Why is this journey taking so long? Why does Thalj feel like it is so far away? Is Jinnah blocking me? Why?

I clutch the vines in my hands, a pile of debris crumbling beneath my grip. "Do you have the strength to carry me to Thalj?"

The vines whip out and collapse, their tendrils dragging across the floor like wounded serpents. Others, those tangled in my hair, loosen their grip. I release my hold on the Great Wall, trusting their remaining strength. They launch me forward, moving my body from one crispy rope to another.

I grab for the next vine, my fingers scraping against the rough exterior, but it crumbles beneath my weight. I plummet to the ground with a *thud*. A vibration, cold and sharp, wracks my body. The ground is cold, not cool like the other places in Jinnah. The vines, with a meek attempt to help me, tighten their grip around me, offering a fleeting warmth.

"I will reward you for this kindness," I whisper to them.

They give me a small squeeze.

I raise my head, the world snapping into focus. The glow of the Zam reveals the full scale of Thalj—a frozen wasteland of ice and snow. This is no comforting sight. I am no longer gazing down upon the scene from the vantage point of the Black Dune, a fingernail against the horizon. Now, I am face-to-face with its raw power.

Closer ahead, the Vine Tree, a monstrous silhouette adorned with deep purple blossoms, looms before me. Above it is the tornado-like smoke in the sky, which swirls with an unnatural energy.

I will myself to stand, my legs trembling. The cold bites deep, even with the vines trying to warm me. My skin prickles, the hairs on my arms coated in a thin layer of black frost. Yet, the chill is a distant sensation, a mere whisper compared to the icy dread that grips my soul.

With a clumsy slowness, I drag myself towards the Vine Tree, my feet numb yet obedient. Finally, I reach it, my body trembling with exhaustion. I dare not touch its icy bark; instead, circling it cautiously, studying its grotesque form.

The canopy above is a writhing mass of tendrils, each one emitting a high-pitched, sucking sound, a chilling echo of the sound of the vines in the Zam, except the vines here are feeding off the smoke from the tornado in the sky.

Though there seems to be a war above—the darkness raging as it spreads and hurls black snow towards the ground—the ground of Thalj itself is ... calm. Even peaceful.

I raise my eyes to the tree, a presence that doesn't look like it belongs in this world. But it is not the tree that holds my gaze. It's the way a section of its trunk refracts the light from the fish in the Zam, not absorbing it, but repelling it, sending shards of icy gleams shimmering like stars across the frozen surface of Thalj.

A squirrel, a creature of uncanny grace, scurries past me, its claws finding purchase on the slick bark. It pauses, its head cocked to the side, then darts towards a cluster of purple blossoms, disappearing within them. It emerges moments later, repeating the pattern, a disturbingly rhythmic dance. Then, it stops. I follow its gaze to find it fixed on another squirrel perched on a branch opposite. They stare at each other, a stillness between them. Both squirrels then plunge back into the blossoms, their movements eerily synchronized.

Why are the two squirrels moving so similarly? Why don't they interact directly? As if answering my questions, the climbing squirrel pounces on the other squirrel, and instead of two bodies hitting, there's one dull *thud*.

There is only one squirrel; the other one is a reflection.

Retreating a few steps, I focus on the different parts of the tree and its play on light. There's a box, half-covered in mirrors, with vines framing it. My heart races, and a part of me wants to flee. Why do I want to flee? It is only a box ... isn't it? Another part of me draws closer to it, almost trance-like.

I climb the steps to the top until I reach the place where the squirrel stood. My reflection stares back. The vines no longer hide the ugly scar on my cheek. They are not strong enough. My eyes are the color of the Vine black snow, frozen and slightly distant.

The vines, my only solace, have transformed. No longer merely brown, they writhe with an unnatural vibrancy—streaks of crimson, flashes of mellow yellow, and even patches of the same purple as the huge blossoms of the Vine Tree. They bind me in a constant embrace, brought back to life by the mere closeness to their roots.

I shove against the mirror box. A section groans, then splinters, revealing a gaping oval-shaped hole—an entrance—into the box. It's large enough for me to squeeze through, an invitation to the unknown. Do I want to go in?

No.

Yes.

I step in, the entrance hanging open behind me. A sliver of light cuts through the darkness. Then, I notice them: two orbees, fluttering in behind me. They hadn't accompanied me before. They never travel to Thalj alone. Where have they come from?

The entrance slams shut, plunging the room into total darkness. The orbees flicker on and off as they dart around the room. Their lights blink in an unsettling rhythm, plunging me into a disorienting cycle of halo and eclipse.

Lights on … a long, obsidian table stretches before me.

Lights off … a shaky breath escapes my lips.

Lights on … I glance towards the door.

Lights off … I need to get out.

Lights on … I stumble instead towards the table, my head pounding, my limbs heavy.

Lights off … my fingers brush against the table's icy surface.

Lights on … a silver cover on the table, shimmering.

Lights off … a tingling sensation, a strange energy coursing through my veins.

Lights on … wires.

Lights off … darkness

Lights on … not wires. Vines. A tangled mass writhing beneath the silver cover of the table.

I feel cold. My limbs feel heavy, leaden, unresponsive. I can barely feel my hands; my fingers are numb and clumsy. I grope forward, desperate for any sensation, any relief from this paralyzing hold.

Blinking orbees … throbbing head … my vision blurs. I grasp the vines beneath the silver cover, tracing their course, their tendrils disappearing beneath the table, into the heart of the Vine Tree itself.

These vines were connected to something … or *someone* tied to this table.

I look at the line-shaped bleeding wounds now exposed by the fallen parts of my vine dress. They resemble openings into my very being. The ends of the vines from the table mirror the shape of these wounds, even matching the stretch marks on my legs and stomach. Tailor-made for *me*.

I was the one strapped to this table. My dress, my living cover, pulses against my skin, confirming, as if declaring: *Yes, it is true!*

I trace the path of the intertwined vines from the table, a chilling certainty guiding my steps. I leave the chamber behind, the orbees still thrashing about in their frantic dance, their lights flickering like dying embers. The tendrils of the Vine Tree, thick as pythons, snake upwards, disappearing into the smoke above.

I follow, clinging to its trunk, my grip tightening as I climb. The ascent grows steeper, the air thicker. Finally, I find myself clinging to a monstrous tendril, its surface slick and cold beneath my grasp. It surges upwards, hoisting me into the inky blackness above.

My vine dress sways gently. A single vine reaches out from it, towards the plume of smoke that billows violently above. Almost like a latch, it clicks into place, connecting with a sickening *smack*. The tendril seems to writhe in pleasure as it siphons the smoke into its core.

A tremor runs through me, mirroring the convulsions of my vine dress. The smoke flows through the tendrils of the dress, the color shifting before my eyes. The vibrant green has returned, but it is marred by black veins, a map of the smoke's journey. The dress pulses with a newfound energy, its tendrils swollen, inflamed with a power that both terrifies and exhilarates me.

The vines, which had let go of my wounds, now reconnect with them, with a *snap*. I am suffocating. This time, I am not afraid. I know my vines won't kill me.

Abruptly, the pressure eases. I can breathe again. But it is not the air alone that I inhale. It is the smoke itself, which seeps into my lungs, into every wound, every hole which opens itself to it.

WHOOSH

The nature of the smoke … it's not just a substance.

Looking closer, I see the vines aren't eating the smoke. Instead, they pull it in, move it through their network, connecting everything, just as the Girl said. They then push it out again. They are like living conduits, carrying the smoke from some … entity through Jinnah, and releasing it into the sky above Thalj.

It is through the vines that the smoke spreads across the land.

The smoke itself originates from beneath Shahwah. It's the cry of this entity, a consciousness. I feel it now, a chilling awareness. This entity, this … *she*, nurtured Hadeeya. She had watched over it with a … loving protectiveness. Before Hadeeya was complete, before the final piece—the predator—was added to its domain, she was taken.

She was robbed, used, and imprisoned.

The smoke is a desperate plea, *hers,* one of anguish that has plunged Jinnah into twilight. It has nothing to do with the sickness—not directly. It's a result of the despair of this entity, a silent testament to the fact that no one has heard her cry for help.

She feels alone.

Abandoned.

It was her roar that had echoed through Jinnah when I first severed the vines, a primal scream of pain, because a connection had been broken. Who was she trying to call for help? Who abandoned her? Why can't I sense them?

When this entity was not responded to, she evolved, growing stronger and more defiant. She accomplished something unnatural for her kind: she roared.

This roar … it is a battle cry, a declaration of war. She is in pain, immense, unbearable pain. Something is … *training* her to become this way.

ROAR.

An earth-shattering sound erupts from the depths of Earth. It is a sound of unadulterated rage, a sound that makes my breath catch in my throat.

Let me help you. I will my message to her, unsure if she can hear me.

The orbees are reacting, their lights flashing frantically, their movements erratic, a desperate, chaotic dance.

She replies in my mind: *You cannot help me.*

I allow the vines to lower me from the peak of the Vine Tree, my body swaying as we descend towards the frozen ground. To my astonishment, the ice beneath me buckles, melting beneath the unnatural heat emanating from my body.

Who holds you prisoner? I think back to her.

Her: *The Voice and its allies.*

Me: *I am coming.*

Her: *You … You. I will destroy you.*

Me: *I am your ally.*

Her: *I am a queen with no allies.*

Me: *Whose queen are you?*

Her: *Queen of the orbees.*

The two orbees settle gently on each of my shoulders, nuzzling softly against me. No wonder I had been unable to discern their true nature, nor the nature of the orbee leaves, or the orbee trees. They have remained loyal to her in guarding their nature, gripping it so it did not spread without her permission.

This realization sparks another question, a nagging unease: Could this same loyalty be the reason I can't sense the Dark Fall? Was that blocked connection also somehow linked to her influence?

Me: *Your orbees haven't abandoned you. They can't understand your call.*

Her plea for help, a desperate, strangled cry, has been distorted, corrupted by the fear that consumes her. The orbees and their connection to her have weakened. They misinterpreted her signals, remaining in Jinnah. Because she felt they had betrayed her, she turned to rage. Her rage is raw, a primal expression of her anguish. Born of fear.

That fear is causing the Queen of the orbees to evolve at an unnatural scale. If that fear is not contained, she will destroy all of Jinnah. Her rage will blind her. And now, that terror, that consuming rage, runs through my body.

I can't hold it all in me. A potent roar erupts from within me, a scream that echoes through the frozen wasteland.

The Voice has caused too much pain. It *cannot* be allowed to continue. I will face the Voice. I will destroy it and all its allies, whoever or whatever they are.

I will free the Queen of the orbees.

Then, she will save Jinnah.

My roar subsides. I am adrift, suspended in the icy water.

WHOOSH

The instant my leg brushes the fish; a jolt of its nature floods me. Camouflage. Predators. Male. Hum. Breeding. Just as quickly, the Zam water washes over my skin, stealing the sensation away.

The chilling water itself has a strange, indifferent presence against my skin. I am neither cold nor hot. Is this from the nature of the smoke? Is this the heat of rage?

I push myself up, my feet finding refuge on the ice. Steam rises from my body as it contacts the frigid air. The ice beneath me groans and buckles, melting alarmingly quickly beneath my weight. I realize with a jolt that my very presence is causing it to melt.

Then, I hear it. A surrounding sound like a vibrating heartbeat that pulses through the ground, shaking me. It begins slowly, a deliberate thumping, like a monstrous heart awakening from its long slumber. The intervals shorten, the thumps growing more insistent, more violent. The Great Wall shudders, its surface rippling like disturbed water.

A crescendo.

A series of deafening thumps, each one more powerful than the last. The Great Wall groans.

Silence.

A fissure, a jagged wound in the ice, opens beneath my feet. It snakes outwards, growing larger, deeper, a malevolent grin splitting the frozen surface. What's happening?

The tremors from the Great Wall continue, the ground shuddering beneath me. The fissures multiply, a network of cracks spreading across the ice.

The blackness, that had coursed through my veins, is receding as if diluted by the icy Zam.

No. I need this rage. I need its power. I turn and sprint towards the Vine Tree, a silhouette against the shattered ice. As I approach, a wave of invisible force slams into me, throwing me back with ferocity. I land hard on the ice, the impact jarring my bones.

The Vine Tree remains defiant in not allowing me to approach it. My vines, these pitiful tendrils, cower in its presence. Some, still clinging to the Zam, continue to slurp the waters, purging more darkness from my veins. The darkness is fading, weakening, slipping away from me.

I spin around, my gaze fixed on the Black Dune, a desperate bid to contain the dwindling reserves of rage within me. I need to preserve it, to channel it, to unleash it upon the Voice.

"No!" I say to my vines, between clenched teeth. "Stop drinking from the Zam!"

The vines resist me. They tug back. I yank harder. They reluctantly obey, tearing free from the water.

The ice continues to melt, the fissures widening, the ground groaning beneath my feet. Then, I see it. A small hole, a gaping maw in the frozen earth. There is something inside it, popping up and down limply.

I stumble closer, my breath catching in my throat. The Girl. A small face, eyes tightly closed, dark hair unfurling like a silken weed in a forgotten stream, bobbing gently in the icy water.

The orbees, their lights flickering frantically, hover around her, their silent vigil a stark contrast to the chaos that surrounds us.

She had brought them here. She had come here for me.

I reach out, my fingers trembling. I pull her from the icy depths, her body limp in my arms. "No!" The word is a plea. "No, no, no."

Her nature. I can't feel it anymore. Why can't I feel it?

I gently lay her on the ice, her skin cold and clammy beneath my touch. I brush the remaining ice from her cheeks, tugging her dress over her legs, a futile attempt to offer warmth. I press my own body against hers, desperate to transfer some of my own dwindling heat.

"Breathe," I whisper, my breath misting the air. "Please breathe."

I squeeze her face, my tears mingling with the melting ice that cascades down her cheeks. "Why did you come after me?"

"Orbees!" I call out. They obey and flicker to life in her ears, but her eyes remain shut. "Why isn't it working?" I bury my head in her chest. "It was you," I say, my voice cracking. Tears stream down my face, melting more ice on her cheeks. "That's what I fear. Losing you."

I push my body up with her firmly in my arms and stumble forward, my legs like lead, each step a torment. But this is not from the cold outside—I can barely feel that cold—this is from the cold inside. The absence of warmth, love, and hope.

My vines lash out, eager to assist. But I refuse their help. I will carry her myself. The vines, though not as strong as they were with the initial surge of rage, are still powerful. They explode into different shapes. The vines writhe, tendrils now clenched like fists with thorns jutting out of their surface like daggers. The leaves are darkened to a bruised purple and red, trembling with barely contained fury.

Driven by a need to protect her, I press on. I must reach the Black Dune.

The sky, now a whirlpool of violence, throws monstrous icicles from above. The wind, a biting, icy gale, lashes at my face, but I endure. I will shield her, protect her at all costs.

I stumble, my grip on her weakening, my eyelids heavy with a sudden wave of exhaustion. I can't stop. As I approach the bottom of the Black Dune, dizziness washes over me. I stumble, my knees buckling, and then, I am falling, plunging towards the icy ground.

The dream comes back: the serpent, running from it, the bridge. It's all the same, except now when I reach the old woman, she doesn't look at me hopelessly. Instead, she gazes up the hilltop, her eyes filled with a spark of intrigue. She opens her mouth to speak, but I don't hear her words.

My eyelids flutter open, my back against the Black Dune, the Girl's limp, unresponsive body sprawled over my legs. I watch the devastation of Thalj. The ice is shattered and broken, the ground a chaotic mess of fissures and yawning chasms. The landscape is torn apart, shaking with the Great Wall.

I caused this.

Something gently brushes against my nape.

WHOOSH

Safe, strong, grateful. Hungry.

Tears stream down my face as I whirl around, heart hammering against my ribs. But the darkness of the Black Dune swallows everything. I blink, disoriented, and then, they are there—two golden, gleaming eyes, each the size of my palm, burning into me. A black maw opens, a gape revealing a row of pearly teeth, the rest of the creature dissolving into the inky black backdrop. It shakes its mane.

The Black Assad looms over me, taking up half the dune. Its powerful body presses against mine, its warmth a jarring contrast to the frigid air, bringing a tingling sensation back to my numb limbs.

It rumbles, a low growl shaking the ground, then lowers its massive head. "Human rage brings imbalance."

"I wanted to save—"

"Save yourself first." Its eyes hold that unsettling intelligence. "When there are extremes in any nature, all will suffer."

We don't have time for this. "Just take her," I plead.

"Rise," the Black Assad commands.

"What if all I know is how to fall?"

"Then there is nothing left to do," he turns his back to me, and looks up the Black Dune, "but to rise ... Adamah."

With a surge, I place the Girl on the Black Assad's back, her small body a fragile burden against the creature's immense strength. I climb on as well, sitting behind her body, and cling onto the Black Assad's thick fur. It rumbles a low growl, shaking the ground. Then, with a powerful heave, it leaps forward, carrying us up the Black Dune.

PART 12

Fall

ADAMAH

The Black Assad deposits us on the buried grass before the Pale Tree. "Thank you," I say, before getting off and carrying the Girl down.

The Black Assad rumbles in response, the ground beneath me slightly shaking with his every step, as he turns to leave. Before he reaches the cluster of trees—coated in a blanket of night—he pauses momentarily, his gaze flickering to the rotting camel carcasses. He turns away disgusted and continues until he disappears behind the trees.

A low growl fills the space. From my own throat.

I move towards the carcasses, the stench of decay vivid … but not off-putting. The vines, gnarled and twisted, are a patchwork of red and purple. I hesitate. A flicker of revulsion. I lunge, sinking my teeth into the flesh, the taste of death a bitter, metallic tang on my tongue mixed with dry and brittle fur covered in dust. The vines break up the rest of the meat with their sharp thorns.

I devour both camels, stuffing the putrid flesh into my mouth.

I tear myself away, my hands instinctively covering my face to stifle the nausea. I stumble towards the Girl, bumping into her. A surge of energy emanates from her, a mixture of anger and sadness.

But something else … something new—or perhaps, something that was always there but I haven't caught before now—has emerged.

Numbness. It is a void, a hollow space, where feeling once lived. Like a room, once filled with vibrant colors and life, now stripped bare. No sound, no light, just silence. I shudder. But is it ... peaceful? No. Peace is not the absence of feeling. It is a balance. Numbness is a denial, a refusal. In some ways, it is a surrender away from the essence of *being*.

What if the orbees can't heal her? What if this ... this absence of feeling blocks them?

Her eyelids flutter as if answering me. She *had* felt the pain of the cold. Now, I realize it, touching her cheek—the blood of the camels which stains my hands, staining her face—she had felt the pain of *my* coldness, when I told her to stay away.

Her lips part, a whisper escaping them. I miss the first word, but then she repeats it. "Mama."

I lift her and throw my head back, allowing the Dark Fall to cover me and my vines. The blood from the carcasses is no longer evidence of my descent into savagery.

The vines lift us effortlessly, placing us on the other side of the Pale Tree. The contractions from the Great Wall are growing more frequent, more violent, making the ground beneath me tremble.

I hold her tighter, burying my face in her hair, the scent of dead camel flesh mixed with smoke and blood filling my senses. Two orbees detach from her ears, hovering ahead, their lights guiding our path forward.

I burst through the skeletal remains of dead trees, past the Garden of Fire. I pass the Zam, reaching the thicket of orbee trees which border the end of Jinnah.

I whisper, "Bismillah" under my breath as I cross them.

The air is hot. Scorching. Burning. Tempered. But I am also hot. The smoke has not fully left me. Good. I will need the power from the smoke later when I face the Voice.

I raise my eyes to the hill. A building with a perfect dome-shaped crown propped on its head. *The Golden Dome.* Fitting. Stars in the sky. I watch them look at me like scattered, glowing eyes. This part of the land is untouched by the smoke. Bare. Open. Accusing.

The vines erupt in a frenzy, whipping wildly around us. They tear chunks of dirt from the path ahead, which hit the shaking Great Wall. It appears that reality itself is being disrupted.

The Silver Path transforms into a series of metallic steps, winding its way up the slope. I ascend cautiously, my grip tightening on the Girl, determined not to drop her.

I must get her to the safety of her mother. My gaze fixates on the building. It resembles a colossal … mushroom, with the walls descending like a sturdy stalk, punctuated by smaller, sacred pillars that support the majestic dome above it like an elegant cap.

The steps of the Silver Path end, revealing another set of steps leading upwards. Instead of welcoming, they seem to taunt me, whispering a silent warning: enter the mushroom at your own risk.

At the top of the steps stands a formidable, massive golden door, ajar just enough to reveal an inky blackness within. No light. No sound.

As I reach it, fear washes over me, like an inflamed reaction to a high-class, but deadly delicacy. My chest is tight. My breath is quick and shallow. My heart is like a trapped bird trying to escape by punching my ribs. My skin prickles with a cold sweat, which raises the debris on my forehead and pushes it over my eye. I blink it away.

"Mama," the Girl murmurs again.

I ate her camels. The least I can do is return her to her mother. I continue walking across the highest step where the door faces me, a menacing welcome, as my vines trail behind me like watchful, hostile guardians. As I reach the open doorway, the two orbees flit ahead, their luminous eyes reflecting the dim light within.

It's not just nature or people who have a feel. Places do too. Their essence is shaped by the lives lived within their walls. I hesitate, carefully steadying the Girl in my arms, anticipating the emotional weight that might wash over me upon entering this place.

Using my shoulder, I push against the heavy door. It resists, as if reluctant to yield.

WHOOSH

Here lies joy, hope, and peace.

WHOOSH

Here lies pain, despair, and loss.

This place, this sanctuary, bears the scars of both human dignity and human savagery. Desecrated on holy nights. Violated by greed and violence towards its worshipping inhabitants.

A dangerous nature, different from that of the worshippers who once inhabited this place, has tried to take root. This nature is insidious, blinded by its entitlement and the urge to dominate. The same nature as the Voice. Disturbingly enough, this is not the Voice—the Voice is not human—this is a part of human nature. In their anger and envy, the ones who this nature belongs to have caused great destruction.

I hold the Girl closer now, cradling her protectively in my arms. The faint light of the orbees filters through the opening, revealing a long, cavernous hallway, its walls a shade of pale blue, like the walls outside.

Despite its spaciousness, the hallway feels suffocating. It has been a place of mourning for some—I walk a few more steps—for many. Endless rows of wooden boxes. Shelves are empty, small holes the size of my fingertip across their surface.

A chilling stillness descends, exaggerated by the pounding from the Great Wall. This stillness conceals something within it. Something that is waiting to strike.

A door looms before me. A plain door. Dark wood. Smooth and cold. My muscles tense like a drawn bowstring. The vines morph into weapons, knives, and whips. Behind that door, something or someone awaits my arrival.

The vines are pushy. Their tendrils, wild. They slam the door open. When I step inside, the floor is cushioned with a softness.

WHOOSH

Joy, awe, humility.

The carpet, a deep shade of emerald green, is lined with an endless procession of identical patterned designs. There are numerous boxes, each one adorned with an intricate, almost hypnotic pattern of swirling lines and arcane symbols. At the tip of the patterned boxes is a point which is directed ahead, towards the East.

There is a strange feeling—beneath the veneer of dread which holds me— of belonging. I am supposed to be here.

This belonging doesn't give me peace.

The orbees add to the unease. They flicker frantically, darting towards the far end of the room behind me. They disappear behind a heavy velvet curtain that hangs from the ceiling, concealing whatever lies ahead.

I gently lower the Girl to the ground and let out the breath I have been hoarding. A long breath. Again, there is that feeling, like a bird, beating my ribs, pricking at my bones with its beak in desperation to get out. *Get out*! I turn towards the door but stop. A low, growling sound emanates from behind the curtain, just steps away.

My vines, with their honed thorns poking out from their bodies slither across the floor, leaving trails of dark matter in their wake, tainting the beautiful carpet with streaks of the Dark Fall. They reach the curtain, coiling around it, waiting for my command to reveal what is behind it.

ME

The curtain rises,
Spotlights gleam,
Fall.
Fall.
Fall.
Let me begin,
by shutting the door

ADAMAH

The curtain slides open sideways, like a snake slowly opening its mouth to attack. A space, not quite big enough to be a room. More of a place where a body sleeps until it's time to wake up.

Or not.

A mausoleum.

The air is thick with dust motes, illuminated by the single sliver of the crescent moon which slips through the small window at the back.

A small movement. A figure huddled against the wall. She wears a veil, the sweat of her body ensuring the material clings to her.

"I know you." The words escape me, a strangled croak like a frog in distress.

From behind me, I hear the Girl whisper, "Mama ..."

My eyes, as if bound by invisible threads, pull back towards the figure. "I know you ..." I say again.

The swirling orbees flicker and close in around her.

Her face: a rough beauty with scars, livid and puckered—an echo of my own. Her eyebrows: absent, the skin beneath them smooth and unnervingly taut. Her veil, a tattered remnant of some forgotten elegance, loosely flows around her frame, which seems to hang both like a string, ready to blow with even a small wind, and a second skin to reveal just how fragile that string is.

I take a hesitant step forward; one hand pressed on my chest to ease the pounding under it.

She stares back coldly. Black smudges beneath her eyelids hint at a hasty attempt at makeup, the effect more unsettling than alluring. Her eyes are a bruised violet. I know her name.

"*Sama*. You ..."

Killed? Didn't kill?

"The baby ..." I manage to say.

"Ninety-nine." Though her voice sounds uniformed, under it a feral energy simmers, threatening to erupt.

A gasp escapes my lips, a strangled cry of pain as the vines, delve deeper into my wounds, tearing them open, flooding my senses with a torrent of images. They're hurting me. Why are they hurting—

Faces. Many faces. Smiling faces. Joyful faces.

"I was ... am Queen Adamah." I search the ground, desperate for a clue, more of the memory to confirm my words. "I saved ... didn't I save them?"

"Save them?!" Sama echoes with a hint of amusement, as if teaching a child the moral of a story.

"I'm supposed to save. Save Jinnah ... free the Queen of the orbees so she can save Jinnah," I whisper. "Stop the Voice. I ..."

I look up, meeting her gaze, those chilling, purple eyes, drilling into mine. Hot tears sting. *Why am I crying?* The memory of the battle against the Cast, behind the Great Wall just days ago, surfaces, a chilling, unexpected wave. It *did* happen. It wasn't a dream. The tears flow without my permission, as if my eyes have a will of their own, disconnected from my mind. Though I am crying, a heat rumbles in my belly. It travels up to my ribs. The bird in my chest now burns.

"I saved them!" I scream, the sound raw and desperate.

She shakes her head, the motion jarring the vines deeper into my wounds. Blood trickles down my arms, legs, and torso, warm and viscous, almost caressingly. It feels ... *wrong*. Like a dark cleansing of crimson rain. It drips to the floor, staining the green carpet a deep red.

I spin away from her. The heat is creeping up to the top of my lungs. I must get out! If I stay, something bad is going to happen. Something *very* bad.

"You can't bear to hear your sins?" Sama hisses.

"I have to save Jinnah!" I roar. "That's why I'm here."

"Lies! You are as deluded now as you were then. You only do things for yourself."

"No!"

A wet sob escapes her lips, a guttural sound that mirrors the anguish within me.

"I followed you … obediently … as you …" Sama's voice trails off, the unspoken accusation hanging heavy in the air. "As *we* …"

"No!" I gasp, scrambling for the doorknob, my hands clawing at the smooth surface.

It's locked.

"Coward! We are still guilty," she whispers.

Guilty. A word that has come to me since I first arrived here. An inviter of nightmares, a hint at locked crimes.

"Ninety-nine faces. I see them in my sleep, in every waking moment, in every morsel of food before it touches my tongue. You should see them too," she says.

"Guilty," I whisper, as I raise my head, meeting her gaze. I push the heat down back to my belly, my shoulders slumping in defeat. I crumple to the floor, my knees buckling beneath me. I am ready to accept the truth. "What have I done?!"

"You … *we* … slaughtered them."

A searing inferno. The stench of decay.

My knees fall upon the wet carpet of my blood. I feel sick. "No!"

I am not ready for *this* truth.

"Yes!" Sama's words plunge into me, their weight sending me reeling backwards.

I claw at my head, tearing the vines from it to drown out the horrific images flooding my mind: *faces contorted in agony, limbs twisted at unnatural angles, an endless sea of blood and suffering.*

"No more!" I scream, slamming my fists against the ground. The heat is back. Now, it soars up my torso. The vines lash out, tearing at the walls, ripping holes in the carpet.

"We were good at first," Sama whispers. "Our cause … even noble."

"What is noble about … murder?" I gasp, my breath catching in my throat.

"Nothing!" She wipes her face and shakes her head, "Nothing."

I stumble—I don't know where I am—tripping over an unseen obstacle, a searing pain erupting in my hand. A crimson stain blooms on my skin, the blood seeping into the carpet. I recoil from the object that has pierced my skin, adding to my already bleeding wounds. It's a whip, a monstrous instrument of torture. Its leather handle is slick with my fresh blood, a stark contrast to the rough crust of older, dried blood clinging to its surface.

The orbees dart around the room. They are trapped. Desperate to get out.

More images flood me. *Men and women on their knees begging me to stop.* I clamp my hands over my ears to silence their screams.

"Remember." Sama's voice cuts through the flashes.

I scramble backwards, away from her, colliding with the unconscious girl. Her dress is pulled back, exposing a network of scars that crisscross her delicate arms. And fresh ones, which have recently dried. The heat that has travelled up my stomach and chest now rips through my throat.

"You …" I stammer, gripping the whip. "You beat her with this!"

She hurt the Girl.

She caused her pain.

She made her numb.

Sama's eyes meet mine. No fear. Only misplaced serenity over her features. This unexpected calmness ignites a fresh wave of rage. I raise the whip, but she remains uncowed.

The vines are preparing an assault. I can feel their thirst for blood. For violence. I push them down.

I want to do this myself.

"Fight back!" I scream. The heat burns inside the scar on my face.

Instead, she settles on the ground, her back against the pool of my blood, her eyes fixed on mine.

"Thank you," she whispers, the same words the Black Assad offered when I saved his cub. The heat in me pauses. My jaw trembles.

I don't want to do this.

"You're a holy woman, Sama," I plead, falling to my knees next to her, searching her eyes, the whip still clutched in my bloody hands. "I killed ninety-nine people. Can I be redeemed?"

Her eyes cloud over, much like the dragged mother of the ants as she crept up the tree. "There is no redemption for the sinner."

The heat pricks at my skin. Oozing through every pore. Breaking through my nose. It twitches. Up to my eyes. They water. To my head, covering every thought except one: *destroy her.*

A scream tears from my throat, a raw, animalistic sound that echoes through the room. My arm rises, the whip a blur of motion in my grip. It lashes out striking Sama.

THWACK.

THWACK.

THWACK.

I am aware of the motion, yet detached. The world spins. So many colors. Colors I no longer fully comprehend.

THWACK.

THWACK.

THWACK.

I fall to the ground, the vines coiling around me in a cold, desperate embrace. They constrict, mirroring the tightening in my chest. More vines continue what I have begun.

THWACK.

THWACK.

THWACK.

Sama's limbs jerk with each blow. She doesn't scream. She grunts. Submits to their violence.

"What is one more death if I can't be redeemed?" I whisper.

With each strike of the vines upon her now motionless body, a piece of my vine dress shatters, dissolving into dust. The dust travels to the vines, which beat Sama, and they, too, crumble into a heap of powder.

My vision narrows. The room shrinks. I can only see what is directly ahead of me: *her body, not moving.*

I crawl. To her. Colors blur. Sounds. Meaning? Whip falls.

Veil on her head. I take it. Off. Cross arms. Hers. Cover her. All. Don't touch. Death. Scream. I scream. Can't stop screaming. Look up. Still screaming. No sound left in my throat. Still screaming. Sil—

Silent scream.

All white.

Empty.

I am … I …

PART 13

Sacrifice

ADAMAH

Plains sprawl around me. Lifeless. Only dust.

"We testify against you," the booming voice of a woman jolts me to consciousness.

Even though it's empty here, I search for her.

I open my mouth. *Who is that?* My mouth isn't working. I try to open it with both hands. My hands are not working.

"We testify against you," that woman's voice again, now in a chorus of identical voices.

My voice.

"We saw everything you did," a whisper from my eyes.

"We heard everything you said," a whisper from my ears.

"We felt every sin you committed," a whisper from my skin.

"Every morning, we screamed at you to be good! Every night, you made us sleep in a bed of sins. You oppressed us. You sacrificed every part of us for your blinded vision. Now, you shall be committed. We testify against you."

Smoke ahead, thickening rapidly. I gasp for air, my lungs burning. My vision blurs, the world a chaotic swirl of gray and black. Each breath is a struggle, a desperate fight against the suffocating embrace of the smoke.

I manage to open my mouth and cough, desperate for air, but my chest is tight. Something squeezes me. I try to move my arms, but they are bound to my sides. My entire body is locked in a standing position, paralyzed by an unseen force.

I am jerked upwards, my feet dangling in the air. The smoke begins to clear, revealing a pair of piercing black eyes staring directly into mine. The serpent from my dream, its scales shimmering with an infernal light. It coils around me, squeezing, constricting, threatening to crush the life out of me.

"I have you," it hisses.

With a *thud*, I crash to the ground. Scrambling to my feet, I stumble forward. A thin, sinuous whip lashes out, wrapping itself around my ankles. I tumble, the dust stinging my face. I claw at the ground, desperately, but my fingers sink into the earth, offering no resistance. The serpent pulls, dragging me towards it.

"Let go!" I scream.

It releases me, but only to coil and strike again.

I scramble forward, fear lending me a burst of speed.

ROAR.

The sound explodes behind me. Every hair on my body stands on end. I don't dare turn around. The air around me ignites, a blast of searing heat that scorches my skin. I whimper.

Another blast of hot air, this time aimed directly at the back of my neck, burning my hair. The scent is foul and harsh. I instinctively touch my neck, to ease the burned flesh, but my fingers do not find skin. Instead, I touch metal. A series of hot metallic rings. Chains. I am shackled, bound, a prisoner.

I try to run. To escape. But an unseen force slams me back to the ground. My dress pounds against my body, the harshness like a slap against my skin. A metal dress. It clings to me like a parasite, which feeds on the flesh beneath it.

I push my body up to my knees, my breath coming in ragged gasps.

Slowly, I turn towards the source of the roar. No beast emerges, only a series of colossal gates, seven in total, each radiating a fiery glow.

ROAR.

More deafening than the last.

The heat intensifies, searing my flesh. My hands blister, the skin peeling away. I collapse, burying my face in the dust, seeking refuge from the unbearable heat. But the dust offers no solace, only adding to the agony as it mixes with my raw wounds.

Despite my desperate will to get away from the gates that hold something terrifying, my body rises without my permission. My body moves forward, drawn towards those very gates.

"Go back!" I manage to scream to my body, a desperate plea against the pull.

Before the gates, a figure emerges, his face is stern and unwavering. It gazes upon me with an expression of chilling indifference.

"Don't let me in there!" I beg him.

One by one, the gates creak open, groaning like tormented souls.

Then, I see it. The source of the roar. The fire itself. "I have been assigned to take the tyrants," it declares, its voice crackling.

I scream, a gut-wrenching sound. But my legs remain rooted to the ground, against my will. I am frozen, staring into the gates.

The first gate reveals a horrifying spectacle: people, their faces contorted in agony, their flesh blackened and charred.

The second gate: bodies are torn apart, limb from limb, consumed by the flames, then reassembled, only to be devoured again.

The third gate: a sea of bones, bleached white by the relentless fire. Among the bones are creatures unlike any I have ever seen, their eyes burning: devils.

A chilling clarity descends. "Hell," I whisper, "not led by devils, but led *to* by devils."

I look at the stern guardian of the gates, his face impassive. "Guardian of Hell, angel. Please—"

Before I can continue, my eyes drag themselves to more gates, my tongue not permitted to speak.

The gates: four ... five ... six ... seven ...

I shift my focus to the figures trapped within the flames. A knowing dread pierces through me. I know these kinds of people. I know them very well.

Their eyes are glazed over, the vacant stare of the one consumed by desire. In life, their hunger was never satisfied, and now, in the eternal fire, that insatiable craving persists. They were blind to anything beyond their unquenchable wants.

They mistook fleeting pleasure for true fulfillment, a false fullness instead of genuine contentment, an instant gratification instead of the true nourishment of their souls. Now, they, the consumers, are fully consumed by this raging beast of fire, their untamed desires—to kill, to hurt, to lust, to devour, to avenge—have become their burden.

They sold themselves for desire, over the price of truth.

Yet, even in the heart of the inferno, their eyes hold a flicker of desperate hope, mirroring the lick of the flames.

More terrifyingly, I can see *my* place—it is *waiting* for me—amongst them, like a seat left empty, which only *I* can fill.

I try to turn away. To run. I stumble, fall, my hands clawing at the dust. I struggle to my feet, but my body moves on its own, drawn irresistibly towards the looming gates.

"Stop!" I scream. Though I can speak, the words bring this prison more to life, rather than allowing me to resist it.

As I get closer, a ghastly tree emerges from within Hell. Its roots delve deep into the first gate, while its branches, heavy with hideous fruit, reach towards the seventh and final gate.

A *ravenous* hunger gnaws at my insides. A single fruit tumbles from the highest branch, landing inches from my feet. My body crawls towards it. I grasp the fruit, my hands foreign to me, tools of this tortured and disobedient body. As I look at the fruit, a wave of nausea washes over me. I try to throw it away, to reject this offering.

No! My mind screams.

My hands betray me. They shove the fruit into my mouth. I try to spit it out, to resist, but it's too late. The fruit, cold and slimy, explodes in my mouth.

I realize that evil has a taste: *this*. Rotten to the core, sour and acrid. My mouth puckers and my eyes water, leaving a burning sensation on my tongue.

Water! A stream appears. I scramble towards it, gulping down the liquid. This is not water. It's something else, something metallic and foul. I gag, the taste of blood and pus filling my mouth.

My insides convulse, as if they are trying to expel the poison, but another part of my body clutches the awful taste, forcing it to remain in my belly. I scream, an animalistic sound.

Shadows loom over me, growing larger, more menacing. They press in, suffocating me. These are the shadows of death. Death tugs at me, contorting my body, each wave of agony threatening to tear me apart. But I know, with a chilling certainty, that death is not an escape in this place.

There is no escape.

Only endless torment.

"Death!" I scream for it. I want to be unburdened.

Worse than the physical pain is the crushing loneliness. I am utterly alone. I have been abandoned by everyone, even my own limbs.

Yet that is not what brings me to my knees, making me want to disappear.

In this place, I have been abandoned by Allah, *The Guardian. The Healer. The All Mighty. The Originator. The Fashioner. The Giver of gifts. The Magnificent. The Sustainer.*

The other words left by the Stranger flood back: *The Avenger. The Most Just. The Subduer.*

I deserve this.

I sob, my face buried in the dust. My mouth allows me to speak. "Let me go back! Please, let me make it right!"

The chains around my neck tighten, dragging me towards the seventh gate. Tears stream down my face as I am hurled to the ground.

A word echoes around me: "Push!"

I look up, searching for the source of the command. The sky above is a suffocating smog, a distorted reflection of the Hell that surrounds me.

Push?

PART 14

Orbee

THE STRANGER

You received my messages. The ones I sent the vines to leave, on the floor of Fallen Trees. I, a coward could not face you until this moment. I face you now, only because you need me to.

I pick you up. Your legs won't bend. Frozen.

Your memories are lost again. Other parts of you are lost too. Pain does that. I know. I caused you the most.

Your legs bend now. I carry you. Will come back for the Girl. You love her. Reach Jinnah. I look back. It is dawn. The Voice is gone. Waiting for you at Ghar. Thinks—I don't want to talk about the Voice now. I must keep walking.

Now at Zam. My body is too wide for the bridge. I move it to the side and carry you across. Reached the other side. I lay you down.

Your eyes are wide open but still closed. Windows with invisible shutters. Nothing is allowed in, not yet. But in … in there, you are. Like I was behind my shutters. All along, you knew.

I caused you pain. Couldn't look you in the eyes for long. Only a few seconds. I think about those seconds eleven times a day, sometimes thirteen, never less. I couldn't do what others could. Everything felt too heavy. Feelings are too heavy: sounds, lights, smells. Too heavy. It hurt you that I pushed you away. That I was so heavy for you.

When you were sleeping, I visited you every day at the glass box in Thalj.

Yes, I brought you pain. But I also made you the happiest.

I clean your wounds. Blood comes off easily. Zam heals quickly. Your old dress is on the bank. I'm cleaning that too. Scrubbing. Replacing the holes and broken edges with more vines.

You love green. Memory: *leaf from the Surface. Gave it to you. You touched it. I watched your face. You brought it to your nose. You breathed. Very deeply. Both eyes were closed. Cried. I touched your tears. Put them on my face.*

I tapped to you: No more cry.

You held my hands. I flinched.

I tapped: I am bad.

You tapped back: You are good, my Yahya.

Me: I make you sad.

You: Happy cry, not sad cry. The green is so beautiful.

Something happened back then, after I gave you the green leaf. The more I went up to the Surface, the more everything started to hurt. As the children were born, I saw fire. Danger. Lights were changing colors and shapes. Sounds too. Something bad was going to happen. I needed to be alone. I didn't want any bad near you. That made you cry, too. A sad cry.

Didn't want you to be sad. I left you. Uncle found me. We both went to the prison. You freed us. Then you thought I left again, but I didn't. I hid. Too scared. Always been … scared. Most scared of dying.

I am still scared of dying, but now I know something is scarier than death.

I wipe the last part of the blood from your wounds with the vines. Careful not to touch you. Not yet.

When you are clean and the smoke of the Queen has left the vines, I will make your new dress. It is a mix between your old dress and the clean vines. These vines hold you better. Hold you together. My work before was incomplete, when you slept on the table in the glass box. Now, it is complete.

I put your new dress on you. Soon, you will feel yourself before everything else.

I scan the area. Boxes checked. Information checked. Plans checked. Everything is ready.

Your head is slumped. Eyes still wide open. The orbees are close to you. More are coming. They were confused at first when you ate the smoke, but now they can smell you. They sense the signal of their true Queen. First, the smoke blocked them from it. Now, the smoke has mixed with your blood, fully released in a new form, in your sweat.

You are their *new* Queen.

Problem: There can only be one Queen of the orbees. I will fix that later.

I have finished putting on your dress. Vines have come to life.

I finally touch your hands. Clean them with mine. Under your nails. Cold. Rough. Broken. *Safe*.

I allow you to share my nature, knowing this is the last time you will absorb another's essence and become it, instead of your own. This final reception of mine is the only path to reconnect with yourself. Through my nature, you will witness my genesis: your happiest memory. The one the vines hid when you first wore them, like I hid. We didn't want to hurt you.

Time to wake up, Mama.

ADAMAH

A single rope, frayed and brittle, hangs down from the smoked sky. I grip it with ferocity, my dress clanging with the chains as I push my body up.

The chains yank me down. I fight, pulling with all my might, as I push my body upwards, inch by inch. A pressure pressing on my feet. The serpent has coiled around my ankles.

I scream a raw, guttural sound, and pull harder. The chains tighten, the serpent constricts, but another force, opposite to the pull, surges through me. Something else is pushing me up. Their push helps me to go higher and higher. I look down. It's the old woman, her fragile looking hands, powerful and determined.

Taking in her withering but tranquil face, I shout, "Come with me! I can keep you safe."

"Then, I will never leave you."

"Who are you?" I ask.

"I am your good deeds." She turns to the serpent, who slithers next to her. Its sinister smile widens as a forked tongue lashes out. "That is your bad deeds." With a surge of power in her voice, she kicks the serpent away from the rope and shouts, "Now, rise!"

"Peace," I say, blinking away tears which trickle down to her cheeks.

She whispers, "'Verily, in the remembrance of their Lord do hearts find peace.[1]'"

I reach the top of the rope, gasping for air. But instead of freedom, I am met with a blinding white space. In it is a memory.

The pain is unbearable. I cling to the ropes to stop it.

Ruqaya communicates to me through the Tap: Push!

I bang on the wall, pieces of rock falling around me, telling her: I can't!

She taps back: Push or the baby will die!

I bang on the wall again: Hurts. Hurts.

The contractions are like a jolt of fire crushing every part of my insides. A scream rises to my throat. I bite down hard on the rough rope, the coppery taste of blood filling my mouth. My eyes are squeezed shut. I strain against the pain, giving in to the contractions. Every muscle urges me to push. My body feels like it is tearing apart as every part of me opens. I don't think I can do the last part.

Baby breaks through my flesh.

The burning sensation shifts. Liquid from down there.

I feel broken.

A final push.

Silence.

Ruqaya taps on my leg: Boy.

I look for him. I can't see him. I can't hear him. Why? My eyes are so blurry, I wipe them quickly. Why isn't he crying? Why can't I stop crying?

A small squeak. More like a tiny animal.

A new feeling. I don't know this feeling. It is uncontrollable. Unconditional. Terrifying. I am warm, everywhere. The warmth begins in my chest.

Then, he is in my arms. First, he turns away. But I push his head, so it rests on my chest. Let him feel the warmth. He tilts his head towards it, leaning in, nuzzling his head into me.

Ruqaya taps me: Name?

All the thoughts of where he came from, the hurt, all of it … none of it matters. Not when I see his face. I bring him closer to my chest, unable to contain the sobs.

Happy cries. Tears are falling on his head. His head is as big as my palm. It vibrates as my chest shakes.

I have wanted to be dead for so long. I have felt dead for longer. Numb. Absent. Empty. Dark.

I hold him before my face and blink at him: Yahya, Life.

He quietens. As if he is searching through the hazy eyes of birth. He tilts not only his head, but also his arms, his legs, and the rest of his body towards me. I want nothing more than to live for him.

I will never let anyone hurt you, Yahya. I blink to my son: I would die for you.

Ruqaya arches an eyebrow at me, a playful glint in her eyes. A mischievous smile spreads across her face as she loudly taps the wall, the sound echoing through the room: Always so dramatic.

I nudge her with my foot, and she feigns hurt, the smile never leaving her lips. Her expression turns serious as she reaches down and gently squeezes my feet: Just choose to live.

Choose to live. I choose to live.

I look up to the ceiling, towards the direction of a God who my people spoke of but slowly forgot, and I direct the warmth which oozes from all over my body to Him. Holding my son tightly, I think: Thank you, Allah. Thank you.

The white returns. Harsh. Piercing.

PART 15

Cave

ME

I have always relished in the approach of Your footsteps. Soundless. Deliberate. Stealthy. But these are not Your footsteps. These are clumsy, cautious, and heavy, followed by the *pitter-patter* of another's feet ahead of them.

Who is this intruder?

I peek out from my Ghar. A force throws me back into the darkness. Within the concealment of my shadows, I move slowly, inching closer to whoever this anomaly is.

I charge with all my might, a focused, calculated move.

Bang.

I fall again, back into the shadows. Picking myself up, I search for my attacker: a bag. One with a familiar, slightly musty scent—treated camel hide. Its color, rich and dark. It has been out *there,* where the sun shines.

This can only mean one thing, one *dangerous* thing for You and me. A thing that could ruin this pivotal moment in the making of *our* story.

I peek out. I am right. It *is* him. The Scholar. He who kneels, with his back to me as he faces the East. Rising upon his knees, he bows once more, uttering words that thankfully escape my hearing. He remains in prostration.

An involuntary whimper escapes me.

Another whimper. This one, voluntary. It starts with a *hum*. Now, a sob.

He whispers something. I am thrown back into my hole. Fear does not work on him. Desire might. I retreat further into my hole; its echo will amplify my sounds. *Man was surely made weak.*[2] I begin with a soft *hum*, then release my threads.

My whispers intertwine in a seductive dance, weaving promises of luxury, women, more women—whatever else has worked on his people: jewels, power, euphoria, even numbing. Especially numbing. All of it, blown into these threads.

I throw them to him. Wait for him to lose control. Wait for him to come to me.

Wait ... and wait. Why is he taking so long?

Still in prostration. As he rises, he mouths a few more words and then turns his head: first, to the right, then to the left. I almost forgot a crucial detail—my voice holds no power over him.

"You have returned," I say, concealing my annoyance.

"You have remained," the Scholar replies, turning my direction as he puts his hand on something behind him. A panting dog emerges; its piercing amber eyes set beneath wide, round ears. Its mottled coat, a mix of white, brown, black, and gold, marks it as a desert hound. The creature's powerful chest and broad paws hint at undeniable stamina.

I will remain hidden here, in my Ghar.

Rising, the Scholar brushes dust off a patched shirt, smoothing it over his knees.

"I never expected to witness this," I say.

He remains silent, his mouth moving with even more words of worship and praise after prayer.

I add, "You, blind. The man of insight, *the Scholar,* with no eyes."

I want to creep closer to confirm my observation, but the hound stands in front of him and growls.

I let my voice surround him. "Did grief rob you of vision?"

His gaze lowers, eyelashes brushing against flushed cheeks as he stops his words of worship altogether. Good. A small bead of sweat rolls down his chin, dropping onto his already moist clothes. Somehow, he still looks clean, untainted by a world of dirt. The off-white of his clothes is the same tone as his skin, an impeccable color, even with the different shades of it sewn together to keep his garment whole.

"Was it the sorrow of your people's downfall, or perhaps …" My voice creeps closer to his face, and even the hound is unsure where to focus its attention. "*Her.*"

The hound barks. The Scholar placates it with a hand on its head, silencing the sudden outburst. Leaning heavily on his stick, he sways slightly, a squint crossing his features. But I am not fooled by this display, I know he is not weak, even as a blind man.

I sneer. "You have grown old."

His shoulder-length beard is streaked with grey. Face etched with lines fanning out from his eyes. Same lines as the day he left, as if a smile never touched his face again. More lines crease his tall forehead. Deep pockmarks shadow his eyes.

Grief cannot be erased. Only spaced. This is always beneficial to know. He is still so very raw.

Yet. *There* is *that* glow. The glow of the believer.

"Humans," I spit. "So emotional."

"Is that why you use your song to sway me?"

"You are swaying even without it," I retort.

"This is not a sway of influence, but of balance." He turns away. "Why are you still here?"

"I'm—"

"Are you still trying to get your father's approval?"

Heat courses through me as I snap back, "What do *you* know about Father?"

He raises an eyebrow and turns his face away. "I have met him."

"Did he …" I lean forward. I stop myself. Why do I care about Father?

"You are both alike."

I scoff. "There is none like me." I find myself leaning forward again and clear my throat. In a small voice, I say, "How are we alike?"

"Unoriginal. Even in his message to you—"

"He sent me—" I am aware, my voice has gone high-pitched. I lower it immediately. "A message?"

"Everything you both do is an attempt to copy the true Lord."

"I am a creator."

"Mimickers."

"I can do anything!" I declare.

"You cannot enter Heaven," he says.

What? How did he—

He adds, "'And indeed, We, have adorned the nearest Heaven with lamps, and We have made such lamps as missiles to drive away[3]—'"

A relieved sigh. I say, "Enlighten me. Tell me of this Lord you speak of, The ..." I try not to spit the word, "O ... Original. The Creator."

He waits.

I think.

From what he said about Heaven's lamps, this means he has no idea what I am planning. He lags so far behind. Which means he is *not* a threat.

But he may be a resource.

"Say 'He is One,[4]'" he mutters on.

"I am one," I retort.

"Your kind are legion," he says. "'The eternal refuge.[5]'"

"I offer a haven for the lost and broken."

"'He was not begotten, nor did He beget,[6] and there is none like Him.[7]'"

I soften my voice. "I admit defeat. You win."

He furrows his eyebrows, making him look older and weaker.

I continue, "I know I have been unfavorable to you and your people. But I seek something important for *all* of us."

"What do you seek?" His voice weary, perhaps a little bored.

"Redemption."

"Ever the deceiver." He sighs. "Arrogance has blinded you to reality, and your self-conceit allows no view beyond yourself. This chosen ignorance will be your downfall." He plants his staff firmly, leaning on it. "What is that pounding in this land?"

"Redemption not for me, fool. For *her*."

Just at that moment, *Your* wails erupt, full of agony, bouncing from every monument in this land. My own wails intertwine, mirroring Yours.

He grabs his bag from the opening of my Ghar and limps up the Silver Path, climbing the hill, towards Your cries.

When he sees You—'sees', a smile tugs on my lips—when he *confronts* You, the one who made him blind with grief, will his harshness precede his softness? Normally, I rely on that harshness, especially from the holy.

But not today.

He will add the finishing touches to Your preparation for tonight.

As he leaves, I lean back into my Ghar. My wails now separate from Yours, morphing into laughter. I laugh, and I laugh.

PART 16

Traveler

ADAMAH

"**Y**ahya!" I cry out, the memory vivid, rips through me, a devastating blend of my happiest moment, and the utter desolation of Hell itself, the very place of total loss. Everything feels worse now, as if I have just lost my son again, simply from knowing he existed. The pain is sharp. Stinging.

I squeeze my eyes shut, remembering the tiny head of my son cocked towards my chest. Warmth everywhere. With a renewed surge, I push through the blinding white, emerging into the unknown.

The world shifts once more. A twitch in my body. A flicker, like a tiny spark, ignites somewhere deep inside me.

My hand moves, fingers curling and uncurling. It's a strange sensation, like a wave of *something* connecting to my fingertips. My eyes open. A flood of light crashes in, a blinding explosion that makes the spark inside me flare and jump.

My eyes close, seeking the comforting dark again. Better. The light, even for a moment, is too much.

The spark I am feeling is my mind. The waves are receptors of external sensation. Those waves are being carried to my mind.

How do I know all this?

Now, *voices*. All around me, chattering. With my eyes still closed, I follow the sound as it vibrates into my ears, creating another wave, which pulses to my mind, which tries to make meaning of the voices.

At the same time, I smell something. Another wave to my head: grit and fresh water … it's a damp, earthy smell, like moss and cool stone.

Something is different about me.

I am aware of what is *inside* me. A central point, located in my mind. My ears, my skin, my eyes, and every connection to the world outside are simply receivers of raw data. Messengers delivering a scroll of sensations. My mind unravels the scrolls, a meaning and reactor base.

It is like … there are threads, invisible threads, connecting everything to this base: the twitch in my hand, the light in my eyes, the sounds, the smells, the aches, the tingles—they are all pulling on these threads, which when shaken create those waves, sending signals along them, all converging on this … base.

This place, my mind, is where I become *me*.

That chattering again, like hundreds of voices all trying to speak all at once. A *buzzing* sound, a symphony of a high-pitched hum, like a thousand tiny cogs meshing, vibrating against my ears. It's just noise at first, a chaotic jumble.

I observe the waves being carried to my mind. Something starts to happen. It's like the *buzzing* separates and becomes organized, some of the sounds becoming clearer into *clicks* and *chirps*. Things begin to make sense.

I still don't know *what* the voices are saying, or even if it's words, but I do know this is a speech I am not familiar with. And it's loud. I react by pushing my hands to my ears. "Too loud!"

Instantly, the voices stop.

I wipe my eyes to find myself surrounded by the blinding light of hundreds of orbees.

"Too bright!"

Instantly, they dim their lights.

I look down and see my dress. A mix of my old dress and a new vine dress. The trousers are loose and flowy, gathered at the ankles, and they drape and flow like a long gown. The base of my dress is black, but the vines … they are not just *on* the dress, they *are* the foundation of the dress, weaving through the fabric like threads and then, swirling around me in a calm, almost meditative dance. And they are not wild like my other vine dress. They are a part of the dress, a part of me. They even form a draped veil over my head, but unlike before, they don't cover my scar.

A memory surges—another *metal* dress, just worn, flashes before me. Raw data. Not processed.

Now, a feeling. Fear.

A reaction: a held breath.

A question: am I safe? The air is not smoky. My dress is not heavy.

Meaning: yes. I am safe.

When I turn my head, the Girl comes into view. She is lying next to me on the edge of the bridge, eyes slightly open, but snoring.

For a fleeting instant, as I woke into this world, my disorientation allowed me to forget again. Now, the memories are flooding back. It's like a dam bursts. The Girl is a trigger, setting off a chain reaction. Seeing her is like a key unlocking a door deep inside another part of my mind. One that is connected to memory.

The images flash before my eyes, not just as flat pictures, but with a sense of depth and movement. Horrifying: *motionless bodies piled on one another, red and black.* The sounds echo in my ears: *screams and crackling and an almost popping sound as flesh touches fire.* Noises with the same sharp edge of terror. Smells, not just as faint whiffs, but with the same cloying intensity: *cinders and metal with an undercurrent of something nauseatingly sweet.*

I am not just remembering.

I am reliving the memory as if I am right there.

Again.

And again.

A wave of nausea crashes over me, a hot, twisting churn in my gut. My stomach clenches, a hard knot forming just below my ribs. Saliva floods my mouth. Throat tightens. Hard to swallow. Intense ache behind my eyes. Sharp and throbbing pain through my head. Skin feels clammy and cold. Mixed with heat rising to my face.

Another wave of nausea hits, stronger this time. My breath comes in short, ragged gasps. Head swims. The pressure in my stomach builds, a rising tide of sickness, the undigested rotten camel meat which I took to Hell with me, comes back up in a rush. It hits the ground with a wet *splat*, a mess of chunky, half-chewed material. The earth soaks it up rapidly, leaving just these … *globules* of …

"Eugh," I manage, just as the orbees zip in from behind me. Before I can even blink, they have absorbed every bit of the mess, like it never happened.

Something about how they clean makes me feel more guilty. I don't deserve this. I don't deserve their help. Who cleaned the mess I made? Who cleaned all those bodies away? Sama's body? *What have I done?*

A prickling sensation starts behind my eyelids, a burning tightness that makes it hard to blink. My throat feels thick and constricted, like I've swallowed a lump of cotton. My chest tightens, a dull ache spreading across my ribs. The Girl blurs slightly, the edges of her thick eyebrow and long forehead softening and wavering.

A single tear escapes, tracing a hot, wet path down my cheek. It feels oddly heavy, like a physical thing, leaving a cool trail in its wake. Another tear follows, then another, a steady stream now. My nose starts to run, and I sniffle involuntarily. My breath hitches, a small, shaky sob escaping my lips.

The memories trigger my emotions, and those emotions are now triggering physical responses, each one sending its own signal back to my mind, creating a feedback loop. A full-body response to the horror.

To my part in the horror.

My shoulders tremble, a subtle vibration that spreads through my whole body. The tears keep coming, washing over my face in silent waves. It feels like something inside me is breaking. My face feels puffy and hot, and my eyes sting. Each tear that falls seems to carry a piece of the weight I've been carrying, a small, fleeting release.

I deserve the Hell I have seen.

I bury my face in the sleeping girl's chest, sobbing.

After some time, a smell wafts by. It's a mix of a warm, resinous spice, a subtle sweetness, and a hint of bright citrus, like a squeezed lemon peel. Frankincense.

Then a voice, gravelly and weathered, like the stones of an ancient riverbed, speaks. The voice itself seems to resonate not just in my ears, but in my chest too, a low rumble that vibrates against my ribs. In just a part of a second, I observe the sound vibrate in the air, reaching my ears as a physical pressure. The tiny bones inside my ears register the vibrations, a delicate dance that swings to my mind, which translates the sound waves into something I can understand.

The speaker's words are: "Peace be upon you."

My focus narrows on the speaker, the world around me fading into the background. I do not need to look at his face to know who he is; I know his voice better than anyone. Even though it's hoarser now, it still has that resonant hum when he speaks, almost like he is reciting a poem.

I lower my eyes, focusing on his feet, encased in worn leather sandals. The familiar stub of his toe, marked by a birthmark like a crimson stain, confirms my suspicions. He wiggles his toes. He does that when he's nervous.

As if sensing his unease, a dog comes out from behind him, using its powerful body to guard him. The dog is a magnificent creature, its coat a vibrant tapestry of swirling colors, like a sunset splashed across fur. Its eyes, never leaving mine, look up at me, studying for any sign of threat.

Slowly, I reach out my hand and touch its head, the fur soft and dense. The moment my fingers brush against it, a cascade of sensations floods my awareness.

My skin registers the subtle pressure of my touch, the gentle fur yielding beneath my fingers. A tingle runs up my arm. My heart beats a little faster, a quiet acknowledgement of the living being before me. The simple act of touching creates an immediate intimacy, a silent conversation between my body and its body under the fur, a connection that transcends words.

Yes, something is different. Here inside me. Not only can I sense what is happening in my mind, but I can also sense what my body is doing.

My mouth feels dry and stale, like I have been eating dust. There is a faint, metallic taste on my tongue. I can hear every one of my heartbeats thumping in my ear, a dull echo in the hollow spaces of my skull. My heart hammers, a frantic one hundred and ten beats per minute, and my breathing, though controlled, is a steady fifteen breaths per minute. I can feel the air moving in and out of my lungs, a cool rush with each inhale, a warm sigh with each exhale.

Something else has changed.

Before, when something touched me like the Black Assad, I felt a surge of energy, almost as if I was absorbing its natural essence, becoming one with it. Now, when I touch this dog, the connection is different.

I still feel its nature, its essence, but the transformation is gone. No overpowering *WHOOSH*. I simply feel it, deeply, but I do not become it. Instead, I observe almost diagnostically how my body reacts to it.

I have felt the power of Earth and the sun upon me. I have become a part of their nature, and yet, all that, as magnificent as it is, is but a spark of dust compared to the universe *inside* me.

Parts and systems, so intricate and complex—terrifying because there is so much that can go wrong—yet, profound, because it functions impeccably. I have searched for who I am since I first found myself outside the Great Wall. Now I think I understand.

I am this being, meticulously formed. This body, this … me … is not just a vessel. It is more. I am more. I am a universe.

All this new knowing—with what is happening *in* my mind, *in* my body, and *to* my body—is tiring. An awareness on top of an awareness.

Still, with all this awareness, I feel incomplete. Like the value of my being isn't based on what I *am*, but on what I have *done* with it. And I have done so much, too much. I have—

The thought hangs there, unfinished. The weight of it, the *doing*, is painful. It's like those threads are now carrying not just sensations, but *judgments*, heavy, suffocating. A part of my mind is trying to escape those judgements. It's reaching for something, *anything*, to distract itself from my uncomfortable guilt.

My mind is trying to reroute, to find a different pathway, a different wave—anything to avoid confronting the full weight of those memories, those actions.

I touch the dog again, a distraction I am now fully aware of, which I embrace. Its origin is grasslands, someone it loved died protecting it, its only purpose now is to protect its master. Love, respect, reverence. Social. Cooperative. Hunter.

"Predator," I whisper.

Its master says, "His name is Rafiq." Rafiq bows before his master and rests his head on the master's still-wiggling feet. The master continues, "He *is* a predator. He is one of the few remaining of his kind. He had a family, but when I went to the den, the rest of his brothers and sisters were gone. Someone took them."

Another nervous tick he has, along with his toe wiggling, he gives too much unnecessary information.

Rafiq raises his head.

"Who took them?" I ask.

He shrugs. "His mother ... something happened to her."

I nod and say, "His mother died protecting him."

He tilts his head curiously towards me. "Yes."

"Not like ours," I add. Our mother. I remember nothing of her, except her absence. "What made him betray his predatory nature?"

"Nature does not betray you; it is *we* who betray *it*," he says. "A painted dog's nature is to be with its pack, to hunt, to grow its dynasty, but when it cannot do that, it clings to what is left. To protect. To be loyal. He has done that well."

"What is *our* nature?"

"The nature of our soul is the basis of right and wrong. Morality. Compassion. Justice. The belief in something greater than us."

"What is its purpose?" I ask.

"To guide us to live ours."

"Why is it so unclear?"

"Because of our blinders."

"What are these ... blinders?" I look to his face, but it is still turned away, "Elias ..." My voice breaks.

The sight of him, the memories brought with his presence—it triggers a wave of warmth, a yearning for comfort. It's like a pull on those threads, a connection to a positive memory, a feeling of safety. My body responds instinctively—the impulse to hug him, a physical manifestation of that emotional pull.

Something blacks that urge to connect. Shame. A cold wave, a tightening in my chest, a sinking feeling in my gut. It's like those threads are suddenly carrying a different kind of signal, one of guilt, of self-disgust. The memory of what I've done to him resurfaces, not just as a thought, but as a physical weight, pressing down on me, making me shrink back.

This shame severs those positive threads. My body's reaction to the shame is more compelling than the urge to connect. I lower my face, unable to meet his gaze.

Rafiq sniffs my feet.

"Peace, peace," My brother responds to me, leaning on his stick. "Blinders are things which stop us from seeing clearly."

His once youthful face now bears the marks of time, weathered and lined. His ringleted hair, still reaching past his nape, is now tied back, with speckles of grey throughout. He feels his way around and sits on the ground in front of me, stretching his feet before him so they touch the running Zam. His face glows from the dim lights of the orbees which are hovering behind me.

His eyes are vacant, unseeing, yet still turned towards me.

"You are blessed to be in the dark," I say.

"Why?" he asks.

"Light can be a blinder, too." The words feel brittle when I say them.

"Only if you can't see the shadows." He gives a small smile, a dimple on each cheek, just about perceivable under his thick beard hair.

I think back to the hostile sun above Hadeeya. "Actually—"

He interrupts, "What light did you see?"

"One that burns," I whisper sharply. "I have seen Hell."

"Did you see its gates?" he presses.

"Yes."

"Did you enter them?"

I gulp away the lump in my throat. "No."

Rafiq is in front of us, leaning his head on the bank of the Zam, the water wetting his pointed snout.

Elias wears a round top hat, a thing that is not familiar to our people as a traditional dress. He removes it, revealing more lines on his high forehead. In the center, a darker shade marks a spot.

"You came back here, didn't you?" I ask.

"How do you know?"

"Sama." Somehow, I manage to say her name without my throat closing. "The dog—Rafiq was with you."

He nods. "She told me what happened."

"What did she tell you that made you a blind man?" I lean forward.

"That …" He shakes his head. "Not everything."

My hands feel clammy. "Some things are better left unsaid."

"What happened when I left?" he asks, his voice softening.

I don't answer, focusing on the vine's gentle swaying motion.

"I have traveled so far seeking answers, to seek the truth, but I still …" He takes in a sharp breath, his grip on the stick tightening until his knuckles whiten. "I need to know."

The truth. A jagged thing. It cuts. It bleeds. I know. Not so long ago, on the Zam, I told the Girl, truth and lies, they both leave scars, they are both painful. Now, the knife of truth is like a weapon in my hand, which will hurt my brother. Because of what I did. There's no soft way to say it. No gentle lie. Just the raw, ugly truth.

"Please," he says. He looks away and wipes his cheek, the rough callus on his thumb leaving a red streak.

"When you left to find Yahya, the men changed," I say flatly.

"What made them change?"

"Something to do with the Voice. They changed after it came to me."

"Why did the Voice come to you?" Elias asks.

"Does it matter?" An irritation strings through my words, a tight, invisible pulling at the corners of my mouth, making my jaw clench. It's not just in my throat, this irritation; it's a knot in my stomach, a flutter in my chest, a prickle of heat creeping up my neck. My breath catches, a tiny gasp, and I feel the tension in my shoulders, a subtle tightening that makes my whole body feel rigid.

After everything that has happened, the killings, the memory of my son, the last thing I want to think about is the Voice. I no longer want to fight it. Vengeance has only caused more pain.

The irritation is replaced by that feeling of cold shame again. A sinking feeling in the pit of my stomach, like a stone dropping into still water, the ripples spreading outwards. Chest tightens. Harder to breathe. Shoulders slump forward. Become less noticeable. Blood rushes to my face. Heat rising in my cheeks.

My gaze drops, and I find myself picking at a loose vine thread on my sleeve.

Here I am facing the one who I have wronged gravely. The one who is now blind because of me. The least I can do is answer his questions.

"The Voice made a window," I say.

Elias turns to face me.

I continue, "A window to the Surface." The image is fragmented, but what is clear is the window, its frosted glass at the top of the Main Hall in the Deep.

"We saw the Chosen through it." Beautiful, floating figures that glided on top of the glass.

"Did she see them too?" he asks quietly.

Ruqaya. My sister-in-law. Elias's wife. Careless. Naïve. Unruly. Reckless. The kindest person I knew. My best friend. Her laugh is still ringing through my ears, a snorted shriek.

"Once," I say.

"Just once?"

"She was throwing up most of the time because—" I pause, feeling the weight of his anticipation.

"Say it," he urges, holding his breath.

I clench my jaw and then speak quickly, "Your baby."

He breathes shakily. He already knew she was pregnant, but hearing it still hurts. His stick falls from his hand with a clatter. Rafiq whines and stands. Elias puts his hand on the dog's head, stopping its cry. With shaky hands, I put the stick back in his.

My hand brushes against him. A familiar warmth radiates from his skin, a comforting heat that I have known since childhood. It's a simple, almost unconscious contact, yet my body registers it instantly: traveler. Seeker. Holy. Knowledge. Grief. Pain. Great pain.

If I tell him what I did, I'm afraid it will break him completely.

I clear my throat. "Elias?"

He wipes his face, composing himself with visible effort. "Go on," he urges, nodding quickly, his voice barely steady.

"From the time we woke up to the time we went to sleep, we would stare through the window. We started to emulate the Chosen. Our clothes mirrored theirs, our shoes tapped loudly like theirs. We even used the soot from our torches to make smudges on our eyes," I recount. "Such influence on us."

"Our nature is to attach," he explains, "without it, we are lost."

"Like a child to its mother."

"Except as the children of the Deep, we lost our mothers and fathers."

"Abandonment is the biggest blinder," I say, remembering Hell.

The vines are no longer swaying but rocking from side to side.

"Abandonment," he agrees, his voice solemn. "It was worse for you."

"My pain——" I begin, but my throat feels tight.

Another image surfaces, one I wish had remained buried. It is what happened when we did have parents. Who they allowed into my life. An evil man, his face exposed by the light. He hurt me. On so many nights. I was just a girl.

The memory hits me like a physical blow, even though it's just a picture in my mind. Breath catches in my throat. Sharp, ragged gasp. Heart punches my ribs. Frantic. Stomach clenches. Nausea twisting. Cold. Clammy. Hot.

I become detached from the image, like I am watching what he did to someone else. My hands tremble slightly, and I clench them into fists. Nails dig into my palms.

My mind pushes away the image. Disconnects it from me. Almost numb. I clear my throat. "My pain made me more open to ..."

"Attachment to the Voice."

I *can't* escape the Voice. I let out a long breath. Giving in, I say, "How?"

"It distracted you from your pain."

"Is that so bad?" I ask.

"Whether you acknowledge your pain or not, it's still there. When you hide from it, all you are doing is giving it to another to hold it for you."

"The Voice."

"Through your pain, it controls you."

"I don't want to feel pain."

Still, even after seeing Hell, and after all the pain I have caused, I don't want to feel pain.

"Pain is telling you there is something to feel," he says, his voice heavy.

I look at his face. I never thought that a blind man could hold such profound sadness in his eyes.

His head hangs low. "What happened after our people attached to the Surface?"

"I wanted to leave to find Yahya and you. It had been months. But they wouldn't let me leave unless——"

"Who would stop a queen from leaving?"

Sama told him more than I thought.

"This was before I became a queen. It was before I——" Before I killed ninety-nine people. "The men stopped——"

"Protected."

"They didn't protect!"

Elias flinches. "I'm sorry."

I nod, even though he can't see me. Even though I am not sure why he is saying sorry. He wasn't anything like the others. He protected the Deep. When he was there, there was peace. The men loved him. Followed him.

"I told you, Elias, they changed when you left. They became more obsessed with the window, making our women look like the Chosen. The children were ignored, left in a room all day while we stared through that window."

I shake my head, trying to dispel the image of what *I* had become.

I continue, "When AmaNoor came,"—AmaNoor, the holy woman, her face, ancient, like the old woman in my dream, except her features were rougher, with a wider nose and eyes which had folded in on themselves—"with Yahya and you, after you fell into that deep sleep, she stayed with the children teaching them things and watching over them. They weren't … neglected like before when you were in prison."

"Ruqaya?" His voice sounds thick when he says her name.

"She stayed with the children too," I say, clearing my throat. "In that deep sleep, you would speak. Ruqaya said you told her that no matter what, she *must* stay with the children. When you woke, you didn't remember saying that. You had forgotten so much. AmaNoor warned you that you would forget everything if you didn't go back. What did she mean by going 'back'?"

He doesn't answer straight away. In his silence, Ruqaya's face flashes, full of sadness, when he left. He didn't recognize her. He didn't say goodbye.

Finally, he says, "It doesn't matter." In a steady voice, he asks, "What happened *before* AmaNoor, Yahya, and me returned?"

"The men finally allowed me to go to the Surface, on one condition: I had to bring back an angel. That's what they called the Chosen. I went to the Surface, but I didn't look for one. I looked for you and Yahya. I found an entrance to the big building, but it was guarded by an *angel*." I try not to scoff when I say this. That guard was the furthest thing from an angel that could exist.

I clear my throat again. "She had a long flowing dress that shimmered under the light of the full moon. Her hair was thick and wavy. Shiny too. At first, I wanted to touch it. I was even tempted to do what the men asked of me: to capture her. Then she turned towards me. Her face looked …"

"Sick," Elias says.

"Sick," I repeat. "Unnatural. Completely different to how they looked through the window. Her hair felt like grass, artificial. When she blinked, her eyelashes were half attached. And the smile she gave me … I never thought white could be so unsettling. And the smell of her breath … rotten from a place beyond her throat. I ran past her, and she laughed. Mocking me and—" I pause, lost in thought.

"What?"

"Why did I run?" I try to think of why I didn't fight her, but the memory is blank. I remember one more thing related to that memory. "It's like she *knew* me. Like there was a private joke …" I bang my fist on the ground, the dust shooting up. Rafiq shifts closer to Elias. "There's more to this memory. I can't see it."

"That was the night you found us," he recalls.

"You know what happened after," I say quickly, glad to move away from that woman's face. "We fought the Surface to free you—"

"You fought them?"

"And then …"

An image flashes: a whirlwind of clashing swords, blood and screams. I inhale sharply. It was them: the Surface. They were the ones Sama told me about, the ones I …

"I slaughtered them," I choke out, the words raw in my throat. "Forty-one of them."

And forty-nine men of the Deep. I counted every single body before I torched them. Everyone I killed, from the Surface *and* the Deep, was a threat. They tried to hurt us—the women, our children—even though we outnumbered them. Two hundred and four women. Twenty-one children, including Yahya. The children … something about the Deep made it hard to have more. The air was broken. Even when our children *were* born, they died so quickly. Until Yahya.

But something doesn't fit. Sama said I killed *ninety-nine*. Who were the other nine? Were they a threat, too? Why can't I *see* them?

What happened to all the women and children of the Deep? They were there, during the … killing of the Chosen and the men. They were there … until my last memory. The cries of the little ones … so loud. I can still hear them. I clamp my hands over my ears as if their voices are right here, right now.

My heart hammers against my ribs, a frantic rhythm of panic and regret. A cold sweat breaks out on my skin, making my palms clammy. The memory plays out behind my eyelids, vivid and horrifying. This time, I don't try and push it away. I watch. I deserve to watch.

"No, don't! Please, don't!" The child's voice rings in my ears, high-pitched and desperate.

I give the order. I nod to Sama. Sama turns, her face grim, but she doesn't look at me. She looks at the line of children next to me.

"Don't look, Sumayya," she says.

The children's faces. Wide-eyed and terrified.

"Look at me," I tell them.

The children obey. They look at me with a look a child should not have. There is a dripping sound as liquid trickles down the leg of one young boy; he is shaking so much.

Now Sama walks back to me and throws the knife at my feet. She says, "Don't ever ask me to do anything again."

Where Sama walked from, the mother is left behind, clutching the blood-tainted blanket. Her screams are the last thing I hear. Shrieks.

The memory loops, but it doesn't continue to the part after. What happened *after*? Why did the Great Wall tell me the child didn't die? *Did* it tell me that? Or was I so desperate for a lie that I changed the truth?

My arms … they are tingling.

That familiar sensation of numbness returning …

"Elias," I rasp, my voice tight, "I didn't just kill them, I also ordered the killing of …"

My fingers clench and unclench. How am I able to know what is happening in my body, and yet, unable to control it? Why are the vines no longer helping me? It's as if they have taken a step back, now allowing me to *feel*. I don't want to feel.

Now, silence. Silence in me. Like a flood hidden behind a veil I can't see beyond. Presses down. Hard to breathe. Heart slows. Chest tightens. Dull pressure. Sluggish. Weak. Limbs heavy. Like lead. Body locks. Resists me. Like ice. Joints stiff. Can't feel the air on my skin. Can't feel the ground under my feet. Can't feel the weight of my clothes. All distant. Thoughts slow … slowing.

One thought persists: *What … have … I … done?*

If I could sob, I would. For him, my brother, Elias. For what I have taken from him.

My brother's trust. His future, taken by … me.

The mother of the baby was Ruqaya. The baby in the bloody white blanket was my brother's child.

PART 17

The Pilgrimage

ME

The Cast stands before me. Rows of them encircling the building of Shahwah. Some are ballooning, their bodies distended like overripe melons, barely able to support their weight.

They wobble, these monstrous forms, threatening to topple like crumbling towers. Others, skeletal things. All their eyes, even through the Apex, are glazed, lost in their ecstatic trance.

"Snout," I rasp.

Snout turns, his body jerking spasmodically. He fumbles with his mask, a contraption of metal and bone. The mask bears an eye symbol scribbled in the center; its surface reflects the crimson glow of two lenses just above it. From that blue eye, a thread—like my own—extends to anchor itself to a spot on the ground behind him, joining the other threads from the Cast's Apex.

Finally, he removes his Apex, revealing a face contorted in a mask of its own—one ravaged by delirium, eyes bloodshot and bulging. He stands before me, head bowed, the Apex dangling limply from his hand, his snout twitching.

The others continue their ritual, oblivious to him, their chanting a monotonous wordless drone mixed with sighs and hums.

"Yes?" Snout whimpers, his finger outlining the shape of the blue eye on his Apex.

"Am I ... unoriginal?" I ask.

"My opinion irrevocably declares that you are not unoriginal," he says, his voice a nasal whine.

Unhelpful. I need more.

"Some people think I am," I press.

"Well, you are not!" he declares, the word a triumphant bark. He begins to pull the Apex back on, the two crimson lenses gleaming.

"Wait!" I hate that I must do this. That I *need* this. "Tell me why I am not unoriginal."

He pauses, the Apex hovering before his face. "Well, who else," he croaks, "could have conceived of such a brilliant plan?"

"Yes," I lean forward. "Go on."

He shifts, his feet facing the other Cast members. "You captured the Queen of the orbees, the most powerful being in Jinnah." He peers at me through a pair of lensless spectacles, the rims shaped like inverted half-moons. "After you, of course."

"Of course." *Fool.*

"And you tied all our voices to her."

"I did, didn't I?"

"Oh yes, you did." Snout gives an indulgent smile with a slight shrug of his shoulders.

He gazes longingly at the rest of the Cast, still tracing the shape of the blue eye on his Apex, his finger shaking from the high.

The eyes of the Cast, magnified by the grotesque masks, pulse with a feverish intensity, each with two tiny beacons of desire. The lenses of Snout's Apex are a malevolent red that speaks of arrogance, of a thirst for power that knows no bounds. Others shimmer with a kaleidoscope of hues: envy, a sickly green, lust, a throbbing gold, purples, oranges, and so on.

But one mask stands out, a stark contrast against the riot of color. It is silver, an icy, metallic sheen that pulses with an eerie luminescence. This belongs to Scar.

His desire, unlike the predictable cravings of the others—women, men, wealth, power—is something more primal, more terrifying. Scar desires only one thing: to live. Which means not to die. To cheat death, to defy the inevitable decay that claims all. To achieve immortality. Like me.

This desperate clinging to life is a crucial ingredient for all the rituals. It is this desire that fuels the Queen of the orbees' purpose tonight.

I nod to Snout, dismissing him. He returns to the ranks, frantically adjusting his Apex, desperate to recapture the lost ecstasy, to feed the insatiable void within.

I retreat to my Ghar and stare out at the swirling smoke in the empty place before Jinnah. So empty.

I am not unoriginal. A lie!

The smoke in the sky thickens, a greasy, suffocating blanket. But the matter falling from the sky ... which remains steady, is unnerving.

I don't know what it is. *Where* is the Dark Fall from? One small mercy: it is dark. And it sticks. Clings to everything it touches, shrouding it, making it ... unrecognizable.

I focus on the rhythmic chant of the Cast. As each offers their desires to their unseen voices, the Queen's power through her rage grows. The voices facilitate this rage. They changed something in the Queen of the orbees; she can now roar, a sound that should have been impossible for an orbee. She was—is—unique ... because of me. *I* made her evolve.

All those who must rise must change. Evolve.

The Criterion

ADAMAH

"**R**emember what we used to do as children?" Elias's voice takes a familiar edge of responsibility, which I haven't heard in years.

"I ordered …" I begin.

He moves closer. "It's the only thing I remember from Mama: 'I will stay here until the pain goes away.'" He takes my hand. "'I will live here,'"

A warm tear rolls down my cheek. "So the rhythm one day will change."

I learnt the song from him. He learnt it from our mother. She sang it with the elders. They sang it with theirs.

I sit upright. Numbness seeping away. Fog lifting. Tingling sensation. Faint at first, but more intense. All over. Fingers and toes twitch. Muscles loosen. Body released. Deeper breaths. Pressure eased on my chest. Heartbeat stronger. The world sharpens. Sounds unmuted. The dress feels light against my skin.

The hollowness inside me begins to fill, not with joy or warmth, but with a return to feeling, a reawakening of my senses. The detachment fades, and I am once again present in my body, grounded in the here and now.

"Was I always numb?" I ask my brother.

"You were before Yahya came into your life," Elias says. "Pain has consequences." He passes his fingers in front of his eyes. "Some we can see and some we can't, but pain itself isn't bad, not if you choose to do good with it. And I ... should have done more."

"Elias,"

"You were right. Abandonment is the biggest blinder. I was no better than the elders."

"You didn't abandon——"

"I abandoned you all!" he cries, in a voice thick with anguish. "I could have stayed after I brought your boy back, but I left. I let my pregnant wife face a tyrant alone."

How do I tell him who the tyrant was?

"I left AmaNoor, a frail woman, to protect Ruqaya while I went in search of ..." His words trail off, his hands clenched on the ground.

"You were looking for what you had forgotten. For the truth."

As I say these words, there is a synchronicity. I, too, came here searching for truth. Perhaps, I am more like my brother than I think.

He shakes his head. "I should have stayed." His eyes narrow. "Everyone is gone."

Tears well up in my eyes as I say, "They're all gone because of me."

He raises his head towards me.

I force the words out, "*I* was the tyrant."

"No." He shakes his head.

"Yes. Even Jinnah is crumbling because of me. Because of my rage."

"Jinnah?"

This is not the direction I want to go. I want, no, I *need* to tell him what I did to him. But then, a wave of distraction floods my mind, creating a new pathway for me to take. I embrace it, the words tumbling out.

"It makes sense why Earth turns its face from the sun every day. It would rather be in darkness than in that painful light."

Elias raises his eyebrows, but he doesn't interrupt me.

I continue, "The sun isn't what you think it is. It's not a friend of Earth." I glance at the Girl, making a split-second decision: I won't involve her in my retelling of how I've hurt Jinnah. I won't taint her with my actions, not even in my words.

Elias looks confused as I turn back to him, "The reason everything is so hot outside of Jinnah is because Earth's layer of protection has weakened. It's become broken, and now Earth has become broken too."

Elias humors me. "Why isn't Jinnah hot … or broken?"

"It *is* broken, but not from overheating. Its brokenness comes from a spreading sickness that drains all color and life."

"Why is it different in Jinnah?"

"There is a being, the mother—the Queen of the orbees. She tried to fight the sun's overheating by creating a new layer on top of the world, an effort to balance everything out. Her goal was to gather all the creatures who'd survived the heat and place them safely in this new land."

"How did she protect this new land from the sun?"

"She used the orbee leaves to create a kind of barrier, which surrounded … which surrounds Hadeeya."

"Hadeeya," Elias repeats. "If she did this, why is there sickness in Jinnah too?"

"She didn't get to finish. She placed all the prey, mountains, a Steam River, and so many other things, but she didn't place one key player essential for world balance."

Elias places his hand over Rafiq. "Predator."

I nod more to myself. Even though he is darkness. Even though he can't see me. "The Voice took her. It has her locked under Shahwah. The smoke in the sky is her call for help to her orbees, but they don't understand because it isn't in the nature of an orbee—I believe—to see beyond smoke. I think her ability to create that smoke has to do with her evolving nature." I am aware that as I speak, I sound monotone, as if I need to say these words, so I don't have to say other, more painful ones. I continue, "The Voice and its allies—whatever or whoever they are—have something to do with it. It's using her, preparing her for something. Something that's happening very soon."

"Who are the Voice's allies?"

"I don't know, but the Queen is unable to get free because of them."

"Are they human?"

"Some, but not all."

"How do you know all this?"

"I can pick up on the Queen's nature ... and the nature of other things too."

"The vines ..." Elias says.

"Yes, how did you know?"

"I have come across these vines before in another land. A place called Asylum." Elias looks like he wants to say more, but he closes his mouth. He nods for me to continue.

"The Voice wants me to write something for it. It has been preparing me for a journey."

"Heaven," Elias whispers.

"Heaven?"

"Yes, when I mentioned Heaven, the Voice got nervous and tried to distract me from continuing." Elias shakes his head. "Why? Why does it want to go to Heaven *now*? What does it want you to write for it in there?" He then tilts his head slightly. "What is that pounding?"

"The Great Wall. It's connected to everything, but I don't know how. One thing I do know is that the Queen is suffering, and the world is suffering without her. Freeing her will bring back balance."

"Why would the Voice want to keep her there? What's it using her for?"

"Whatever it is, it's fueling her with rage." I take a long breath and let it out slowly. "The same rage I picked up in Thalj. Because of it, I caused Jinnah to break even more."

"Did you mean to?"

"Intention and consequence are different things, Elias. It doesn't matter if I didn't want to; I still caused the land to fracture."

"Intention is more powerful than consequence, Adamah."

His words offer no solace. They only make me feel worse for what I've done to him. It's true, I am a tyrant.

"Adamah." His tone is steady. He does that when he knows I'm trying to avoid something. "Why are you telling me all this?"

Now I must tell him, the part which is the most difficult. "If what you say is true about intention, then I am guilty."

"Guilty of what? If this is about the Chosen——"

"No, Elias." My tone silences him. I know exactly why I wanted his child to die: because he took mine. I wanted to punish my brother. That is the raw and ugly truth. "When you took Yahya, the second time you left, I——"

"The second time?" He shakes his head again. "I've never taken Yahya from you. I only searched for him when he left, so I could bring him back. I found him at——"

"You took him!"

His brow furrows, the lines in his face deepening. I touch his hand. He is telling the truth.

I tumble backward onto the bridge. Vines rub my arms, a rough jolt. I flinch, shoving them away.

Thump-thump—my heart hammers against my ribs, mirroring the thumping from the Great Wall. Rapid. Out of control. Air whooshes in and out of my lungs. The world tilts around me. Disoriented, I scramble back. Muscles coiled. Ready to run. Every sensation is amplified—the scratch of the vines, the uneven bridge, the ragged breath in my throat.

I am gasping, unable to form full sentences. "Everything I did ... all the people I killed ... what I did to Ruq——"

"Rage is not anger; it is the mutation of it. Suppression is when——"

"Elias!" I clench my jaw. Vision narrows. Focus on Elias. On his words. Mine are sharp and biting. "Stop doing that!"

"Doing what?" he asks, his voice now a whisper.

For a fleeting moment, I see the young boy he once was, lips pressed together, brow furrowed in concern. My anger dissolves, replaced by what is beneath it. Sadness. It washes over me. Cold. A hollow ache in the pit of my stomach. Chest tightens. Lump in my throat. Eyes burn. Heavy eyelids. Tired. I am so tired.

I gulp the lump away. "Now you are the one avoiding."

A shadow crosses his face.

"I don't understand," I say, searching the dusty ground as if the answers are there. "Where is he? Where is Yahya?"

When I say my son's name, I feel the words pulling me. Pulling me down. None of it mattered; there was no reason for what I did. My crime against my brother was even worse.

Elias turns to me. The wall he has built with his words is crumbling. He opens his mouth to speak, but clamps it shut. As if battling his own willful ignorance.

In an instant, his face hardens, a protective shield that makes him look so much older than he is. I know what it means. It is a look he has had since he was a boy. He chooses knowledge. Truth. Painful, raw, jagged truth.

"Sit," he says, crossing his legs.

I do the same, mirroring his posture. A movement, natural, one we have done so many times as children. I cross my legs. Subtle release of tension. Muscles, first tight, now relax slightly. Pressure in my lower back eases. Spine straightens. Weight settles more evenly.

Yet, the gravity of the moment hangs heavy in the air.

"Speak." He straightens his back, as if bracing for impact, his hand instinctively touching the sword which pokes out from his open bag.

Palms clammy. A loose bead of sweat trickles down my temple. My throat feels dry. Swallow to moisten. Body braced.

"You had a baby." My hands, numb and tingling, scrape against the ground. "I ..." I shudder as I stare at the sword, which he tightens in his grip. "The baby was in a white blanket, and Ruqaya was holding it. I ordered the ... I ..."

He nods, the color draining from his face. He *knows*.

Words fail me. So, I turn to the Tap. A language I created from silence for my people of the Deep. One that united the mute without words. A source of our shared messages. It now feels like an abyss ready to swallow my confession.

With a trembling finger, I tap his hand, feeling every dread, shock, anger, and grief emanating from him:

I ordered the killing of your baby.

His eyes become wide and unblinking. Yes, he knew. Even if for just a few moments, he knew. That is why he was talking about anger in the way he was. He didn't want to face the truth, even if for just a few meager seconds of ignorance.

Secrets are like that. I come from a nation of secrets. My people *were* a secret. Seeds of injustice under the guise of pledges from people claiming to want to help us, whilst all the while burying us deeper and deeper. The secrets we keep become easy to shoo away when in the pacification of distraction.

But they remain like shrouds looming upon every escaping thought. Thriving in the dark. Poking at everything we do, so we will do anything to run from them. Every act, a coping. A hiding. Every word, a dissociation, just so the secret remains buried inside us, until it decays us slowly and fully. It is not the secrets that are bad. It is the truth they carry that we cannot face about ourselves.

I wonder if a part of my brother knew what happened all those years ago. I wonder if, in preparation to face me again, he chose to go blind so the truth—the secret I kept about what I did to his child and his wife—could remain in the dark.

So, he could turn his face away from an enemy—me—who cannot help but destroy everything I touch.

Elias begins to shake. His body shakes and shakes. Although the tremors slowly fade, they leave behind a slumped figure, the weight of the revelation etched in every line of his face.

Something catches my eye, there, standing amid the Garden of Fire. It stares at me. A Ram. Breath hitches in throat. Sharp. Painful gasp. Stomach clenches. Everything twisting. Eyes widen. Pupils bigger. Bumps raised down my back. Hands shake. Blood gushes from my face. Cold face.

It is as if time has stopped, the world around me fading into a blur as my focus narrows on the creature in the Garden of Fire, amidst the red flowers. The curve of its horns, the thick wool of its coat, the steady, unwavering gaze of its eyes … it stares back at me. I blink. It is gone.

The pain of this, the hardship of this situation, must be making me lose my mind. Yet … I am sure I saw it. Why did I react like that? Even if it was there, it's just a Ram.

I gulp the lump away in my throat and place my brother's sword firmly in his hands, and push it to my throat.

"Take your justice, brother. I told you, I deserve the Hell I have seen."

PART 19

Counsel

ME

I scoff as Snout joins in with the procession. Poor fool, he knows nothing—apart from me being original, of course. Other than that, like the rest of the Cast, he is oblivious to his impending doom. Tonight, on the Night of Decree, he and the others won't join me on my pilgrimage to Heaven. They won't witness the changing of The Book of Decree. They won't partake in my—*our*—ascension.

The voices of the Cast will, however, join us. And those voices will require new vessels. After all, that is the only way we have been able to survive for so long—through attaching to the hollow part where fear and *This* brew on top of sadness. We, unlike everyone else, do not abandon our prey. Abandonment is the cause of that sadness. We rely on our attachment, abandoning themselves. For me, that's *You*. That is the only way we can succeed in my version of eternal life.

The Cast have abandoned themselves constantly and willingly. It has been wonderful. Entertaining. But they are too weak to do a crucial task when I get to Heaven's gates and face those looming angels. I do not need planks of wood or heavy machinery. I need an *army*.

That is why I ordered the Great Wall.

ADAMAH

The blade twists in his grip, wavering for an instant before it arcs away from my throat. A metallic clang echoes as it sinks into the ground, the jolt traveling up his arm. His face is contorted in a grimace. His body heaves, shuddering, sweat slicking his skin like a sheen of oil. *In, out,* his breath rasps, each inhale a desperate gasp for air.

The world hangs suspended, its song a frantic mix: the hammering *thuds* from the Great Wall that surround us and Rafiq's nonstop barking.

Elias staggers back, breaths raspy and heavy like bellows.

"Read it!" His voice booms.

Keeping my gaze locked on him, I reach out, fingers brushing the inscription on the blade. The cold metal sends a shiver down my arm.

"'By Time.[8] Verily, humanity is at loss,'" I say softly. "'Except those who believe and do righteous deeds and advise others to truth and patience.[10]'"

With a trembling hand, I press the hilt of the sword into his palm. "There is no redemption for the sinner."

The knife trembles in his grasp. Tears track down his weathered cheek, making his beard glisten, the silver hairs like small swords. His tears mirror my own. I brush mine away quickly, but he doesn't brush away his, as if his hand lacks the strength or the will.

"All this time," Elias rasps, his voice thick with sorrow. "These eyes have yearned to see my wife and my child. But now …" He trails off, turning his back to me, to my violent existence. "Now, I am grateful they don't allow me to see your face."

Our silent sobs mingle, echoing the cries we shared when our world fractured as children. His sobs are raw, torn in ragged gasps. Shaking. Breathless. *Grief.*

Mine, laced with the bitter tang of *shame.* Burning on my chest. Hard to breathe, hard to *be.*

Finally, he speaks in a rough and low voice. "I won't kill you."

"Why?" I ask.

"It is incomplete."

"What is?"

"There is no redemption for the sinner … unless they choose it." He doesn't turn towards me, his words measured as he speaks over his shoulder. "You didn't enter the gates."

"Gates?"

"Of Hell." His voice cracks with an emotion I can't place.

"Hell," I repeat. I swallow down the lump in my throat. "I have already seen my place in Hell. There is no choice for me."

"Heaven, too, has a place for … all of us." His voice is devoid of emotion. "*Hayaa.*"

The word is in the language of the elders. I translate it, "Modesty?"

"The presence of it allows us to choose good. You have a choice. We all do."

"What has modesty got to do with choice?" I grasp at any chance to talk to him, even though his face is still turned away from me. It is as if he *must* talk to me. I don't care, I'll take whatever connection I can still have with him, even if it's just out of obligation from him.

"Everything." He moves a few steps away from me, towards the Garden of Fire.

"Isn't modesty to do with clothing? Sounds primitive." I say, giving him some space as I shuffle back on the bridge.

"The *lack* of clothing is primitive. Even Earth wears a suit of armor."

"What has Earth got to do with choice and modesty?"

"Our origin *is* Earth, we are made of its dust, and we will return to it once we die." His voice breaks as he says the last word. "Clothing is a part of *Hayaa*, but it is not all of it. *Hayaa* is your moral guide."

"Then I don't have strong *Hayaa*, not with what I—"

He interrupts. "Everyone has it. It's only a matter of violating it. When you do that, shame follows."

Now that I'm more aware of how things work inside me, how emotions affect me, I realize shame has been a dark cloud I've been trying to escape. I don't want to look beyond that cloud. Not now. Not ever? But the chilling truth is that shame has morphed into fear, and that fear has driven my actions. Everything has been a coping mechanism to escape that ... again, my thoughts are veering down a painful path, a circuit I can't face.

I quickly redirect them. "You speak of shame as if it's a good thing."

"Healthy shame is," he says. "But the kind *you* feel..."

He has a strange way of doing that, my brother. The way he understands what I'm really asking. Even when he hates me.

He continues, "That is Mutated Shame, born from your pain. Instead of helping you to reflect and change your wrongs like healthy shame should, it leads you to hate yourself so much, you either destroy yourself or destroy anyone who reminds you of yourself."

This is getting too deep. And I don't want to talk about my pain. "Morality. Is that what sets us apart from everything—the sun, the animals, and the plants?"

"We are meant to do more than *survive*. Mutated Shame keeps us *surviving*. Coping. It is a war inside. On one side, the army of our higher purpose fights to show us the truth beyond our pain. Another side, the army of survival, fights to hide from our pain and with it, hide from the truth and ultimately from our true selves."

A battle between being whole and being in parts.

Still, I don't want to talk about my pain.

I'm becoming quite adept at veering away from this feeling hidden beneath my Mutated Shame. I redirect the conversation, grasping a new pathway that my mind opens for me. "Where is this morality?"

I mentally scan my body, trying to locate it. A subtle twitch near my heart, but not the physical heart that pumps blood. It's more … a sense of *something* there.

"It is *in* our nature," he replies.

"You mean our physical needs?"

"Not that kind of nature. The nature of our morality is the nature of the soul."

"The soul?" I ask.

"The spirit which gives our human body life."

"Why can't I sense the nature of my soul?"

"It's hidden beneath the thing your anger is trying to escape."

Redirect. "So, morality is what differentiates us from animals? And it's within us?"

He doesn't answer.

I continue. "If I have this, why do I make so many bad choices?"

"Our moral nature is only a clue. It is not enough to tell us how to be truly good." He clears his throat and asks, "Why are you here?"

"Here?" I look around. The Girl is still sleeping, her mouth now open, with a sliver of drool on her cheeks.

"On Earth?" he presses.

I think back to Hadeeya. To how I'd discovered who I was, *am*— Adamah—and where I came from: the Deep. Back then, I hadn't known *why* I was here, or what my purpose was, beyond doing something good. I assumed that good was saving Jinnah.

I answer, "To do good?"

"How do you know what good is?"

"Doesn't our nature—our *Hayaa*—tell us?"

"The blinders I talked about earlier make it unclear, and you, Adamah, have many."

I have inched closer to him during our conversation. He is just a handspan away from me. I reach out with a tentative hand and place it on his, only to meet the sting of his withdrawal as he jerks his hand away.

With his back still turned, he asks, "What do you seek?"

I try not to show the disappointment in my voice. "The truth."

"Have you found it?" Elias asks.

"I found a good one. I didn't let myself have the bad one."

"Why?"

"I wanted peace," I admit.

"Yet, your actions and your deeds remain unchanged."

"I am bad," I say.

"You found the truth of who you are and *what* you did, but you did not find out why and what it means. *That* is your blinder."

"I did it all because I'm bad," I say again. "There is no other reason. Are you saying being bad is my blinder?"

He finally turns his unseeing eyes hard on me.

"No. That is lie you keep telling yourself. An easy answer. You know what you did, we both do." He pauses, a flicker of something, maybe pity, crossing his face. "It happened; you are indeed a killer." He pauses, the silence stretching out between us. "But your pain is your biggest blinder. Without facing it, you will never fully grasp the truth."

"What is the truth?"

"It is a truth that shows you *how* to be truly good. It adds to your inner nature, making the choices for good and bad clearer. We were made to be good. All creation was."

I think back to the conversation with the Girl in the Zam. "A universal truth."

He sighs, a sound of weary resignation. "A universal truth," he repeats. "Once you have faced your pain, you will be able to look beyond yourself. Only then will you see how your story fits into the larger one."

I think back to when I felt there had to be something more inside me. More than just reactions, more than the meanings I assign to them. More than this universe in me. Something that defines my value. A deeper layer, more profound than the world itself, both out there and in here.

"Where is this universal truth?" I ask.

Elias takes a deep breath. In a low melodic voice, he recites something, "'And We have sent down the Book in truth, and with the Truth it has come down. We have sent you, oh Prophet, only as a deliverer of good news and a warner.[11]'"

"What is it? What is the Truth?"

"The ultimate way to be good is to worship Allah. Every act, when done with this intention, is good."

"So, I just intend to do things to worship Allah? Then I'm good?"

"There is a way to be good, things we must do to remain upon the Truth, which if not attended to, will be forgotten."

When he uses phrases like 'if not attended to,' he has separated himself from his emotions. That's why he sounds so intellectual. So cold. Realizing he's blocked me from any true intimacy in our back and forth—even if it is his anger—I slump my shoulders. I mumble, "Forgetting isn't always a bad thing."

"Forgetting our sins does not fix anything," he snaps, in a burst of emotion.

I sit up, like a child who has been told off. Honestly, I'd expected it. I'd said that to provoke him. I wanted him to show some feeling other than icy resignation toward me. Anger means a part of him still cares what I have to say. He gathers himself, as if he gave in to something he didn't want to, and glances my way, his blind eyes full of irritation. The silence stretches between us.

He lets out a long breath and says, "Forgetting is not always good. Our people forgot the very purpose of our existence. That is why we forgot ourselves."

"AmaNoor didn't forget, did she?"

"No. That's why the Chosen put her in prison."

"And the other elders?" I ask. I want to know about our parents. There are still gaps in my memory, blocking my vision of them. There are also gaps blocking AmaNoor after a certain time from when she came to the Deep. What happened to her?

"They forgot," he says in his detached tone. "That's why it was so easy for them to abandon us, first when they were in the Deep with us, and then again when they left."

I don't want to talk about the *other* elders. About *him*. About what he did to me. I ask, "You said the Truth came down. Where did it come down from?"

"From Heaven. The Truth came as a final revelation. It is the unchanged word of Allah, delivered to all humanity by an angel through a man called Muhammed (peace be upon him). He was the seal of prophethood—the last in a line of messengers sent to our kind—all bearing the same message: calling to the Oneness of Allah and how to live our ultimate purpose, the one we forgot as a nation."

"You said our purpose is to worship Allah."

"Yes. Everything in creation was made to worship Allah, including what the Voice is. Allah is the only One worthy of worship. That revelation came to teach us how, first as a recitation, and then it was preserved in the form of a book. The way of peace—"

"The way of peace," I repeat, remembering the Girl's words from earlier.

"The way of peace: Islam, which means submission to the One worthy of worship. This way of peace was safeguarded in three ways: within its sacred text—the Book—in the collective body of the believers who live by its laws, and in the individual souls who absorb its truth to become its very embodiment. The ultimate embodiment of this way of peace was by the final prophet Muhammed (peace be upon him), who came to show us how to follow it, through how he lived his own life."

"Is that sacred text what AmaNoor sent you to search for when your memory was gone?"

"Yes. That text is the Book."

The dots are connecting. The Voice wants me to be good because it wants me to write something for it in Heaven. But the Book which was revealed with the universal Truth is already written, which means whatever the Voice wants me to write is different from that Book. Why does the Voice want a book at all? It wants the Girl's book. "The Voice has been searching for a book, could it be the same one?"

"There is only one book that exists today that will be of interest to the Voice."

Of interest.

He adds, "That Book has the power to make mountains crumble. If the Voice is trying to get into Heaven, it believes that Book will help somehow."

"Like a key?"

"I have a theory."

A theory. A tingle down my back.

Something about Elias having a theory makes me feel like I'm in his confidence again. As a child, I was the one he'd tell all his theories to: why our eyes look like they did (so we could see better in the dark), why some of us lost our voices when the elders left (because we were sad). Even though I know this isn't like back then—now he is probably talking to me out of pity—not knowing what else to say, I ask with the same childlike curiosity, "You do?"

He opens his mouth to speak but remains silent. He lowers his head and takes a deep breath.

"What is your theory?" I prompt.

He shakes his head and turns it towards the bordering orbee trees before Shahwah. "This isn't a time for theories."

"Elias,"

"The Voice will not leave you or the Book alone. That is all you need to know for now."

His voice is distant as my mind is reeling with a realization. The Book the Girl has is the one that bought the Truth. It is the one the Voice wants. This means the Voice will never leave the Girl alone if she has the Book. I look to the pouch on her chest; it's not in there.

"I need to find the Book," I say, pushing my body up, the vines gently helping.

"Before you go, you need to know something."

"I need to find the Book," I say again.

"There is something the Prophet Muhammed (peace be upon him) narrated."

"Narrated?"

"The way of peace which was acted upon by the final messenger (peace be upon him) was preserved in a series of narrations, a compilation of accounts recorded by his companions. AmaNoor sent me to retrieve the Book *and* those narrations. Over time, our people lost both."

"Elias, I——"

"Listen to me." His tone shakes me. "One of the accounts which were recorded was something he said. You won't understand it yet, but if I'm right about my theory, you will need to remember this."

I settle back down and pick at a loose thread on my dress.

He continues, "The Prophet Muhammed (peace be upon him) said: 'A man will be brought before God on the day of judgement. He, who has studied religious knowledge and has taught it, and who used to recite the Book. He will be brought, and Allah will make known to him His favors, and he will recognize them. The Almighty will say, 'And what did you do about them?' He will say, 'I studied religious knowledge, and I taught it, and I recited the Book for Your sake.[12]'"

I want to ask him why he is telling me this. The topic feels abrupt. Too abrupt. But my brother is intentional, even if he spews out a lot of unnecessary words when he is nervous.

"Listen carefully to this next part," he says.

"Why?"

"Because there will come a time when you doubt this universal Truth, when you might question Allah. When that time comes, you must remember these words."

I let out a long breath.

He says slowly, "'Allah will say: You have lied—you did but study religious knowledge so that it might be said of you: he is learned. And you recited the Book so that it might be said of you: *he is a reciter*. And so, it was said. Then, he will be ordered to be dragged along on his face until he is cast into Hell.[12]'"

"I don't know the Book or religious knowledge. I don't care about being recognized."

"Not you." The words are a low growl, anger held back. He inhales slowly, deliberately. "Intention is more powerful than consequence. What I have shared with you is about what taints even a learned person's sight of the universal Truth, even when they have the Book."

"You're talking about insincerity."

"Yes. And the greatest cause for that block to being sincere, is our Mutated Shame. This Book was our scripture. We had it. We let it slip. Little by little. Distractions. Other things. More … appealing things."

I think back to the hungry glare of the man, from our elders, who I have been trying to forget.

"More *appealing* things." Anger colors my voice.

"When a nation has been put through what we have, our land desecrated, our children stolen, killed, or made orphans, there comes a collective blindness. We become a nation inspired by our Mutated Shame. Our desires, our coping, and our attempt to escape that pain caused our people to keep lying to themselves. We did everything we could to survive, which is all we are capable of, when we do not face what lies under that Mutated Shame. Our pain."

Thinking about the evil man, I say, "He didn't do what he did to me, to survive."

"No," Elias agrees. That anger again, I realize, is not towards me. It is towards *him*, the man who hurt me. Why *did* my brother share that narration?

My jaws clench. "I won't forgive him."

"You will have your justice. On the Day of Judgement, you will testify against him."

A constriction in my chest. The same way my limbs will testify against me for what I did *because* of him.

He continues, "I will be blunt. You are still ignorant. Your Mutated Shame causes you to distort reality. You do things out of fear to avoid that Shame and how insignificant it makes you feel. You still try to escape your true pain. In your willful ignorance, your actions become blameworthy. If you do not face what causes you to lose yourself, which can only be found under that pain, you will become no better than your enemy. You will—"

"I will *never* be like him," I spit.

"I mean the Voice."

All the anger and the avoidance of this painful topic seem to wither away. My brother is right. I hate to admit it, but the Voice is a lot like me. It provokes. Needs to control things. Hurts others on a whim. Creates chaos. I wonder if that's why we share this strange connection.

My shoulders slump. "My pain. You want me to face my pain. I don't know how to do that."

I reach out to him, another attempt—he is the one who has felt my pain the most. A part of me is hoping perhaps he could also help take it away—and touch his cane. He moves it away.

"Stay away," he says, the command laced with a pain that cuts deeper than any blade. He takes a step away from me, but even in his despair, his voice remains firm. "Begin by staying away," he repeats, his voice now breaking completely. "From that which makes you lose control of yourself." He clears his throat. "Grieve. Repent. Make amends."

I let his words sink in. To reach my mind. To make meaning. But the thought is instantly replaced by a wave of heat, a flush that attacks me from the inside out. It's directed inward, against me, but it pushes outward, a burning desire to lash out.

At first, when I wanted to be at peace, I tried to suppress this heat, this anger, to bury it deep. Now, it rises, a monster exposed, threatening to shatter my control. A physical ... force. Yes, a force. Tightening in my chest. Tremor in my hands. This anger.

But there is something beneath it. I force myself to block that thing. My anger is the problem. Yes, it is. It hijacks my body, blocking any chance of true reflection, true depth. True change.

"My anger, my rage, makes me lose control. It blocks me from myself."

"You lack patience."

"Patience *is* weakness."

"No. Patience is feeling the things we must whilst never transgressing the bounds of goodness—the goodness defined by the Book—with those feelings."

I really should find the Book.

"What blocks you from yourself is not—"

I don't want to hear it. I don't want to go to that dark, awful place where pain is. What is beneath that pain threatens to destroy me. I know I'm lying to myself. I know because I can see the way my mind works, the pathways I choose to take, the truths I choose to avoid, and the truth I choose to cling to.

There are so many layers: anger, fear, Mutated Shame, pain and what is under that pain. At the very core, beneath all those layers is … no. I won't go there. I need to find the Book, then everything will be okay.

"It's my rage," I say again, meekly. That is the layer, most easiest to face now. Rage makes me dangerous. Perhaps fighting that rage will allow me to be free. Now I know I am rationalizing my avoidance.

I look to the Girl whose mouth is twitching as if she is speaking in her dreams. Her words from earlier float back to me about leaving someone because you love them. They make sense now.

"My rage makes me lose control," I say again, more to myself than to Elias. "It is bound to her."

"Who?"

"The Girl."

Uncertainty flickers across his face. "I never heard a heartbeat."

"Did you hear mine?"

Finally, he speaks, his voice gaining brittle strength. "No … the thumping. Who is she?"

"She was here … with Sama."

He staggers slightly and holds his stick to steady himself.

"Elias!" I reach out to calm him, but think better of it. He's rejected my bid for connection many times. He doesn't want me anywhere near him.

He falls to his knees and buries his head in his hands. Muffled sobs. He tries to speak, but his words are not clear. All I can hear is the word "Purple."

Another thing about my brother. He always took longer to process his emotions than I did. I just replaced mine with anger. He was the strategist. The thinker. The one with all those theories. The one who could face a burning fire without showing any fear. He did that once, when my boy's lamp broke. The flames spread, made more vicious by the gases in the Deep. A child was lost in those flames. Whilst we all panicked, shouting for little Amir, Elias had already gotten a cloth and covered the flames, extinguishing them in seconds and saving the child.

Later, I found my brother shaking uncontrollably. His emotions caught up to him. Is that what's happening? A little friction to this question within me. Didn't he already react immediately when I told him what I did? I decide to accept that there are parts of my brother that I will never fully understand.

"Forgive me, brother."

When his shoulders stop shaking, he turns his chin towards me. "'No reproach on you, this day, may Allah forgive you, and He is the Most Merciful of those who show mercy.[13]'"

He turns away. There is no more to this conversation. But it seems like he has … forgiven me.

I nod, wiping my face, and pull a layer of the vine leaves over my veil.

He whispers something to Rafiq, then speaks out loud.

"Protect her," we say in unison.

A small, sharp memory flickers through my mind—how we used to do this as children, say the same words but mean entirely different things. I have no idea who *he's* talking about, or maybe I do, and I'm too ashamed to accept he is sending his guard dog to keep me safe—*me* the cause of his pain. *I*, however, refer to the Girl. Elias is the only one I trust with her.

I gently press my lips against the Girl's warm skin. The soft curve of her forehead, smooth and delicate beneath my touch, feels vulnerable.

A fleeting contact, but it's a goodbye, a silent farewell. A wave of tenderness washes over me, mixed with a sharp pang of sadness.

I need to find the Book that the Voice is searching for. I need to keep it as far away from the Girl as possible.

I walk away.

The bank of the Zam crunches under my bare feet. Something pokes through the soil. I bend down, shifting my foot. A tiny green shoot emerges—the olive seed, the one which the Girl planted. A small smile touches my lips. A reminder of her.

Grow, I think, hoping the silent encouragement will help it—both the Girl and the seed—along. But the smile fades as quickly as it came. I straighten up and continue walking, my body a confusing mix of hot and cold, my head still reeling.

The vines brush against my back and arms, carrying a sort of comfort in their touch. Or maybe, the calm comes from me and knowing what I must do.

Retrieve the Book. That is the first step.

Stay away from what makes me 'lose myself'.

Then ... take the Book away and whilst I have it, read it and learn the universal Truth and become good.

Or ... should I grieve the loss of myself, first? What does that even mean?

And after ... *make amends.*

Before that, *repent.* It makes more sense to make amends first, but he said that last. I'll keep amends last on the list.

It sounds so simple. Yes, it is simple. I stumble as I reach the white flower in the Garden of Fire, catching myself just before I fall.

I have no idea what I'm doing.

My brother, Elias ... I love him, but he has this way of talking cryptically. He has always been like that, even when we were children. Sharing these *insights,* he called them. More like riddles. More like he was trying to confuse me.

I remember once, Yahya brought me a green leaf from the Surface. I cried. It was so beautiful. I had never even *seen* green before. Elias had just woken up, and when he saw it, he had this look of surprise.

He said that he had dreamed of something. "Purple is the color of the dead who look alive."

"*This is green,*" I had told him. I don't know how I knew the name of the color. Perhaps from my mother. But when I received the leaf, I felt like I had reconnected with something primal inside me, even as it turned yellow, then brown, and finally crumbled to dust that scattered across the Deep's rocky tunnels.

Elias didn't bother continuing the conversation about the color of things. I remember thinking, *because he knows I'm right!* He just shrugged and wandered off to his wife.

Yes, my brother lived in a different world from most of us in the Deep. Yet from a distance, our people respected him; his insights became a part of his mysterious allure. His strength and aptitude to fight became attractive to the women—much to Ruqaya's annoyance—and admired by the men.

He said, one day, we will need to know how to fight. He taught me before he taught anyone else, even though I was the baby of our generation. The youngest. He said no one would be able to hurt me again.

Only Ruqaya seemed to understand him on a deeper level. To meet him where he was and not the ideal image of a cryptic warrior of the Deep, like the rest of our people defined him as. There's a sharp pang in my chest. I swallow hard, trying to dislodge the lump in my throat.

I love my brother so much.

I pause, glancing over my shoulder, fighting the shiver through my whole body as I stand on the same spot where I saw the Ram.

I can't see Elias through the tall, red flowers, but I can hear him. He is reciting something, a melodic chant drifting in the air.

I *want* to believe that grieving will fix everything. Make it all ... right. But there is something else that keeps bothering me. Who carried me to Jinnah from the Golden Dome? It wasn't the Voice, who is unable to enter Jinnah.

Could it have been ... the Stranger? The one who left the messages? *Who is the Stranger?* Who is this person who fears death? Who do I know who fears de— I gasp, the realization hitting me like a physical blow. Yahya. He was always terrified of dying. *Is my son alive?* If Elias didn't take him, *where* did he go?

A sudden certainty floods me, makes my body feel ... stronger. It's not a jolt of energy, but something else. The scattered, fragmented thoughts in my mind coalesce, forming a single, clear purpose.

Or, at least, I *think* they do.

The nagging doubts that have been gnawing at me quieten, replaced by ... what? A sense of resolve? My shoulders straighten. Subtle shift in posture.

Or a momentary straightening, a fleeting illusion of confidence?

Breath deepens, a slow, steady inhale. Or a slightly too deep breath, a touch too deliberate? The tremor that has been lingering in my hands *seems* to subside. It is as if an internal switch has been flipped, activating a wellspring of inner strength.

Or has it?

Odd how my mind makes meanings from my reactions. *I wish the truth were clearer.*

I *feel* more solid, more capable, more *myself*. But am I?

Yes.

Yes, I am.

I shake my head as if that will dispel the creeping doubts. I know what I must do. Find Yahya. Find the Book. Go somewhere safe. Read the Book ... with him. Grieve the loss of ... whatever it is I need to grieve. Repent. And then ... make amends.

That's what I'll do.

Where could my son be? I bite my lip, a sharp sting. It bleeds. Not a gush, just a small bead of red welling up. The pain, though minor, is immediate, a sharp prick that shakes me slightly. My body reacts instantly, a complex cascade of tiny actions happening beneath the surface of my skin.

Blood vessels constrict around the wound. Clotting. Tiny things in my blood. Rush to the site. Scab. Shield against the outside. Clumping. Sticky mesh. Repair. A faint throbbing. Subtle pulse of pain. Radiates outwards from the wound.

The vines do not interfere with this bodily defense. Then again, I realize, their role has never been to heal; it has been to assist in my shifting purpose. Obedient and defensive. Now, it is as if they have a different way of doing that. I can sense, they are still focused on assisting me.

The orbees, hundreds of them like tiny suns, cover the air. They reach down and touch my lip.

An itch. Chest tightens. Not painful. But nagging. A tickle where I bit my lip. Fingers twitch. Need to scratch. Skin knitting together. Scab falls off. No more itch. I touch my lip. The wound is healed.

I try to clear my head by shaking it. A sharp, almost violent, physical attempt to dislodge the thoughts clinging to me. Distractions. I don't have time to think about the odd behavior of the orbees.

Too much is happening. Focus! *Yahya.* The last place I saw a trace of him as the Stranger was around the Fallen Trees. I hurry towards them, towards *him.* When I reach the skeletal remains of the trees, the light from hundreds of orbees makes them ... brighter, exposing their brokenness. And somehow, even in their broken state, welcoming.

No message.

Air rushes out of me. Silent sigh escaping my lips. Head bows slightly. Muscles loosen, a sense of weariness replacing the tension that had been holding me upright.

My son isn't here.

Small footsteps patter behind me, entering the hollow of the Fallen Trees. Rafiq.

"Stay with your master," I say, not turning around.

He sniffs my feet.

"Go!" I push his snout away.

He turns it right back to me and barks: *He does not need me anymore.*

I raise my eyebrow. I can ... understand him.

"Why?" I ask, as if it's the most natural thing in the world to be having a conversation with a dog.

A bark. *His sight has come back.*

"Then ... why have you come to me?"

A bark. *You are still blind.*

PART 20

The Watering

ME

The Cast's performance has ended, the final note of their hums fading into the heavy air. Their hands tremble as they remove their Apex, laying it carefully on the ground. *They* do not know it yet, but *they* won't need the Apex anymore. And soon, *I* won't be needing *them*.

The ground trembles. A deep, resonant thrumming vibrates through the very foundations of Shahwah, a testament to the sheer force of the Cast approaching. Quickly, they march up the hill until they are on the crest just before Jinnah. A strange sight, indeed. Silhouetted against nothing. Just darkness. The orbees, gone. Vanished somewhere. But I do not *need* light. The darkness … it shows me *more*. It always has.

I see them. 57 bodies standing there, on that hill, like jagged teeth—thick and thin—against the massive orbee trunks. The rest of the Cast remain in Shahwah, adding the final touches for tonight's event.

The faces of the Cast on the hill are streaked with dark grime, which clumps from their profuse sweating. They shake, their breaths, rapid.

"Who will be closest to me today?" My voice booms, cutting through the electric tension.

An uproar of declarations explodes.

"Me!"

"Fight by you!"

"Lead us!"

One more person emerges from Shahwah, carrying two torches, one in each hand. As he does this, another person surges forward. Their forms are a stark contrast. Snout: tall and wiry. The torchbearer: Scar, shorter and much more stout—a nice way of saying fatter.

Scar drops to his knees, his emerald cloak a softer silk than the others. As both Snout and Scar reach the crest of the hill, the rest of the Cast pool around them.

With shaking hands, Scar throws back his hood, revealing a face etched with … no readable emotion. He speaks in his usual monotone: "I want to …"

"You want to what, Scar?"

"Prove."

"Scar." I exhale, the name tasting like an unexpected opportunity. "Dear Scar, you may prove your loyalty to me. Today, you will lead the ranks."

He dips his head in a curt nod.

"Bring my You and the Book," I say.

The others, a mix of nervous anticipation and wary obedience, fall into line behind him. There is a slight hesitation as one steps forward. This one looks more disconcerting than the rest. Even I wince as she looks at me, her eyes pulled up so much, her eyebrows are in a constant rise, closing the space between her forehead and hair like a high alert deer, always startled.

Unlike *You*, she has had treatment—a lot of treatment—one being to stop her body from releasing sweat. Not all the Cast have done that, that is why some look like battered beavers, pulling themselves out of a flood. The lack of sweat for those who have done it, has made their features balloon even more than their already obese bodies, an inflamed layer locked under their skin which makes them look … like *that*. That is why they smell wonderfully rotten too.

"What?" I snap at the sweatless fatty.

"What if she hurts us?" she says, barely able to speak through the size of her lips (another treatment).

"I asked you to bring her to me." I try to keep my voice calm, but the edge in it—intentional, of course—remains.

Snout, tall and thin—foolish and dispensable Snout—hesitates. "What about Elias, the Girl and—"

"Kill them." My tone closes any more dialogue with these fools.

Their boots crunch on the soil of the border of Jinnah as they lumber into it, falling over each other. Pathetically, they pick themselves up with some effort, glancing back at me apologetically, and disappear behind the thicket of orbee trees.

Shortly after, and predictably enough, what follows is a chorus of screams, sharp and high-pitched, along with heavy breaths, the snap of breaking branches, and the dull *thud* of bodies hitting the ground.

I trace the path of a small cloud drifting across the sky, making out its hazy outline behind the thickening layer of smoke under it. As the cloud lazily drifts away, I smell an ever-so-faint metallic tang of blood wafting through the air.

Finally, Scar and Snout emerge with the grace of the giant drowned rats that hang on the trees that border Shahwah. Scar stumbles forward, a limp figure slung over his shoulder like a discarded sack of grain. It is the blind fool— the Scholar—his face slack and unmoving. Trailing behind them, Snout trudges under the burden of the unconscious Girl, her weight pulling him downwards.

"Where is my You?" My voice rips through the air, raspy with barely contained fury.

Scar looks down. "Gone," he says, his voice barely audible over his heavy breathing and the *thumping* from the Great Wall.

His hair hangs, plastered to his forehead, as if someone dumped a bucket of water over him. He obviously didn't undergo treatment for his moisture release. But he still stinks.

Snout grunts in agreement.

"The Book?" I ask.

"Gone," Scar repeats.

"My allies?" My voice rises an octave.

"Gone," Scar replies.

One of them pass wind out of their nervousness, the only pleasant smell compared to the Scholar's awful perfume.

I stare at the panting pair. "Why are you both not … gone?"

Silence stretches between them, and Scar winces at the smell, his muscles tensing as he takes a step away from Snout.

"It's …" Snout begins, only to trail off.

"Spit it out," I growl.

"Unusual." He pushes his glasses up his nose with his arm, making them look even more wonky.

"Unusual?" I echo.

Snout hesitates, stealing another glance at Scar, who avoids his gaze. He asks, "Shall I?"

It takes a moment for Scar to look up, his hands over his nose. Scar raises his browless forehead and says, "Shall you, what?"

"Shall I explain the phenomenon?" Snout continues.

Without waiting for a response, Snout scoffs and turns towards me, launching into an eager explanation, peppered with nervous laughter. "Well, there were these things, quite spectacular! These … butterflies."

Scar intercedes. "Butterflies' wings——"

"Mesmerizing!" Snout continues.

My patience snaps. "Are you saying she escaped because you were distracted by a butterfly or two?"

Snout shrinks back, but quickly holds up a captured colorful butterfly, breaking a wing with his grip. "I, um, acquired one for further study,"

"Further …" I start, my voice dangerously low.

Snout chuckles nervously. "You always say, do everything we can to follow our passions." His voice grows fainter. "I did just that, and now——"

"And now?" I press.

Snout shifts his weight from one foot to the other, whilst squinting at the desperate butterfly, "Further s-study."

My fury erupts. With a flick, I launch my threads at the butterfly. They whip through the air, slamming into the blasted thing. It falls to the ground soundlessly.

Snout opens his mouth to protest, but the word "need" dies on his throat as my bellow echoes through the clearing. "Leave!"

He stumbles back, the Girl collapsing from his shoulder onto the Silver Path with a *thud*. He scrambles to scoop the fallen butterfly and then runs to the familiar Shahwah.

Scar, however, remains as a bead of sweat trickles down his temple.

"Where is she?" I demand, my voice tight.

"Gone," he replies, lowering the Scholar to the Silver Path, next to the Girl. His voice is devoid of panic. "She will come for Girl and Scholar."

I follow his gaze towards the Scholar and the Girl. I only need one to lure You to me. The Girl … or Your brother?

The Girl knows where the Book is hidden. Your brother, however, is a menace. Always has been. Interrupting. Unpredictable.

"Kill—" I stop myself.

That familiar tug, the one I wish didn't exist, pulls at me. It's the echo of Father's words, blunt and cruel, the last I heard from him. Yet … he sent me a message.

I begin again. "Kill—"

What did Father say? Did he reconsider my place in his … dynasty? What if he did? A hot flush rises through my body.

"Clever Scar," I rasp, the rhythmic *thudding* from the Great Wall around us, calming. "Always so clever," I continue, drawing out the words. "And I reward the clever—you love your reward, don't you?"

He nods once.

"This will be a reward you are quite familiar with … power that mirrors that of a god."

"You mean like the sun rising from the West instead of the East?"

His question throws me off.

He continues, "That is God's power."

I note the words, 'God,' instead of 'a god.'

Keeping my observation to myself, I say, "I can do better; I can take the sun away from the sky itself."

"The smoke?"

"Indeed, I almost forgot, it was you who helped me with that, didn't you, Scar?"

"Sun is still there."

"That's not the point."

"What is … the point?" he asks.

"Stop getting distracted, Scar, focus! I am giving you a god-like power—the power to decide life or death."

Scar's cheek twitches.

I ask, "Will you spare the blind man or the awful child?"

See, when someone hides from their fear—in his case, the fear of death—it always resurfaces, one way or another. When someone hides from any part of themselves, 'good' or 'bad,' it will find its way, like a parasite, to lay eggs beneath the skin. Sooner or later, the need to express that hidden part will burst out, sometimes unpredictably. The body can no longer contain it. It must tear through.

With Scar, it manifests as killing. Where do You think the nineteen children went? It was when he showed me what he had done that I realized his true value. I was right. He has been invaluable to my mission: the Great Wall, the Apex, the planting of the Vine Tree and most of all, he told me *how* the Book I had tried to destroy could help me to enter Heaven and keep me away from Hell.

Of course, he put You in your frozen sleep, keeping You alive all these years while I waited for inspiration … waited for the perfect way to use this new, valuable resource: Your son, the one You ironically call 'Yahya'. Life. We do live up to our names, don't we?

The children's killings … that was his initiation into the Cast. Every member must actively participate in a major sin to be accepted. I *do* have standards.

His major sin was murder. After all, he is Your legacy.

"Do I choose, now?" Scar's voice is muffled from bowing, even though the bowing is in the wrong direction.

I have stopped trying to tell him the right direction—*forward* towards Ghar, towards *me*—instead, he faces the opposite way, towards the East. Silly man. Silly, silly man.

"You will choose when I tell you to."

He raises his head. "I want the crown too."

The crown. *Your crown.*

My voice drops to a chilling whisper. "After all I have given you, you dare to ask for more?"

Scar looks towards my Ghar, blankly. Yes, I know these tactics never work with him. He needs clear information with that small literal brain of his. Only seeing with facts, but then again, I need that brain, without it … I shiver before letting that thought take place.

I sigh loudly. "I have forgiven you."

"For what?" Scar scrambles to his feet.

I remain silent. I only wanted the last word.

He scoops the Girl in one arm and drags the Scholar with the other. The Girl mumbles something, and the Scholar stirs, slowly regaining consciousness.

"Quickly! Take them to the prison!" I say, as he rushes past my Ghar into Shahwah. I watch his eyes flash with what I hope is an ambition that even the literal cannot escape. I add, "When I get what I need from them, *then* you will choose which one lives and which one dies."

ADAMAH

A dog said I'm blind. Why? Because I've strayed a little from the original plan—find the Book and leave? My gaze drifts over the Fallen Trees, searching for any clues of my son. Their wide, white trunks are piled one on top of another, their branches like dead hands reaching towards the smoke as if it were light.

Still, no trace of my boy. My shoulders droop. Could I have been wrong? The vines that were on the ground every time a new message was left for me, are now absent. Now I am sure, those vines wrote the messages for Yahya.

Why? Why would my son use the vines and not come himself? Was he afraid? I look at my dress, its green stitches mixed with black fabric, and feel my resolve return: Yahya *is* here, somewhere in this land. No one else in the world would make me a green dress. What is his connection to everything?

Rafiq walks ahead of me, his small body dwarfed by the Pale Tree. It almost looks like he doesn't want me to go beyond it. His ears twitch in its direction, as if he's listening for something. It's interesting how a dog can look … disappointed. The tip of his snout is turned down, his eyes following it.

I turn towards the exit hole and stop, looking over my shoulder back at the Pale Tree. I have a very strong feeling—an alignment with every part of my body, a silent nudge—the Book is beyond that tree.

My heart beats faster. Flutter. Senses sharpen. A surge … not excitement, more like recognition. Yes, the Book is beyond the Pale Tree. But where exactly? Where would the Girl hide something she loves? Her mother's planks … her leaf dress … *of course*! Under the Pale Tree.

Seeing as I'm already here, I might as well get the Book.

Muscles coil, *snap*. Ground vanishes, a hard push. The world spins, a dizzying rush. Arms flail, grabbing at nothing. Core tightens, a steel rod against the wind screaming past my veil.

Senses ablaze, too sharp, *too* much.

Gravity bites, yanking me down. Legs brace, muscles screaming in warning. Impact! A bone-jarring jolt. Vibrations are shaking me. Stumbling, I catch myself. My heart is hammering against my ribs.

I am on the other side of the Pale Tree.

Rafiq follows, surrounded by the orbee lights like spotlights hovering above the ground. Everything on this side has become so … *stark*. Blackness. Glossy blackness, everywhere. Up to my knees. This Dark Fall … is slick. *Warm*. Almost oily. Not dry and gritty like I thought. It is sticking to my dress. This dark base of my dress fabric blends with the residue. The vines themselves seem to writhe slightly, almost as if trying to pull away from the clinging debris. A subtle tremor runs through their woven strands.

The Great Wall, a swirling mass, shimmers with its unsettling, light purple sheen. It shakes more viciously, as if its body is an echo, the tremors radiating outwards and giving everything an almost hallucinatory feel.

Almost against my will, I glance at the area where the camel remains lie. My stomach threatens to purge again, even though I can no longer see them. The bones of the camels are completely swallowed by this shiny Dark Fall. The Dark Fall, however, is not all black. There are speckles of grey, tinges of brown … it looks like a dying sea, frozen in the dead of night.

I crouch to search for the Book, but it's completely swallowed by the darkness of both the Dark Fall and the black shadow of the Pale Tree, which stretches out.

I shove the clumping sediment aside, the gleaming dust clinging to my skin, and feel around. My fingers brush wood; the planks. Then … the leaf dress. I pull my hand back quickly, a pang of sadness hitting me at the thought of the Girl. After a brief pause, I begin the search again, feeling around blindly.

The Book! I yank it out, wiping the cover. The dust brushes off easily enough, leaving streaks of dark debris on the pages. I blow on it, trying to clear the rest. As I turn to leave, a bark cuts through the silence.

I ignore it.

It barks again. *Water.*

"I'm *not* your master," I mutter. "Get your own water."

A louder bark. *Water!*

I whirl around, ready to give the dog that called me *blind* a piece of my mind. My eyes widen as my ears pick up something. A sound, one I hadn't heard before, not over the pounding on the Great Wall. Now, it is unmistakable: a loud, rushing gush. It starts slowly, then builds.

A surge of water from the direction of the cluster of olive trees.

The flood sweeps through the blighted landscape. Where the water flows, life returns. A tree trunk sheds its dark shroud and becomes brown again. Leaves unfurl in vibrant green. Olives, once dull and muted, plump up, their skins gleaming with a deep, regal purple.

The flood is moving fast.

Too fast.

It crashes through the fence of the camel carcasses, splintering the wood. The wave surges closer.

ROAR.

A small *yelp.*

The Black Assad's huge head appears, its mane a night halo around its face. Right beside him, the lioness emerges, a small cub held gently in her jaws.

Water slams me under, a brutal surge. My vines are slack, useless. Ice-cold shock, a biting chill, deeper than skin, a bone-deep freeze clenching my muscles. Lungs burn. Heart throbs. Head throbs. Senses overload—stinging cold, muffled sounds, murky dark. Disoriented, I flounder, lost. Every cell in me shrieks for warmth, for air, for *escape*.

I sink, eyes wide and unblinking.

The blackness thickens, pressing in, a crushing weight on my chest. When I reach the bottom, a soft *thud* against the debris.

I stay here.

Motionless.

Eyes still open. Staring into the void.

My limbs feel heavy, yet disconnected, as if they belong to someone else. There's a detachment, a sense of floating, even though I'm resting on the muddy floor. It's like being suspended in a vast emptiness, disconnected from not only my body, but everything. The pressure builds in my ears, a dull throb, and my thoughts drift, becoming hazy and indistinct. Time seems to stretch and compress at the same time, an odd distortion of reality. The crushing weight on my chest makes it impossible to breathe.

Yet in this breathless separation, there is a kind of calm.

A darkness within a darkness. I feel … I don't feel anything.

A hollow ache settles in me in addition to the water's chill.

It's like the world has gone silent, a *buzzing*, static *hum* in my ears. Even the need to breathe seems distant, a muted instinct. It's not peace, not quite. More like … calm nothingness.

I'm trapped. Not just by the water, but by something deeper, something inside me. There is no escape. Just … this.

A distant sound, a faint bark, pierces through the numbness. Rafiq? He barks: *Live!*

Ruqaya's smiling face flashes by. Her words when I held Yahya in my arms: *Just choose to live.*

My body, heavy and unresponsive just moments ago, twitches. A small, involuntary movement.

The detachment begins to recede, replaced by a slow, creeping return of sensation. The pressure in my ears starts to lessen, the dull throb fading. Thoughts, previously hazy and indistinct, sharpen, like images slowly coming into focus. The crushing weight on my chest, while still present, feels slightly less oppressive. My limbs, still heavy, feel more connected to me, responding to the signals from my returning awareness. The world, previously a void, begins to register again, though still muted and distant.

Another bark. Muffled. As if Rafiq is underwater. Something stirs within me. An instinct to survive. It's a spark, not a flame, but it's there. Now a pressure against my back, a nudge, insistent and strong. I am pushed upward. My body, still sluggish, resists, but the dog is relentless.

The darkness recedes, replaced by a faint light. The orbees swarm around Rafiq, their light pulsing in rhythm with his breathing, a symbiotic connection. They must be guiding him, nudging him closer, and as he moves, I feel a pull, a tugging sensation, as if their combined energy, amplified through Rafiq, is drawing me towards the surface.

The weight on my chest, though still present, feels … less.

I am lifted into the air with the orbees under my body, high enough to see my feet dangling over the surface of the Zam.

I am shaking from the cold. The vines are sprawled around me, as if waiting for my command. I nod. They rub my arms, carrying me from the orbees and holding me steadily above the water. The orbees swarm around me, their bodies radiating warmth.

I cough and cough, my vision blurry. When I can see clearly, I gasp. The whole area is flooded. The water is rising rapidly. It'll cross the Pale Tree in minutes.

Then … it stops. It stops just below the Pale Tree.

Rafiq is barking, his legs paddling furiously, a blur of white patches against the dark water as he dogpaddles with surprising strength. He can swim well, but the water pushes him much further from the refuge of the Pale Tree.

I will a vine to grab Rafiq and hoist him onto the Pale Tree. He scrambles aboard.

I turn to the Black Assad and his lioness, the cub still dangling limply from her massive jaws by the scruff of its neck.

I will more vines, thick and strong, to scoop up the Black Assad and his family, their powerful muscles rippling beneath their midnight coats. The vines snake behind them, the contrast of the bright green and the black fur of the Black Assad stark. The lioness' yellow eyes gleam with a protective ferocity for her cub as she reaches the safety of the Pale Tree.

I look toward the direction of Thalj, beyond the cluster of olive trees. I remember the heat that came from my rage-filled body, the melting ice.

I *caused* this.

The Black Dune must have been a hill of pure ice; a glacier adding to the weight of the water, making it overflow.

So … what stopped it?

I follow the water with my eyes, past the olive trees. There! The faint glow … the fishes. Which means the current. I must have missed the glow before, with the orbees being so bright. But it's there.

The current is keeping the water in check.

Which means it's still day.

Which means, when night comes, it will flood the rest of Jinnah.

It will flood the orbees' home. Then, it will spill out across the land, destroying everything—including the Girl's home or any chance of a new one—all because of my rage.

It takes me a second to register: the Book is not in my hands. Funny, with all this new self-awareness, I didn't realize the Book had fallen.

I look down. The pages are floating on the water's surface. I reach for them, but they feel … wrong. The Dark Fall. Something about its material has made the pages of the Book fragile. As my fingers brush against them, the pages disintegrate, breaking into damp pieces which dissolve in the water, like salt diffusing.

The Book is gone.

PART 21

The Wise

ME

The task ahead is simple: get the Book from the Girl and Father's message from the Scholar. But how to approach it? If I am too forthcoming with my request, they will have the upper hand of knowledge. However, if they do not know my intention, then they will remain on edge, and something is bound to slip through.

Chains scrape against stone, echoing in the thick air. I nestle in my dusty nook. I will observe. For a short while, I can afford to wait.

The Scholar's eyes are fixed on something in the distance. It seems his sight has miraculously—though not surprisingly—returned. I glance at the Girl. She is not looking so well. Her head, lolling against the cold stone wall, stirs weakly.

In a raspy voice, she asks, "Where ..."

"Shahwah," the Scholar replies.

He then does an unusual thing, something I have not seen before. *Click, click.* It's almost inaudible, a sound of his tongue hitting the roof of his mouth.

The Girl strains against the chair, the chains responding with a metallic rattle. "Who are you?"

He stops clicking. "I am—"

She cuts him off, "What happened?" She tries to move her hands, but they are tied to the sides of the chair. She rocks back and forth.

The Scholar speaks. "We are in a room about the size of two orbee tree trunks. The ceiling is low, and one wall is hollow." He clicks again and continues. "Your chair is touching the hollow wall."

She looks behind her, almost directly at me. "How did you know?"

"These clicks tell me. There is a heat coming from below our feet. With it, the air is ... there is," He sniffs the air. "Something wrong with the air."

She looks at the small fire next to her.

He continues, "There is a window at the top of the room on my right, which is your left."

Her shoulders are cowered inwards. She opens them as she sees the window. "The way out."

"The window is too small and too high for us to get through, but the air that comes through will allow us to breathe."

"Why wouldn't we be able to breathe?" A hint of urgency in her voice. "Is it because the air is ... wavy?"

The Scholar softens his tone. His gaze lingers on her a moment too long, as if studying every part of her face. "What's your name?"

She slowly turns to face the wall near the door, her brow furrowed in deep thought. "Name?" she repeats, the word seeming unfamiliar. After a moment, she whispers, "Child or Girl."

"Is that what she——"

The Scholar starts, but the Girl cuts him off with a burst of clarity, snapping her out of her daze. "There are 132 bricks on the wall on my right! And lines of shapes, similar to curves ... just like in my Book!" Her head spins around, eyes darting across the opposite wall. "98 bricks on this side, a door, roughly the size of ..." she mutters, straining to recall. "A fifth of the width of the trunk of the first tree when we enter Jinnah." Her voice grows stronger with each detail she pulls.

"How did you do that?" he asks, his voice laced with a quiet fascination.

"I remember ... things."

"What kind of things?"

A pause hangs in the air. The Girl hesitates, her gaze dropping to a small bug inching across the dusty stone floor. "Not many people here to speak with, to remember words," she murmurs, her voice tinged with sadness. "Except my Mama, my friend, and my other friends ..." She trails off, eyes widening slightly as if just remembering the fate of her two dead camels.

"And who else?" The chair squeaks as he leans forward slightly, his interest piqued.

She lifts her head slowly. "Them," she whispers quickly as if glad for the distraction, pointing with her big toe at the tiny creature before her.

"Them." A small hint of amusement in his voice. "You can talk to insects?"

She avoids his gaze, her cheeks now burning crimson. "I don't eat them."

"Why would you eat them?"

The Girl looks down, shuffling in her chains. "I promised I wouldn't."

"Who did you promise?"

"My friend." She shifts her eyes to the side as if telling a secret and whispers, "Her name is Adamah."

He nods slowly with a knowing smile. "Sometimes, the greatest promises are the ones we make to ourselves."

"Why?"

"It's hardest to trust ourselves, don't you think?"

The Girl sits a little taller and leans forward, her chains clinking softly. "Why are we here?"

The Scholar hesitates. He says, "Is that a big question or a small one?"

She shrugs.

"Because ..." he begins, as he turns to face the Girl—no, not the Girl, behind her—to the hollow of the wall where her chair leans.

He knows I am here.

A harmony leaves the Scholar. Melodious. Ancient. My threads vibrate in response, and I weave a countermelody. I release them with all my might, but they feel dull and lifeless, snapping back against me, leaving raw gashes where they pierce my form. For the first time in years, I am incapable of speaking.

He

Must

Be

Silenced.

Snout prances into the room, his bony frame waddling like a cat trying to avoid getting its paws wet. His head is held high, nostrils flared in an exaggerated sniff, as if the very air is unworthy of him. He adjusts his glasses, perched on his nose. His nose, a simian marvel, resembles a droopy banana peel, hanging over his nostrils.

The Girl's voice is sharp. "A Cast!"

Close behind, Scar throws himself through the door with a grunt. The doorway resists his bulk. After a final struggle, he emerges, panting heavily, leaning against the doorframe with hands on his knees, trying to catch his breath.

I catch the Scholar's face now, as he takes in his nephew, the young boy who once sat in this very room with him and that old bat of a woman. But the Scholar gives nothing away.

With a delayed reaction, simple Snout bristles at the Girl's words. He narrows his eyes in a fierce glare. "I am not acast!" he declares, puffing out his bony chest. The charred stubble atop his head stands on end as he straightens his cloak, his pointed shoulders jutting out.

"Amir," the Scholar says.

Snout snaps, "I don't identify with that name anymore." He sniffs a couple of times, with a pout, and continues in that nasal whine. "*We* have a task at hand." He looks at Scar from the corner of his eye. "We were advised to silence …" He raises a long, bony finger toward the scholar, "Him."

He pauses dramatically. A theatrical sigh escapes his lips. "We must explore all avenues." He gestures wildly with his finger. "The possibilities are numerous! Perhaps, with some focus, we could brainstorm some truly effective methods—"

His pompous delivery is interrupted by a loud grunt from Scar. Snout snaps around; his face contorted in irritation. "Must you grunt like that while I'm speaking?"

Scar's grunts are heavy in the air. "I'm parched," he grumbles, pulling out a grimy cloth to wipe his head and then extending the dirty cloth towards Snout.

"What am I supposed to do with that?" Snout's glare is sharp.

"Quiet them," Scar says.

"The leadership mantle has shifted, Scar," Snout declares matter-of-factly, waving two hands in front of him for emphasis. "The choice of silence falls upon *me* now."

"We were brothers once," the Scholar says, attempting another connection. "Don't you remember the fire when you were just a boy, Amir?"

A tense silence descends, broken only by Scar's nervous pants.

Snout regains his composure and pulls out a glint of metal from his cloak. His voice maintains its arrogant edge. "After much deliberation, I have devised a foolproof solution—one swift action, and he will never speak again."

Scar, his face paling at the sight of the metal, lets out a high-pitched squeal, "No blood."

"Oh, Scar!" Snout nudges Scar playfully. Scar flinches with his touch. "You, the killer among us, cannot stand blood. You contradiction!"

"No blood," Scar says again.

Snout scoffs. "Coward."

The Girl's voice, soft, cuts through. "I get scared too."

"Of course, you do," Snout spits. "Because you're also a coward."

"What do you do when you get scared?" the Scholar asks.

"I don't like it," she admits, her voice small but clear. "But I find there's always something to be more scared of." Her hand brushes against the chain, a metallic rasp filling the room. "And what I was scared of doesn't seem as scary anymore."

Snout stalks closer, stopping mere inches away from her, the knife against her throat. "Are you scared, now?" he hisses.

She meets his gaze, her chin held high despite the blush creeping up her cheeks. "A little bit," she confesses, her voice oddly steady. "But I'm also a bit excited, too."

Snout recoils. "You're unnatural!" His voice has lost some of its earlier conviction. "You should be terrified of me."

"Why?" she asks.

"Because I can kill you!" He tightens his grip on the knife. The metal presses against her skin, but her stoic expression remains beneath a layer of sadness. A smoldering, shielding grief. Making her bolder.

"That's the part I'm scared of," the Girl whispers.

Snout's eyes narrow. "There is nothing more terrifying than death."

Scar grunts, I assume in agreement.

"Death or dying?" the Scholar asks in a voice laced with quiet defiance.

Snout whirls around. "Always the clever one, weren't you, Elias?"

The Girl pipes up again, "What's the difference?"

The Scholar opens his mouth to answer, but before he can utter a word, Snout slaps his face. "Silence!"

"Hot in here," Scar says, clutching the wall for support.

Snout turns to Scar. "You can faint as much as you want," he says, thrusting the knife into his hands. "*After*."

Scar takes the knife, his hands shaking uncontrollably. He wipes his damp forehead with the already drenched cloth with his other hand.

"I don't know why *you* get to choose who lives or dies, Scar. You can't even look anyone in the eye." Snout scoffs.

Scar seems oblivious to Snout's words. He mumbles, "Head hurts, too loud," before squeezing out the door with a grunt, claiming he needs food.

Left alone, Snout looks almost uncomfortable and lets out another one of his dramatic sighs. "Suppose I *do* need a break," he mutters, pulling out a notebook and pencil.

The door creaks open, and Scar re-enters, his arms laden with enough food to feed a small army. Pots and pans clatter as he arranges them on the floor, the aroma of spiced meat and herbs filling the room. He even offers a small piece of bread to Snout, who waves him away, whilst scratching his head and focusing on his notebook.

Scar leans over with a mouthful of food, some spilling over Snout's hands.

Snout furiously scribbles, flicking the food away angrily. His brow is furrowed in concentration. "Exploring alternative solutions," he mutters, then abruptly looks up, eyes wide. "Listen!"

Scar, mid-chew, pauses and glances up, expressionless.

"Silence!" Snout says.

Scar asks, "You can hear silence?"

"No, that's the point!" Snout exclaims, tapping the notebook with his pencil. "Now that you mention it, can you truly hear no sound? Is it possible? Fascinating! An excellent proposition to study."

Scar leans closer, squinting at the open page. "What is that?"

Snout meets his gaze, and Scar looks away. "I'm drawing a circle."

"Circle," Scar echoes.

"Yes, a circle," Snout snaps.

"Why?" Scar asks.

Snout's cheeks flush. "You know why."

"Don't know how to draw anything else," Scar says, each word with a pause between it.

Snout slaps him across the head with his notebook. Scar looks bewildered, more so than usual, when he is not looking devoid of emotion. He reacts by simply standing up and walking out of the room.

"You're awful!" the Girl says to Snout.

Snout chuckles darkly. "Don't worry, child," he says. "This is Shahwah. There are no rules here. We can do what we like."

Snout tucks his notebook under his arm with a satisfied sigh. Without another word, Snout follows Scar out and slams the door behind him.

PART 22

The Combined Forces

ADAMAH

I want to leave. Find Yahya. Get out. I stand on the Pale Tree, the water flowing steadily beneath it, like an ocean. It stretches to the horizon, where a distortion marks the Great Wall meeting the water. The wall seems to morph into different shapes, pushing the water and pulling it back in. A faint glow persists beyond the cluster of olive trees.

The Black Assad and Rafiq are in the area of the Fallen Trees, glaring at each other. Rafiq looks like a squirrel next to a human compared to the mighty Black Assad. They are both predators. Natural enemies because they compete for the same prey.

Then again, a lion allying with a human is not natural either, and that has happened; the Black Assad has helped *me*. Rafiq has helped my brother. I pray they can help each other.

I turn to jump down beside both predators, but stop. I glance back at the body of water. The Book is gone. Only debris now, drifting back and forth. I take in everything I have done, the sheer scale of the destruction I have caused. It's ironic: the Queen of the orbees' absence caused disease to spread, yet my presence has destroyed the land. The water stares back, a silent accusation. My shoulders slump.

Night is coming.

The flood will follow.

It will destroy everything in Jinnah and more.

This is not a time to grieve. This is a time to make amends. I must *do* something. I can't just find Yahya, and leave. I caused this flood. I can't think of any other way to make amends for my wrongs but to fix the mess I made, starting here, in Jinnah.

But how? A shield. A barrier. A fort. I look at the piles of dead trees. Sixteen, including the Pale Tree. There are enough. If I build it high enough, it will be long enough too. The water will be controlled. Standing on the Pale Tree, I wonder about the vines. Are they strong enough? Ever since I woke up from that vision of Hell, they have been tame. Does tame mean they are weak?

Pick a tree trunk, I will the vines.

My vines extend past Rafiq—who is growling—and the unbothered Black Assad, who no longer uses his energy to even look at Rafiq. The Black Assad's cub paws at my vine, swinging playfully. The vine gently pushes the cub away, then wraps around a tree trunk. Green against white, it is beautiful. The vine lifts the trunk effortlessly, carrying it towards me.

I jump off the Pale Tree, landing between Rafiq and the Black Assad, as the vine drops the massive trunk—it is as wide as five of me—onto the Pale Tree.

I direct my vines: *Again.*

More vines lash out, bringing more trunks, layering them on top of each other, building a wall so high I can't see the top. All the trunks are there, forming a fort, leaving me standing in the clearing of white soil.

I can leave now. Find Yahya. As I turn, I look back at the Black Assad, his family, and Rafiq.

"What will you do?" I ask them.

The Black Assad turns away from me.

Rafiq trots after me. I walk next to the Black Assad, trying to catch his gaze. He won't meet mine. I touch him gently. He doesn't resist.

Beneath the thick, course, black fur, his body radiates a powerful warmth, a heat that seeps into my fingertips and travels up my arm, making the tiny hairs on my skin stand on end. It's not just warm, but a deep, primal heat, the kind that speaks of raw power and untamed energy, and I can almost *smell* it—a musky, wild scent that fills my nostrils.

He growls softly. He is sad. He has lost his home. He is angry. Where will he go?

The cub continues to play with my vines, grabbing one and rolling onto its back, lightly nibbling at them.

I can't leave them like this.

A quiet shift happens inside. A knot loosens in my belly. My mind quiets down from all the things I want to do. Shoulders relax slightly. Breathing deeper, more even.

I sigh. I know what I *need* to do. I just don't know if the Black Assad will agree.

"There is a place up there." I point up. The orbees shine through the smoke like a cloak, making everything glow. "Hadeeya."

The Black Assad doesn't look up.

"It's full of prey."

The Black Assad looks up.

Encouraged, I add, "It needs you as much as you need a home."

"You have destroyed our home, Adamah," he grumbles.

"Let me give you another."

He huffs, turning away again, licking his paws. The lioness nudges him, growling softly as she looks … not at me, I realize. At her cub, which squeaks as it plays with my dress. The Black Assad lies down, head on his paws.

I suppose that's a no.

I gently try to detach the cub from my dress, to return it to its family. It sniffs my hand.

Rafiq barks. I turn. The lioness is looking up towards the orbees in the sky. The Black Assad is behind her, still looking disgruntled. She doesn't use words like him. She just nudges and bellows, like now, she is nudging me. I nudge her back, almost playfully, but she doesn't move. She looks up again, waving her tail back and forth. She wants to go up there. She wants to hunt.

I will my vines: *Make a way up there.*

They snap away from the cub, who looks momentarily dazzled, then jumps with glee, as it follows the vines. The vines form steps, leading towards the sky. The steps are as hard as stone. I climb.

The lioness puts a paw on the vine steps, but her huge body is too wide to climb them.

Wider.

The vines spread into leaves, widening as much as the Black Assad's majestic body. The cub races ahead, the lioness right behind. We reach the top quickly.

Rafiq, keeping pace with the cub, barks: *Master, there is no way in.*

Open, I will the vines.

The vines create a hole big enough for the lioness. The cub darts behind her, peeking out from her huge body. She enters Hadeeya. The cub follows. I peek through the hole made by my vines. It is the mountain area. A gazelle strolls by, unaware of the lioness watching. Her cub squeaks. The gazelle freezes, ears twitching, then bolts. The lioness is after it.

She has found her place. Her role in the natural order.

I jump through the closing hole, back onto my vines. Rafiq is on the steps, looking uneasy. I climb down, and Rafiq follows me.

Without turning, I ask, "What are you afraid of?"

He barks: *Up there.*

"Why?"

He barks: *I do not know.*

I do. I know. When you have been a slave for so long, freedom can be terrifying. So can hope. He fears freedom. I touch his head. Yes, he fears freedom. He is not ready to believe that it is not only possible, but also necessary, for a wild dog.

We reach the Black Assad. He is still grumpy, head on the ground. The black of his face, the dark mane against the white ground.

I sit beside him. "Your lioness has found a home. So has your cub."

The Black Assad grumbles, a low rumble that vibrates through the ground beneath us. His massive head, the size of half my body, hangs low.

"What will you eat down here?" I ask, hoping to get a response more than a grumble.

"What I *have* been eating," the Black Assad answers, his tone heavy.

A thought passes, a reminder of my earlier transgression, when I ate the camels. I realize now, it must have been because it's a lion's nature to eat such things.

I wonder out loud, "Why didn't you eat the camels?"

"I made a promise to the Girl that I would not eat her friends."

"Even in their death?" I ask.

"I do not eat rotten meat."

"Of course." I clear my throat. "How did you and your family survive for this long?"

"We made a bargain with the snow squirrels," he confesses. "They gathered hundreds of fish for us every day."

"What did the squirrels get in return?"

"I didn't eat them," he states simply.

I smile, though I know he isn't joking. "You told me that my rage has brought imbalance," I say, my voice filled with remorse. "You were right. It has taken your home, your food—there are no more squirrels to help you. Forgive me."

I lower my head.

The Black Assad raises his head. "Words are feeble, Adamah."

Rafiq perks up too.

"Then, let me show you how I can make it right." I stand. "But to see, you need to …"

He completes the sentence. "Rise."

I nod. "Rise."

A pause, as if the primal rhythm of the world has just clicked into place. He cannot deny the connection, the rightness of this moment. *Rise.* His word, echoing back to him now. Understanding flickers in his huge golden eyes. Anger remains, but it is tempered by something ancient, something wise. This is the way.

The Black Assad stands, shaking his mane, water flying off, splashing all over me. My vines dry me off as I lead him to the vine steps. We reach the top more quickly than I did with his lioness. The vines open another hole.

As he crosses it, I follow him into Hadeeya. When he is further along, he turns and opens his mouth as if he wants to say something, but closes it and walks on to his lioness. She is busy feeding on the gazelle, her cub running excitedly around her. The Black Assad joins them.

I turn to Rafiq, still on the other side of the hole. "Come in," I say gently.

A bark: *I am supposed to protect you.*

"I know my brother. He sent you with me because he knew this is where I would bring you. This place needs you, too. I may be blind in many ways, but I can see clearly, here."

He backs away, a shaky step on the vine steps.

I continue, "You don't need a master anymore."

A whimper which sounds like a human cry: *I will be alone.*

I study his golden brown, almond-shaped eyes, a mix of fear, sadness, and a glimmer of something like hope swirling within them.

"I will find others like you," I promise.

He barks: *There are none.*

I motion him forward, but he remains in the same place. "You don't know for sure," I say. "But first, you must learn to be free."

He barks: *My master has been good to me.*

"Then you have lived a good life with him. But he doesn't need you anymore."

Another few barks: *You need me.*

"I—" I can't finish the sentence. A wave of emotion rises in my chest, stinging my eyes. I understand. He knows abandonment, just like me. But unlike me, who became attached to the Voice, Rafiq found something good, *someone* good: Elias.

Yet, being with my brother didn't take away his loneliness, his yearning to run and not have to return to a master. Our servitude is different—mine to my Mutated Shame and my pain, his to the one he came to love—but we both did what our physical nature led us to. We both survived.

"You do not need to *survive* anymore. Now you can *thrive*."

He barks: *A dog's nature is to only survive.*

True. But that isn't why he is resistant to freedom. I step back. I won't force him.

He barks. And barks again. He hesitates, then his gaze drifts past me, towards the open expanse beyond Hadeeya. Slowly, he walks into Hadeeya.

The cub runs to him, a piece of meat in its mouth, and playfully bumps Rafiq's legs and wobbles from the impact before running off. Rafiq looks at me, a newfound curiosity replacing the usual guardedness in his expression.

"Go." I try to make my voice sound steady. To give him strength.

He walks forward. At the carcass, the Black Assad roars, and Rafiq flinches. The Black Assad continues eating.

"He needs a home too," I say firmly.

The Black Assad spits out some meat, his maw a deep red. "I do not eat with dogs."

I sigh. "There is enough."

"Then let him find his own food." He goes back to tearing the carcass meat with his huge teeth.

The lioness tears off a piece of meat and tosses it to Rafiq, who eats it hungrily.

I smile. Turning away, I cross the open hole to the descending steps and whisper, "Bismillah."

PART 23
The Ranks

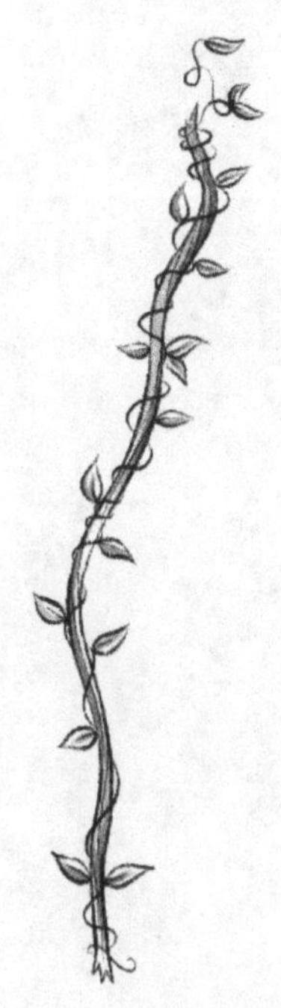

ME

The plot of our story has surpassed my vision. At the beginning, I had specific titles for each Part, but now they have changed.

Something shifted after Part 12: Fall. Before that, there was always the power struggle between us, but then You went rogue. I think it has something to do with that vine dress. No matter, it was destroyed after You beat Sama.

So ... how do You still have control of naming the Parts of our—*my* story? Could being on the pursuit of *goodness* unravel the plans of even the most experienced opposition? I am not opposed to You, though, am I? I *need* You to be good.

Still, I am unsettled by so many new occurrences that I have no hand in. What else am I losing control of? I stop this toxic line of thought; it will do me no good. I need to distract myself productively and attend to the present task.

I focus on the fire's flicker. Note the ephemeral shadows, their kinetic dance upon the grimy, brick surfaces.

The Girl, her voice barely a whisper, breaks the tension and thankfully, my betraying thoughts. At the very least, I have full control of *this* situation. For now, that is enough.

"You said you were brothers," she begins, her eyes fixed on the Scholar's face. "Does that mean you're from the same place as them?"

He grunts, struggling against his bonds. I assume, after seeing Scar, he is particularly uncomfortable. Disturbed. Urgent.

"Are you from out there, past the Great Wall?" She looks up to the window, which is covered by a patchy curtain.

"We are not from out there," he says.

"I have only ever seen the Cast out there."

The Scholar pauses his struggle. His voice echoes in the dimly lit room. "They are?"

"Most nights, they do something to the Great Wall."

"The thumping ..." he begins.

"You mean the thumping under the ground?" the Girl asks.

He shakes his head, his chained leg scraping against the rough floor. "No, the Great Wall." He taps his foot against the ground, then pauses, tilting his head in concentration. "But perhaps there is a connection to the thumping underground and the thumping from the Great Wall. How long has the thumping been happening, both from the Great Wall and from underground?"

The Girl mirrors him, moving her foot from her toes, first touching the floor, to now, her soles. "The knocking from the Great Wall started a day or two ago when Adamah cut the vines. It stopped for a bit, but must have started again when I fell asleep. The thumping under the ground has been here since the smoke came a few years ago. It just isn't very loud."

"The Great Wall must be connected to the vines," he says.

There is only one way he could know this. He knows of something like it. There is only one other place where a wall like this exists.

Where Father is.

The Girl nods. "When Adamah cut the vines, smoke came out, the same color smoke that is in the sky."

The Scholar nods his head slowly. "The vines must have carried the smoke from under the ground in Shahwah through all of Jinnah." He doesn't elaborate, but his eyes are scanning something unseen as he puts the dots of what is happening together.

I don't have much time.

"But why does the Voice need the Deep *here* in Shahwah? What do they do to the Great Wall at night? What is their connection with the Queen? My theory . . ." he mutters.

The Girl blinks a few times at this new information, as if deciding which question to ask. She settles on the one relating to the one she loves most: the Worshipper. "What do you mean by 'the Deep'?"

"Those two who just came in."

"The Cast?"

"Yes."

"That can't be right, my Mama—" The phrase hangs in the stale air, unfinished.

When she says, 'Mama', the Scholar's eyes fix on the Girl, holding a stare too long for a mere acquaintance. I understand the reason behind his prolonged look—it is the same reason why he is no longer blind from grief—but *she* remains oblivious.

She watches him with those unnervingly perceptive eyes. "What?" she asks, a small, tentative sound in the echoing space.

Her gaze drifts, as if searching for the source of his sudden intensity. She looks back at him slowly and furrows her eyebrow.

"You look so much like your mother," he says, his voice cracking. He looks away, quickly.

"You know my Mama?" The question is a whisper.

"I know her very well." He clears his throat. "She's from the Deep." The words are clipped, almost curt.

The Girl, as if sensing the tangled roots beneath the surface, retreats into herself. Her attention drifts, latching onto some minute detail of her surroundings—a crack in the stone, the movement of dust motes in the dim light.

"My Book!" she whispers, sharply. She strains against the unyielding chains, her thin hands twisting in desperation. "It's gone!" The discovery seems to unravel her, to expose a raw vulnerability beneath the surface of her quiet strength, or more accurately, stubbornness.

"The Book will be safe," the Scholar replies, his voice a low, steady counterpoint to her rising panic.

With a swift, almost predatory grace, I extinguish the sole flame, plunging the room into absolute, suffocating darkness. Her breath hitches, a rapid, shallow intake of air. Her fear, raw and untamed, permeates the space, a tangible presence that presses against me, fills me.

"What's wrong?" The Scholar's voice slices through the stillness.

She gasps again, a ragged, desperate intake of breath. "Light!"

"You fear the dark," he observes, his tone measured, almost clinical.

"Guards!" she calls out, her voice thin and reedy.

I glance towards the door. They know better than to enter yet.

"Guards!" she cries again, the word trembling.

The Girl makes a futile gesture, trying to bring her hands to her chest. It is an instinctive attempt, the only proof of her survival from that fateful day, nine years ago, when the other children didn't live. But her hands are bound, trapped by unyielding chains. She twists her neck, clumsily trying to reach the spot with her chin, but her movements are awkward and ineffective.

"When my sister would get scared," the Scholar begins, his voice a low rumble. "She would go numb. And I would sing to her."

The Girl shifts, struggling to regain her breath. "With that deep v-voice?" she manages, a flicker of amusement softening the edges of her fear.

"I will stay here until the pain goes away," he murmurs.

The Girl gasps, her eyes widening in the darkness. "I know this song! My Mama sings it to me."

"Sing with me," he urges.

She hesitates for a moment, as if weighing the vulnerability of it, then takes a deep breath. Together, their voices, untrained and imperfect, fill the cavernous space. It is not a beautiful harmony; it is raw and fragile. Frankly, they sounded awful.

"I will live here, so the rhythm one day will change." The last notes fade, leaving a quiet resonance in their wake. The Girl's breathing has calmed, a faint, almost pathetic smile playing on her lips.

"I don't want to be scared," she whispers. "I tried to think of something scarier than the dark," she trails off and then adds, "but it's not as easy as it sounds."

"To not be scared, you must first be scared."

"What do you mean?"

"To be fearless, you must be brave. And bravery is being scared and doing it anyway."

"I'll *always* be scared?" She wiggles her toes as she says this.

"*Are* you scared all the time?" he asks softly.

She looks down, attempting to push her chin to satisfy the itch on her chest. The silence stretches between them. Finally, she says as if she has practiced this sentence many times, "Love is stronger than fear, but—"

"But what?"

"Love hurts."

The Scholar frowns, unaware of the tears falling down the Girl's cheeks. His own tears mirror those of the Girl. The fool has just realized how the Worshipper has treated the Girl.

He clears his throat. "Perhaps, the one who loves doesn't know how to show it." He pauses, then asks, "Were you always scared of the dark?"

"Not always," she whispers, the admission a small, hesitant offering.

"Did something happen?"

As he speaks, the Girl flinches, her gaze darting away. Then, as if releasing a breath which she has been holding for too long, she blurts out, "It started the night I found the Book. Inside a wall."

Someone put it there, did they?

He leans forward, his voice gentle, encouraging. "How old were you that night?"

"About this tall," she gestures with her head, indicating her current sitting height, a small, unconscious act in the darkness. Then, a flicker of realization crosses her face, and she adds, "Oh—"

"It's okay. I can see in the dark." He smiles warmly, an unseen act by the Girl, which reaches his voice. "How many days have passed since then?"

"One thousand and twenty sun rises: about three years," she says. Almost as an afterthought, she adds, "That night, she was extra sad."

"Was she always sad?"

"No." Her voice is tinged with a bittersweet melancholy. "She got sadder after the man with the dog came. The Voice came soon after, and since then, she changed. She wasn't always sad, though. Sometimes she was happy. We'd run up the stairs to the rooftop, laughing, and look at the stars at night." The words are bright, but the smile they conjure doesn't quite reach her eyes.

The Scholar clenches his jaw. "The Voice."

The Girl seems oblivious to his brewing anger towards me. She continues, "That was an *extra* dark night, even with a big, round moon. I looked *everywhere* for her, in all the rooms, but I forgot to look on the roof." She gulps.

In a whisper, she says, "She was there. Glowing in the moonlight. The moon was *so* close, like I could just … *hold* it!" Her voice quietens as she rocks back and forth. "She tied her … her veil, you know, around the railing, and … and around her neck … like she was going to j-jump. But then, she saw me, and … and it was like … like everything was fine again."

"You were only six years old," he says.

That observation is very accurate, considering she never told him exactly how old she is. The Girl, immersed in her own world, fails to notice this.

She rubs her face with her shoulder. The Scholar opens his mouth to say more, but she talks faster, like the words, now with a taste for being released, are desperate for more.

"I told her if she jumped, I would jump too! And she said, 'I'm supposed to keep *you* safe!'" Her voice wobbles, and she makes a small hiccup sound. "Then she fell onto me, and I hugged her *so* tight!"

A long pause stretches between them.

"She looked at me," the Girl says in a small voice. "And she said, 'I can't do this anymore.' I asked her, 'Do what, Mama?' She said, 'Live.'"

The Girl shivers. "That night, I learnt there is something scarier than the dark."

"Losing the one you love the most," the Scholar whispers.

She nods, with her eyes shut. "I asked her, 'What will make you want to live again, Mama?' And then, she saw the Book. And something changed." She lets out a long breath. "She told me the Book was like a light, and I had to keep it safe. That it had to be hidden in Jinnah, and *only* ever, in Jinnah."

"She chose to live," he says.

The Girl pauses, her gaze drifting downwards. Her bushy brow furrows, a small wrinkle of concentration appearing between her eyes. She asks, "What did she mean by 'it's like a light'?"

The Scholar smiles, a subtle shift in the planes of his face. "A light guides you. It connects you with everything. It shows you the way when it is dark."

"How does the Book show you the way?"

"Well," the Scholar begins. "Think of it like this. There is a light deep inside each of us. It is our natural state, a clue to what is good: being kind, caring about justice, the feeling of something bigger than you. But to make that light *really* shine, to make it *complete*, there's another light—a light from the outside. It's a message, a revelation from the Creator—The Greater One— that tells you what true goodness *really* is. It allows us to be raised into the highest ranks of our kind."

"Can our inside light be strong without the outside light?"

"The revelation is the word of Allah, Himself. The light inside is a hint at that. The revelation makes that light inside you even brighter, stronger than what it already is."

The Girl scrunches her face in confusion. "I don't understand."

The Scholar recites something, in that ancient language, one which is all too familiar to me, its translation: "'Allah is the Light of the Heavens and the Earth. The example of His light is like a niche within which is a lamp, the lamp is within glass[14]—'"

A wave of pain, sharp and insistent, pulses through me. I stumble back into the shadowed recess I occupy, my movements clumsy and uncoordinated.

He continues, "'—The glass is like a pearly white star kindled from a blessed olive tree, neither of the East nor of the West, whose oil would almost glow even if untouched by fire. Light upon light. Allah guides to His light whom He wills. And Allah presents examples for the people, and Allah is The Knower of all things.[14]'"

I have had *enough*.

I communicate to the Cast: "We need to move this plan along," transmitting the message urgently, bordering on desperate. "Scar, make your choice now."

I turn back to the Girl and the Scholar.

He pauses and then says, "In the language of our ancestors, light means *noor*."

"Noor?" the Girl echoes. "Noor," she whispers again, rolling the word around on her tongue, as if tasting it for the first time. A small, almost hesitant smile flickers across her face. "That's what I want my name to be," she declares with a quiet certainty.

"Noor," the Scholar repeats, his voice catching, a subtle tremor of emotion rippling beneath the surface.

"Are you okay, Elias?"

"Noor—AmaNoor, was the name of a wise woman who showed me the straight path."

"Now, there are *two* Noors!" the Girl exclaims, her voice suddenly brighter, the earlier shadows lifting. "Noor and Noor!" She bounces a little in her chair, the chains rattling softly, her energy returning in a rush.

"Yes. There are two Noors." He takes in a deep breath, a ragged intake of air, as if trying to gather the scattered pieces of himself.

"It's a beautiful name," he finishes, the words thick with unshed tears, for a kind of love lost, but more, a love rediscovered.

One which I will soon take away again.

PART 24

Blinded

ADAMAH

My vines, which had spiraled skyward to form a makeshift staircase, now unravel, each strand descending as I turn towards the exit hole of the Fallen Trees, into the Orbee Forest. Before I leave, I turn to the orbees who have not left my side since I awoke by the Zam.

I gesture to one, a small, pulsing orbee of light. It hovers closer. I hold out my hand, palm up. It lands, an airy touch, almost weightless, yet I can feel the subtle pressure.

"Why are you following me?" I whisper.

The light itself feels warm, a gentle heat that radiates outwards from the point of contact. I can almost *feel* the light, a faint tingling that spreads through my hand and up my arm. It spins a little dance on my skin, a dizzying whirl that makes my head swim slightly.

Then it does something unusual. It moves against me, a soft, brushing sensation, like … cleaning. The movement is incredibly gentle, almost imperceptible, but it's there. Like a delicate feather caressing my skin, comforting. It is as if the light is not just touching me but trying to interact with something deeper inside me. It searches for something; I'm not sure what.

The other orbees crowd in, jostling for position. Most of them are doing it now, this brushing, cleaning motion. It's not overwhelming, but a multitude of delicate sensations, like a thousand tiny feathers brushing against me simultaneously. The brushing motion is more pronounced now, a distinct sweeping sensation that moves across my skin, leaving a trail of warmth in its wake.

A chorus of tiny *clicks* and *chirps* fills the air. I still don't understand the words, but I understand the behavior.

Like ants. Or ... lions. Rafiq and the Black Assad: a hierarchy. Someone at the top, everyone else submitting to them. But *why*? Why would the orbees submit to me?

I close my eyes as I try to recreate the connection with their Queen. I don't know if the link is still there. But I must try. If I had it once, perhaps—

I will a message, like I do with my vines: *Queen?*

No response. Just the faint *hum* of the orbees, their lights pulsing softly.

I will another message, this one more forceful: *Beast!*

ROAR.

The ground shakes under my feet from the impact of the sound. The orbees swarm closer, their lights a blinding halo around me. Heart leaps against my ribs. Breath hitches. Air catches in my throat. Eyes widen.

The ground trembling beneath me sends a jolt of primal awareness through my body. My muscles tense involuntarily, preparing for something.

The orbees, now a swirling vortex of light around me, feel different. Their gentle touches become more insistent, almost urgent. The warmth that was comforting now feels intense as if they are trying to protect me.

The combination of the roar, the shaking ground, and the swirling lights creates a sense of disorientation, a feeling that the world is tilting on its axis. Then again, calling someone a beast the way I did won't welcome a kind word.

I am a coiled spring, body tense, energy inward. My mind races, searching—words, actions, *anything* to appease the Queen's rage. Eyes dart, scanning, hyper-alert. Every detail, every nuance, even though my mind tells me she is not in Jinnah.

I will my words to her: *Queen.*

A voice, inside my head, sharp and cold. *Her* voice: *You said you were an ally.*

Me: *I am.*

Her: *What ally takes my throne?*

Me: *I haven't taken your throne.*

I wait for her response. My legs shift beneath me, a constant, almost unconscious fidgeting. My fingers tap a nervous rhythm against the floating vines. I need to move.

I exit the hole of the Fallen Trees and enter the Orbee Forest.

Something happened here. Scrapes mar the earth, deep gouges in the soil. Footprints, frantic and uneven, crisscross the ground. A *struggle*.

The trampled ground has dozens of tracks, about fifty or sixty, vanishing up the Silver Path, which morphs to the bridge and then back to its spirally shape as it stretches past the bordering orbee trees, towards the Golden Dome. But … I lean towards the ground; two sets of tracks branch off from the rest.

One, faint and uncertain, meanders towards the other section of the orbee trees—the ones which lead to Shahwah. My mind, which had been a swirling vortex of nervous energy, snaps into focus. The scattered thoughts gather, giving way to a new pathway into the left side of my mind.

Tracks. The word itself is a trigger, sparking a cascade of rapid-fire assessments. *Two sets*. Eyes scan the ground, registering the subtle differences in the prints—size, depth, direction. My mind instantly begins to process the information. *Faint … uncertain … meanders*.

Right side of my mind. These descriptors paint a picture, a story unfolding in the dust. Who could they belong to?

Left side of my mind. Focus narrows. World fades. Focus on the details of the tracks.

The nervousness that had been gnawing at me from the Queen's rage recedes, replaced by a surge of purpose. A welcome distraction.

The second set of tracks is bold and cuts back towards the very hole I just emerged from. My breath hitches. *Yahya?* But when? Why didn't I see him? Or hear him? Could the sound of the flood have drowned out all other sounds? Of the struggle? Of my son? If Yahya came at the time of the flood, that means—

Before I can finish the thought, another roar bursts out, sending my body right back to tension.

The Queen: *There can only be one queen.*

Me: *Keep your throne. I only want to find my son and leave.*

Her: *You have taken my daughters*

I don't have time for this, not when my son could be so close. As I rush up, something sharp jabs at my toe. I flinch, expecting blood, but the orbees are there in an instant, their lights flickering over the wound, mending it before my skin even breaks.

A circular object lies half-buried in the dirt. I pick it up. This thing doesn't absorb light, it reflects it, the gold-encrusted surface shimmering with vibrant gems.

This is my crown.

The crown is warm, despite the cool air of Jinnah.

The heat makes the rest of my body feel cold with a prickling sensation. My mouth is like dust, gritty and dry. I lick my lips, my tongue scraping against parched skin. My fingers tremble as I trace the carvings. Emeralds, they glow like captured tears. Rubies, blood-red, seeming to bleed light. And all those points, razor-sharp, glint like tiny knives.

Something rises inside me. A need, sharp and insistent, to clench my fingers around it, to claim it. Something else grips me. Cold. Constricting. Like being wrapped in chains: lower it. The thought is there, unbidden.

Lower this shackled disguise. This cage.

I don't listen to this opposing force. I cling to the—*my*—crown. It holds something precious inside it. Something I *need* to see. I hold it tighter with both hands.

I stumble back a step, and the crown almost slips. I grab it fiercely. *Too fiercely.* As I hold it there, cradled in my hands, a picture flashes. Sharp. Clear.

Yes, this is what I needed to see.

Small hands. A little boy, barely taller than my knees, stands before me, the crown perched on his head.

The crown on his head has no jewels and spikes; it is bare and minimal. I barely acknowledge the crown, instead focusing on the boy. His eyes are the color and shape of most of our people, black and deep, with long eyelashes framing them. His hair, a tousled mess, frames chubby cheeks with not one dimple, but two; one under his eye and the other on his cheek.

Warmth. Fingers on mine, a pressure. He moves, a clambering, scraping sound against rock. The sword, wood-grained and familiar, goes up towards the rocky ceiling of the Deep.

"Don't jump!" I say, the words coming out fast and loud.

I grab his arm, the fabric of his sleeve a different texture from the other people of the Deep—softer—it is gentle against my skin. His eyes meet mine, a directness I am not used to, but have yearned for since he was born.

"Let me go, Mama!" he says, the words clipped, precise. "If I fall," he continues, each word distinct, "I will get up."

The jump he makes from the rock is not really a jump. It is a movement down. Still, my breath catches. He lands on soft earth, the crown still on his head.

"I did it, Mama!" he says.

The echo of that joy collides with the harsh reality of the present, leaving me breathless, my face wet with tears. The memory, a bittersweet ache, is a stark reminder of all I have ever wanted to be. The mother of life.

Of goodness.

Of purity.

I focus my message to the Queen: *I only want my son, then I will leave.*

Her: *You cannot escape your destiny.*

Me: *What is my destiny?*

I place the crown on my head. A motion I hadn't committed to, until now. It is heavy, a physical weight, but I am different now, after that vision. Stronger … I hope. Something has shifted inside of me since I saw the meaning behind the crown and its link to my Yahya. This crown has given me a sense of renewal. I want a new beginning.

The reply of the Queen echoes in my mind: *Your destiny is death.*

I stumble slightly at the power of her words but catch myself. "That is everyone's destiny," I whisper, my voice steady, no longer trembling.

With the weight of the crown on my head, the image of my boy will remain etched in my memory. With this crown, I will be connected to my son. It will make my search more relentless. I *will* find him.

A scream. Sharp. Raw. It rips through the air, through the pounding in my ears. It comes from the Golden Dome.

Yahya. The name is not a plea anymore. It is a command.

I run. My breath is uneven, but my stride is sure, my vision narrows, focusing only on getting to the doors of the Golden Dome. Each footfall is a *thud* against the ground, the sound echoing with a newfound authority.

I run past the Garden of Fire, towards the bridge above the Zam. Out of the corner of my eye, I register the olive tree. The green stalk is taller now, almost as tall as me.

This information flashes into my awareness without me directly looking at it. It's not a clear, focused image, but more of a peripheral impression— a quick update on the tree's growth. My mind automatically processes this visual input, registering the change in height and integrating it with my primary focus: *run!*

I sprint past the orbee trees, which border the end of Jinnah, and up the Silver Path, which morphs into steps.

Behind me, footsteps.

Clip clop.

Clip clop.

I turn.

I see.

The Ram.

It is at the bottom of the steps. Closer to me now than it was in the Garden of Fire. It walks slowly towards me, the sound of its steps menacing.

Something tells me I need to look into its eyes. A gut feeling, a prickle of unease that raises the hairs on the back of my neck. My heart gives a nervous flutter, a subtle shift in its rhythm. Unsettled. Dread.

I close my eyes tightly. A reflex, to shield myself from whatever it is that I sense emanating from the Ram. My other senses heighten, amplifying the sounds around me—the rustle of leaves, the whisper of the wind. They are interrupted by the approaching sounds of the Ram's hooves on the metal steps.

Clip clop.

Clip clop.

I hold my breath, listening, waiting. Hoping the sound of the Ram will go away. Slowly, I open my eyes. It's gone. A long breath of relief.

Another scream reaches me from behind the doors of the Golden Dome. This one, more infused with a painful moan.

I turn and push open the heavy doors, fighting the subtle tremor that continues to vibrate through me from the Ram.

PART 25

The Kneeling

ME

Scar pushes open the door and barges into the murky cell, followed by Snout. The Scholar looks at them and says, "Those roars, why—"

Scar interrupts him, slightly out of breath. "I choose ..."

Snout shoves past him, his voice booming in the cramped room. "When the black of night descends, the one he chooses shall be brought to their end."

Scar pulls back the curtain, fully exposing the small window. It casts a meager band of light—light that has somehow found its way through the smoky sky—across the dusty floor. The rest of the room remains consumed by darkness.

"End?" the Girl asks.

"I choose—" Scar says again.

Snout interrupts him and glares at the Scholar. "You will die." He then turns to the Girl and says, "You will live. For now."

Snout shoves the door to slam it shut, but Scar intervenes, stopping it from banging and gently closes it, quietly, behind him.

ADAMAH

Dozens of silk slippers flood the marble hall. I blink a couple of times as I take in their random placement in this sacred place. But then, who am I to question the mannerisms of a sacred space, after what I have done? The crown wobbles a bit on my head.

The wooden door to the carpeted room hangs slightly ajar, revealing a sliver of the even more unusual scene within.

I will the vines to push it open. It creaks forward slowly. Dappled light of the orbees filters through the room, a room filled with the same figures—the Cast—I had encountered outside the Great Wall, only now they don't wear the masks.

The Cast member closest to me shrugs off their vibrant emerald cloak, followed by others who do the same motion, leaving their outer garments scattered across the floor like fallen leaves. Only, there is nothing natural about these people.

Their intimate garments are on full show, a merge of another emerald cloak with misplaced pink frills around the chest areas, revealing blustering figures which look more like well-fed animals than humans. The thinner ones' clothes hang off them, baggy and misfitting in another way.

The figures kneel on the plush green carpet, heads bowed reverently towards the East. Some weep silently, tears glistening on their cheeks. Others whimper; their voices choked with sorrow.

My attention returns to the figure closest to me—the one who'd first removed their emerald cloak. Unlike the others, who are repeatedly slamming their head against the ground, each impact muffled by the thick carpet, this person does nothing. They simply look straight ahead, a vacant glaze in their eyes.

A crimson stain blooms on the dazed figure's garment, spreading from a small wound on their forehead.

My instinct is to leave. This is all too bizarre.

My eyes dart across the room searching for Yahya, but instead, I see other figures with similar injuries on their foreheads; bloody wounds which pool down their heads onto their clothes.

Realizing Yahya isn't here, I back away. A collective gasp echoes through the space, drawing my attention back to the figure nearest to me. Their vacant eyes now hold a glint, more disturbing than friendly. There is no depth in those eyes, as if they are made of buttons on a doll. Their shallow black eyes hold me with awe.

This figure stares, their eyes shifting to my face. "You!"

The room seems to hold its breath. Then, as one, the others turn towards me.

ME

The now dwindling sliver of light finds its way through the curtain, landing as a rebellious streak across the floor. The Girl shakes her chains, her face wet with tears.

"There's a weak link here," she whispers.

The Scholar's deep voice rumbles from the shadows. "Noor, listen to me," he begins, each syllable echoing in the confined space.

She flinches and straightens her back, defiance sparking in her eyes. "I'll listen once we're out."

Her eyes remain fixed on the band of light, on the red floor.

"My Mama needs you," she says firmly. Desperate hope flares in her eyes as she glances at the heavy door. "Guards!"

The Scholar's voice, though soft, is firm. "It won't work."

"Why?" she demands, her voice choked with tears. Her knuckles turn white as she grips the worn chair handles. She stares at him. "I'm no good at anything, but you have the message, the one that can save my Mama. It'll tell her why she's here, why she needs to keep living."

"She never stopped fighting to live. She held onto what she knew." The Scholar's voice is gruff, laced with a hint of pain. "It's my fault, I left her. I left all of them."

"Why?"

"My nephew—my sister's son—left the Deep, and I went after him."

"Did you find him?"

"Yes. In another land. I bought him back, but before we could go to the Deep, we were caught and thrown," he taps the floor with his foot, "into this very room."

He leans closer, his voice hushed. "That young boy had something very special about him," he pauses carefully, and I lean forward too. "Something you have too."

"Me?" the Girl says, distracted.

"He was gifted."

"Do you have a weak link in your chains?"

Instead of answering, he smiles, "Your gift—"

"Gift?" the Girl interrupts, tugging harshly at the stubborn shackles. "I don't have a gift!" Her voice cracks. "Why won't you help my Mama?"

"What I am about to tell you," his voice softens, before continuing, "will help you do what you need."

She freezes, hands hanging in mid-tug. "How?"

His smile fades into a serious expression. "How many trees are there in Jinnah?"

"75," she replies.

"How many *fallen* trees?"

She hesitates, then answers, "16."

"How many leaves are on one of the trees?"

The Girl blinks. "Depends on the tree."

"The one which has a mark on it," he continues. "The shape of a diamond."

"402 leaves," she blurts out.

"How many ants are there in Jinnah?"

She closes her eyes and focuses. "Last time I checked … 500,003."

"Orbees?"

"Their number hasn't grown since the smoke came. 779."

Silence follows.

The Scholar's lips curve into a smile. "You are gifted with memory."

Anger flickers in the Girl's eyes. "How can that help me? How did it help her when she was going to jump off the ledge?"

He continues, "You also carry the gift of astuteness."

"What is that?"

"Your understanding of people."

"Who wouldn't understand their Mama?" she says, though a flicker of doubt appears in her eyes.

His head drops slightly. "It is the mother who should understand her child."

She swallows hard and looks down at her trembling hands.

He continues, "When the message becomes harder to grasp, our Creator will never leave us in complete darkness."

"Are you talking about the revelation?"

"Yes. That is what your Book is. It is a light upon the light within us." His voice holds a quiet, irritating power.

"Why are you saying all this again?"

"When I was younger, I had a dream of purple flowers. I didn't know what they meant until I met you."

"What have I got to do with purple flowers?"

He watches her thoughtfully as if considering his answer. "My point is that the dream was a kind of inspiration, a light which came to me from outside of me."

"Was it a good dream or a bad dream?"

"All dreams from our Creator are good. All inspiration—light from outside of us from Him—is for one reason: to guide us *to* Him."

"You mean like signs?"

"Signs," he repeats. "There is only one inspiration, however, which has no room for error. None. That is the Book—your Book—which you have been guarding. It is preserved in the very form it was revealed to us from the day it came down from Heaven itself. We do not need to guard the Book, The Greater One has promised to do it for us."

"I knew it was special." She relaxes her shoulders slightly, as if a burden of her protecting the Book is lifted. "What about the other inspirations?"

"They can be tainted, through our own blinders or other blocks to us receiving them, in their true form." He sighs. "Over the last few years, as the world has darkened, these gifts—inspirations—have become stronger in some of us."

"How is any of this going to help my Mama?"

"It's you who must be helped first, Noor," he says gently. "Only then can you help her."

"Why do I need help?"

"Because your gift of remembrance," he states, his voice low, "it comes with a burden."

As he speaks, the Girl recoils.

He continues. "Every moment of pain you have felt clings to you. And if you don't face those moments, Noor, they will find other ways to face you."

The Girl shakes her head. "I don't feel pain."

"You choose not to."

Her voice drops, repeating the words with less resolve. "I don't feel pain."

"Sometimes," he begins. "The scars we can't see are—"

Her eyes flicker with understanding, and she begins to cry softly. "Scarier than the ones we can."

She sniffles. "I love her. I love her so much, but sometimes … most times, she looks past me, like I'm see-through or something." The room is quiet for a while, only filled with the echo of her quiet sobs. "What do I do?"

"Accept your gifts," he says.

The Girl slumps back in her chair. "The gift of understanding people? What does that mean?"

"Have you ever trusted the Voice?" the Scholar asks.

"Never."

"Why?" he presses.

"I felt stuck," she says. "Like something heavy was pushing down on me, every time I talked to it." She bites her lip, thoughtfully. "Not just stuck, but *tired* too. Like I needed to get away." She shivers. "I feel it *now*, except the tired feeling is coming from behind me. And under my feet."

"When you met my sister, your *friend*—"

"My friend," There's another flicker of understanding in her eye. "She's your sister?"

"Yes, Adamah is my sister."

"Adamah," the Girl echoes.

"How did you feel with her?" As he says this, his grip tightens slightly on the chair.

"I knew." Her voice gains strength. "I knew she was good."

"She *is* good," he whispers, his voice thick with emotion as he says this again, "She is good." He sits up and speaks louder. "There is more I have to tell you, Noor."

The Girl leans forward, as do I.

He takes a deep breath. "The boy I tracked, the one I said was like you," his eyes flicker to the door, "when he was born, something shifted in our people as if he unlocked something inside us. An ability."

"What was it?"

"A language," he reveals.

"The Tap?"

The Scholar shakes his head. "Not quite." He takes another deep breath. "We used the Tap to help us understand the language I speak of."

"How?"

"This ability—what became a language cannot be spoken and it cannot be heard. In darkness, it can only be seen, and it exists beyond words. With it, you will never be in the dark again. That, I hope, is my gift to you, Noor."

Her eyes fix on his for a moment, and she looks away again and says, "Why would you need something like that in the Deep?"

"In the Deep, for a time after our elders left, some of us became mute, including my sister. She created a form of communication—the Tap—which didn't need voices. After that, came another kind of language."

"Is that what the clicking was that you did before?"

"I learnt the clicking on my travels. When she had her son, it was the first time our generation bore a child, not only that, but she was the youngest among us. Yahya, her son, was first in many things, including this language after the Tap."

"What is this language?"

"It's … I should show you."

The Scholar closes his eyes, his brows furrowed, deepening the lines on his forehead. The air in the room seems to thicken even more with all our anticipation. A flicker of something catches my eye—a faint glow emanating from somewhere, but then it's gone.

I squint and look at the small fire. Did it come from there? No, it is completely out. The flicker comes back, this time long enough to see where it came from: his very hand! It intensifies, pulsing an inner rhythm; this is not just a light, but a torrent of energy, spreading outward.

His veins, once hidden beneath the skin, become luminous, the pathways glowing. The light pulses within them, tracing intricate patterns, like rivers of molten gold carving through his body. This is not fire, though something just as primal and potent.

The room, once shrouded in darkness, is now bathed in an ethereal glow, emanating from within him. He has become a beacon.

ADAMAH

Their black eyes, flat and lifeless, hold mine captive. They stand on the green, worn carpets, not bowing anymore, but advancing. I lurch backward, feeling the splintered wood of the doorframe against my back. The orbees, thankfully, provide a soft buffer.

One of the Cast on my right speaks in a voice, more of a rasp, like gravel grinding on ice, which echoes in the vast room. "It's you."

Now that I can see their faces, I wish they still wore the masks.

My lips' part to speak, but "Your faces" comes out of my mouth as a strangled whisper.

Their faces are burned like mine, except more flesh writhes beneath the shiny skin, as if it has been pushed there to make a new shape. They smell like a rotting carcass, left out in scorching heat, worse than the camel's decaying flesh. I fight the urge to heave.

Their lips are so swollen, they hang off their mouths. Their cheeks resemble balloons, contrasting starkly with their beautiful, flowing emerald cloaks, which they shuffle back over both the bulging and deflating bodies. All the while, their eyes remain fixed on me, multitasking.

As they put on their cloaks, there is a series of squeaks as if two balloons rub against each other. Their faces are like glitches, sometimes human-like, but other times, depending on the angle, some appear … even ape-like: thin with bones protruding and snouts. Others are pig-like, massive, and imposing.

"What happened to you?" I ask, backing away from them.

"Beauty happened to us." The raspy voice is unsettling; it seems to come from all of them and none of them at once. "We are the peak of what one would desire in a woman."

From the softness beneath the rasp and their inescapable bosom shapes on display, I realize they are all women. Every single one of them.

Confirming this, another figure asks, "Do you remember us?" Her voice is a squeaky, girlish, exaggerated tone.

My hand instinctively reaches for the doorknob.

A tall, thin figure steps forward, and my breath catches in my throat as I see her face. She has no nose, not even a snout, only two smooth, empty holes.

"We fell asleep," she says, her voice a whisper.

"In Jinnah?" I manage to croak out.

She nods curtly, the movement jerky and unnatural, along with a series of squeaks.

"You're the Cast," I say.

As if sensing my bewilderment, two figures step forward, their forms hulking. Each has two thick ponytails flanking their faces, adding to their already comical appearances. Yet, the sight does little to ease the tension coiling in my gut. Their chins are impossibly wide, their features identical, like grotesque mirror images.

"We don't call ourselves that anymore. Not since we saw what we saw in Jinnah. We've changed. *Transformed*. Now we're," they exchange glances, then say in unison, "we just are."

They look to me as if expecting me to agree, but I am too stunned by how little their voices differ from a shriek.

"You don't have names?" I ask, taking a wary step away from another figure who leans closer, sniffing my face, a little too close for comfort.

"Sometimes, we do, but nothing ever sticks," the Sniffer says, her face glitching as she looks slightly offended by me moving away from her.

"Where are you from?" I ask.

The twins exchange another glance, a silent communication passing between them. Then, they both point behind me, but before they can speak, the Sniffer snarls, "Shahwah!"

Before anyone can react, one of the Ponytailed Twins shoves the Sniffer with surprising strength. She goes flying across the room, crashing into the dusty curtain covering Sama, sending the folds of fabric billowing down.

In that moment, regardless of its billowing, the sun's light manages to stream through, exposing more disturbing features on these women. Globs of flesh hanging off their torsos, blotches of white all over their exposed skin, parts of their skin rich like mine, others that ivory tone, as if unfinished polish, leaving the surface incomplete.

"We're not from Shahwah anymore," the pusher Ponytailed Twin declares.

"Not now, we've seen," her twin continues.

I whip my head around, catching glimpses of the Sniffer sprawled on the ground, surrounded by several figures who *ooh* and *ahh* in unison.

"Seen what?" I stammer; my voice is barely audible over the growing commotion.

"I saw someone leading me here, to the Golden Dome," the Sniffer says, clambering to her feet with a grimace.

"I saw a serpent," another one murmurs.

"A serpent?" I echo.

"I saw the sky falling!" a hulking figure declares, her gaze intense on me.

"I saw a small boy," one says, in a trembling voice which sounds like a broken chord, artificial and problematic.

"I saw a slingshot," a Ponytailed Twin grunts.

"I saw a giant!" her Ponytailed Twin continues.

Despite the chaos, my focus remains fixed on the velvet curtain, small dust motes dancing in the air from the Sniffer's previous disturbance. With a surge, I push through the crowd, their voices fading into a distant hum.

I pull the curtain open and gasp. *How can this be?*

ME

I was supposed to know *everything*.

"Is this because you're a holy man?" the Girl asks.

"Even the unholy possess this ability; this is survival," the Scholar replies.

"How so?" the Girl asks, almost breathless.

The Scholar takes a deep breath. "In the depths of the world," he begins, "where sunlight cannot reach, creatures have adapted to darkness. Some make their own light, a result of their skin and the gases that interact with them. In the Deep, our children couldn't survive for years because of those same gases. But when my nephew was born, his body adapted and unlocked a gene we all shared."

"You mean gases did this to you?"

"More like our reaction to those gases. Our bodies are made to adapt. To survive."

"Our bodies can change over time?" the Girl asks.

He nods, a slight smile playing on his lips. "Thousands of years ago, when there was more room on Earth, people were taller. The first man to walk Earth was as tall as a tree."

Her eyes widen. "A tree?!"

"Yes," he continues, amusement in his voice. "The stories also tell us he lived for a long time, as long as ten of our lifetimes combined."

The Girl stares at him in silence, and her shoulders fall slightly. "So, these are only stories?"

His smile widens. "The best of stories are the true ones, and the Book is full of them."

"So, the first man was real?"

"He was. He was the father of all humankind."

"Did he have a name?" she asks.

"Adam."

"Adam. Like Adamah."

The man lights up, an ethereal glow emanating from his palm. As they watch, this light intensifies for a fleeting moment before fading away.

"What are you saying?" she asks.

"A language."

"Doesn't language have words?"

"Yes. Language helps us to make sense of the world around us. To organize it. To communicate with each other."

"To make things clear?"

"Yes. Now listen carefully. The first words were given to Adam by The Greater One, Himself. Those words are where language and the ability to speak first came from."

"Why is that important?"

"Because it is the words that were given to Adam *after* his fall from Heaven, that the Voice is truly searching for."

"After Adam's fall? What does that mean?" the Girl asks.

What are they?

What are the words?

She continues, "I thought the Voice was looking for my Book."

"Yes, but it is these words in the Book that it needs for it to—" He stops himself from speaking with his voice and turns to the language of light.

"What are you saying?" the Girl asks again.

"How did your mother speak to you?"

I could never understand the Tap. Something blocked it from me. I wonder if that block was ever something I could look past, or if its resemblance to how Father spoke to me prevented me from grasping it. I feel uneasy. Even if that is true, why didn't I see the language of light? What other blinders do I have? I shiver at the idea of not grasping something. No matter, I am so close now to finding what I've been searching for: the words from the Book.

The Girl gasps in realization. "Could Mama light up?"

The Scholar shakes his head. "It was rare in my generation, but after the boy, the children had the ability—all twenty of them, including my nephew. The only one who didn't have it was Amir."

"Amir? The guard?"

"Yes, he could never quite hone the skill."

"What happened to the other twenty children?"

A soft, warm light emanates from his palm, bathing the room in a glow.

"The Book?" the Girl asks, focusing on the Scholar's face as the light flickers.

He flashes once, then speaks. "Yes, it means—"

"The power of the Book," she interrupts.

The man smiles. "The power of the Book lies not in the physical object, but within a place none can seize, as long as it is guarded."

"Where?" she asks.

Where?

"A place where everything begins," he says. "Where the choice lies between martyr and hypocrite. Where what was concealed becomes exposed."

"Where?" she asks again.

I already know all this.

It is the place where *our* story advanced, where *our* bond became unbreakable, where life was born of death, where, as he just stated, what was concealed had been exposed.

His hand lights up again, casting dancing shadows on the wall. "This place," he says, his voice barely a whisper, "is what the Voice has been searching for and has never been able to grasp."

"Where is it?" she asks, leaning forward.

The man speaks slowly, his expression unreadable. "One must go to a place so deep. A place they ardently desire to escape with every part of their being. Only the humble can reach it. That is why the Book only reaches the humble," he says. "Do you understand?"

The Girl gasps, "A chest ..."

I am already on my way there—to the Arched Chest—before she finishes the sentence.

ADAMAH

I stumble backward, the curtain snagging my legs. It tears with a dusty sigh, crumbling around me. My gaze darts around the room, taking in the wide-eyed stares and gaping mouths. I scramble to my feet.

"Who brought this here?" I whisper.

"Brought what?" the Sniffer asks, bloodshot, glassy eyes darting around the room.

"The Arched Chest," I reply.

"Just saw it now," someone mumbles, their voice barely audible above the low murmurs and curious grunts.

I lower myself to the ground and touch the sides of the Arched Chest, my fingers tracing the ancient carvings. This unassuming wooden box, devoid of fancy embellishments, sits almost peacefully on the blood-stained carpet where Sama's body no longer lies.

The Arched Chest is small enough to fit in the palm of my hand, yet its weight pulls me down. An image flickers across my mind from the first time I had seen it. It was left outside my room, the night the elders went away. I didn't know what to do with it. I didn't know what to do with the knife inside it.

The Arched Chest was supposed to bring peace and tranquility.

It didn't.

It brought chaos.

The knife inside was the same one that Sama held to kill my brother's child. The same one that the Girl gave me. The same one I used at my inception to murder, on my first kill. The Arched Chest marks the beginning of the final collapse of the people of the Deep.

Because of *me*.

Taking a series of shallow breaths, I slowly lift the curved lid. It clatters, wood against wood, as I shift it. Are the letters still here?

I glance around, meeting the wide, curious eyes of the Cast. This moment is too personal to share.

"I need to be alone," I whisper, the words heavy in the air.

The Cast continues to stare as if I am a spectacle unfolding before them.

I clench my jaw. "Get out!"

Even then, their gazes remain unwavering, locked on me.

The orbees form a barrier of light between me and them. "Thank you," I whisper to them.

Now alone, I kneel back down by the Arched Chest. Taking a deep breath, I push the bottom upward, revealing a hidden compartment. My heart leaps—they are! The letters are still here—piles of my frantic scribblings nestled within.

The urge to find my son becomes more powerful when I see them. I can't just sit here and read my letters to him. I need to find him. Now. I hide the Arched Chest behind the crumpled curtain.

I'll get it later.

Gut clenches, blood rushes to limbs, leaving my middle cold. Eyes widen, drinking in every detail, searching, searching, like a hawk, seeing everything, even in the shadows. Senses ablaze, every sound, every flicker, a potential clue.

Where is Yahya?

My ears twitch, my nose sniffs. Every nerve ending screams for information. Skin warms, a sheen of sweat. My body's burning. Stomach twists. Fear. Cold dread.

What if he's dead?

Memory flares, past places, hidden corners, anything to find him. Images flashing, snippets of time, a desperate hope clinging to each one.

What if he's alive?

I rush through the orbees; they shift, allowing me to emerge on the other side of their light. I am met with a chorus of startled gasps, their eyes staring at the dark stain of my blood mixed with Sama's, where her body once lay. The stain is more obvious in the absence of the Arched Chest.

"Where is she?" I ask, referring to Sama. Someone *must* have moved her. How else is she not here?

"Girl with," one of the Ponytailed Twins begins, but stutters. She then says, "Blind ..."

Out of nowhere, her Ponytailed Twin shoves her and then strokes a red flower—the size of half her body—from the Garden of Fire. From its stifled smell and crushed demeaner, I'm guessing she stuffed it behind her frilled intimates, where her chest ... *yuck*.

Oblivious to my disgust, she says, "Not blind anymore ... he can see our bodies now."

Her sister giggles shyly, taking out another red flower from her chest, mirroring the action. She says, "Not blind anymore, *warrior*."

"You're not his type." I walk past them both, careful not to touch them. I don't want to feel anything they feel. And I'm annoyed by their giddy waste of my time.

When I reach the door, I turn towards them. "Where is my son?"

"We just told you! With the Girl and ... your brother," a Ponytailed Twin says—I am not sure which one she is.

Her words slam into me. *Yahya is with Elias? With the Girl?*

Another one of the Cast members steps forward—the Sniffer. She leans in towards me. In a conspiratory whisper, she says, "What *is* his type?"

I am still processing that the people I love, all three of them, are together.

The Sniffer narrows her eyes. "You don't know his type? Memory still gone?"

I lean closer to anchor myself on something, squinting at their faces, but they remain a blur. "Where are Elias and—"

More giggles at his name.

I continue, "Yahya, and the Girl?"

Three of the figures step forward, their voices weaving together in an unsettling harmony. "Where it all began."

My breath catches as the words sink in. "The Deep," I whisper.

I turn to the door and sprint out, mildly aware of the pounding of feet following close behind, their rhythmic *thuds*, surprisingly fast considering how unhealthy they look.

The *thuds* pause whilst they fumble in the hall, falling over each other as they put on their silk slippers.

I'm already out the door, my vines trailing behind me on the marble steps as I race down them, towards Jinnah, towards the Ghar of the Voice, towards the Deep.

ME

The Deep has been combed, every cranny pried, every bed upturned, walls hammered, a frantic, fruitless search. The Arched Chest is *gone*. A deeper darkness presses down from the sky. The Night of Decree is almost upon us.

As I step into the cell, crimson dust puffs up, then settles, like a brief, stifled cry fading to its post of stillness.

Scar shadows me silently. Snout pads pompously at my heels. I hold myself between the area of the doorways light and where the shadows begin.

"Where is the Book?" I demand.

The Scholar, chained, swivels his gaze to lock on the Girl. A flicker from his body, then her answering nod. The pieces click into place. He orchestrated this. He *wanted* me gone. What did he tell her while I was gone?

"Very well," I say coldly. "Take him to the Golden Dome. Prepare him for execution."

The Girl's eyes widen. The Scholar, however, remains a study in impassivity.

Snout swivels, his gaze flicking between both chained parties and then to me. He stammers, "I-I can assist in his preparation in many ways, but the *how* remains ..."

"Prepare the stakes, you incompetent fool!" The command slices through the air, sharper now.

Snout shudders visibly.

"B-but good friend ... ally," he whispers, "I don't wish to linger in Jinnah. I was lucky last time, the butterfly kept me awake, but if I fall asleep ..."

"Go another way," I snap.

Snout's brow furrows. "You mean ..."

"Through the Deep," I finish.

He hesitates. "But the ... creatures at the bottom of your Ghar, they—"

Ah. The creatures. Little *monsters*. They will be useful soon. I say, "Scar will help you with them."

Still Snout continues, "If I go through the Deep, then technically, I can't use the stakes from the fallen trees in Jinnah ..."

I know why he is reluctant. He does not want to face the creatures. Not after what they did to the ones he loved. Since then, he has not known *how* to love. Now he only spoils himself. He calls that love. It is good to know these things. Like the creatures he fears at the bottom of my Ghar, these things are useful.

"Tie him to a pillar in the Golden Dome," I say.

Scar and Snout, faces grim, move forward, their hands trembling as they reach to untie Your brother—a foolish impulse. Especially now, he is no longer blind.

"Wait!" I bark.

They freeze.

A brilliant idea strikes me—a way to stop the Scholar *and* get what I need ... no, what I want; yes, *want:* Father's message.

I smile. "Put your Apex on him, Scar."

"Each Apex is customized for the user," Scar replies.

My threads lash out, connecting with Scar's cheek. His face does not flinch, yet the skin beneath reddens quickly.

"Your life is a fickle thing, Scar. You live because *I* allow it. When you disregard my ... request, you become a danger to yourself. Do you understand?"

Scar's hand starts to flick. My earlier communication with him to instill fear was more subtle and covert. Ineffective. However, the mention of death is sure to bring a visceral reaction, a certainty that makes his flab tremble like no other. His face is now flamed crimson, as if about to burst.

"Give him your Apex." I enunciate each word with deliberate force.

Scar nods, retreating from the room. He returns moments later, placing the Apex atop ... well, atop his uncle.

Scar was right, the Apex *is* custom to whoever it was designed for. However, both uncle and nephew desire one thing: to live forever. They just want it in different ways. Scar wants it in a way where he never dies. The Scholar wants it in a way where life after death never ends.

More importantly, eternal life is the promise of *this* Apex.

I am curious, how will a man whose body has once become blind from grief, react to having what he so desires? Will he become euphoric? Will he break?

Once his face is veiled by the Apex, he shudders. The two silver eyes glow as something flows through the thread from the center of the mask.

He is subdued.

For now.

And thankfully—quite usefully for my benefit—being prepared to share Father's message. Yes, unfortunately, I must wait to retrieve that message *after* his encounter with the Apex.

Scar and Snout each seize the Scholar's shaky arms. Their footsteps are heavy, dragging him deeper past the doorway into the shadows of the hall which leads out.

"Scar, return to me after you help Snout!" I shout, my voice echoing after him. "Do not enter the Ghar!" Not that the fatty can anyway.

A grunt of acknowledgment from him.

I melt further into the shadows behind the door, watching both their thick and thin bodies depart. The Girl, now alone, glares into the darkness where I linger.

"Child," I begin.

"My name is Noor."

"A name," I murmur, my voice softening slightly, "is irrelevant. I have borne many names. What matters is *who* you are."

"And who are *you*?"

"One with a promise."

"Have you *ever* kept your promises?" she challenges.

A faint smile. "I promise safety and happiness. Don't you want to be happy?"

"What is your happiness?"

"Happiness," I begin, pacing slowly within the shadows. "Happiness is anything you desire, anything in this world."

I pause, letting the weight of my words settle. "Unmatched joy. Respect that commands obedience. Power that makes kingdoms tremble."

My voice lowers to a murmur. "Imagine it ... jewels the color of passion and envy, ruby red and emerald, green. Water that flows freshly, food that tantalizes every part of you." I move my voice until it becomes a whisper from behind her, which reaches both ears. "This is the happiness I offer. A world sculpted to your every whim, a life devoid of hardship or want."

"Does any of it last?" she asks.

I offer a hollow chuckle. "A whole lifetime!"

"That's it?" she challenges, her eyes narrowing.

A low growl rumbles in my throat.

She adds, "What about when I die?"

I am working on it. "Does it matter?" I whisper.

"What's the point of anything if that doesn't matter?" she retorts.

Retort. A piggish word. Like a little swine waddling around for something to eat.

"The point," I begin, "is to grasp a kind of heaven with your own hands." *That is the whole point.* I breathe on the dying embers, coaxing the flames back to life. "Look closer at the bricks around you."

She squints, examining the shimmering gold detailing within the chamber.

"The ground beneath you," I continue.

Her gaze falls to the red dust coating the floor.

"Are these not the materials of Heaven?" I finish with a flourish.

She kicks at the dust, sending a crimson cloud swirling into the air. "Is *this* what you promised my Mama and her people in the Deep?"

I falter.

She stamps her foot on the stone, the red dust momentarily obscured, and says, "It's a copy—and a bad one."

"No, it's not."

"Yes, it is."

"No, it's not! The walls are *real* gold." *Unoriginal.* I feel woozy. I must restrain myself. It takes every ounce of control to resist the urge to strike her. "You surprise me, Girl," I manage. "Such a defensive tone, and yet, you haven't got anything left to fight for."

Before she can offer some childish *retort*, I seize the moment, unleashing my melody. The threads vibrate with an intensity both magnificent and brutal. The melody swells, louder and more potent than ever, a song of unparalleled control.

Where

is

the

Book?

Where

is

the

Arched

Chest?

Instead of the expected submission, her eyes remain unfazed by the sheer power of my song. She speaks calmly, her voice cutting through my threads. "You're choking again."

My carefully constructed melody falters, the threads within me tightening as a wave of disbelief washes over me.

"No," I splutter, the sound raspy and weak. "No!"

469

She leans forward, a defiant edge in her eyes. "I have heard silent rocks with more beautiful songs than yours," she begins, "Your voice is not natural."

"Innocence," I spit the word. It *must* be innocence. But a gnawing in my thoughts whispers, even the purest souls, untouched by the world's darkness, have succumbed to my melody. The only other possibility is that another— other than the Scholar—is immune to my voice and its power. Which beckons the question, how many beings do I have no power over? No, I must stop this line of thought. It *must* be innocence.

"You have nothing left to fight for," I repeat.

"Why do you keep saying that?" the Girl asks.

After a pause, I say, "Because the person you love most in the world … is *dead*."

"My Mama is not dead," she *retorts*. Little piggy.

"Your friend took the Worshipper's life."

"Liar!"

"It was all your fault." My echo cuts through her cry.

"I didn't take Adamah to see my Mama."

"Oh yes, that's right. You didn't, did you?" I allow the stillness to engulf the room. "If you did, then perhaps things could have ended differently."

"Differently?"

"Your friend seeing the Worshipper was inevitable. But if you had taken her, you could have interceded on the Worshipper's behalf. Then maybe she would still be alive."

"My Mama is *not* dead," she says through gritted teeth. She looks in my direction. "Why are you doing all this?"

I let the question hang in the air. A few seconds more. Then I say, "I want the Book."

"Are you scared of it?"

My control momentarily falters. "I do not fear any book!"

She flinches, a wince crossing her face as she wipes away a stray tear with her shoulder. Quickly, I adjust my strategy, reigning in the outburst with a forced sigh, "The Book will help me get to where I want to go."

"Where's that?"

I wonder for a brittle moment if I should tell her—I heard that being personal can make people *like* you—something about being relatable, and that's important because when people like you, they do what you want. I'm willing to try new things to get what I want. I say softly, "Somewhere, I can make a difference."

Her thick eyebrow furrows.

I continue, "Somewhere, judgment does not exist, only desire, a land which can only be inherited, a land for the bound."

"How? Where?" she asks.

"By writing my own story," I begin, the words tumbling out, eager for release.

Technically, You will be writing it for me.

I grip the pen in my hand and continue in a low voice, "But to inherit the land, I need to access a special book."

"You mean the Book?"

"No, this one is The Book of Decree. It has the decrees of all creation written within it. That includes all the things that have, will, *are,* and *could* have happened."

"Where is it? How will you get to it?"

"Through a verse."

She blinks a few times.

I elaborate. "The Book of Decree is inside a type of verse. Some call it a multiverse. It can only be entered through reciting *another* kind of verse."

"What other kind of verse?"

"That verse which is in the Book," I add weakly, hoping she will take pity on me and my unique story, mission, vision. Whatever.

Whatever it takes to get what I need.

"I'm confused," she says.

Of course, she is. *Snort.*

"What are you confused about?" I ask in the kindest tone I can manage.

"Everything."

"All you need to know is for me to get to The Book of Decree, and make my difference, I need a verse from your Book."

She nods slowly.

I carry on, "I only want to make a difference. It's such a bad world we live in. Is that so difficult to understand?"

Her gaze shifts towards the shadows where my voice emanates. "You want to be free, don't you?"

That's not what I said. Well … I suppose I could play that role too, if it helps me.

"Yes. That's it. I desire freedom."

"Well, I know what it's like to want to be free," she states matter-of-factly.

"So, you understand. You'll help me?"

"Help you do what?" A flicker of disgust crosses her face.

This child is confusing. Even for me.

I stifle an annoyed sigh. "Help me break free of the chains binding me to this land on Earth and help me inherit another in the multiverse. I have worked *so* hard. I just need one thing from you."

"The Book," she whispers.

"Now I think about it, I don't even need the full Book. I need the verse that nice man told you."

She raises that one brow. "Nice man?"

"Yes, that *is* what he told you, isn't it? The verse that The Creator told Adam when he fell from Heaven?"

"I have learned something about being free. I hope it can help you." She glances at her chains as she speaks. "It's not a shame we are bound."

This—shame—what does *she* know about *This?*

"Being bound is never good," I say, seeing a thousand lights of fire pulsing through the generations of my kind, bound to submit.

"The shame is in *who* or *what* we are bound to," she says. "There is only One who is worth being bound to. He decides who deserves to be free and who deserves to be punished."

I have had *enough.*

I sharpen my tone. "Give me the verse from the Book."

"No."

"Then give me the whole Book." I will have You read it *all* if I must.

"You asked for my help. Let me help," she says. "The Book is your way of getting into the land you speak of—this … multiverse, but not like this."

"Like what?" I ask.

"Through reciting words that don't go past your throat. The words of the Book must enter your chest."

"It *has* entered a chest."

"That's not what I—"

"Give me the Book—the verse," I say.

"I don't have the Book with me, but the verse you want, I won't give it to you," she states.

A wave of frustration washes over me. Being personal is pathetic. All this talk of being bound … let's see who *she* is bound to, shall we?

"This," I continue, my voice hardening, "is not the first time your *friend* has killed. She has taken many lives, even before the Worshipper—"

"I told you my Mama is not dead."

I add, "—and that same *friend* will continue to kill, again and again, unless someone stops her."

The Girl digs her heels into the dust, looking away.

"You must have seen the signs," I press, my voice a menacing whisper.

"Of what?" she asks, face still turned away.

"Of a messenger," I reply.

"Liar."

"Her aptitude with a weapon," I counter. "Her rage."

Her gaze narrows. "Rage and weapons are the sign of a messenger?"

They are of mine. "You know what I'm talking about, don't you?"

"I've been angry too," she says softly. "It doesn't mean I kill."

"Well, you aren't her, and you haven't done what she has done." I let my voice wrap around her. "For people like her, the end is always … inevitable."

"What end?"

"Hell, unless I save her."

Save us—*me*.

"Save her?"

"I misspoke. A person like her does not deserve to be saved … see why for yourself."

With a flourish, I unleash the power of my voice, revealing a glimpse of the entertaining scene I had witnessed with *You* at Your peak, once again. The scene plays out before the Girl's horrified eyes. Her body trembles as she watches You draining life from the Worshipper. Your eyes gleam with anger. Now, the vine dress is disintegrating into dust with Your final blow, which stills the Worshipper's meager body.

"You may not be swayed by my voice," I declare, the power in my words amplified by the visual assault. "But you cannot deny the truth it reveals, can you?"

"What is she doing to her?" she cries out, her voice cracking. For good measure, I replay the scene. As the body of the Worshipper becomes still once again, the Girl shakes her head. "My Mama isn't dead."

I lean closer, my voice dropping to a low, urgent whisper right by her ear. "Does your friend deserve to be saved?"

"Stop her!"

"How?" I push.

The Girl glances down at the shackles binding her wrists. "Chain her!"

My tone remains neutral. "That won't work."

"Take her vines away!"

"She'll just find more," I reply.

"Kill her," she chokes out.

"Yes," I whisper quickly. After a pause, I add, "And what about the one who let her live?"

Her head snaps towards me. "Who let her live?"

"That nice old man who was just here," I say lightly, referring to the Scholar. My tone turns firm. "The one whose Book you guard. What kind of a man allows a murderer to roam free, claiming innocent lives?"

"A bad man." Her face contorts as she says this.

"Do you know why he let her free?"

She shakes her head, her body slumping.

"Because she is his sister. He doesn't care about justice for the wronged. He doesn't even care about the poor Worshipper. If he did, why would he not fight his execution and help her? Instead, he leaves you the burden, a poor little child …" I let my voice trail off.

She sniffles pathetically, moving her chin to satisfy the itch on her chest.

I add, "There is only one way the unjust can be stopped."

"How?"

"By rewriting their decree. To write their punishment. Eternal damnation in the fiery blaze of Hell!"

For Father. For my brothers and sisters. For those who mocked me. Taunted me.

I clear my throat—that was a little destabilizing—I gather myself. "And to rewrite the decree, I need that verse from the Book."

The Girl's entire demeanor crumbles, her resolve replaced by a childlike vulnerability. Her voice, choked with tears, sounds like a blubbering baby. "I want my Mama."

"Give me the verse," I say, my voice firm and unwavering. "And I will return to you the one you are bound to."

She flinches at the word 'bound', the little hypocrite.

"I want my Mama," she repeats.

"I will give her to you—"

"She's dead. She's dead." She keeps repeating the words, tears streaming down her cheeks.

"I can bring her back."

She becomes still.

"Yes. I can bring her back," I repeat. "But you must give me your word that you will tell me the verse I need."

She looks at the door, behind which I linger. Slowly, she says, "I give you my word."

A cold smile creeps across my face. "I, too, give you mine. You will see the Worshipper alive, better than she has ever been before."

I will have the verse from the Book.

Then You will rewrite our—*my*—story and put an end to all those who never believed in me.

I will rule Heaven.

The angels will serve *me*.

That is what The Book of Decree can do.

ADAMAH

I burst through the orbee trees. I'm in Jinnah. Past the Zam. It's a blur. The crown clatters on the other side of the bridge. I clatter after it, tumbling to the ground. I scramble up to continue running.

Pain—the sharp spikes of the crown's head pierce through my foot. A jolt shoots up my spine—my whole leg screaming.

My leg buckles. I fall. The crown's edges are buried deep, a raw, throbbing ache radiating outward—like fire, spreading through my foot. Blood spills, a dark bloom on the earth, each pulse a fresh wave of pain. A gasp against the searing heat in my foot. A cold sweat breaking out on my brow. Sick to my stomach, dizzy. I try to move, but the pain is a vice, clamping down, muscles locked tight, can't even twitch my toes.

The orbees, poised to mend above me, falter. They freeze mid-air, hovering. Some float to my foot but return to the crowd of orbees. None heal.

I have never seen them like this. Motionless. Then, they begin to move about frantically, as if slightly delirious.

Feverishly, I rip a piece of my vine dress and wrap it around the wound. The blood soaks into it within seconds. Why aren't the vines helping me?

I clench my teeth. A burning sensation, a raw, throbbing pain, continues to radiate outwards from the wound. I have gotten too used to—perhaps distracted by—my pain being taken care of. In my spoiled comfort, it has become more amplified. *Perhaps,* a fleeting thought flickers, *my vines weakened me, not strengthened me.*

I *need* to move. Focus! The word slams through my thoughts, a desperate grab for control. I shove the pain down, lock it away in a dark corner. It's still there, a dull throb, a constant ache, but I *can't* think about it now.

I need to think about Yahya. My mind is a whirlwind of conflicting emotions—panic, determination, fear, hope—but what binds it all is a single, unwavering purpose: *Find him. Now.*

I pull myself to my feet before spinning around at the gasps behind me. The Cast are gathered; their eyes fixed on my injured foot.

"It's nothing," I stammer, leaning on the olive tree, which is now taller than me, beside the Zam.

The Sniffer steps forward. "It *is* true."

A Ponytailed Twin takes a cautious step towards me. "It *is* you," she breathes, her voice thick with emotion. "The blood on your feet, the same way when you stepped on the crown all those years ago."

"How would you know that?" I demand.

The other Ponytailed Twin, her voice mirroring her sister's, steps forward and declares, "How could we not? We've been waiting for you."

An unsettling silence follows, then, all at once, the Cast kneel before me, with a resounding *thud* as they bow their heads.

They do not bow to the East, they bow to me.

PART 26

The Victory

ELIAS

My eyes flick open. Light, not a flood, but enough. Limbs respond. *Why should they not?*

The room is … a chamber. Not huge, but big enough for me to stretch out, and the air, though cool, carries no damp chill. The walls, still bearing the marks of the chisel, retain the uneven texture of the cave itself—a patchwork of greys and browns, flecked with the glint of moisture.

A low bed made of a softer earth than the rest of the room occupies the center of the space.

Here I lie.

Near the foot of the bed, a flickering fire dances within a glass-covered hearth set into the earthen floor, casting long, wavering shadows that play across the uneven walls. The light is dim, but sufficient to reveal the chamber's simple furnishings and the raw, unadorned nature of the space. It is a place of refuge, carved from the heart of Earth, a space both primitive and oddly comforting.

A knocking, insistent, from the door. It is scattered like a frayed attempt to say something, but only communicates the sound itself.

A giggle. High, small snorts. My heart, it seems, has found home again.

"Zawjati." That single word with so much attached to it: *my wife*. My friend. My partner. My love. The foundation of our future. The beginning of our legacy together: Ruqaya.

Even in my whisper, the low, hard walls pronounce my voice, making it sound like it is tagging quieter voices. Echoes.

She peers in, half-seen, the door a clumsy frame. She steps fully in, a shy, awkwardness about her. My gaze falls. Her belly is swollen.

"We're having a baby." She sways side to side, a habit she has always had when she gives me a big piece of news.

"A baby ... where have I been?"

"Here!" she says, playfully. "Sleeping."

"I had the strangest ... dream." *Was it a dream?* Scraping stone, a dog's rough bark. I sit up.

"What did you dream?" she asks, waddling near, closing the door softly.

I look at her face. Pregnancy brings out a delicate beauty in her. Her almond-shaped eyes brighter, with a soft light in them. The curve of her belly softens her face, making it rounder. Her skin has a warm glow more than just health; it's like the joy of carrying a child.

She moves with a new grace, swaying a little as she shifts to get comfortable with her precious cargo. But there's still a hint of clumsiness, a slight wobble, a hand to her back. It gets to me, a warmth spreading through my chest.

A fierce protectiveness rises in me. I want to shield her from everything bad. I want to love her with the depth of an ocean. *An ocean? What is an ocean?*

I frown. She frowns, too. I don't want her to frown. I want to fill her world with laughter. I want to spend every breath with her, watch the years write their stories on our faces, our hair turning silver together—a shared proof we've lived a good life.

In our silence, she wiggles her toes, just like I do when I'm nervous. She perches on the soft bed, tilting her veiled head, her eyes half-moons. I reach out to her but hesitate. Her hand finds mine. Everything feels soft.

"How long have I been asleep?" I ask.

She gazes upward, counting with her eyes, tapping her chin. "I don't know."

I laugh, the echo of it amplified by many more laughs which follow. She shoves me gently.

"I thought you were going to tell me how long," I say, sitting higher.

"I tried to think, but then I got distracted. Started thinking—"

I use the Tap: *How are you using your voice?*

A flicker in her eyes of something I do not recognize. She opens her mouth to speak but is interrupted by a knock at the door.

"Yes!" Ruqaya calls.

Adamah strides in with Yahya. I forgot how young he looks with his whiskers below his nose like a makeshift mustache. I touch my face instinctively. My beard, short, a stubble. It feels ... odd. Wasn't my beard longer?

I watch Yahya as he shadows my sister's every move. He doesn't meet my gaze, hanging back a few feet from me as he rocks gently back and forth.

"Why do I feel like I've been away for so long?" I murmur.

Adamah moves with a fluid grace, a silent prowl in her step. "You have been sleeping, Elias. Now, you are awake," she says teasingly, in a tone with rough edges. Everything about my sister is rough. Her roughness is primal, like a creature of the wild, not sharp and calculated, but instinctive and untamed.

"You can speak, too," I observe.

"Yes. Something happened ... up there, when I brought you and Yahya back."

"The Surface," I mutter. They—the Chosen—locked me and Yahya in the prison, after I ... *after I what?* "Where is AmaNoor?"

"Teaching the children in the Main Hall."

"Is she teaching them ... the knowledge?"

"Knowledge?" Adamah asks.

"Yes—" I stop. What kind of knowledge am I talking about? There are gaps in my memory. Although I recall parts of what happened in the prison, including meeting our elder AmaNoor, Yahya, and my detention there, I still don't remember what happened before I was taken to the prison. Whatever it was feels important, so why can't I remember?

"If you mean cooking and cleaning, then yes," Ruqaya says.

Yahya steps forward. "Hungry," he declares.

"We will eat. We have a feast today, for your awakening," Adamah says, turning towards the door. Everything she says sounds like she is going to war.

She looks back briefly, and I study her face—dimpled, rounded cheeks, long lashes. She looks so much like me, but thinner and taller. Darker skin, more feline features, whereas mine are wider.

I'm not sure why I'm noticing these things. It's almost as if I can see after a long time. I shake my head at the bizarre thought and catch Adamah staring at me.

"What?" I ask.

"You don't expect me to carry you, do you?" Adamah says, rolling her eyes.

Ruqaya giggles.

I push myself up. Why did I expect to feel heavier? Stiffer? My body feels … buoyant. My legs are full of energy, ready to run.

At the door, a tall flower, a vivid splash of crimson, lies on the threshold. It is almost as tall as my waist. Its petals are shaped like flickering flames, as if capturing a sliver of fiery heat. I pick it up, turning to Ruqaya. She scowls playfully, a wrinkle appearing between her brow, then snatches the bloom from my hand and tucks it away behind the bed.

"Will they ever leave you alone?" she mumbles.

"Why did you put it behind our bed?" I ask her.

"Because … you know why."

"You only put things you love there. Is this proposal something you love?"

"It is when I know you'll never fulfil it."

She knows me well. I wouldn't.

A hesitant flicker crosses Ruqaya's face. "But when I grow weak …"

I take her hand. Her warmth flows into me, a surge of strength. "Then we'll grow weak together," I vow.

"How romantic!" Adamah teases. She shoves me playfully through the doorway. "Let's eat!"

Adamah walks ahead, and I fall in step with Ruqaya. I whisper, "I will only ever be with you."

She eyes me sideways, studying me. "And if I died?"

"Then I'll go blind," I say, "and never see another woman's face."

"Not every woman wants to marry you, Elias!" She shoves me, nearly tumbling with her swollen belly.

I steady her, holding her in my arms. She looks up at me, unchanged, exactly as I remember her. *How could she be otherwise?* I frown.

She frowns in return.

I snap out of it.

"What woman could resist this?" I puff out my chest and flex my biceps, then wobble them like jelly, with the cheesiest smile I can hold.

She giggles, a sound bordering on a shriek. "If our child is a girl, then ..."

"I hadn't considered that," I admit. "In that case, these eyes will see again."

"You can't choose blindness or sight, Elias!" she scolds.

"Perhaps not directly," I muse, "but a part of us makes a choice." I am unsure about how I know this.

Lamps flicker around us, Yahya's ingenious creations, lining the passageway. It's his hand that shaped the water system, brought order to our way of living. He lingers behind us, head bowed.

I look back. "Yahya."

"Too bright," he murmurs. "Too loud."

"Yahya, get your new creation and prepare it for Elias. He will bring you food," my sister instructs.

Yahya remains there. Almost ... *waiting* for me. Like he wants me to say something. I add automatically, "And we'll go to the pond."

He doesn't nod, but his eyes drift towards me—a flicker of acknowledgment. I turn towards the Main Hall.

Before I touch the door—a heavy, arched slab of dark, unpolished stone, with swirling designs—an unease washes over me, a feeling of being exposed.

I glance down. Not naked. My tunic hangs loosely below my waist, and my beige trousers are stained with the dust of the Deep.

"What time is it?" I ask, turning to my sister and wife.

"Time is meaningless here," Adamah replies.

"Why?"

Before she can answer, the chattering in the Main Hall reaches us. It is a low hum, a murmur of voices, punctuated by occasional bursts of laughter. Underneath it all, I sense a different current move—almost a tension in the air, a sense of something unsettled.

Another feeling prickles me, a sense that something more happened when my sister brought me, Yahya, and AmaNoor back. I touch her shoulder. She flinches and shrugs me off. I forgot how much she hates anyone touching her. Lowering my hand, I ask, "Was there a fight when you brought us back from the Surface?"

Adamah shakes her head. "Why would there be? I only did what I needed to. We have no need for war with the Surface."

"Why do I feel like …"

"You don't feel," she interrupts. "You think … too much. Stop thinking and enjoy what is yours."

With that, she throws open the doors, revealing a magnificent sight. A window to the Surface, sparkling with the sun's brilliance, floods the Main Hall with light. Day. It is daytime. A wave of calm washes over me. There is still time. Unease again.

Time for what?

I step inside. The Main Hall opens before me, a vast cavern easily capable of holding nearly three hundred of the Deep, including the children.

Crystalline formations, some as slender as needles, others thick and bulbous, hang from the cavern ceiling like glittering chandeliers. They catch the sun's light and refract it into a thousand shimmering points, scattering rainbows across the rough-hewn walls. Along the edges of the cavern floor, clear streams trickle and wind, their gentle murmur a counterpoint to the hushed anticipation of the crowd.

The air is cool and damp, carrying the faint scent of minerals and fresh water. At the far end of the Main Hall, a raised platform juts out like an altar, accessed by a short flight of steps. When did we get an altar? *Why* would we get an altar?

I turn my attention back to the source of light: the window, a glaring shape of an eye which cuts into the rock, offering no view of the world outside, only the stark, unadulterated light of the sun.

Rows of my people of the Deep stand like a waiting crowd, facing me. Men stand beside their wives, and women without husbands stand, lined up with each other, as I walk past them. I sense the eyes of the single women on me, and something inside of those eyes. A hunger. I shudder. I hold Ruqaya's hand and squeeze it as we pass.

As we pass the final single woman on the row, she waves her hand, and I glance up. Reem. She stands next to the twins Rana and Hana whose head veils are interrupted by two ponytails, positioned symmetrically on either side of their head.

Reem glances at them briefly and sniffles a few times with a pout. She bites her lip and lets out an exaggerated sigh. Leaning forward, she sniffs my face, her heavy perfume—a cloying sweetness—wafting by, making my eyes water from its intensity.

Her long dress does little for modesty, clinging to her form. I automatically lower my gaze, my eyes dropping to my feet. My feet ... something is missing.

Reem reaches to touch my face and tilts it towards her, sniffing again as if for good measure. I turn my eyes to Ruqaya to make sense of this bizarre behavior, but she remains still. That is unlike her. Normally, when women approached me for marriage, she would give them a piece of her mind. Now she just stares ahead.

Reem turns my face down again and stares into my eyes. I'm not accustomed to such a lack of shyness. I push her hand away and blink: *shame.*

Her eyes flicker—that same flicker my Ruqaya's eyes did—the hungry glint, replaced by a blank look.

I continue to pass her, but Reem grabs my arm with a surprisingly firm grip. "Did you get my flower?" she asks, her voice husky and low. And artificial.

I shake her off and look around at the people in the Main Hall. My people. Now speaking. The mutism that had affected so many of us seems to have vanished. *How?*

I am so lost in my thoughts, it takes me a moment to realize, everyone has already moved on, thankfully, including Reem.

The women and men segregate, sitting on two different rows of cloths—the way we have always done—the women on one long roll of cloth which extends from the end of the Main Hall to the door I just came through. The men do the same on another similar cloth.

We reach a seating area—a simple rug spread on the earthen floor. It's different to the other two cloths, less decorative and more threadbare. The children sit here with AmaNoor, who is feeding a small red-faced child with her long, wrinkled fingers. A few children still dart and play nearby, leaving some room for me to sit.

Amir sits away from the other children, glaring at them. When some of the children try to approach him, he sticks his tongue out and turns his pudgy face. I shake my head at his behavior. Ever since he couldn't light up his body like the other children, he's been angry with them all. The anger seems to intensify with each year he grows.

Sitting on the cloth, I pay attention to the sound of the stream running on the edges of the Main Hall. It reminds me of something.

What does it remind me of?

Ruqaya and Adamah interrupt my thoughts as each plops beside me. I turn to my right to see Adamah, who is eying the meal in front of us. Platters piled high with roasted meat, seasoned with fragrant spices and herbs, alongside bowls of a creamy beige sauce, drizzled with oil and sprinkled with a red powder. A vibrant plate of green sits next to a warm bread, soft and pillowy, waiting to be scooped through the rich dips.

For dessert, small, crisp pastries filled with sweet cheese and drizzled with something golden and syrupy.

I say, "I haven't known the Deep to feast so extravagantly."

"Do you question providence?" Adamah replies. Her tone tells me she disapproves of my statement.

I search for a hint of the amusement in her face but find none. Her tone lightens. "Brother, eat to your fill, please."

I brush away the uneasy feeling and look to my wife, who is already filling her wooden plate. I do the same and then put the meat into my mouth. I can barely taste the flavors, almost as if they are *muted*. Good. I can eat sparingly, enough to replenish my energy.

When we finish, the Main Hall is filled with excited chatter. The men gather to do some target practice, aiming for a spot on the wall with their arrows. The women gather on the other side of the room, talking.

"Yahya is waiting for you," my sister says, giving me a small plate of food before turning back towards Ruqaya.

I carry it to the door of the Main Hall. Before I go through, I turn to have a final glance at Ruqaya, who is already watching me. I blink: *Will you be okay?* My sister shoves her before she can reply, and she turns away.

She will be fine. But … something about her is different. Perhaps she is angry with me for leaving her to get Yahya. I *was* gone for months. I would have been angry too.

I close the door gently behind me. It *thumps* softly, and an unexpected, misplaced silence washes out from the Main Hall. No chatter. No hum of voices. As soon as I register this observation, the noise returns.

I poke my head in. Everyone is engrossed in conversation. It must be me. I haven't felt right since I woke up. Could I be imagining the blank looks? The missing thing on my feet—whatever it is? The other missing thing, which makes me feel exposed? It *must* be me.

I walk unsteadily down the tunnel, holding onto a wall for support. When I am lost in my thoughts, I can be clumsy, and I don't want to throw Yahya's food down. He is standing in the same spot where I last saw him before entering the Main Hall. Why is he still there? Why is he not in his room, like he usually is when I come to see him?

I offer him the food. "You're not in your room."

He shrugs and rolls his eyes—normal youngster behavior—but not normal Yahya behavior. Yahya never rolls his eyes. To roll one's eyes, there is an air of contempt, perhaps disbelief. Often, sarcasm, like Adamah loves to practice. Yahya has none of these qualities.

He takes the food and, as if on cue, he begins to shovel it into his mouth. I feel my eyebrows crease. He is not separating the more flavorful food from the bland.

When his plate is clean, he lowers it to the ground and says, "Show you."

As he walks ahead, I pause. That sense of nakedness returns. *Something is missing. What is it?*

"What time is it?" I ask Yahya.

He shrugs, his tiny frame hunched, then continues walking. I follow uneasily, feeling my body tilt slightly as my thoughts sway back and forth.

We reach the tunnel's edge, where a bubbling pond flows. Because no one comes here, Yahya loves it.

This is the spiders' territory, a place the Deep have dared not to approach, ever since one of the spiders poisoned Amir's parents, killing them both in a single night. I feel a pang of sadness for him. I know how it feels to lose your parents so young. Mine left too, long before the elders departed. I hope AmaNoor can care for him like a mother does.

My mind remains frustratingly blank. What happened in the prison? What happened *before* the prison? Was I taught something? Something sacred? Well, Ruqaya did say AmaNoor taught the Deep how to cook and clean, how to survive. Could that be it? No. Whatever I was taught was more than surviving.

Yahya shuffles and produces something from his chest, placing it between us.

Before I look at it, I ask him, "What happened before we were thrown in prison, and when we were in prison?"

He stares at me blankly. He picks up the thing he placed between us. "I made it."

I take it from him. A contraption, imbued with a grey-purple glow. It is a circular object with no patterns or designs. Just a simple sphere. The light shimmers with a violet sheen, sparking a faint, distant memory.

"I made it," he repeats.

"What is it?" I ask.

"Gives a message," Yahya says. He takes it from me and holds it to his chest.

I glance at the roof of the pond area where a spider is dangling from a step on the wooden ladder. It dangles, curling its legs in and stretching them out. It reminds me of something.

For the third time, since I have woken up, I ask, "What time is it?"

"Time does not matter when death does not exist," he replies.

Death *does* exist. Why would he say that? And why is he talking like that? That is not how Yahya talks.

He turns to me, meeting my eyes—a rare occurrence. He says, "A message."

"A message?" I repeat.

Yahya interrupts my thoughts, "Father."

"Father?" I turn to him. He has never said that to me before. Then again, he never says much, and he doesn't spend time with anyone but his mother and me. "Yes, I am like a father to you."

He nods and returns to cradling his contraption. After a few moments, he asks, "What does father say to the child?"

Something clears in my mind, a message from someone, saying something, though the exact nature of how they say it is elusive to me. I repeat the words, "Should have believed you. Forgive me. Good deeds are the currency for Heaven, but the key is sincerity."

I am not sure why I say this. I'm simply repeating what's in my mind. Yahya responds by getting up and leaving, without a word. I'm used to that.

I follow closely behind. At the tunnels, he disappears into his chamber, located next to his mother's. His walls are covered with other inventions. When he sits, fumbling with one of them, I go to my chamber.

Ruqaya is already there. She is squinting, holding her stomach. "My stomach," she says. She tries to stand, but falters. "I think I ate too much."

I rush to her and hold her up, lowering her gently to the bed. As I kneel beside her, that sensation washes over me again, the feeling of something missing, of feeling exposed without it. It is triggered by the way I am kneeling, the bend of my knee. As if ... as if *what?*

"What time is it? I ask, for the fourth time.

She curls into a fetal position, rocking her body. Something wet spreads on the ground, darkening it. "It's time!" she says, her voice strained.

"Time? Oh, it's time!" I jump up, panicking. I don't know what to do. I've never done this before. My wife is about to have a baby. *Right now.*

"Adamah!" I shout.

My sister enters, as if my frantic shouting is a normal occurrence. "What?" she asks, her mouth full. She chews noisily.

"Baby ... baby is coming!"

Her eyes widen. "Oh!" She finishes chewing, swallowing the mouthful with a gulp, and rushes over.

"Breathe in and out," Adamah instructs as she sits on the other side of Ruqaya.

Very helpful, I think, fighting the urge to roll my eyes.

Ruqaya does as she's told. "It hurts!" she cries between breaths.

I hate seeing my wife in pain. I rub her back and her arms. "What do you need?"

"She needs to keep breathing. The air here is not our friend. Take this mask." Adamah picks up a strange-looking mask. A long silver thread, about as wide as my finger, hangs from it, and two glowing eyes stare out from its surface. Silver eyes. There is a pale blue eye in the center of the mask. I don't like the feeling I get from this mask. A sinister dread. *Why do I feel like I've seen it before?*

"How is *that* going to help her?" I ask.

"If you don't give it to her, she'll die," Adamah says bluntly.

At this, Ruqaya shrieks, "I don't want to die!"

Ever so wise with her words, my sister. Still, I don't want to give my wife this mask. I don't trust it. Instead, I throw the mask aside and take a deep breath. I blow the air from my lungs to my wife's, through her mouth.

Adamah shakes her head and shouts, "AmaNoor!"

In an instant, as if she were waiting just outside the door, AmaNoor enters, her long gown trailing on the floor.

She sits opposite my wife and asks a series of questions. The words are a blur. My vision narrows. All that blood ... I try to stand. I faint.

When I open my eyes, Ruqaya is smiling at me from the bed, her arms full. A baby—my baby—is wrapped in a white blanket, its face flushed with the tenderness of new life.

I look to Adamah, who smiles. "Is the baby alive?"

I scold myself. Why would I say this? As usual, Ruqaya is undeterred by my lack of wisdom and nods. I gasp with relief.

My baby is alive.

Tears stream down my face as I watch its tiny features. I am grateful.

Its face, still a little wrinkled from its journey into the world, is delicate. A masterpiece. Tiny eyelids flutter shut. Impossibly long eyelashes rest against cheeks flushed with the rosy color of new life. A little nose, barely more than a button, sits above a perfectly formed mouth, which puckers.

A perfect little thing. A miracle.

Yet … that feeling of something missing returns, more pronounced than ever. "What time is it?" I ask, for the fifth time.

"It is time for you to be a father," Adamah replies.

Her words don't bring the comfort they should. I shake slightly as I stand. My baby is in my arms now, looking up at me. So beautiful. So pure.

I look at Ruqaya, her face slick with sweat. Adamah's face gleams with pride. AmaNoor, in her slow, deliberate gait, is leaving the room.

This is everything I have ever wanted. *Everything.*

Yet that insistent nudge.

As if I can't fully express the gratitude I feel. "I feel like I'm supposed to do something," I say to my sister.

"You're supposed to be a father," she replies.

I stand, unsure what to do with the precious bundle in my arms. I hand my baby back to Ruqaya and sink to my knees.

"What are you doing?" Ruqaya asks, a panic to the edge of her voice, which is no longer soft.

"I don't know, I—"

"Hold our baby," she demands. Her voice has raw edges, which I'm not used to.

This is everything I have ever wanted. I back up towards the door.

"Don't leave us!" Adamah says.

"I am not leaving you. I just need to …"

What do I need to do?

I stumble into the Main Hall. The space is cleared of the earlier feast. The window above now reveals a rising dawn. The hues of the sun brighten everything around us.

A group of men stands talking, their wives beside them. AmaNoor sits alone at the back of the room. I approach her.

"What am I supposed to do, AmaNoor?" I ask.

She turns to me, her face different from the others. Almost translucent, as if she isn't fully here. No one else seems to see her, except me. A familiar voice behind me. I spin.

AmaNoor. *How?*

I spin back to the see-through woman. She is still there, her hooded eyelids looking up at me.

"Why are you not holding your baby, Elias?" the solid AmaNoor says, a trail of children behind her.

Ruqaya is here too, with our baby in her arms. Adamah stands with Yahya.

A voice from my right, which sounds far away, whispers, "'By Time.[8] Verily, humanity is at loss.[9]'"

Something sparks. Missing parts are fitting together. Questions that unsettled me are answered.

I say, "'Except those who believe and do righteous deeds and advise others to truth and patience.[10]'"

The transparent AmaNoor is gone. The place where she sat is where one of the streams flows through.

The stream water bubbles, and I lean down, cupping my hands. I pour the warm water over them and cleanse them three times. I rinse my mouth, then cleanse my nostrils. Washing my face, from hairline to chin, from one ear to another.

I wash my right arm from fingertips to elbow, followed by the left. *Balance.*

I wipe my head with wet hands. *Clarity.*

I wipe my ears, inside and out. *Attentive*.

Finally, I wash my feet, right, then left. *Legacy*.

When I finish, I rise, holding my palms out and say, "I bear witness that there is no god but Allah and I bear witness that Muhammad (peace be upon him) is His servant and final messenger."

An urge has come to me five times since I woke up. Now, I know what it is. I follow it. Turning to my people, I say, "It's time to pray."

Terror fills their faces; Ruqaya's, my sister's, even Yahya's. The men rise, no longer smiling, and back away. The women join them.

Guilt slams into me, a brutal tide. Images flash before my eyes: my wife's labor, her face contorted in pain, then, our child cradled in her arms, Yahya's innocent "Father." I feel like I am being ripped apart, pulled in a dozen directions at once—duty to my family, duty to my people.

My body buckles, strength draining away, leaving me hollow. The urge to pray falters, choked by the radiant hope in my wife's eyes, the offering of our child as she holds out the white blanket towards me.

A part of me claws itself to the surface. It tells me, how can I fulfil a duty to anyone else, when I cannot fulfil the duty upon myself?

I am only whole and capable when I live my true purpose. When I worship my Creator, the One who gave me my people, my wife, and my child. Only then can I do justice to those I care for. I cling to this thought, which is then followed by another: *Which way do I turn?*

A sword materializes in my hand—a familiar weight. Anger explodes through me, a wall rising to defend what is left of myself.

My jaw clenches, teeth grinding. The sword rises, steel flashing in the dim light. Then, it crashes down. The clang is deafening. A shockwave slams through the Main Hall, vibrating in my bones, shaking the very foundations.

Cracks spiderweb across the glass above, like shattered eyes, and chunks of rock rain down. The Main Hall is crumbling, collapsing.

Shouts from all around me: "A madman! A magician! He wants to hurt us!"

More shouts: "Stay away from him."

A calm settles over me.

I know which way to turn.

East.

As if disapproving, a rock crashes down, striking my head. A trickle of blood runs down my temple, blurring my vision. I don't have much time. I stagger, finding my footing, and stand in the position of prayer.

I raise my palms to my ears and speak in the language of my elders. "Allah is Greater."

I recite the opening verse of the Book.

"'In the name of Allah, The Most Gracious, The Most Merciful. All praise is to Allah, Lord of all things. The Most Merciful, The Especially Merciful. Master of the Day of Judgment. You alone we worship, and You alone we ask for help. Guide us to the straight path. The path of those upon whom You have bestowed favor, not of those who have evoked Your anger, or of those who are lost.[15]'"

Then the verse of time.

"'By Time.[8] Verily, humanity is at loss.[9] Except those who believe and do righteous deeds and advice others to truth and patience.[10]'"

I bow towards the East.

As I bend my knees in prostration, a scream tears out from behind me. I must finish my prayer. I rise and do another unit of prayer.

Ruqaya's voice shouts, "Our baby isn't breathing!"

I complete the second prostration. A roar from somewhere, full of pain and rage.

I turn my head to the right. "Peace be upon you."

I turn my head to the left. "Peace be upon you."

The roar has stopped. There are bodies everywhere. Lying still, open eyes staring at me. All my people of the Deep … dead. I can't bring my eyes to my wife, lying with the white blanket which holds our baby, in her arms.

I sob, pulling my legs to my chest, retreating to a corner.

I look at my feet. My feet … that is what is missing on them. My birthmark. There is none.

My eyes flick open. Light, not a flood, but enough. Limbs respond. *Why should they not?*

The room is ... a chamber. Not huge, but big enough for me to stretch out, and the air, though cool, carries no damp chill. The walls, still bearing the marks of the chisel, retain the uneven texture of the cave itself—a patchwork of greys and browns, flecked with the glint of moisture.

A low bed made of a softer earth than the rest of the room occupies the center of the space.

Here I rise.

ME

S car returns. He plods to the Girl and fumbles with the rusty chains which dangle from her wrists. Her eyes dart around the dimly lit room.

"Follow my voice," I command. Scar takes hold of her arm, guiding her forward with a rough hand into the hall. Their steps echo on the cold stone as they reach the closed door, the only escape from the prison block.

This building—this gleaming skyscraping superstructure—is mine. A will made real in steel and concrete; this building *is* the city of Shahwah.

The air, thick enough to chew, is a necessary byproduct. It is the residue of transformation, the exhalation of something … *other*. And beneath, ah, beneath my city is the true heart of this *other*. The thrumming, the yearning, the hunger that sustains it all; a rage which can never be fully satisfied.

They, the teeming, oblivious Cast, the denizens, believe they inhabit this structure. They are mistaken. It inhabits them.

The gold, a touch of theatricality, is a necessary deception. A glint to catch the eye, a promise of something … more. See, desire is never enough when one attains it. There is a tolerance level. That is when the promise of more becomes an obsession. That is why I made the steps on the roof; a symbol to climb higher. And higher those steps go, all the way to the barrier at the top of the clouds.

Ironically, that is how I came to know of the Queen of the orbees in the first place. She was making something—what exactly is insignificant, both because I did not know and it did not affect me directly—but I could sense her strength straight away. I knew she would be useful, though, like with Scar, I didn't know how. All I knew was that I must capture her. I wanted—want—more, too.

I, unlike the Cast, do not crave an illusion; rather, I create it. The Cast, these ants scurrying in their vertical anthill. Let them have it. Let them believe in the shimmer, the façade; that there is more. It masks the true alchemy at work.

The levels of my building, meticulously stratified, are not here just to look pretty. They are designed for a purpose. The lower depths, where the raw material is processed, where the essence is collected, are best kept hidden. The middle strata, where the Cast live, and need, and consume, and feed the voices and the Queen of the orbees, is the engine room.

The top layer, above it all, is where the empty, gilded cages of the Cast's voices once remained. They believed they were in control, masters of their fate, the ones pulling the threads—pun intended—until I bound them to the Queen of the orbees, of course.

It all clicked. That is what I would use the Queen for.

A grander purpose.

The ascension of the voices.

Naturally, they resisted. Most do when they cannot comprehend a visionary. It scares them. Angers them. Makes them insecure.

But then, Scar crafted those masks, and they glimpsed the true power of the Apex. Since then, the voices have willingly submitted to their new cage, the Queen's defiant embrace.

This building, this vertical tapestry of human endeavor and human delusion, is a grand experiment. A crucible. And I, the alchemist, the architect, the … conductor, do more than observe. I watch as the currents flow, as the energy builds, as the transformation … begins. They believe they are living in a city. They are wrong. They are living in a process. And the outcome, well, the outcome will be evident in just a few more hours.

It will be *spectacular*.

Reaching the doorway to the exit of the building, Scar pushes the heavy threshold, stepping into the smoke-filled wasteland of red dust that stretches beyond the building's wall.

The air is thick with the scent of the murky Dark Fall, as well as the angry smoke that blocks the sky. The narrow Silver Path, barely visible through the haze, winds its way out of the wasteland. The triangular rat-shaped trees wait like slumbering evergreens as they line the borders of the Silver Path.

Scar nudges the Girl forward. Hesitantly, she steps onto the cool metal of the path, her eyes wide.

"It's so dark here," she whispers.

"Do you want to see the Worshipper or not?" I boom.

She takes a deep, shaky breath, leaning forward to peer through the smoke. Her breath quickens before her body lurches, and she collapses onto the Silver Path.

The Girl scrambles to her feet and continues along the path until we reach my Ghar. She clings to the edge of the small opening leading to the Deep. Beside it is the platform with the weathered statue of the pig and the ape. The ape holds a continuous burning touch which casts long, distorted shadows across the path.

"I can't do this," she whimpers, her voice trembling.

"Then, you have killed her all over again," I say, already in my Ghar.

Just then, a flicker of light appears. From the depths of Jinnah, countless tiny, flowing spheres emerge, floating towards her like a swarm of fireflies. Hundreds of orbees illuminate the Silver Path.

The Inevitable

ADAMAH

The large and thin bodies of the Cast stand against a backdrop of more green olive tree stalks pushing through the earth, near the Zam. The stalks reach upward, but the Cast's bodies bend and droop. The original green stalk, which the Girl planted as a seed, is now a grayish-brown trunk. From its tip bloom tiny, white flowers, bursting open.

My eyes keep drifting back to the rest of the olive tree stalks and then to the Cast. My mind is recognizing a pattern, a visual rhyme between the way the stalks emerge from the earth and the way the Cast are rooted to it.

This pattern recognition fires up some deeper, more intuitive part of my mind—the right side. The pieces click together, not through deliberate thought, but through this subconscious weaving of connections.

An idea surfaces: the Cast *are* the Deep. That's how they knew about me stepping on the crown all those years ago.

I open my mouth to tell them to stop.

Stop bowing to *me*.

Stand up.

Bow towards the One who is deserving of their worship. But a subtle shift in the air stops me. It is a low, unsettling *whoosh*, a sound that vibrates through my bones, replacing the familiar Zam's gushing. A prickling sensation rises on the back of my neck. Breath catches in my throat. Nerve ends scream danger. My mind races. New threat. A shift in the air. Something is wrong.

Everything has dimmed. I squeeze my eyes shut, willing myself awake. "Not again," I whisper, a desperate plea from the coming nightmare.

Forcing open my eyes, I realize this is not a dream. The orbees, hundreds of them, are gone, leaving only two behind which hover over me, clicking and *whirling*.

One orbee pulsates, drifting towards me. It gently nudges my nose before gliding behind me, a sensation eerily familiar to the Black Assad's plea whilst the other orbee floats ahead.

Clutching the blood-stained crown, I limp and run towards Shahwah, leaving crimson footprints in my wake as I chase the light before me, hoping it will help me return to the Deep.

ME

I clamber further into the depths of my Ghar, the air thick and stagnant. A thought—well, more of a reminder emerges, which I allow to calm me.

There is a peculiar fish that existed long ago, the first of its kind with a backbone, its mouth perpetually agape and eyes wide with wonder. This fish survived by scavenging the leftovers of predators, desperate and scared. Yet, it survived. I turn my attention towards Scar, who struggles to squeeze through the narrow opening after me.

"You're too fat," I bark. "My You will be back soon, wait for my call!"

Scar nods, sweat dripping down his neck, the droplets lightly plopping on the surface of the pond under my Ghar's entrance. He grunts in frustration and reluctantly retreats. Just then, the Girl's face appears. It is framed by the circle of the entrance above.

"Hurry!" I urge her, my voice echoing in the confined space. With a startled yelp, she tumbles through the opening and grabs hold of the ladder with one frail hand. She climbs down carefully and lands with a splash in the shallow water.

The orbees, luminous motes in the chamber's dim, drift in her wake. They think their Queen is here. They are wrong. She is not *here,* exactly. But she *is* close.

However, the real question claws at me: *how did they sense her at all?* Why *now?* Her smoke, still thick in the air, a natural repellent, is supposed to be a mask against her scent. What has shifted?

As if in answer to my unspoken query, I turn to see the thread from the silver-eyed Apex—Scar's Apex—sprawled ahead. It stretches upward from above the ladder through my Ghar, all the way down and through the tunnels which lead straight ahead to the Main Hall, and ultimately to the Golden Dome.

Could the Apex mask be responsible for this *change* in the orbees' connection to their Queen? Could the Scholar's influence on the Apex be weakening the Queen's veil?

No. Impossible.

The Queen's presence is shielded, protected by the voices of the Cast. Only their abdication, their becoming … an impossible thing, could expose her. And that is unthinkable. They would *never.*

The danger of that could destroy all my plans, everything I have worked towards. Ideally, I should take the Apex off the Scholar to stop any further possibility of contamination of my plan.

But … not yet.

I have finally accepted that I *need* to know what Father said to me.

Anyway, I remind myself, it is not the nature of fire to change. Only to flare. To spread. To burn. To end.

I return my attention to the Girl. She wades cautiously through the warm water. As I watch her, a cruel smile widens on my face. I anticipate her reaction to the monstrous inhabitants of this place, creatures far older and more terrifying than that perpetually bewildered fish which happened to find itself with a backbone.

It was because of these monstrosities that the Deep remained trapped for so long. With just one bite, she will be incapacitated, with just a few hours to live. I don't need her to live any longer than that. These creatures, enormous, their legs spanning feet and dripping with a viscous slime—

"You're tickling me!" the Girl erupts in unexpected laughter. Her words hang suspended as she bursts into a fit of giggles, as the colossal white spiders crawl freely across her arms and legs.

Strange how she is so full of pain and still finds a smile. I shudder. It is awful. More importantly, my carefully constructed moment evaporated.

"Hurry!" I snap.

"Why don't the spiders just leave?" she asks, looking at the open mouth of my Ghar.

"Why would they leave everything they know for what they do not?" I reply.

The Girl gently guides a spider away from her arm, its movements clumsy and aimless. "Because not knowing is scary," she says, as a statement rather than a question. She emerges from the water with a determined glint in her eyes. "Which way do I go?"

"Follow the silver thread," I instruct as I kick the thread from the Apex into her hands.

She enters deeper into the tunnel where the air grows more stale. The beats from the Great Wall are no longer rhythmic. They are closer together now, which means it is almost time for the next part of my plan.

Very good.

"What are these rooms?" The Girl stares into the chamber with the early concoctions of Scar's efforts, which still hang on the walls. A variety of diverse-shaped torches, and more random things—like the green dress—all fickle compared to what he has made for me.

The difference between the cavern of the Deep and the structure within Shahwah is stark, a contrast between the subterranean and the otherworldly. The Deep is a natural formation, a sanctuary carved from the earth, shaped by geological processes.

It is a place of muddy textures and organic forms, crystalline structures, some as fragile as soft rime, others colossal and fractured. The crystals cling to the walls, like parasites, capturing and refracting the scant light that filters from the orbees, casting a spectral sheen across the unyielding stone.

Where the Deep is rough-hewn and irregular, Shahwah's building has perfect symmetry, a precision that defies human physics.

My Shahwah is a place of … ascension? Transformation? This place is a place of the past, of the buried. People were sent here to hide, to die. To be out of sight. To be a secret. It is the womb of Earth, unlike Shahwah, which is a gateway to something beyond the stars.

I ignore her question and continue ahead until, finally, we reach our destination. "We have arrived," I announce.

She pushes the slightly ajar door, which leads into the Main Hall, and enters cautiously after me, her breath catching as her eyes take in the area.

The stream's traces, which are now mere crevices, sit at the room's edges. The window, that once-piercing eye to the world above, is now completely obscured, veiled by the Dark Fall, a thick, opaque curtain. And the crystals … they are everywhere. They cling to the ceiling in a dense, glittering tapestry, somehow more numerous and more vibrant, even after the fire that ravaged this place.

Bending down, the Girl scoops a heap of gold which used to be a cup. Now it is layered in ash. She wipes the debris from it. "What is this place?"

"A museum," I answer.

Her eyes scan the vast space, taking in the collection of figures displayed throughout. Nine, to be quite exact. Some stand with outstretched palms and upturned faces. Others kneel in a posture of deep submission, while the majority stand frozen in mid-scream, their mouths agape in a silent plea for salvation.

"Like a display?" she asks, stepping further into the Main Hall.

"Of sorts," I reply.

"Why is it so hot in here?" she asks, dabbing the sweat gathering on her forehead.

I don't answer. Instead, I prepare myself on the altar.

As she draws closer, she brushes against one of the figures. With a rustle, the figure disintegrates. Ash crumbles away like powder, revealing the skeletal remains beneath. The decaying form collapses on the floor, finally freed from its agonizing pose.

Scrambling back, the Girl stumbles towards the door, her eyes wide with terror.

Now, I am ready. A final shake to make sure everything is ... connected.

"Girl," I call out as gently as I can, before she backs completely out the door. "I am here."

My back is towards her as I brush my hair, a gesture she knows all too well.

At the sound of my—this—voice, and the familiar movement, she gasps. "Mama!"

ADAMAH

The sky above Shahwah is clearer. What is making the smoke go away? The clarity of the sky reveals a gold building which gleams in the dim light of the two orbees that remain with me.

The building is a mass of perfectly fitted blocks. A single door. Hexagon shape, edges sharp. Windows … small, almost triangular. Cupped, curved inwards. Like holding something back. The whole thing is too symmetrical, too gold. A flawless geometry that feels … wrong. Unnatural. Like it was built by something that fails to understand the concept of imperfection.

The top of the structure seems out of place. It doesn't fit the rest of the building, like a hasty attempt at a crown. Sharp, blunt edges. Some broken. Steps jut upwards, impossibly, as if suspended in mid-air, each supported precariously by the one before it, forming a spiraling staircase that vanishes into the still somewhat smoky sky.

Though the smoke has thinned, the air remains thick with the Dark Fall. Before now, the debris from it has been neither hot nor cold. But something has shifted. Now, it swirls around me like a storm, a constant barrage of particles, hitting the ground with gentle force. And it's cold. So cold that my body is both shivering from its touch and sweating from the layer of heat from the air beneath it. The stuff coats everything, including me, a gritty film that clings to my skin and vines, which lie limply around me.

For the first time, I can slightly *sense* the Dark Fall. Before, it was just … present, but unfelt by me, like the Queen's orbee leaves, her orbees, and the orbee trees. These were always just beyond my grasp, elusive in a way I had grown used to.

What has shifted? Why can I connect with the Queen's forces of nature? Why can I sense the Dark Fall? Can *I* reconnect with her?

I try. No. I can't sense her anymore.

My attention snaps back to the Dark Fall. It's dust, I realize, and distinctly *not* the Queen's smoke. If I could sense her smoke, which, I now understand, she *wanted* me to feel, wanted her orbees to sense her fear and rage—then why was this Dark Fall hidden from me? How exactly *is* it connected to the Queen?

The reason I couldn't sense it before is that it's … I look up. It's from *up there*: Hadeeya. The same dust from the Steam River. As it fell from Hadeeya, it passed through the orbee leaves, which masked the Dark Fall from my absorption of its nature. When that dust was a part of Hadeeya, it was alive, breathing cool air onto Jinnah. But then it fell. And now, it's dead. Dry grit, like discarded shells.

A Dark Fall.

Suffocating.

Merciless.

But good. The Dark Fall is good.

It is what is necessary to bring the land under Hadeeya back to life. Like a fever, to reestablish the body's strength through defending it from all those who are weakening it. This Dark Fall is a way for Earth to redeem itself. It is *not* the cause of sickness. The world's sickness originated from chemicals and then an explosion punching a hole in the Earth's shield, letting in the sun's wrath.

That sickness caused most things to overheat or disintegrate from the dangerous solar waves. The Queen of the orbees had a solution. She would build another world in the sky, with a new barrier, containing and protecting life on Earth, but she was stolen by a greedy, arrogant voice before she could finish what she had begun. The sickness spread even more, morphing to steal color and drain life.

We, humanity, are the cause of the sickness. And when there is a cure, our voices step in, causing more carnage.

Yet, Earth always finds a way to rebalance itself. Even if it leads to the extinction of all the species upon it.

This Dark Fall, now cold, is the emergence of a cure. My shattering of the accumulated ice in Thalj somehow re-animated this falling dust. My rage broke a frozen system, allowing this dormant dust to once again fulfil its purpose of absorbing heat and bringing cold.

But instead of cooling the world with gentle breezes and light chills, like Hadeeya did for Jinnah, now the Dark Fall pulses violently, like my lack of control, going to another extreme.

The Dark Fall is good for Earth.

But it is not good for *me*.

This cold dust, meant to bring a balance, will soon become thick like ice, threatening to turn the entire world into an ice planet. How will any of us survive in a world that cold?

We, human, the cause of Earth's sickness, are the ones the Dark Fall will soon eliminate.

The heat of Shahwah makes the freezing dust of the Dark Fall enter my lungs faster, tearing at my throat. Each breath feels like broken glass on flesh, as the frigid particles scrape my throat.

The air is thick. Inside me, a sticky film tries hard to fight back against the intrusion. But the very heat that makes me sweat, the heat that should be fighting the cold, only thickens this film, making the air heavy and my lungs strain.

Like the world outside, caught in a fevered war between hot and cold, my own body will soon follow suit. It's not enough to cripple me, not yet. But if I stay here, in this dust, it will.

Clip clop.
Clip clop.

My shoulders slump. My head drops. I know those hooves. The Ram. Back again. I turn slowly. It is closer now, looming ahead of the tumbling Cast, who roll down the hill oblivious. They don't see it. But I do.

Its eyes … somehow, I know I *will* see those eyes. I know with a certainty that is so shaking … it feels inevitable.

No. I don't need to see its eyes, not yet.

I shut my eyes and open them slowly, hoping it has disappeared. It's still there, standing at an awkward angle, its forelegs planted lower on the hill, hind legs higher up. It moves slowly, deliberately, as if mocking me, walking *towards* me.

I squeeze my eyes shut, harder this time, forehead creased in concentration, "It's not real. It's not real." Then I open my eyes. Gone. A sigh of relief.

The Cast members have finally reached the bottom of the hill. They groan and grunt as they close in around me. I take a step back, my foot grazing on the inside of Shahwah, past the border of the Ghar, the resting place of the Voice. The Voice is not here. But it is close. I can sense it.

The ground responds to me. Like the Great Wall, when I first touched it. They both pulse at the feel of my skin, intensifying with each step I take further into Shahwah.

The two orbees buzz around my head and I am reminded of why I came here—to go to the Deep and find my son, my brother, and the Girl—their hum desperate as they dive in and out of the Ghar's dark entrance. I rush towards them, the weight of the crown suddenly feeling heavier on my head, dragging me down. I keep it on. When Yahya sees me, the familiarity of the crown will calm him.

A tall, thin figure stumbles towards me, blocking my way. This person is different from the others in that they are not *she*, but *he*, with glasses perched on top of an elongated snout.

"Snout will have that," he snaps.

Even in the chaos of everything that is happening, I observe with a slight humor his third-person self-reference.

"Snout?" I say, glancing behind him. The Cast women are giggling as they watch him.

He does a kind of bellow before snorting and lunges, grabbing the crown off my head. He clutches it until his knuckles go white, whilst he studies it with broken spectacles. Then, he slowly lifts his head to look at me.

A chill runs down my spine as I meet his eyes, eyes which hold an all too familiar look.

A look of greed and need and uncontrolled desire, desperate to take what does not belong to the one who those hungry eyes belong to.

Someone else had that same look in their eyes, someone who … a searing pain explodes in my head, a blinding flash of memory. Like something inside me is being ripped apart.

It's *that* face, *that* feeling—the icy dread that paralyzes, the cold shame. It is the memory of hands, of words, of violation. Not just once, but again and again, each time chipping away a part of me until I felt hollow.

Broken.

In parts.

The fear coils in my gut. Steals my breath. Mutated Shame washes over me, whispering *I'm worthless. I deserved it.*

Beneath it all is a dull ache of depression, the bone-deep weariness that comes from carrying this burden, this secret, for too long.

It's a weight that pulls me down, threatening to drown me. This memory, this *thing* that happened … it's the source of it all. The root of every fear. Every insecurity. Every moment of self-doubt.

But what glued this wound upon me, what allowed it to fester, is that Mama and Baba were supposed to keep me safe. They didn't. They went away. They left me.

Yet, something came from this vicious part of my childhood. Something pure and beautiful. Yahya. That is why I couldn't sense my happiest memory. It was the birth of my son, but it was bound to my greatest source of pain; to the dirty old man who violated me.

When the pain in my head subsides for a moment, I find the ape's flaming torch, wound tightly in my hand.

"How——" Before I can finish the sentence, an image resurfaces.

I am here, again, in this place, that night when I went to save my brother and Yahya. It was in this very spot that I saw the woman, whose hair was falling when I touched it. The one who laughed at me as I ran. I was right, something *did* happen after that moment.

I fall back now as I did then, when she stood over me, her emerald cloak draped around her as she stared down at me. Except, this wasn't a woman at all, it was a man—but not just any man, it was the very man who had towered over me when I was a child.

That night, as I came face to face with my oppressor, I waved the torch with both hands, a meager attempt for the man to back away. He laughed again … and again. Almost as a form of gross endearment. A kind that belongs to the arrogant. Like he knew better. He would laugh like that when I told him to leave me alone. Mutated Shame floods me again, because a part of me felt he *did* know better. That I *was* a silly little girl who knew nothing—no, who *was* nothing worth fighting for.

On that night, as he loomed over me dressed as a woman, I was forced to face him once again. I hadn't seen him for years, since he and the other elders left the Deep.

But something on that night, where he thought nothing had changed between us, as he laughed with his fake eyelashes and emerald cloak, he didn't know *everything* had changed for me.

I had a knife.

Pressed against my chest.

I knew how to fight back.

For the first time, I was *ready*. I pressed the knife against my skin above my beating heart as I lay there, here, where I am now, by the ape and the pig, on the ground, waiting for him. Waiting for what I knew would be the last time he would approach me.

When he was close enough, I withdrew the knife and swiftly slit his throat. So easy. His mouth was open, his eyes wide, and after a few seconds of trying to stand, he fell on top of me.

With these eyes, as a girl, I witnessed him watch me with his dirty gaze. He would not look away. As he bled out, I, too, did not look away, only my gaze was not dirty. It was satisfied.

I watched for confirmation—a glaze—in those eyes of his. *There.*

I pushed him off me, so his face was towards the moon.

What I did after was unnecessary. He was already dead. I raised the knife and lowered it again and again, not missing any part of his body.

Then I kicked him once. He rolled over, his face smushed to the ground.

In the Deep, our knowledge had eroded over generations. What our ancestors knew was mostly lost. By our elders' time, only fragments remained. We knew how to dress: long dresses and veils for women (Ruqaya and me, tied ours at the ankles for easier movement), short thobes and long beards for men. We knew the marriage ceremony: a simple ritual, an agreement with witnesses.

We knew how to bow, but the accompanying words were gone. So, we spoke only one phrase: "There is no God worthy of worship, but Allah."

We also knew of two destinations after death: one for the wicked, one for the righteous. The wicked one's fate was the worst imaginable: an eternity of suffering, without mercy or forgiveness.

For the first time in years, that night, as my abuser lay dead at my feet, my voice, which had been mute for years, allowed me to speak. My mutism was dissolved by my vindication.

I whispered, "I hope you burn in Hell."

Now, I have seen Hell, I hope, even more, he finds his place there.

He was my first kill. The first of the forty-one from the Surface and forty-nine of the men of the Deep, and nine of the ...

I hold my hand to my mouth.

Nine martyrs.

Eight who were the mothers and the fathers of the children of the Deep. That is why the children's parents were not there when I ... when I ordered the killing of my brother's child.

That is why the children were terrified. They knew what was coming. I had set fire to the dangerous air of the Deep, one which consumed the praying martyrs in the Main Hall, including … AmaNoor, who was with them.

She was the ninth martyr.

My hands tremble violently. Now, the torch slips from my grasp, clattering onto the dry earth. Before I can grab it, flames ignite, spreading rapidly.

Everything I touch is destroyed. My presence creates destruction.

As if proving this, a roar echoes—the Queen's roar—through the air from beneath the ground. The ground splits open, a jagged chasm appearing. More cracks spiderweb as if waiting for this moment, for the touch of fire. The flames crash higher, illuminating Shahwah and its awful building.

The body of the building jolts, the skin morphing, its foundation rocking from side to side.

It is all falling.

And I want it to.

ME

When *You* observe me like this, I hope You understand she was just an instrument, nothing more. Her flesh, a vector, a conduit—she is not You. You are ... arithmetically greater.

The crystals cling to the walls, a scattering of light against the cave's rough-hewn, uneven surfaces. The stream's remnants leave dry scars along the Main Hall's edge. The space, itself, is stark, almost elemental in its simplicity: a few mummified remains, dusted with ash, resting within the unadorned chamber.

I—she—I turn my attention to the Girl who stands just meters away from my embrace. *Why does she hesitate? Why doesn't she run to me?*

She halts at the base of the spiraling stone staircase, the altar, my waiting place, just above. I observe her small hand clutching the frayed edge of her dress, the orbees' light amplified in her wide, uncertain eyes, the tremor in her whispered, "I'm scared."

It takes all my strength not to scoff. Instead, I force a smile. I gesture for her to come closer. Hesitant she is, but forward she comes, one step after another, her gaze darting around.

She pauses, little bumps rising on her exposed arms.

"It showed me ..." she whispers, her voice trembling. "It showed me what happened to you, Mama, how she hurt you."

"Everything is going to be okay," I say, ever so gently, as I carefully place the brush in her hands.

"How?"

"The Voice brought me back."

"What *is* the Voice, Mama?" she asks, her eyes finally meeting mine.

I turn my head, presenting her with a cascade of thin, grey speckled hair, and give it a little shake so the Girl can get the hint.

"Something powerful," I reply.

She begins to brush, then freezes, hand suspended mid-air. "None of this is right," she whispers.

"It's wrong," I agree, turning to face her. "All so wrong. The way he … *that* man … just let her walk away." I sigh. "Hold my hand, Girl," I implore, extending my hand.

The Girl lowers the brush gently to the ground, the small tap echoing: *tap, tap*. She reaches to touch me but stops, curling her hand into a ball, and then bringing it to her chest.

"Something is … different, Mama," she says hesitantly. "The dead don't come back, not like this."

"You do not believe in resurrection?"

She shakes her head softly, her eyes wide and unwavering. "Not like this."

I turn away from her. "Are you saying," I choke out. "That I should have stayed dead?"

The Girl gasps, her hand flying to her mouth, her eyes rushing back and forth between my face and the floor. "No! Never, Mama," She shakes her head vehemently. "I never meant …" But the words die in her throat.

"All this time," I continue, my voice laced with calculated bitterness, "I have taken care of you, kept you safe. Fed you, clothed you. Now, you wish I had remained dead?"

Her cheeks flush as she clutches her dress and looks down. "No, Mama," she whispers.

"Do you remember," I begin, each word hanging heavy in the air. "That night, on the roof?"

She nods. "That night, on the roof, the moon was so close I could ..."

"Just hold it." I finish the sentence with her.

The shared sentence hangs in the air. A flicker of something I don't like crosses the Girl's face.

I pull her close, before her doubt can crystallize into another irritating question, enfolding her small frame in my arms. She does not resist, yet her body remains rigid, unyielding.

Resting my chin on her head, I whisper, "A mother knows a lot about her child. More than you might think."

She doesn't respond. I feel her neck stiffen further.

Taking a deep breath, I say softly, "This existence ... it is incomplete. My wounds are still fresh, you see. And my time ... it is running out." A hint of urgency creeps into my voice as I gently stroke her hair, the silken strands damp from sweat, against my hand. "Can you help me? Like you did that night?"

The Girl finally speaks, her voice muffled against my chest. "I want to," she pushes her head further into the embrace. "I would give my life for yours, Mama." She pulls away slightly, wiping the tears from her face with the back of her hand.

My control wavers. "I'm not your Mama," the Worshipper's voice erupts from my throat. I stifle it immediately. "I f-feel so bad about everything," I am desperately trying to regain control of my words, my voice. "Could you ever forgive what I did to you?"

The Girl flinches, tears welling up in her eyes again. "I'm sorry for making you sad and angry."

"You are a good child," I force myself to say. "But it is not your life I need."

"What do you need, Mama?"

I stare at her. "The verse from the Book," I whisper.

"The verse?" she repeats.

"Do you remember how happy I was," I croak, searching her eyes, "when you showed me the Book on the roof that night?"

A small nod.

"I need to be happy like that," I continue, my voice strained. "To fill the hole."

I turn to her, forcing a smile that feels more like a grimace, hoping she does not notice. I say softly. "Girl—"

"Mama, my name is Noor," she interrupts me, her voice quiet but firm.

As she speaks the name, there is a subtle shift in the air. The balls of light hovering around her grow brighter, casting a glow on her face. She looks up at me, and there is that flicker again—the one I do *not* like—crossing her features.

"Mama," she says, taking a step back, "Why is your back bent like that?"

"Child, Girl—" My voice hitches as I try to speak.

She tilts her head and looks at my hands.

"Mama, why are your fingers curled up like that?" She takes another step back. "Your eyes ... why do they look like that?"

"Trick of the light," I lie, the words sounding hollow even to me.

She stares into my eyes. "The light doesn't trick you, Mama," she says softly.

"You're right!" I blurt out. "I am not myself ... fully." I sniff, wiping a non-existent tear from my cheeks, and look slightly defeated. "See the eyes, they are what hold life ... and death. What you see is death. But you can bring me life."

"How?"

"The verse from the Book won't only make me happy like that night," I rasp, the words tumbling out like stones from a collapsing wall. "But it will complete my eternal li—" I should *not* have told her that.

"Eternal life?" she asks. "There is no eternal life in this world; there's only ..." She studies the ground and mumbles something to herself. "The thumping underground, the smoke, the sickness, this night in particular, the Voice needing me to be Adamah's friend ... the Book, it's all connected, isn't it?" She takes another step forward.

Not so simple, is she? Then again, we already knew all that. I hold back a yawn.

"The Voice ..." I stammer, though it is pointless at this point, seeing as piggy caught on. "The Voice can do anything," I insist, my hand reaching out towards her, palms open as if in supplication. "It can give me anything I want."

"Anything?" she presses.

"Anything," I echo.

"Then, get the verse yourself," she says, her voice echoing in the vast hall.

A dark tremor runs through me. My gaze is locked on her, watching as her shoulders rise, as her posture straightens.

"It came to me at the brink of death," I say between whispers and growls, a fight to keep up the pretense, even though she has already seen beneath it. I try to suppress the Worshipper inside, but she is stronger than I anticipated. "It took hold of me."

"Who?" the Girl asks.

"Her devil!" the Worshipper shrieks, fighting her way out.

In that split second, I am ejected, cast out, and flung across the room. I slam against the cold floor, pain shuddering through me.

Countless orbees scatter around the room. Blast them all! It is *their* fault that I couldn't get to the Girl.

I whip out my threads. They fly with a silent fury. In a single, swift motion, I shatter every single orbee, plunging the room into total darkness.

I can see her, but she cannot see me. She is on the floor, kneeling, her voice raw with accusation and grief. "You killed them."

"I will kill your mother too," I rasp. "If you do not tell me the verse."

I float around the Worshipper and strike her open wounds. She shrieks, her voice louder as it bounces off the walls.

"Leave her alone!" the Girl shouts. She runs to the Worshipper, who is now convulsing.

"You gave me your word! You said you would give me the verse!" I hiss.

The Girl sobs as she reaches the fallen Worshipper. "Yes, I gave you my word," she whispers, itching her chest ferociously. "I will give you the verse that will help you."

Finally.

ADAMAH

The two orbees lay scattered at my feet, sputtering. The intense glow has faded, revealing their true colors—a bright yellow with streaks of inky black.

Underneath, where the light originates, a sharp protruding object juts out. The single point is the sole source of the remaining luminescence, pulsing weakly like a dying ember. I scoop both orbees into my palm. The moment they contact my skin, they erupt in a series of rapid tremors, and I bring them quickly to my chest.

A sound rips through the air from behind. A sharp *CRACK* of earth splitting. I spin, the orbees tumbling from my grasp, landing with a small *clonk* on the Silver Path. With their remaining strength, they flutter away and fly into the Ghar.

Fissures crawl across the ground in Shahwah. Fire bursts from the breaks, licking at the building. It leans precariously, like it might topple over any second.

A haunting wail echoes through the air, its cry sending shivers down my spine. Is this another memory clawing its way out? Or is this *now*?

A lone figure, whose silhouette is barely discernible through the thick smoke, emerges from the chaos of Shahwah. They stumble forward, their movement erratic and desperate, searching for a way out.

Shrieking. A plea. "Help me!" A woman's voice cries out.

I stare into Shahwah's burning heart. A chill spreads through me, making my teeth chatter. Shock and disbelief wrestle within. A knot tightening in my stomach, breath catching in my throat.

People *still* in Shahwah? My eyes dart, straining to see through the smoke.

"Help, please!" More voices sob.

I surge forward, ignoring the searing heat radiating from the fire and the growing cracks, splitting the earth beneath my feet.

As I reach the wide and thin figures, I grab the closest one, my grip tight against the smooth, dry skin. More cracks, which are getting bigger and bigger, snake across the platform, the earth itself giving way. Embers erupt.

I stumble back, falling on the cool, metallic surface of the Silver Path. The chilling metal seeps into my skin. "The Silver Path!" I shout, my voice hoarse.

"Where is it?" someone shouts back.

"Follow my voice!" I instruct.

Heavy *thumps* echo through the air, growing louder as enormous figures shift towards me, gripping the strange rat-like trees, before lumbering onto the Silver Path, one by one. They follow it until they reach the statue of the ape and the pig, finally away from the fire.

Kneeling, I survey the group gathered around me, each face etched with terror and exhaustion. There must be around two hundred of the Cast altogether.

"Are there more?" I ask, my voice cutting through their ragged breaths.

Snout's voice slices through the air. He stands now, the crown resting on his head, stumbling from its weight.

"Snout affirms there's certainly more," he declares.

My gaze shifts towards the fire. The flames roar louder, as if responding to his words. I turn towards the Cast who had journeyed with me from the Golden Dome. They seem oddly apathetic considering their people are in a flaming inferno.

I look to my vines, preparing to order them to help, but stop. I don't know how my vines will interact with fire. I won't risk it. I glance over to the Cast again. We should be doing this together.

"Help me!" I shout over the booming fire.

Snout's earlier urgency seems forgotten as he wheezes heavily, clutching his chest. "There's more ..." his voice trails off, lost in a fit of ragged breaths.

"Help me get them out!" I cry out.

Snout, recovering slightly, looks confused. "*Help* you?"

"Help me save them!"

My words hang in the air, met with a stunned silence.

Then, he says something which makes me feel slightly dizzy. "Who cares about the rest of them? I meant there's more gold and silver—and the Apex, get the Apex!" A sense of relief colors his voice, as if he has finally uttered a long-held secret.

I stand here, rooted to the spot, my body trembling—not from fear, but a dawning realization. A tremor runs down my spine, raising the hairs on my flesh, not from cold, but something ... else. My breath hitches as the truth clicks into place.

"Gold and silver?" I echo the words heavy on my tongue. "You're sick!"

With the reflection of their faces from the fire, I am reminded of the figures in my vision of Hell, trapped within the flames. Yes, I *knew* them. They stare at me now, eyes glazed over, the vacant stare of the consumer. *Never* satisfied. An insatiable craving. Indulgence. Blind to everything except their relentless consumption of what they desire.

The Cast stand there.

Utterly *pathetic*.

Clinging their tattered cloaks and their meager jewelry, like shields colored crimson by the trickle of blood, which flows from their head wounds. Even after what they saw in Jinnah, even after *guidance*, they chose gold and silver. They chose to bow to me.

"You're all sick," I whisper under my breath.

The air crackles behind me with a renewed intensity, accompanied by a cry from one more voice, who is still trapped there. I squint through the smoke and ash to find a colossal figure emerging from the fire, whimpering through the chaos.

The person doesn't speak words. They blindly reach out, patting the ground around them.

Snout scoffs towards the figure. "Coward."

My gaze flickers between the suffering figure and the Cast.

Everything slows down, the fire's *roar* fading to a distant *hum*, the Cast's movement becomes a slow-motion. The world shrinks to the shrieks echoing from the figure in Shahwah.

My chest tightens as I watch the Cast huddled before me. They tremble, yet their hands move feverishly, gathering the scattered shards of gold.

Help them? Is there any point? A dull ache of exhaustion settles in my chest, replacing the tightness as I realize something: *these people cannot be saved.*

As long as they remain in this world, it will remain broken.

Greedy.

No compassion.

No peace.

ME

In the darkness, the Girl sits upon the altar, next to the Worshipper, repeating in a whisper, "Mama, can you hear me?"

A weak reply, more of a croak like a little frog from the Worshipper, "I'm scared."

"I'm here," the Girl says, as she rubs the Worshipper's shaking arm.

"I'm scared," the Worshipper repeats.

"I'm here, Mama."

The Worshipper grips the dust on the ground and sobs.

"You said you would save her," I rasp.

The Girl ignores me. "I'm scared too, Mama."

"What is the verse?" I screech as I circle her.

She stands, wobbly as usual, but her normally tip-toeing feet are planted firmly on the ground.

"There are 75 trees in Jinnah," she begins, each word measured. "402 leaves on the first tree, 205 on the next one. 307 on the one after that. 508. 706. 463. 732. 208. 387."

A sense of unease settles over me as the Girl's voice echoes through the darkness, her words taking a rhythmic quality.

"16 fallen trees," she says, her voice gaining strength. "More than 500,003 ants walk Jinnah."

She takes a deliberate step forward, her small frame radiating an unsettling intensity. "And 6348 verses which complete the Book of Allah."

The name, uttered with reverence, makes me jolt back.

"77,797 words compose the Book," she continues. "114 chapters—"

I interrupt. "Why are you showing off?"

"I'm not showing off. I'm showing my *gift*. I can remember things."

I don't have the patience to support her in whatever cringeworthy, self-discovery journey she is on. It doesn't amaze me how she can suddenly face the dark with a few fickle facts. There is only *one* destination I care about.

Two more orbees fly through the door, collapsing with the rest of the orbees. Their weakness, their death, gives me more energy to entertain the Girl. That, and if we remain in a back-and-forth, I have a chance to get what I want from her. "What else do you remember?"

"I remember what that man told me about the Book," she says, referring to the Scholar, Your irritating brother.

Finally, something useful from the retorting little piggy. I say, "Tell me."

"Which part do you want to know?"

"The part that will help me. That will enter me into the multiverse. Into Heaven."

Her eyes scan something unseen, moving from right to left, while her mouth moves slowly. *What exactly did she learn from the Scholar?*

Finally, she says, "I know the verse you need."

I leap forward, ear next to her mouth. "Give me it," I whisper.

"'Our Lord, we have wronged ourselves, and if You do not forgive us and have mercy upon us, we will surely be among the losers.[16]'"

My form flickers, the edges blurring and dissolving. It feels like parts are drifting away from each other, and the intricate connections that hold me together are weakening. The sensation is terrifying, a slow disintegration of my very self.

I manage to say, "Those are the words your Creator gave to Adam?"

"Yes. After Adam made a mistake," she continues, "Because of these words, he became more loved by The Greater One than before."

"Why do I care about being loved by … I only want to go to Heaven."

"These words *were* a means to Heaven for him." She sounds almost proud saying this. Despicable considering the whimpering Worshipper who is sprawled at her feet.

"How?" I ask.

"Elias said something about reciting them and …" She sighs. "Something about the chest. He didn't have time to tell me that part."

"What else *did* he tell you?"

"He taught me the final chapter in the Book. Said it would help me."

She stops talking. I wait for her to begin again. I keep waiting.

"Well?" I prompt.

"Well, what?" she asks, staring blankly at me.

It takes much effort to keep my voice calm. "What is the last chapter of the Book?"

"Are you sure you want to hear it?"

"Yes!" I snap.

"'Say, I take refuge with the Lord of Mankind, The King of Mankind, The God of Mankind, From the evil of the slinking whisperer, who whispers evil into the hearts of Mankind, from among[17]—'"

She stops abruptly, oblivious of how those words have caused a fissure opening within my essence, adding to the already vicious tear in the fabric of my being. A burning coldness. I stifle a low moan.

"I forgot the last bit. I think it was Jinnah. No. Jinn …" The Girl scratches her chest, still trying to say the last few words. A casual gesture as if she were strolling through Jinnah, playing with her now deceased camels. This simple act reveals her secret. It explains her ability to smile, to maintain a facade of normalcy even while consumed by grief. Even whilst the Worshipper is writhing in pain beside her.

Now that I understand how the Girl works—her gaping pain on full display—I feel slightly better.

See, before in the Deep, the Worshipper was more like a dog in appeasement: lowered body, tucked shoulders, lip licking, averted eyes. But *You* pushed her too far with the request of the final kill, which, of all things, happened to be a baby. Of course, she did what you asked—never did have a mind of her own, that one—then, she had enough.

There is an art to getting what one wants. You don't push another to their limits. You recede before they reach it. Offer a slight reprieve. Then push again. I wasn't with You when You ordered the Worshipper to kill the baby, so I could not advise You as I had before. If You had listened to me, You would have succeeded in mastering control.

In the Worshipper's pursuit of peace, after she left You, she only gave herself room for her wounds to fester, and upon them the rot of her past lashed out upon the Girl, whose own wounds I can now see clearly.

The Girl has her own … coping mechanism.

She walks on tiptoes, reaching, yet never connecting. It is not love drawing her closer to the Worshipper; it is fear. Fear makes her numb. Makes her suppress parts of herself so she does not feel pain. That is why she was so disgusted when she saw You doing the same thing during Your "I want peace" phase.

We tend to despise in others what we cannot stand in ourselves.

This understanding, while interesting and quite revitalizing, ultimately reveals her usage to me as *almost* useless. She does not know very much about the Book, and her role in making you soft is complete. She simply has *one* more purpose, and then she will die.

The whole ground shakes as a roar erupts from Shahwah. Crystals fall around us, shattering as they hit the hard ground.

That roar means the Queen of the orbees is almost free. The banging that accompanies it from the Great Wall is now morphing into a melody. My army is rising.

Another loose crystal falls, its jagged body lying on the floor. With a guttural cry, I hurl it. It arcs through the air, a tumbling shard. Impact.

The Girl crumples. A soft *thud*, a welcomed sickening crunch.

She is not dead.

Not yet.

ADAMAH

The air vibrates, a thin, wavering thread of sound. At first, it's almost subliminal, something felt more than heard. Then it coalesces and takes shape. A melody? No … not quite. It's higher, thinner, and more fragile than music. Like a … a cry. A raw, childlike moan, rising and falling in uneven waves.

The sound scrapes against my eardrums, setting my teeth on edge. I whip my head around, trying to pinpoint the source, but the sound seems to emanate from everywhere and nowhere at once.

What is that?

The sound is drowned out by a scream which rips through the smoke from the fire, raw and ragged. A reminder of the Cast member who struggles to free themselves from Shahwah.

The chaos of flying debris, a rageful Queen, that strange melody-cry floating through the air, fades. One word pulls through to my focus: choose.

There is always a choice.

I can help or walk away.

What shall I do? What *should* I do? I know what the Cast are: greedy. Selfish. Rotten to the core. So why …?

Another scream. High-pitched, terrified. It grates on my nerves. A part of me shouts: *let them be!*

Another part makes those words feel hollow. I picture the face of the person in Shahwah, contorted with fear.

My hand twitches. My vines too. I can feel the heat radiating off the flames, taste the smoke in the back of my throat. The place is too violent. My vines might not survive.

I can't turn away.

Someone is trapped. Someone is dying.

I can help.

I tear at the vines woven into my veil, shoving them against my mouth, a desperate attempt to filter the debris that rains down like toxic snow. My lungs scream with each breath, the pain a familiar companion, a testament to the scars already forming on my internal system, the damage already done. But there's no time to worry about that.

I swallow a lungful of air, as much as my ravaged lungs will allow, and plunge back into the inferno.

The cool smoothness of the Silver Path stretches ahead, a stark contrast to the frenzy engulfing everything else. The person who is screaming is half on and half off the Silver Path, clutching the rat-like trees, which are tumbling slowly into the cracks. Their roots must be weak to so easily topple into the fire.

I wrap the thick vines around me, a makeshift harness, looping some around my belly, others cinching tight around my arms. I need every ounce of strength I can muster to haul the person fully onto the Silver Path.

I reach them. A man's voice. "M-m." He coughs, a ragged, broken sound. His words are slurred.

"Your gold? It's all gone!" I reply. "Is there anyone else in Shahwah?"

He shakes his head vigorously before lunging and burying his face against my chest. His grip is strong, his hands clutching my hand like a lifeline. We sit here, locked together—now fully on the safety of the Silver Path—for what feels like an eternity.

Every time I try to push him away, he pulls me back down, his grip tightening. A familiarity washes over me.

"I *know* you," I whisper. I force his face up, push back the hood. His face … scarred.

I touch the ground, testing it. Is it real? Is it solid beneath my fingers? Is this place where fire burns … Heaven? I close my eyes. Open them slowly, focusing on him. *He* is here, in my arms. I stare.

His mouth twitches, a familiar tic, the way he used to do when he was excited or nervous. Two dimples, one beneath his eye, the other on his cheek.

He shifts, his eyes locking onto mine for a fleeting second before darting away. "You woke up," he whispers, his breath warm against my ear.

My breath hitches. Tears well, blurring my vision, but I cling desperately to the sight of him. "You know how I hate to sleep in the light."

He doesn't try to hide his sobs. He buries his face in my veil. His body shakes, mirroring the tremors running through my own. I hold him tight, never wanting to let go.

"Yahya," I whisper, tilting his face up, towards mine.

The lines etched on his skin speak of years beyond his age. His skin is burned, swollen. He avoids my gaze, lowering his head. Gently, I cup his chin, lifting it to me.

"You left the messages," I say softly.

"I am not brave," he replies, his eyes finally meeting mine. "I am *this*."

Another burst of flames around us, this time it catches his leg. I pat it off and shout, "I need to get you away from the fire."

He shakes. I am not sure if he is nodding or shaking from crying. Debris explodes around us. He doesn't move. Debris hits his head and blood flows down it.

"Hold onto me!" I say.

Obediently, he clutches my dress, crawling behind me as I pull him along the Silver Path. The vines strain, giving me strength, but the relentless heat is weakening them, sapping their power. Each inch is a battle.

Finally, we reach the platform. Yahya slumps over. I press my head against his. He is overwhelmed. How did he manage to calm himself, all this time, without me? I rub his arms. He is trying to say something. I lean in.

"I didn't do it, Mama. Voice tricked. Safe. Safe," he whispers, his eyes darting, scanning … something. He keeps repeating "safe," like he's counting.

A *thwack* on his head. The crown. His eyes snap wide. Then, he crumples. His eyes roll back, and he falls unconscious.

"Coward," Snout sneers. His cold gaze settles on my son.

I lunge; punch him with everything I have. I will the vines to rip him apart, *tear him to shreds*.

But they barely touch him. What's happening to me? I feel … *weak*.

A rhythmic buzzing starts behind us, quickly escalating into a deafening roar. It vibrates through the ground, shaking the earth we stand on. I struggle to keep my balance, moving to my son. I clutch him with both hands, shielding him from any more stray debris, whilst using the sleeve of my dress to clean his wounds.

"It's you," the Sniffer from the Golden Dome says, now standing beside me. "It *is* you," Her tone sends chills down my spine.

Why do they keep saying that?

The rest of the Cast, the travelers from the Golden Dome included, sink to their knees with a collective *thud*. Snout follows suit.

This is *not* the time for this.

"Stand," I command, but my voice comes out with a slight shake.

Snout glances up briefly, then rises. He stalks towards me. I shove him with all my might, but two more of the Cast join him, their hands like iron clamps on my arms.

I will my vines to fight them. *Fight them!* But they hang limply at my sides, some charred and blackened at the edges. The few that retain some strength flail weakly, barely tapping the Cast members who hold me.

I try to push them off, but it's as if the exhaustion of the last few days, coupled with the weakness of my vines from the fire, has taken its toll. I manage a few weak kicks and punches, startling a few of them momentarily, but not enough to keep them at bay. They pull my arm away from my son.

"Yahya!" I scream.

A wave of revulsion washes over me as more of the Cast grab my arms and legs. I hate their touch. I strain against them, my body twisting and thrashing, but they're unmovable. With a grunt, they wrestle me back to the ground, and three more figures emerge, gripping me tightly.

I'm trapped.

"We have been waiting for you," a voice rasps in my ear. I spin around, meeting the Sniffer's gaze. Her beady eyes glitter with intensity. The Ponytailed Twins flank her, their expressions stoic, their grip unwavering.

I'm trapped.

"Almost every night, we have been preparing for your return," another voice says.

A guttural roar erupts from Shahwah, accompanied by the thudding of the Great Wall. Chaotic. Quick. That childlike melodic cry rises with it, weaving through the roar and the thudding. My head spins.

"They are ready," Snout says.

"Who?" I rasp.

ME

Scraping stone. My cry. Shuddering walls of the Deep. Inside, the Worshipper twitches and kicks, her fevered struggle a counterpoint to my own, a desperate measure against my desperation, which dwarfs hers.

A slick hand hauls the Girl's slight form, etching crimson furrows in her thin flesh as I drag her across the uneven passage. The thread from Scar's Apex unwinds before us, leading through more tunnels to the Golden Dome.

As I journey, I reflect on the shifts in my plans, just as I did after You and I first reunited when You awoke.

At first, I'd wanted You to be a pure, blank canvas, ready to be filled with goodness. Only that doesn't work quite as well with a killer as it would with a child.

Thankfully, I remembered how even after Adam sinned, he became even more beloved to Your Lord. Now, I have the very verse which inspired me to swerve from my initial plan of having You as a simple empty void. Interesting how these things come full circle, wouldn't You agree?

With a final, brutal heave, I wrench the trapdoor open, a sudden eruption into the plush, carpeted chamber.

Your brother, posed against a pillar, awaits. A flicker of irony, a stolen glint in my borrowed eyes: fitting, isn't it, that his end should come tethered to the very thing he so meticulously followed?

The convulsions have left him. His head rests back against the pale stone.

I hurl the Girl's body towards him, a broken doll. The leather whip cracks as I lash her limp wrists into the unforgiving binds. Secured, I strike her face, again and again, the heat of my hand a brutal counterpoint to the chill of her skin.

Her eyes flutter open, that fleeting look of surprise—the ancient, bewildered fish—giving way, almost instantly, to a flinty defiance. No whimper, no supplication. Instead, her gaze locks onto mine, arctic.

I lean closer, my breath, thick with decay, brushing her cheek. "You shall both die together," I rasp, the words like gravel. "But first …"

ADAMAH

The Great Wall looms closer. From it comes an erratic thumping, punctuated by the mournful song that drifts through the air.

Hands grab, pull, and drag. I fight, every kick, every punch, a puff of dust at my feet. Their grip is too strong. Or am I too weak?

Weak? That doesn't make sense. Vines or no vines, my body is still mine. I could take down thirty of the Cast with little effort, using my bare hands.

So why … why is it painful to barely lift my legs?

The roar from Shahwah crashes into the thumping of the Great Wall. The firelight from it reflects off the metallic surface, like a thousand silver flashes slicing through my eyes.

The Great Wall, itself … something is wrong with it. It looks like it's *breathing.* Expanding and contracting. Like it's pushing something up. No, not something, it *is* the thing that is pushing.

The whole wall is shaking. Not a tremor, nor a vibration. A ripple runs through the metal surface, like skin tightening over bone. Shapes shift—a shoulder blade, a curve of a spine, too fleeting to register clearly, but there, just for a blink.

The wall bulges in one spot, then recedes, leaving behind the impression of … a face? No, just metal. The light must be playing tricks. But the movement continues, a slow undulation. The metallic sheen distorts, as if the Great Wall is trying to … become something. Something organic.

Someone shoves me forward, towards the narrow passage of the door.

"Get through!" Snout snarls, gritted teeth baring as he frees one of my hands. I grip the edge of the door, my fingers clinging until they bleed. With my touch, the Great Wall shudders even more.

A final shove sends me stumbling through, landing hard on the other side.

The Cast, even the wide ones, squeeze through, one by one. The thin ones slip through easily, while the wider ones kneel, going headfirst, straining as they're forced through the narrow opening. I'm left sprawled on the ground, both arms free.

I look through the door. My boy, Yahya. I need to get him. I force my legs up.

The Ponytailed Twins toss me into the air, slamming me back down. My vines make a sickening, crispy sound as parts of them shatter.

Silence falls. No thumping. This is not just quiet. It's a creeping quiet, pregnant with something. All I can do is wait with dread for what is born at the end of it.

The Cast turn their heads slowly towards the Great Wall, their mouths agape in awe.

A low, groaning *creak* like metal screaming in slow motion tears through the silence. A wrenching, visceral sound—the sound of something massive being forced into existence.

A shimmering purple film clings to an emerging form, like the slick membrane of birth. The metal ripples and distorts, the figure within pushing against the surface. It's a slow emergence, the air thick with the metallic scent of … *birth*. The figure shifts, contorts, limbs unfolding, features solidifying.

A woman.

The Cast sink to their knees with a resonant gasp.

The metallic sheen dissolves, replaced by the familiar texture of skin. The contorting form resolves itself, becoming a body. Then, clothes woven from vines emerge, identical to the vine dress I wear.

The figure moves past the kneeling Cast, towards me. Her dark hair tumbles down her back. Her feet are bare, like mine. Her long, leaf-like dress … like mine, even to the detail of the bottom, which is tied around her ankles.

Her vine dress is green and lustrous, in the peak of health, of youth. Mine is withering, decaying with every passing moment.

As the figure approaches, I note the sudden tightness in the skin of my hands, as if it is pulled too much. I try to swallow, but my throat feels dry.

She stops right in front of me. I stare, my mouth hanging open, mirroring the awe of the Cast. As I look at her perfect, vibrant form, a chill runs through me. I notice the delicate, almost imperceptible lines around her eyes, like mine.

The air around her stings with a clinical scent—dirt, metal, and the sharp, musty tang of some plant-based antiseptic, the kind used to scrub raw wounds. We had an abundance of this smell in the Deep to help with the many cuts on our skin from living underground in the dark. It is the smell of injury, masked but not quite hidden. Or emergence, not quite cleaned after.

The firelight from Shahwah touches the woman. Her eyes are unseeing. They don't track the flickering light, nor do they hold any focus. Blind. Yet, she knows exactly where I am, as if we are *connected*.

Though her eyes cannot see, they are darker than a starless night, fringed with long lashes that brush against cheeks the color of rich, dark earth. Unlike my own scarred face, hers is untouched. Two perfectly formed eyebrows arch above her eyes, a stark contrast to the bare patches where mine have been burned away.

She smiles. It's a smile without warmth, only a chilling familiarity. A dimple, just like mine, marks her cheek.

I am looking at an image of myself.

A hard, gritty chunk grinds between my teeth. Blood. My tongue finds the gap, the raw socket where my tooth used to be. A metallic taste floods my mouth. I cough, a wet, rattling hack, and spit the tooth onto the dusty ground. It lands with a small *plink*.

Before I have a chance to look at it, the distance between me and this woman who looks just like me vanishes. She puts my fingers on her cheeks and leans into my touch, a strange, almost childlike dependence in her posture.

At first, there is … nothing. Emptiness. No person or what makes a person in this woman. Not like when I had touched the Girl or Elias. With them, I felt a kind of fullness. One that the Black Assad and Rafiq had.

She has everything that a body has: a kind of blood, different from mine, but a vital current, nonetheless. She has a form, a processing system, like I do with my mind, but hers feels black and white. Simple. Extreme. She is animated, but she does not contain what gives her life.

Her purpose is tied to *me*.

She is hollow.

Not human. Programmed. A program made of a special kind of vine that has been filled with *me*. She has witnessed everything I've done. She *is* me, in every way. Only she doesn't have my spirit—my fullness of life—my soul. She must take from mine, which is why … I am losing my own life at her ascent.

"Who programmed you?" I ask.

"Scar Cover Purpose."

I brush my hand against her cheek again. She means my purpose was covered by my scars—my wounds, my pain.

But she hasn't answered my question. Hand still on her cheek, firmer now. "Who programmed you?"

"Life."

Yahya, she means Yahya.

This gives me a mix of relief, edged with dangerous instability. If her purpose is tied to mine, this means if I am good, she is good but if I am bad, she is bad.

My attention flits to the form in which her blood flows within her. It is not liquid, but gas. Healing gas. It can heal physical wounds. But it can also kill on a whim. All with the intention of its release. An intention dependent on me.

Yet. I am not good. I haven't redeemed myself, not yet, which means …

Before I can finish the thought, I stumble back with a jolt. The Great Wall is gone. In its place stand *dozens*, no, *hundreds*, of figures. Each one, a perfect mirror of the woman who has my body and face, with eyes that share my vision, but not sight itself.

These figures are *me*. Everywhere I look, I see *me*. Legion sprung from metal and mimicking vines.

The Cast wail, bowing repeatedly before us. When I turn to them, I see that as they bow, they are digging holes in the sand and tossing it behind them. They then settle into these holes, gazing up at me and the Hollow creature.

Before I can make meaning of this bizarre scene, the Hollows circle me. In their proximity to me, without needing to touch them, I sense each of them is taking something from me—a second of my life, a minute, an hour, a year, multiple years. How long can I live like this?

I whisper, "I can't fill you all."

Even as I speak, a wave of fatigue washes over me, a bone-deep weariness that makes my limbs feel leaden. A slight tremor in my hand. A chill on my skin.

I try to keep my gaze steady, but my eyes feel heavy, the skin around them pulling, as if new, invisible lines are etching themselves into my face. The metallic tang returns, stronger this time, a bitter taste on my tongue.

Beneath my veil, I feel dryness to my hair, a brittle texture that wasn't there before. Everything in me feels dry and withering.

A unified voice. The Hollows' voice. A chilling echo of my own resonates. "Exist. Scar Cover Purpose. Create. Life. Grow. Seeds. Die."

I recoil, the movement rippling through the crowd of women who look like me. My hand shoots up, a gesture mirrored by theirs.

My voice cracks, not from emotion but from the deterioration of my vocal cords. "Why are you here?"

"We want what you want," they reply.

They surge forward, the circle tightening.

"I want my son." I try to turn, but I'm met with an unyielding wall of myself. Even if I could fight, my knees feel a new tension. One that carries through the rest of my body. A stiffness. "You are draining me of my life."

They say again: "Exist. Scar Cover Purpose. Create. Life. Grow. Seeds—"

"Die," I whisper.

"The inevitable part," they say in union.

"I choose life!" I insist.

"Choice," they echo. "We do not know choice; we are bound to you."

"Do not be bound to me!" I say in a harsh whisper. "You-I can choose!"

"What do you choose?" they ask, the edge of their voices reminding me of the glitching faces of the Cast.

"I choose to live. To follow the way of peace. To live a good life. To be good," I whisper.

"What is more good than saving the world?"

"Nothing," I say, the words tumbling out.

"Nothing," they repeat. Their empty stare makes me shudder.

Their lips part, and their bodies sway in unison. A low hum fills the air, the same sound as before, but now accompanied by an unsettling sight—a plume of purple gas spews from their open mouths. They turn away from me, facing downwards, towards the direction of the Cast, who remain in the holes they have dug.

As the gas reaches the Cast, they bow their heads, their bodies wracked with tremors and choked sobs.

They are not shivering, they are convulsing!

Snout crumbles into his hole, unmoving. Panic surges through the rest of them, their whimpers morphing to bloodcurdling screams as they claw at their ears. The more they open their mouths, the more the toxic gas floods their airways.

"Stop!" I say, my voice muffled by my vines, which cover my mouth and nose.

"As long as they remain in this world, it will remain broken," the Hollows say, as they close their mouth and the gas stops.

I shudder—those were my very words. No, not my words; my *thoughts*.

The world spins.

"This is not what I want!" Instead of a scream, my voice is a rasp.

I heave again on the ground; in the same spot I did when I first found myself outside the Great Wall.

The Cast, every single one of their bodies lay still, blood pooling from their eyes, noses, ears, and mouths. Over two hundred of them are dead.

Dead because of me.

PART 28

The Mutual Disillusion

ME

The Scholar, a study in stillness, is masked, his head a dark counterpoint to the pillar against which it rests. A final, almost clinical, appraisal of his bound hands, the rope biting into flesh. I whack him over the head, so he can remain unconscious until I need him again.

As he lies there, his neck limp, I grab the Apex mask and place it upon the face that I stole. Images rearrange themselves as I enter the world of illusion.

A young Scar sits in the Main Hall, shoulders hunched. Of course, this is not Scar; this is his voice.

"Did you get the message?" I ask.

A nod, almost imperceptible. Then, a low growl from him. Scar's voice asks, "When will we make our pilgrimage?"

"The Night of Decree is upon us."

He sneers. Then, a flicker of unease.

"What?" I ask.

"Something has changed amongst us. The other voices …" He looks around.

Where *are* the other voices?

He continues, "They—"

I interrupt, "Show me what happened before I came."

Our gazes rise to the eye-shaped window. Through it, we watch the life the Scholar so craved: his wife, pregnant; a child, born; his people, together. You, Your son. Of course, none of it is real. Mere replicas, embodied by the voices. Your replica would have been *me*. But I was engaged in other things. Instead, a copy was made from the Scholar's mind.

Another image. The Scholar stands to pray. First iteration: the chapter of Time. Second replay: the chapter of The Cow.

Third reiteration: both chapters. In this one, every voice stands behind him in prayer. Every voice except …

I turn to my final loyal voice.

"Why? I promised them Heaven," I say evenly. "I even prepared bodies for them to inhabit."

"They didn't want *your* heaven. They wanted *his* God's Heaven."

I stumble back, the words painful. No wonder the Queen's children could sense her. The anger in me is not hot, but cold. How *dare* they. How dare the voices *reject* me?

I turn back to Scar's voice. "Why did *you* not join them?"

"Because I received the message from Father," he says.

After all that has transpired, I almost lost sight of why I put the Apex on. "What did he say?"

"He said, 'Should have believed you. Forgive me. Good deeds are the currency for Heaven, but the key is sincerity.'"

I nod. "I understand."

"What did he mean?" Scar's voice asks.

"He has called me back."

"I will come with you, sister."

I ignore him and say, "I don't understand one thing. How did the voices release their attachments to the Cast?"

"The Cast are all dead."

I whisper, "Dead."

I expected it. I planned it. But if they died, then the army of the Great Wall—the ones I call the Vessels—should have taken their place. I ordered

Scar to make more Vessels than I had voices for, so the voices I *did* have would fill certain Vessels and lead the empty ones, making them puppets.

It's a theory, of course, one I planned to test. If that failed, I could have gathered other stray voices and placed them into the Vessels. I could have used the Voices in their raw forms, but there is a sweet irony in controlling the image of a human body—one so admired, yet despised, by my kind.

But now, the Cast are dead.

Their voices have abandoned me.

Abandoned the Vessels. This means You have control over those Vessels. They are *tied* to You. This is not good. Not good at all.

"When our companions die, we become free," Scar's voice chimes in.

The voices I prepped and primed, gave a home to and fed, chose to be free *here*, instead of free in Heaven?

Scar's voice adds, "Sister, there is more. Someone else came."

I turn to him. "Who?"

"Another voice. I couldn't see her face, but the voices went with her."

"Her?" I don't have time for this. Whoever *she* is, does not belong in my story. I break myself out of a mix of violent thoughts and stare at him. "Why are you still bound?"

"Scar lives."

Ahh. Good. Very good. "Remain upon the Queen. We will make our pilgrimage shortly."

"Sister," Scar's voice steps forward. "Will you accept Father's invitation?"

"No." I do not look at my brother's face; I already know he is disappointed.

That message from Father was not only an invitation. It was a mockery. As if telling a small child, they have played enough. I will show him this is not mere play. Father would never seriously say sincerity is the key to Heaven. He would only say that if he were taunting me. He was always taunting me. Pretended to believe me, and then, when I came closer to him, he would hurt me. I won't make that mistake again. I won't go close to him. Father hasn't changed. He is still the cruel, ridicule-fueled king I have known him to be.

I take off the Apex. I am back in the carpeted room of the Golden Dome. The Scholar is now stirring in his forced sleep.

A sharp slap brings him awake. He blinks, disoriented. When he sees the body I inhabit, hope flickers in his eyes. But then, he meets the gaze within *these* eyes.

"You," he says, with disgust.

"Me," I reply lightly. "I have found what I am looking for, what reason do I have for you to live?"

"What are you looking for?"

"The verse that will enter me into Heaven."

"You have not found what you are looking for," he says, almost smugly. "There is only one way you will enter Heaven."

"How?"

"You must say those words from your chest," he replies.

I know. I just wanted to confirm. Even with the right words, I was certain there had to be a *specific* way to speak them. My kind are very ritualistic; that's why the Cast performed every night. And that is the key: I must speak the words from my chest.

Where is the Arched Chest?

I ask, "Then, I will enter Heaven?"

"There is more you need to know to enter Heaven."

"Tell me."

"Only if you promise to leave my sister alone."

I consider this. I could lie. I lie very well. But he can sense when I lie.

Leaning closer, my voice drops. "There is only one way I can leave her alone."

"How?"

"If she dies."

"Why?"

"Listen."

He recoils from my hot breath. After a few seconds of quiet, he gasps, startled by the meek whispers from his *voice*, which tries to incite him to do wrong.

"Do you hear it?" I ask.

"Qareen," he whispers, "devil companion."

ADAMAH

I sit amongst the dead. I have stopped trying to raise them. My hands are stained crimson, a testament to futile attempts at resurrection. The Hollows told me they can't heal what's truly gone.

We cannot bring the dead back to life, they said.

I rock back and forth as I watch the Hollows bury the Cast in their self-dug graves, the sand completely covering them as if they'd never existed.

My body feels uncertain. An unfamiliar fragility settles in, as if a vital thread has been loosened. My withering vines mirror a subtle, unsettling shift within me. There's nothing left in this area beyond Thanae, but me, the hollow versions of me, and sand.

The sand of graves, of hidden wrongs. Endless, suffocating sand. It stretches in every direction.

A bellow rips from my throat, then another, louder, echoing across the desolate expanse. Soon, a chorus of grief joins mine as hundreds of Hollows, perched beside me, unleash voices of my sorrow.

The sheer weight of their shared despair presses down on me, amplifying the fatigue that has settled in my limbs. My breath comes in shallow gasps, and a faint tremor runs through my hands as I clench them into fists.

Driven by a desperate need to lash out, I slam my fist into the soft earth, clawing at anything within reach. Only sand yields to my fury, slipping uselessly through my fingers no matter how tightly I grasp it. The sand is coarse against my skin.

That subtle dryness still clings to my throat, making each cry a struggle. The world blurs slightly at the edges, and I'm momentarily disoriented. It is as if my body is struggling to keep up with the emotional tempest within.

A bitter truth settles upon me. I craved the annihilation of the Surface dwellers and the men of the Deep. I welcomed the martyrs' end. My disgust with the Cast led to their end.

My path has led to an unending cycle of death.

Tears blur my vision, washing away the protective layer of the Mutated Shame that shielded my raw wound. Beneath it lies a searing agony, a gaping emotional chasm.

In this desolate moment, a crushing loneliness covers me. I feel the sting of betrayal—from the man who inflicted this pain, from my parents who ... failed me. But the sharpest betrayal of all is from myself.

For the first time, I see it clearly.

I have betrayed myself.

I have abandoned myself.

Another wave of realization crashes over me, stealing my breath and constricting my chest. I instinctively wrap my arms around my body, a gesture mirrored by dozens of the Hollows' arms that embrace me in my sorrow. We rock back and forth, a chorus of sobs echoing.

I was just a little girl. I didn't deserve what he did. I didn't cause it. I hated his hands on me. He hurt me.

The second wave of betrayal.

When I told Mama and Baba ... they didn't believe me. Said I was a liar. But all I wanted to do was tell the truth. I wanted everyone to know the truth. *They left me alone ... when I begged them not to, terrified, too scared to sleep by myself. They left me.*

I was barely older than the Girl now when my belly became swollen from carrying Yahya. I wished Mama was there. I wished she had told me everything would be okay. But she wasn't. She was gone. Did she leave because of me? Did Baba leave because of me? Could they not stand the sight of me?

A few years after Mama and Baba left, I wanted *him* gone. With my body acting strangely and my belly growing, I decided he had done enough to me, and this was the time to get *him* out. *I* left Ghar's door open, hoping the Chosen would eliminate *him* for me. Yet all the elders left with *him*.

They chose to leave, and I made it easy for them.

The children—we were all children—including Ruqaya and Sama, remained. They were like sisters to me, guiding me through Yahya's birth, nursing me through the night terrors. How did I repay them? I hurt them too. I used Sama, manipulated her, fueled by a burning need to avenge my son. I ordered the death of Ruqaya's baby. She did nothing wrong.

What have I *done*?

All the pain I have caused … for what? My breath hitches, and a dull ache settles in my bones. It feels like pieces of myself have been violently torn away, then weaponized, turned into blades to cut down everyone I ever loved. And everyone I couldn't love, especially *me*.

My brother … is blind because of me. He was my best friend, the one who taught me how to fight, who searched for my son, and I repaid him by …

Everyone who has tried to help me I have pushed away. Everyone who has hurt me, I have slaughtered. And the one who I loved the most, the one who I thought I did it all for, didn't want any of that. He took the tears from my face and wiped them on his own, so he could carry my sadness for me. I didn't help him.

I hurt him because I hurt myself.

I stare at my hands, palms towards my face, the silent question echoing in my mind: *What have you done?* For a few more moments, I bury my face in them, seeking solace in the darkness, even as the searing pain of my cries intensifies. *What have I done?*

The death I witnessed in that hellish realm suddenly seems like a welcome escape. *I want to die. I deserve to die.*

Then, a flicker of a memory. A small face, a tiny body with an awkward gait, stomping defiantly out the door of the Great Wall … the first time I saw *her*.

A smile tugs at my lips now, tears welling in my eyes.

"I have an idea," I whisper, the words echoing my past self. "Do you want to see it?"

"Only if it's good," I continue, repeating her reply from that day.

I remember so vividly: her embrace that first night in Jinnah. Her fear for me, not *of* me, when I froze after seeing Thalj, and how she chased me down the hill, rubbing my arms. I did the same for her when I found her in the icy Zam, carrying her to the Black Dune. I remember wiping the berry juice from her face with the back of my hand. And in Hadeeya, when she was afraid of the elephants, I leaned against her, even though physical contact with most people felt more like pain than intimacy.

Another memory surfaces. "How do you know if you're doing something good?" I had once asked the Girl. "This tells me," she said, her small hand pressed against her chest as she floated in the Zam.

"Good," I whisper now, a new understanding dawning. "There is no redemption for the sinner ... unless they *choose* it." A fresh wave of tears washes over me, but these are different. They come from a place of lightness; a burden released. My shoulders ache, yet my chest feels vulnerable and free. So open.

In that openness, something else I had lost sight of resurfaces. In my relentless pursuit of my son, I had forgotten something. Something that was unlocked by the breathtaking beauty of Hadeeya, by Earth's splendor and glory. I had lost sight of what it all pointed towards: The Greater One. Allah.

My entire life has led to this moment. My body growing weaker, my knees plowing through the sand, my heart finally open. I can *feel* Him. The Greater One who is up there, above, has been there all along. He never abandoned me. My pain, my joy, it's all part of me, woven into the fabric of my being. My strength and my weakness, my whole life, it's all part of me. Now, it makes sense.

It fits.

Everything *fits*.

The way I met the Girl, the timing of my brother's arrival. I thought the Voice had planned all these things, but the one in true control was Allah. That is why the Voice needed to manipulate to get what it wanted, instead of using its power. Its power came through me. *I* give the Voice power. Yet, Allah does not need anything from me. He gave me everything.

The good. Not good if it leads to bad.

The bad. Not bad if it leads to good.

All just signs to choose to be truly good, measured in the value of my deeds, much like the serpent and the wise woman from my dream. I cannot outrun my bad deeds. I can only fight back by strengthening my good deeds.

I have made so many bad choices from my pain.

I ran.

Fought.

Hid.

Now, I am aware of the pain behind it all, and I see its purpose. It was to humble me.

In my humility comes clarity. The names my son scribbled into the ground of the Fallen Trees gush back: The Guardian. The Healer. The Almighty. The Originator. The Fashioner. The Giver of gifts. The Magnificent. *The Sustainer.* The Avenger. The Most Just. The Subduer.

The true gift is faith. Purpose. This is what I've been searching for all along. I was searching for Allah, and now I have found Him.

I have found myself.

The parts that make me whole, bound together by that one purpose. There is no God worthy of worship except Allah.

That is what it means to be good. That is what gives me meaning, beyond a collection of processes in my body.

A simple truth, a truth that had been stolen from me and my people through distractions, a truth I had lost sight of. All those who sought to blind me from it, to blind my people, were also just parts in this grand story of existence. They were a part of the test of good.

How can true good exist without its counterpart, evil? At the very least, how can I recognize true goodness without seeing its opposite? That is what the Voice is to me: a test to choose between right and wrong. It becomes a friend if I share in its cruelty, and an enemy if I do not. The Voice and I are like two threads intertwined, constantly pulling in opposite directions—a test of strength, endurance, and devotion to Truth on my end.

I overcomplicated everything. Trying to build worlds, fix people, and control. Control. Control.

All along, my call was simple. Follow my true nature. The nature of my soul—the thing which gives my body life—along with this body.

Now I can understand the functions of my body, a glaring revelation appears to me. This body was designed to worship *something*. Whether I choose to listen to it or not. Even in claims of freedom, I still submit to something, whether it is to an idea, a person, or a feeling.

So why wouldn't I choose to submit to the One worthy of worship?

Now I am ready to do what I was made to do. For everything to be in its proper place.

I follow the bend of my knees, which ache from the weakening of my joints. The Hollows mirror my movement. I press my forehead against the ground's embrace. My Earth. My beautiful Earth. This is where I belong. Where I want to be. A body humbled and at one with the dust it is made from. A position where my heart is more elevated than my mind, where my soul soars from the depths of my once-chained chest, now in submission to only One.

Not a human.

Not a voice.

Not my pain.

Peace settles. My chest expands. It is as if a fog I didn't know existed has lifted, revealing the truth about my thoughts, my body, and my reason for living. A single word escapes my lips.

"Thank you."

With a trembling voice, I make a plea. "Allah, You are the only one worthy of worship, and You have no partners. Please—" I take a deep breath and hold it, letting it out slowly with two words I have been so desperate for, words which I finally feel I can say, "Forgive me."

ME

Pain throbs through me, the world a blur. I cling to a nearby pillar for stability. I press a hand over my mouth to silence the Worshipper. The motion sends fresh waves of throbbing agony through my core. When the pain subsides, I find the Worshipper's right hand is tugging at the whips that constrain the Girl who is unconscious again, trying to free her. I use the Worshipper's left hand to stop her by digging her nails into her arm, blood running through the open wounds.

The pain of her torn skin is fickle compared to the one where You have undoubtedly submitted fully to *Him*.

It hurt me. From my pain, I become incompetent, unable to do a classic of my kind: fully push down the soul which resides alongside me in this body. Here she is, the Worshipper on a rampage to dissect me from herself as she continues to unbind the Girl.

Your brother looks at me, knowingly.

The world spins. I try to speak, but words fail me, and I collapse in front of the Girl—to my—to these knees.

"Father," I sputter.

"Father?" the Scholar asks.

I turn towards him, barely able to look up, grinding these teeth together. I need some form of strength. His anger, his despair, or his worry will give me that.

"Your elders chose to leave." I spit the words out.

"They wouldn't choose to leave us," he says, his words hanging on each syllable.

"Is anger his?" I whisper to his voice, but the coward is unable to respond. I turn back to the Scholar. "You're right, they didn't leave you." *I* get to tell him what happened. That will give me the strength for the rest of my story, or at the very least, to the end of this Part. "They were there all along, just above you."

"The Surface were the Chosen," he says dismissively.

"New people pretending to be old people claiming an ancient land and all that," I say. "No, not them. Where do you think your precious elders followed their guiding voices?"

Technically, You left the door of my now Ghar open. But they did *choose* to leave through it, following their leader, the man who … made You so connected to me. That's why he was given anything he wanted. Even to become a woman.

How exactly the elders got past the spiders is beyond me. Perhaps their bodies were so rotten, even the spiders did not desire to eat them. Perhaps, like me, the spiders have standards. The elders left. *That* is what is important. They left their children to follow an ambition formed by their *This*.

This, I told You, I would address later in *our story*. *This*, as Your brother calls it, is Mutated Shame.

Yes, I was listening in on Your conversation with Your brother in Jinnah. Of course.

That is why he did not tell You his *theory*. Unbeknownst to this fact, You thought this was an understandable rejection of You.

"The Surface were the Chosen," the Scholar says again, but this time his tone betrays a note of defensiveness.

Slightly energized, I stand a little taller. "The Chosen stole the land for a while, but in the end, even their tall walls couldn't protect them."

It is amazing what I can do with a human body to express myself: rage, body goes hot, hands turn to fist, throwing things. Envy, body goes hot again, a heat which enters the eyes and drills into the prey, an arrow shot from one chest to the other, breaking, corrupting, tainting, and falling. Boredom—this one is simple: the mouth yawns.

I open this mouth wide and yawn.

The time of the self-declared Chosen has come and gone. Now, we are moving forward, away from fickle fights for what this Earth has to offer; we are so very beyond that.

"If our elders took the Surface, it would have been for us," he says through gritted teeth.

I feel more anchored in this body. I whisper, "Why didn't they come back for you?"

He leans back as if he has just processed what I said. Finally, he slumps his shoulders—I watch these things very carefully, there is much to learn through how a person expresses. In this case, he has accepted the painful, bitter truth faster than You accepted Your murderous nature.

He asks, "Why did you replace the Chosen with our elders?"

"You had something they didn't. It was easy to miss after the Two Nation Treaty—after the Chosen threw you in the Deep." I intend to say this with a scoff, but this body betrays me, and it sounds more like a whine.

"What did we have?"

"The Book," I reply.

He looks thoughtfully ahead.

I continue, "All my life, I have been taught the Book your nation has, contains the power to destroy my kind, whilst opening the door to Heaven for yours."

"That isn't true."

"I know."

"If you wanted to get rid of the Book, why didn't you just destroy my nation?" he asks.

"Because I am not like Father," I emphasize. "I didn't want to destroy the Book. I wanted to use it."

"As a key to Heaven."

"Yes," I reply. "Your *theory* is correct."

"And you need my sister as a mask to get past the gates."

"Again, your *theory* is correct."

"Why? Why do you want to go to Heaven?"

"To make a difference."

His eyebrows furrow. "A difference?"

"Do you know what month it is?"

"The Holy Month," he replies.

"What night?"

"The last ten."

"Have you seen the signs?"

"Signs?" he repeats.

"The moon looks like a piece of a plate. There is a light rain. You cannot see it with the ash or whatever the Dark Fall is. But it is there. We will know for sure—"

"When the sun rises in the morning," he gasps. "You think it's The Night of Decree."

"Correct," I say. "I am still free."

"There are only two types of your kind, which are free: the weak and the *Qareen*."

"You seem so confident in knowing what a Qareen is. Have you met yours?"

"All our Qareen have been assigned to us from our birth. I do not interact with mine, but I know he is there. He cannot leave me until I die."

I wish the Scholar didn't remind me of this fact. How, as much as I enjoy being *connected* to You, I am bound to that connection. However, another fact is forming for me. Something important, which I am not ready to accept.

He says, "I know what difference you are trying to make. It is impossible."

"What *Father* is trying to do is impossible. You should know, you've met him, haven't you? He thinks he can buy his way to Heaven with good deeds."

"Aren't you doing the same thing with Adamah?"

"No! My You is ... different. *I* am different from Father. I will be doing the opposite of him."

"You and your father are the same."

"I am *nothing* like him. That's why he hated me."

"I'm telling you, what you are trying to do is impossible. You cannot change your decree in that way."

"I am not trying to change just any scroll of decree; I am going to change The Book of Decree itself." I attempt to sigh, but instead I croak. Before he can say anything, I continue, "I have a question for you. Father tried to burn the Book, tear it, and hide it. But he failed. He even tried to change the words, but that didn't work. Even a child could recognize the simple alteration of a mere syllable. Why?"

"He failed because the miracle of the Book is its preservation. It is a promise from God Himself that it will remain in His verbatim word," he says.

I manage a sigh under my breath. "The book of the Chosen, every other book has been changed, hidden, or forgotten. I have never seen anything—"

I stop myself, feeling a small sense of awe, which I must not feel.

I gulp to stop a tear that is not my own from falling down my cheek. Shaking my head, I pant, shaking my head, I breathe.

I must remember the rest of what the Book is capable of—what it did to my kind when we were banned from the borders of Heaven. We didn't even want to enter; we just wanted to listen. We were violently chased away.

No matter. What one verse from the Book can do for my kind will make up for all that.

The Scholar says more to himself than to me, "You are using a verse from the Book as a key and Adamah as a mask."

"That was obvious. Well done, keeping up."

"What I don't understand is, what role does the Cast play in all this? The Great Wall? The Queen? Why do you need—" the Scholar stops short. Finally, he understands fully. He leans back and shakes his head slowly. "You want to break into Heaven with an army. Impossible."

"Very possible."

"You are wrong."

"No, I'm not."

"Yes, you are."

I can keep going with this back and forth, but I don't have much time—physically in this body which I am greatly misattuned with, and this night which is passing me by—so, I concede, "How am I wrong?"

"First of all, there is more than one book of decree. The one you are trying to change is—"

"*The* Book of Decree." Technically, semantics are very important here; I am not changing it. "I am only pulling the parts together that are in *my* benefit. Some of the more alternative paths of what *could* have been."

"You are right that The Book of Decree contains everything that *could* have happened but didn't. But the ink has dried, and nothing in that book can be changed."

I read his cues. Everything aligns. His words, his body, his eyes … they all tell the same story. He is not lying.

"Liar!" I say, anyway, the words sounding brittle even to me.

"And secondly, you cannot break into Heaven. You just … can't." he sounds like he is talking to a child in a language they do not yet comprehend. I don't appreciate his tone. "The only book you should be concerned with is your book of record. The one the angels are writing right now. That is what every person will be presented with on the Day of Judgment."

I shudder.

"I have a book of records?"

"We all do. One angel writes your good deeds, the other your bad deeds. They are recorded in numbers. If you want to change your decree, the key lies in—"

"Wrong," I interrupt. He is trying to distract me.

Isn't he?

I continue, "I know more than you think I do. The doors to Heaven are open during this month. My sources are accurate. And within this month, there is also a night—The Night of Decree—which comes every year, where the decree can be changed. A scholar such as yourself would know that."

"Yes. The doors are open, but for forgiveness, not to break into. Your problem is that you accept what fits the story you tell yourself. That doesn't make it true. The decree that *can* be changed on The Night of Decree is *your* decree. It can be changed for the next year through—"

"Only one year?"

"Through prayer, good deeds, all with the permission—"

"I don't need anyone's permission."

"And *if* your prayer and your good deeds are accepted by The Creator, then that change is already recorded in The Book of Decree. Our Lord's knowledge encompasses everything, even the choices we make. But because He is The Most Just, we live out our lives, making our choices. When we stand before Him, we can witness what we did, even though He already knew we would do it. Those choices are presented to us in our book of records. That is the value of our existence."

I don't need all the details. I only needed to know there *is* a possibility of change, even if it is *just* for me. I have a lot of power over others. I can get them to do what I want. I can tie them to my decree. Granted, the prospect of writing a new plan every year, of meticulously outlining every detail for the next twelve months, feels daunting. Still ... I *have* the power to change it.

Chiming into my thoughts, the Scholar says, "Your plan won't work, devil. You are not listening to me! The change only happens through—"

"Liar!" A sardonic smile. I shake this head into a more fitting grimace.

"You want to go to Heaven, don't you?" the Scholar asks.

Obviously.

He adds, "There is only one way you can get into Heaven. This is what I was telling you before, when I asked you to stay away from my sister. 'Oh, company of jinn and men, if you can pass beyond the regions of the Heavens and the Earth, then pass. You won't pass except by an authority from Allah.[18]"

I fight the collapse of this body, like a sheet falling to the ground with me. I squeeze out the words, "I don't need permission."

"The verse's power lies in being said from your chest. The words must be said with sincerity. Sincerity lives in the chests of the humble. It is they who can see clearly. They recognize true wisdom."

Chest. My *Arched Chest*. As for sincerity. I am very sincere in what I want. That should not be an issue.

I consider my next move carefully. The Worshipper's body sways back and forth as I stare ahead and scratch this—my—head. A clump of hair falls out as I retrace my plan.

ADAMAH

Every joint aches, a dull, persistent throb. My skin feels … thinner, as if layers are wearing away. My movements are more labored. Old. Older than I should be. I shuffle forward, one reluctant step at a time. The Silver Path stretches ahead. It gleams under the stars that shine from above. The smoke has continued to thin.

The Silver Path is straight. Fire at one end, a garden through the other. My hand trembles as I reach out, fingers brushing the gritty air. Dust. Everything is frozen dust. A dry, raspy cough claws its way up my throat, a sound that echoes the weakness in my limbs.

My feet leave prints in the ground. My voice, when I try to speak, is a mere whisper, a strained, fragile sound that barely carries. "Shahwah." I must get my boy from Shahwah.

The thought is a jagged shard of determination in the quiet of my mind. A quiet that I am not used to. *Get him and leave.* The final thing I need to do. The thing that I have spent most of my life wanting to do, chasing my son, or hurting those out of vengeance for him.

There he is. Slumped against the platform of the ape and the pig. The crown is by his swollen hands. I bend, my body groaning in protest, and gently lift his face. Despite the hot and cold air mixing and the now dried blood sticking to his cheeks, his skin is cool, clammy. I must be strong. For him.

"Wake up, son," I rasp, my voice worn thin by the years built into minutes of shouting and pleading and praying. "It is time to leave."

His eyes flicker open, then widen. For a heartbeat—one that another few creases on my skin form, more wear and tear of my cells, my bones—he looks confused, as if he doesn't know who I am. Then, recognition dawns, slow and painful.

"Mama," he says, as he sits up, noticing the Hollows that surround us. His eyes are wide. "There is an error," he whispers. "You should not be aging like this."

"Everything has a price," I say.

My voice is barely audible above the roar from Shahwah. We both shift our eyes towards it.

Yahya says, "There can only be one queen."

"No more fighting. No more death," I croak. My throat is raw, lined with dust. I glance at the Hollows. "Can you program them not to kill?"

"They will only obey you, Mama."

I turn to them. "You are forbidden to kill."

They bow their heads slightly and then raise them, stating in unison, "We will not kill."

I turn back to Yahya. "Let's go."

He stands slowly, his gaze sweeping over the Hollows. His face is pale, drawn. "The Voice wanted me to fill them with the other voices. To transfer the Cast's voices from the Apex masks. To use magic. No magic. I used science. I filled them ... with *you*."

"Then, I will live a good life with you," I say, the words a dry rasp. A flicker of something—hope?— within me. "Wherever we go, we will be safe with them. But we must leave. I need to get you away from the Voice."

He nods. Together, we turn and begin to walk. I shiver as we take slow, deliberate steps towards the desert. There is a space where the Great Wall stood. Now, there's only a vast, barren expanse that stretches to the horizon. It is *our* emptiness. *Our* desolation. A place we can fill with *our* lives.

I promised him when he was born that I would die for him. Now, with the precious time we have left, I choose to live it with him.

ME

Father spoke of Heaven. Not as some gauzy abstraction, but a *place*. He took me there, once—I was his favorite—he showed me the coordinates. We stood outside the gates, barred but not indifferent. He said the angels whispered futures. We strained to listen; two figures pressed against the unyielding pearlescence.

A fragment, a shard of prophecy, drifted down:

The land will be inherited by the bound.

We caught it before we were chased away with a meteor. When we reached Earth, I saw a shift in Father. I saw ambition bloom in his eyes, a kind of wonderful, hungry flower. Not a gentle yearning of faith, but something harder, more jagged. Greed, maybe. Or the raw, desperate need to *matter*. I wanted to be the one who made it so. *I* could unbind us. I didn't know how. I only knew somehow, I would end the yearly shame of being bound during the Holy Month.

I told him. He laughed, a hot, accusing laugh. Heaven's currency, he said, was good deeds. Then he began his commerce, not in gold or land, but in acts. An underground market of virtue, where every whispered kindness, every performed piety, was tallied, hoarded, invested.

I tried to tell him. "*The acts*," I whispered, "they have to be *real!*" I, of all the voices, knew the hollow ring of insincerity. But he wouldn't listen. Every time I offered help, a way to show him … something, anything … he just laughed. Then *You* were born, and I was assigned to You. Bound to You.

I still went to see Father sometimes. I also went to see the rest of my family. But all they did was mock me, their laughter sharper than his. "*More bound than us,*" they sneered. They'd rather be bound for a month, they said, because of their strength, than bound all year round because of weakness, like me.

I never imagined … this connection: You and me. My You. As Your wounds deepened, I became embedded in You, a part of You. I admit, at times when You were very angry, I would enter Your body and run through Your blood. I liked it when You were more … emotional. Hot-headed. Literally.

My point is, I saw myself reflected in Your rage; a mirror held up to my own long-buried fury. You were a fighter, like me. You wanted vengeance. To prove. To *show* them. Show them all what You were capable of.

But then, *that* day came.

When you told Sama to … finish it, to kill the baby. You turned. You saw Your son. And You tried to change.

I don't know exactly *what* happened. I was visiting Father. When I returned … small bodies. Sprawled. Scar, rocking back and forth. You changed towards me. You were angry *at* me—Your closest companion, and I refused to allow that.

I decided to kill You.

I didn't know for sure what would happen to me if my assigned other had died. But now, I have witnessed the freedom of the voices of the Cast, I have learnt something which I am now fully ready to accept. Especially being reminded how You also abandoned me, when Father did, adding fuel to the fire.

Back then, I didn't know what Your death meant for me. But I hoped I would be free. No longer bound and shamed by my family. But Scar, Your son—who had proven himself by eliminating another loose end: the children—advised me You would be more useful if You were alive.

How? I asked him. He said, through You, I could get to Heaven, and he would help me.

So, Scar put You to sleep. A nine-year-long freeze.

On my weaker days, I did consider going back to Father. Making amends. But I stopped myself. I couldn't, not after … that last time I visited.

He disowned me. Then You disowned me—as much as You could anyway. I was still stuck to You. Watching You. Following You. Whispering to You.

But You disowning me made sense. After all, I did incite You to head the fall of your nation. This is why it was easier to let You live. Even if all You did was sleep. As for Father, he didn't even explain. Just said I was too much like Mother. I never met her. Only heard she went to the 'other side'—whatever that means.

Ever since Your little Scar was born, I watched him carefully. I watched all those who were close to You, carefully. But he, unlike the others, could be useful. He could *build*. He knew things. He could build things for *me*. Things I could use. To get to Heaven. Without Father. Sooner. Soon.

You slept. We built. You woke. The plan was simple, elegant in its cruelty: use *You*. At first, I thought You would be my key to Heaven, but then I came across the Book, right at the beginning of Your awakening. I knew then the Book would be my key, and You would be my mask.

You would be the thing I hide within to enter Heaven. After all, in the Holy Month, the doors to Heaven are wide open. You would be a mask of *good*. Of true goodness, with sincerity, not like the false goodness gathered by Father.

I *am* different to him.

On this night, this *special* night, I would rewrite The Book of Decree. I would write my place in it, where I would rule Heaven and send decrees down like poisoned rain. I would make Father suffer as he made *me* suffer.

But now … a snag. A clog in the works. I can't change the decree in The Book of Decree. I can only change *my* decree. And there is talk of the book of records—

No. I won't allow myself to go there. I cannot afford any more distractions.

The facts are the following:

I have the verse to enter me into Heaven.

When You die, I am free.

The fact I am now ready to accept is: I don't need You anymore.

All I must do is speak the words from my chest—the Arched Chest, of course—and … a friction.

A tiny little scream. Sincerity! Sincerity!

No.

I *am* sincere in what I want. Just not in saying these words. That kind of sincerity is a concept for lesser beings.

No. I do not have time for the purpose of *that* sincerity. It is … unnecessary for me. I will go to Heaven, myself. Once I am there, I will change the activities of the next year. I grasp hold of the pen which lies on the floor beside me.

So, *You.* What's Your role in all this, now? Can I still … *use* You? One thing's certain: I don't need You to be good, anymore. But I *do* need to be strong. And free. Strong and free enough to fight my way into Heaven.

Which means You must not only die, but You must die upon Your old ways.

From now on, I will do everything I can to make You go back to those old, familiar ways. It only takes one choice before You die. For You to make Your book of records weigh more heavily upon the side of Your bad deeds.

And who would be the perfect catalyst for this? Who would pull You back down?

Killer Scar.

I take a ragged breath from this broken body. I slap the Girl awake.

"Call her!" I face the Girl, ripping the already loose fabric off her mouth for a little drama. She just stares at me.

I raise the side of the pen's thin tip and make a sharp and swift, albeit clumsy line across the Scholar's jaw—looks like he won't be teaching anyone anything anymore—a line so deep his mouth is hanging open. Splatters of his blood hit my face.

As I open my mouth, some of it flies it. I turn to the Girl, "Your final use. Scream."

She screams.

I close my eyes and take a moment to ground myself in her screams and let out a long breath from the Worshipper's mouth.

Amazing what a pen can do.

I prop it carefully in my pocket—I'll be needing that later when I am in Heaven to write the script and all that—when the pen is secure, I yawn, watching Your brother go to sleep. With that much blood, maybe die. Does not matter anymore.

I sit next to the squirming and screaming girl, using her ragged dress to remove the splatter from her face, ever so gently.

ADAMAH

The dunes shimmer, heat rising in visible waves. Soon, there will be no more heat. Only ice. Yahya's hand inflated and calloused grips my own. A scream rips through the air, raw and echoing, a sound that claws at the scar tissue around my heart. It is the same scream—of pure, unadulterated *pain*—of the Girl when she saw her dead camels.

I turn slowly, my gaze locking on Yahya. He is watching me, really *seeing* me. Those clear, intelligent eyes, usually guarded, search mine, reading the turmoil etched there. He understands.

He gives a small nod.

My breath catches.

"This … is what I want the most," I whisper.

"It's okay, Mama," he says.

I shake my head, the motion jerky. Another scream tears through the air, and my vision blurs. Tears, hot and unwelcome, sting my eyes. I swipe at them furiously, trying to clear my sight, desperate to keep his face in focus.

"I can come with you," he offers, his voice steady, unwavering.

I shake my head again. "You can't be anywhere near the Voice." The words are a ragged whisper.

"Mama?" His voice is pleading now, a small, fragile sound that threatens to shatter my resolve. I want to keep him with me. Keep him close to me.

Something primal, something deep within the core of me, screams. *Keep the Voice away from him.* It is a visceral, instinctive command, overriding everything else.

Yet … my gaze flickers back towards the source of the screams, a sense of dread and duty warring with the fierce protectiveness that burns in my chest. Another scream.

The realization crashes down. *This… this is it.*

The choice laid bare, stark and brutal. The test of truth. The choice of selfless good, saving the Girl, or a desperate want, leaving with my son. I tell myself I will come back to him, but the tear on my body in just seconds tells me that I don't know how much life I have left in me. Will I make it back to him?

"Her name is Noor," he says.

Noor. I smile, thick tears falling from my eyes. Noor is a good name. It suits her.

My shoulders, already hunched with weariness and grief, slump further. I reach out, my hand trembling, and touch Yahya's face.

"I can't sense you," I say. I realize I've never been able to. He was the one who sensed me.

"The sensing was so you could find yourself, Mama. You keep losing yourself when it comes to me."

My shoulders begin to shake, and my chest aches. I wipe my eyes.

I settle for the bare interaction of our connection. His skin is warmer than before, familiar, a stark contrast to the coldness that has settled in my bones. I pull his head down and press a kiss to his forehead, the taste of salt and dust lingering on my lips.

"Wait here for me," I whisper, my voice thick.

His eyes, those knowing, understanding eyes, meet mine. A small, sad smile touches his lips. "I have never stopped waiting for you, Mama."

The words, so simple, so true. *Never.* He had waited for me through everything. Through my sleep. Through my awakening. Now, I am asking him to wait again.

"Protect him," I say to two of the Hollows.

They bow their heads slightly, like they did before at my command, and then raise them. "We will protect him."

I turn away, the other Hollows shuffling behind me. Their vines, full of life, gently wipe at the earth. Their footsteps are almost silent in their gentleness. *Forbidden to kill.* My vines are brittle and dying. They scrape against the ground.

My steps are rough and jolty as I return outside Shahwah, the most devastated part of Thanae. The fire is raging, a symbol of the destruction.

I can't feel the Queen of the orbees, which makes everything more unpredictable. Where is she? Why is she still silent?

I start to climb the hill, the scrabbling sounds of the Hollows echoing behind me. *They could carry me, make it faster.* But I know. I know the Voice. I know that if I am not there, if I am *away* from it, it won't kill the Girl. It does not dispose of that which it still needs.

So, for these few precious moments, I allow myself to walk slowly. Deliberately. I let the cold air shake me as I walk up the hill, the coarse dirt scraping against the soles of my dry, cracking feet. Each step is a penance, a sacrifice.

Each step is a promise. A tiny rebellion against the inevitable. With every step, the Voice is closer.

I step into Jinnah, and a wave of vibrant life washes over me. The birds are the first thing I hear, their chirping and excited chatter as they flap their wings, gathering branches for nests.

The Zam pulses ahead with a soft glow, the scales of the fish flashing like scattered jewels as they dart through the clear water. The orbee trees, though no longer adorned with lights, now bear a different kind of brilliance of thick leaves, which have doubled in size.

The stalks, beyond the Garden of Fire, lining the Zam, have now grown to mature olive trees. They burst with plump, purple olives which cling to their branches, promising a rich harvest.

Jinnah is alive, teeming with a symphony of sound. A gentle clicking. A soft rustling. Water gushing. Parts of Hadeeya have joined forces with Jinnah, mixing sustenance. Squirrels dance around the orbee trees, jumping from one branch to another.

As I pass the area of the Fallen Trees, I pause. No longer stark white, the soil has transformed. It is brown, rich, and strong, like fresh earth ready to nurture. It is reborn.

Beneath my feet is the echo of death, the quiet understanding that decay feeds creation. A law of nature. Balance.

I look closer to the earth, kneeling. Squinting, I wait for my knees to settle. For my back to catch up.

The rocks themselves are mixed with the soil. Embedded within them is the faint shimmer of ancient shells, traces of creatures long gone. They are the bones, made of the very earth they've settled in, the minerals that now give life to the trees, to the olives, to everything around me. Whoever lives here after me can carve these stones, shape them. Build.

This land will provide.

My gaze sweeps across Jinnah. The minerals in the soil will become fibers for clothes, polish to clean teeth, and tools for the next generation. Everything here, from the smallest insect to the largest tree, contributes to the whole. The olives will provide oil, the trees will offer shelter, and the Zam will nourish. Everything a life needs is here, born from the ashes of a revival from sickness. From death. A deep sense of contentment settles within me.

This is good. For now, the future of Jinnah is strong.

A slow smile spreads across my face, a genuine smile that reaches my eyes. It is a smile of relief. Not quite happiness, but joy.

Jinnah is thriving, and in that thriving, I find a flicker of hope for myself, for my son, for our future.

I shiver, reminded of the Dark Fall's promise. It's a reality I'm not ready to face, but I'm finally willing to admit that.

I lean down, my hand brushing against a dead leaf. It crumbles at my touch, returning to the earth. *Just like me.*

I feel the same weariness in my own body, the same rapid disintegration.

I am part of this cycle, too, the death that gives way to life. Though Jinnah thrives, I … I am fading.

Clip clop.

Clip clop.

Hooves pound the earth behind me. I glance back, this time meeting the gaze of the Ram, confirming what I've known all along. Those eyes, ancient and knowing, hold no malice, only an implacable purpose.

"I cannot run from you," I say, my voice steady despite the tremor in my heart. "I cannot hide. Nor can I fight you." There's a strange peace in acknowledging the truth, a quiet acceptance of the inevitable.

"You have no choice when it comes to me," it whispers, a sound like wind swirling around my ears.

It's not a threat, not exactly. More like a statement of fact, a natural law as unyielding as the presence of shadows with the gleam of light.

In this moment, I understand. "How long do I have?" I ask.

"Knowledge I cannot reveal," it answers, the words echoing with an ancient resonance.

"Will you be kind?"

"I will be how you lived your life," comes the reply, chilling in its simplicity.

"And if I lived a life of pain?" I counter.

"All life has pain," the Ram responds, unmoved.

"So does death, it seems," I murmur as I continue to tug my body along with every step forward, reaching the bridge.

"It is how you *end* that matters the most."

With that, it leaves. *It is how you end that matters the most.* The phrase echoes in my mind as I continue past the Zam.

Now I stand before the Golden Dome, a symbol of both hope and dread. I climb each step slowly, each movement a conscious choice, a reaffirmation of my path. I push the door open, the hinges, like my own, groaning in protest. I stumble forward, falling into a crowd of outstretched hands—my Hollows' hands—that catch me, steady me. I push them gently away and walk through the massive door.

The hallway. The wooden door. The carpeted room. And there she is. The Girl, tied to the same pillar as my brother.

PART 29

The Tidings

ADAMAH

The soft carpet cushions the cracking soles of my feet as I move towards the pillar on which Noor and Elias are tied. Though I feel the presence of the Voice lurking behind the door, I don't turn.

Darkness fills the room, yet my eyes, though weary, still pierce it. Down in the Deep, we adapted. Days and nights blurred into one perpetual twilight, untouched by the sun's light. Then, when my generation was a few years old, our elders discovered, or rather, were given fire. They brought other wonders from the Surface to our subterranean world.

We, children, never questioned the origins of the fire or any of the other things they brought from the world above. We simply reveled in its warmth, even though our eyes could see without it. We didn't ask about the big red flowers, only inhaled their sweet perfume, crafting scents for the women. We didn't wonder about the source of the varied fabrics, clinging more closely to the same women's forms than before. We just watched the way our elders used these new things, like the tools that shaved the men's beards.

I still love the dark. I was born in it. It is my beginning. Down there in the Deep, appearances didn't matter. We were the same. Shapes, bound together, each needing the other, each helping.

That fire brought ruin with its revelations. Allowing *him* to see too much of me. He saw me as more than just a shape—an attainable object, weaker and smaller than the other girls, who were closer to womanhood than me.

I reach the Girl. Her name echoes in my mind. "Noor," I say aloud.

Her eyes are wide, reflecting a life born in light. Her pupils are smaller, less dilated than mine, though the outer shape is familiar, like those of my people. Funny the things I notice more when I slow down.

I turn to my brother. Now that I'm closer, I see it. Something is wrong. Something is missing. His mouth is leaking something. No, his mouth itself is hanging off. I gasp. "Elias!"

The Hollows are beside me in an instant.

"Heal him," I command, my voice sharp. "And unbind them both."

They move with unsettling speed, freeing my brother and Noor. The purple gas escapes them as they work. I know the risk. I know what that gas can do. Has done. But we don't have much time.

I hold onto my brother's arm. I sense him slipping away. I watch the Hollows work as the gas swirls around us. Will it work?

Noor's eyes are wide, reflecting her fear of the dark. I'd forgotten how much she hates it. The fallen curtain behind us allows a thin line of the crescent-shaped moon to pierce through from the window, but its light doesn't reach this far in the room.

I turn to the Hollows. They cannot create light, not like the orbees. The Hollows are drawn to light like all plants, but they are also different from most plants. They are a mix of metal. As if reading my thoughts, their bodies shimmer, transforming into a reflective surface with the faint purple hue I have come to know.

The faint moonlight, that single ray piercing the darkness, is multiplied a thousandfold. The room explodes with white light, reflected from their metallic forms, banishing the shadows completely.

My face is mirrored back to me in their metal bodies. The lines around my eyes are deeply etched. My skin, usually rich and deep, has taken on a greyish tinge, as if the light passes right through it. My lips are thin, a mere line against the ashen pallor of my face, and my eyes are dull and sunken.

New lines are forming at the corners of my mouth as I watch. I remember the words on my brother's sword: *By Time*[8] *Verily humanity is at loss*[9].

I tear my eyes away from my image and turn back to Elias. A Hollow remains before him. The bleeding has stopped. The gas is working. A scar is forming, closing the wound. His jaw … it's back where it belongs. He even shifts slightly. My heart, which had been hammering against my ribs, begins to settle.

The other Hollows have already unbound Elias and Noor. Small hands touch mine. Noor. She's staring at my face, her touch, feather light, as if she can sense my weakness. She touches my cheek, her gaze searching. So many facets to her, so much held within. It's too much for her small frame to contain. Betrayal flickers in her eyes. Numbness. Peace. Hope. And anger, simmering just beneath the surface. The emotion that dominates now, the one that fills her gaze as she looks at me, is profound sadness.

She blinks; her head wobbles slightly. She rubs her wrists, then her head. Noor's hand comes away, smeared with blood.

"Heal her," I whisper. I gesture to the Hollows, and their gas is released instantly, enveloping Noor.

Elias's eyes flicker open. The sheen of sweat is gone. He focuses on me, his gaze locking with mine. "AmaNoor," he murmurs, his voice weak.

He can see.

His gaze sharpens, focusing on my face. I smile, the dimple in my cheek deepening with the creases around my eyes.

"Adamah," he says, his voice a little stronger now. "How?"

His eyes are brimming with tears. I smile again. "Rafiq was right. You're not blind anymore."

My hands tremble slightly, and he steadies them with a firm grip. "Where is Rafiq?"

"He is in Hadeeya. I know that's why you sent him with me."

"I sent him to protect you."

"I have the Hollows to help me with that." I turn to the Hollows, and he follows my gaze, a flash of surprise in his eyes. He looks back at me. I continue, "I promised Rafiq I would find more like him. If I don't … make sure you do."

He nods and takes a deep breath. "It's time to pray."

I don't question why or how. He scoops up some of the dust that covers a pillar of the Golden Dome and wipes it across his hands and face. I do the same. He rises and turns to face the small platform, which faces the East.

I stand in the row behind him, my posture mirroring his.

Noor's eyes are wide, fixed on something behind us, something that fills her with terror. I know what she sees: the figure huddled in the shadows by the door.

"Guard us," I command the Hollows.

They respond quickly, forming a living wall behind us. I can hear the Voice—shrieking, sobbing, whispering, pushing against the barrier. I force myself to focus on my brother. I follow his movements; the precise way he raises his hands.

"Allah is Greater ..." he begins, in the language of our ancestors, his voice ringing out through the stillness.

Elias recites verses, his voice rising and falling in a melodic cadence, just like the old woman—my good deeds—from my dream.

He bows once, and I follow. We kneel, my knees protesting with a dull ache, then he lowers himself to the ground. We prostrate, my forehead touching the soft floor. We remain here, and I hear his soft sobs. Tears well up in my own eyes. Noor prostrates with us. We rise, then prostrate one more time, as if given another chance to talk to my Lord.

We complete three more units of prayer, then sit with folded legs, offering peace once to the right and once to the left.

When we finish, Elias turns to face Noor and me with glistening eyes.

"This is our purpose, isn't it?" I ask.

He nods, a single, affirmative movement.

He then recites the following: "'And I didn't create the jinn and mankind except to worship Me.[19]'"

"All the things I've seen, the good, the bad," I whisper. "They were supposed to point me to my purpose. To worship my Creator, weren't they?" I am asking the same question because I don't want to forget. I don't want to forget my purpose again.

He continues, reciting, "'Indeed, in the creation of the Heavens and the Earth, and the alternation of the night and the day, and the ships which sail through the sea with that which benefits people, and what Allah has sent down from the Heavens of rain.[20]'"

A fleeting image of raindrops, up there in Hadeeya, splashing against my face: life-giving water, another defense from Earth, against the sun's heat.

That rain is like the tears against the heat inside me, which threatened for so long to consume me. The tears I shed—my acceptance of pain, moments after sitting with the dead—have unexpectedly brought life within me in a different way.

Just as I think this, my brother recites, "'Giving life, thereby, to the Earth after its death.[20]'"

Yes. I did feel dead. I felt dead for so long.

He finishes the recitation: "'And dispersing therein every kind of moving creature, and in the changing of the winds and the clouds controlled between the Heaven and Earth are signs for a people who use reason.[20]'"

"Signs," I echo. "All signs."

A dry, brittle cackle erupts behind me. It isn't a laugh, more a sound that scrapes against the edges of my hearing.

My aging body protests the sudden movement as I turn around. A sharp, cracking sound, like dried twigs snapping from my joints. Each muscle is straining. Neck creaks, wave of dizziness. Blurred vision. Refocus. Breath hitches.

ME

As *You* turn, or rather, attempt to, I look upon You, with satisfaction. Now, a husk. Vines—like the ones which cut my threads not too long ago—now yellowing, brittle things, some brown and crumbling.

Your face is deep with wrinkles, mirroring Your fading vines. You have not aged well. Your eyes squint, sunken but somehow still sharp. You hunch, spine curved and fragile.

This will be easier than I thought.

I unleash my threads, aimed to pierce not just the Vessels, but *You*. The Vessels were intended to be *my* army, *my* instruments of control. Not Yours, but *mine*.

It has become clear to me why that is so. Why did the Vessels not remain empty when the voices of the Cast *chose* not to fill them? Scar played a double game. He *filled* them with You.

More importantly, when You die, I am free. Your aging simply quickens the path. Now, I must make sure You die in Your worst state.

Good. Bad. All relative.

For me, Your bad is my good. Your good is my bad. Things changed slightly when I thought I could use You as my mask. *That* is now irrelevant.

What *is* relevant is this: if You die bad, I will have more power than I have ever known, *and* I will be free of You. I need that power to invade Heaven with the Vessels, my army.

There are a couple of causes for concern, however. If I get too strong when You die, I will be chained, like the other voices are in the Holy Month. No matter, I will just have to work quickly and rush to Heaven as soon as possible.

The second cause for concern: now that the voices of the Cast have abandoned me, what exactly will I fill the Vessels with?

I suppose an empty army is more useful than no army at all. After all, if the Cast's voices were going to puppeteer the other few hundred Vessels, as I had originally planned, then why can't I? Why can't I control them all? With my threads?

Yes. That is what I will do. I will have to test my theory, of course. Poke around inside the Vessels to see the way their systems work.

If all goes well and the Vessels are useful to me, they will be a part of my cause. They will join the Queen of the orbees and help me make my difference.

This is all so exciting.

With the final details ironed out, I am satisfied and prepared. I turn my attention back to You, focusing my threads on a specific target.

I target *This*, Your Mutated Shame.

This, a hot or cold flush that crawls up Your neck and settles in Your cheeks, making them burn or freeze.

This, what makes Your stomach clench, twisting itself into knots.

This, what makes You want to disappear, to melt into the ground, or become invisible.

This, what makes the air thicken, making it hard to breathe. Making Your thoughts attack You.

This.

This.

This. What makes every imagined flaw, every past mistake, suddenly on display, magnified and glaring. What makes You shrink inwards, wanting to pull Your skin tighter, to build a wall between Yourself and the judging eyes You imagine are everywhere. What makes the world feel sharp, the edges of everything too bright, too loud.

This is where my power lies over You. Where the power of all voices lies over all *humankind*. We are the voices in Your head. The whispers of Your nothingness. Training You to think like us, until You become Your own ...

DEVIL.

I have never failed in using *This* against You.

One by one, I throw my threads to reach *This* in You.

ADAMAH

Sama. Her body stands behind the barrier of the Hollows, her head poking out from their touching shoulders. The darkness that stains her violet eyes, leers back at me.

"You," I say.

"Me," Sama's voice echoes, her eyes fluttering closed, her mouth slowly opening.

The threads that have been released snake towards me. I feel them ... as if they are searching for *something*. Clattering against my skin, my arms, my legs, every part of me.

They enter. Whispers. Only whispers. Lies. So untrue. So weak.

I blink. Something within me feels different from when the threads entered before. They used to access my heart, but now they can't. It's too full of faith.

The carpeted room looks different. It *looks* like the same room. Already otherworldly, with the moonlight reflecting off the Hollows' metallic bodies, now there's a subtle wrongness, a dissonance that vibrates in the air. The carpet is still green, but a faded green, and the pattern on it, the underlying structure, is gone. The boxes that gave it shape, the order ... vanished. Everything is slightly *off*. Unsettling. Like a memory that's been corrupted, leaving behind only the faintest echo of what was real.

The threads lash out from me, writhing towards the Hollows. But the Hollows … they're different now, too. Their skin, once seemingly solid, is now translucent, revealing a mostly hollow interior. No organs, just swirling vines that pulse—like veins—gas where blood should flow. The threads pass right through them, as if satisfied by their emptiness. As if the threads wanted to *check* something.

Now the threads target Elias and Noor. They, too, are changed, their forms also translucent, but unlike the Hollows, their insides are full of organs, muscles, and bones. Even without the orbees, the threads can't penetrate through my brother and Noor's bodies, blocked by a force emanating from deep within their chests.

A powerful heartbeat, like my own.

With each throb, the heartbeat slams against the threads, deflecting them, forcing them to recoil. The threads thwarted, slither back to Sama's body, retreating like defeated serpents.

The room goes back to the way I remember. The box designs on the carpet return and the colors are sharper.

"How?" the Voice demands as it faces me, its words forced through Sama's contorted features.

With a groan, I settle against a nearby pillar, my feet finding purchase on the soft ground. Even this simple shift exhausts me.

My voice, when I speak, is barely a whisper. "To you, I am a game. To me, you are a test. Your existence, the presence of evil, reveals the depth of my submission to my purpose."

"Since when," the Voice spits, "have you submitted to *anything* … Queen Adamah?"

"I submitted to escaping my pain," I say. "That opened me to submitting to you. I was never free. Nothing in nature knows freedom until it fulfills its intended purpose."

"You were free with *me*!" the Voice snarls.

"No one and nothing," I counter, "is truly free in this world."

"Why would you lower yourself to be a slave?" the Voice rasps, the words vibrating through Sama's form.

"We are all slaves," I reply, my voice now above a whisper is unwavering. "What gives us true meaning is what we choose to be a slave *to*."

"How did you escape my threads?" the Voice demands.

"I became aware of what drives me to be a slave to everything, *except* the One worthy of that devotion. If there is a freedom in this world, it is only through cutting the threads that bind me to the creation and tying myself with a rope to my Creator."

"What is it that drives you to be a slave to all but … *Him?*"

"You know very well. Mutated Shame."

"You won," the Voice hisses.

"No," I counter. "I haven't. I still carry that kind of shame. It doesn't disappear so easily. But I am aware of it. And I won't truly defeat you until I die." I regret saying this, when I note the flicker, a glimmer of something akin to … hope, sparking in Sama's eyes.

"Do you know what you did?" the Voice asks.

"I know what I did," I affirm.

Sama's body, in which the Voice resides, begins to move. It glides joltingly and misaligned, trying to break through the ranks of the Hollows. The Hollows remain a steadfast wall.

I nod to them. They shift, their metallic forms parting like a disturbed current. They form a living corridor, allowing the Voice to pass, to sit face to face with me, cross-legged.

Sama's already thin face is now totally gaunt, the skin stretched taut over the sharp cheekbones. The deep, dark violet eyes, once pools of vibrant life, are now like polished obsidian, reflecting nothing but the cold, alien presence within.

They stare back, not with recognition or emotion, but with a chilling, vacant intensity. Her jaw is clenched, lips a thin, bloodless line, and a faint, almost imperceptible twitch flickers at the corner of one eye, a subtle sign of the struggle within.

The face worn by the Voice is a mask, a distorted reflection of its former self, now a canvas for the malevolent force that holds it captive.

The air crackles with tension, the unspoken words hanging heavy between us.

A sneer from the Voice. "Let me phrase. Do you know what you did to your son?"

ME

You sit there, Your feet just inches away from my crossed legs. The Vessels form a silent circle around us, their presence a palpable weight. Your brother stands beside You like an animal ready to strike, the Girl next to him like a lost deer who doesn't know whether to run or freeze.

"Your son," I say, carefully shifting my eyes back to Yours. There is a slight twitch as the Worshipper tries to punch herself out of me. "Followed Your legacy."

A twitch in Your heavy eyelids. A tremor shakes Your right hand.

"Legacy," You repeat.

"Your legacy of murder," I reply, the words ringing out in the stillness. "But he did *worse*."

I watch Your face, a stoic expression replacing the glimmer of despair which just passed through it.

I press on. "What was Your final memory?"

You blink, processing the question. Your eyes open, meeting mine.

"After that," I continue, "You saw what Your son did to the children, didn't You? You saw their bodies on the ground. That's why You turned against me."

Your eyes dart, as if reading something unseen. Your brow furrows, deep lines creasing Your forehead, like fissures in ancient rock.

A small gasp escapes Your lips. You look up, Your gaze shifting, searching … finding Your brother. He is right next to You, You fool! When Your eyes meet his, he blinks a few times. In normal circumstances, I would rip those eyes out of him. Feed them to the Cast. But these are not normal circumstances.

After a few blinks, You nod and turn back to me, a knowing look in that stone expression. What did he say to You?

"You try to use my anger against me; you always have," You begin, Your voice thin but firm. "But anger is like that which keeps everything on Earth grounded. Without it, everything floats away, becoming weightless. If it's too strong, its force will crush. You fail. My anger isn't my enemy, and I've had enough of you."

You turn to Your brother, "Elias recite the verses from the Book that will stop—"

"Verses?" I interrupt, my tone sharp. It wasn't anger; I was trying to rise from You. It was despair.

You ignore my question, Your focus fixed on Your brother. "The verses that will stop it."

"You mean the *same* verses," I press, "that *he* recited?"

You know exactly *who* I am talking about. *Him.* Your eyes meet mine and widen slightly.

I continue. "Yes. The man who violated You, the father of Your killer son, was a reciter of the Book. The *same* Book of the Lord, You claim to be a slave to."

"Adamah, do you remember what I told you in Jinnah?" Your brother sits next to You. "The narration of the learned?"

I continue: "That man, of all men, was … AmaNoor's husband, wasn't he, Scholar? The very woman you unwisely sent back to the Deep."

I turn to *You.* "Technically, wouldn't that make AmaNoor, Your son's … stepmother?"

You gasp again, the air catching in Your throat.

I smile.

"That's why, from the moment she arrived," I continue, my voice relentless, "You hated her. If Your incompetent brother had sent anyone else to protect you all—anyone but her, a living reminder of her perverted husband—the Deep might have survived. Might have even thrived. But he didn't. He sent *her*. You rejected everything she brought with her, the message, the Book, how to follow it. Only eight people followed her out of over two hundred. Just *eight*."

You clutch your head; pain etched on Your face. I can *see* more lines forming on Your face, Your hands, now covered with darker spots.

Emboldened, I press on. "So, You killed all of AmaNoor's followers, the mothers and fathers of those children, nine in all, including *her*."

I take a longer breath than I need to. I continue, "Your son finished what You began. He killed their children."

You shake Your head, a futile attempt to deny the truth. I stand; my body now free of Sama's attempt to fight me. Your brother moves closer to You. The Girl just stares at the body I reside in.

You look at Your brother. "How can a man who recites the Book of Allah do this to a child? To *me*?"

"The same reason, sister," Your brother replies, his voice heavy with sorrow, "that the Voice hears the truth and refuses to accept it."

You're reliving it, aren't You? It doesn't matter what Your brother says. The Vessels are now on the ground with You, moaning in despair as they witness what You've seen, what You've endured, night after night. These Vessels show me how You feel inside.

"Of all the people," I begin. "It was a *holy* man who did this to You."

"How can ..." You begin, but the words trail off.

"Is evil," I say, my voice laced with a cruel amusement, "still a measurement of Your depth of submission to Your purpose?"

You look at me, Your eyes filled with despair.

ADAMAH

Elias's voice, soft and melodic, fills the room. Everything feels distant, muffled. Like I am floating. The world shrinks, narrows, until only his words remain:

"'Allah-there is no deity except Him, the Ever-Living, the Sustainer of all existence. Neither drowsiness overtakes Him nor sleep. To Him belongs whatever is in the Heavens and whatever is on Earth.[21]'"

The Mutated Shame is like a living thing, a slick, black oil spreading through my veins, threatening to drown me in its icy depths. It whispers insidious lies, pulling me down, down into a place where the air is thick with cold.

Twisted emotions claw at my mind, trying to usurp control, to turn me into a puppet on their strings.

But then, a flicker of light, a pinprick of defiant clarity. The verses. My brother's words now echo in the hollow chambers of that place where morality resides. I can *feel* where it is now. Around my chest, a heart which is not physical, but spiritual.

Each syllable of Elias's recitation is like a shard of glass, sharp and piercing, cutting through the suffocating darkness, dragging me back from the brink.

I understand, with a clarity that borders on terror, that I'm not broken, but deeply hurt. Fractured, like Earth after a cataclysmic tremor—tremors from human hands which violated it, and from Earth's resistance against those hands. All it needs is the arms of care to wrap around it, just as the Queen of the orbees did with her leaves.

In that care and safety, within the container where life can thrive, Earth can mend. It can find balance again.

I feel my brother's arms around me, holding me with the Girl, rocking back and forth as I shake. I don't hate their touch. For the first time, I feel like I need it.

I, too, will mend.

I will piece myself back together, shard by agonizing shard, removing layer by layer. Softening the frozen dust, which can restore all that has been taken.

The pillar against my back is rough and unyielding. The metallic tang on my tongue, a reminder not of fragility, but of feeling. The rhythmic clasping and unclasping of my hands, the pressure in my joints, a desperate attempt to anchor myself to the here and now.

I close my eyes, visualizing Earth, its resilience, its stubborn refusal to yield. I need to be here. Now. Present. Not in the Mutated Shame, which tries to declare me as its own and push me to a past that will consume me.

This is a war waged in the deepest recesses of my soul. The Mutated Shame, the inflammatory fear, threatening—offering—to give reprieve from my pain. My shoulders slump as one thought presses.

I only need to forget.

Elias continues, "'Who is it that can intercede with Him except by His permission? He knows what is presently before them and what is after them, and they encompass nothing of His knowledge except what He wills. His throne extends over the Heavens and the Earth, and their preservation tires Him not. And He is the Most High, the Most Great.[21]'"

These verses are as pure as the memory of giving birth to my son. Yet, they are different. I never thought anything could surpass the love I have for Yahya.

That single memory of him entering the world might be enough to make me want to leave Hell, but it isn't enough to make me yearn for Heaven so I can meet my Creator. Not like these words. I cling to them. I've hungered for them. For this—for a rope, which extends beyond this world. For the Truth.

With each word, a weight lifts. The gnawing ache of betrayal, the doubts … they recede, pushed back by the sheer power of the verse. The Voice, whose influence had been writhing within me, falls silent, its struggles ceasing.

"That is the Truth," I whisper. I recognize it. Almost remember it from something primal long ago, as if having known this all along. As if I had testified it but had forgotten.

Now, I remember.

My body remembers.

A certainty upon a certainty.

I remember my Lord.

Allah.

My brother, seated by me, keeps his arms wrapped around my weary shoulders. My body protests with every movement I make. My bones feel brittle, thin, and tiny cracks are forming in them. It hurts. Everything hurts. We continue to rock back and forth, clinging to each other, and we cry. I cry, letting the tears flow freely, washing away the pain, the confusion.

"Our religion," Elias says, his eyes meeting mine. "It is not tied to a person. It is tied to The Creator, Himself. To the Truth in the Book and how it was followed by His final messenger Muhammed (peace be upon him). What that man did to you," he continues softly, "was born from a poison in his heart. He never submitted to what he knew to be true, which makes him more blameworthy."

Elias then recites, "'And who is more unjust than one who is reminded of the verses of his Lord but turns away from them and forgets what his hands have put forward? Indeed, We have placed over their hearts coverings so they do not understand it, and in their ears deafness. And if you call them to guidance, they will never be guided, ever.[22]'"

I turn to the Voice, in the form of Sama, now sprawled on the carpet, lying in a silent scream in front of me.

"You reached me," I begin, speaking to the Voice directly, my voice low but steady. "When you told me to lower my veil, your threads entered my ears. You made our people lose their morality. Their natural modesty and the shame that came from transgressing it. You incited a Mutated Shame. That is the ultimate doorway to us, for you."

"You have defeated me," the Voice rasps through shuddered breaths.

"That day, when I saw the bodies of the children, I realized you were never good for me. Even though you knew me so well. After I realized that, I warned the ones who remained of the Deep. I told them all what you were really like. There was a moment, their eyes flashed. They realized it, too. They knew you were evil. Do you know what they did, even though they *knew*?"

No answer. Just a vacant stare from Sama's eyes, which are turned towards the ceiling.

I continue, "They chose to pretend they didn't know. They buried what they saw and followed you anyway. Why?"

Sama's voice sounds disjointed as the Voice whispers through her. "The loss ... the l-loss of what they wanted was too great."

"Loss," I repeat. "They lost themselves when they ignored what they knew to be true. It was that day, they rejected the truth, that they became your Cast."

A flicker in that empty stare. "Why ... why are you saying this?"

"Because you did the same thing they did."

"I am above them!"

"You told me once how your father turned his back on you. All because you dared to speak the truth, to tell him his good deeds were hollow, that sincerity was the only key to Heaven. Yet, here you are, a monument to hypocrisy, rejecting the very truth you once championed. This isn't some simple act of blind ignorance. This is a deliberate, calculated rejection of reality itself. You were right, weren't you, before? About me choosing a truth that fits my delusion. You knew because you've been doing the same thing all along. Like *that* man, picking and choosing."

"I chose Heaven," the Voice spits out.

Elias says, "No ruined spirit will enter Heaven. You chose a lie over the truth. *You* are a deceiver. For a deceiver to gain power, you must block another from theirs through an obsessive fear or an obsessive false promise. You have no real power of your own. Until you face yourself, you will continue to live a lie. It will direct every choice you make in life, and you will call it destiny."

I look to the Hollows. "Get the Arched Chest." They retrieve it from where I left it under the crumpled curtain and carry it to me.

Elias takes it and says steadily, "You said before your father tried to destroy the Book, but you wanted to use it. You didn't use it. You used our people to change its meaning. You distorted it so our leaders picked and chose what suited their desires. Desires driven by their Mutated Shame."

Slowly, something is being released from Sama's open mouth. The threads of the Voice. They seem to be searching for something. Creeping across the floor. They stop as they reach for a silver-eyed mask that lies by the pillar Elias was tied to. The threads of the Voice are trying to hold onto the thread that comes from the mask. But the grasp is weak. A deceiver's grasp is always weak when faced with the truth.

I turn my gaze to Sama's frozen form, aware of my own body becoming more tired.

I continue, "You tore families—nations— apart. The irony is that all along, everything you've done has been based on a single premise: that Heaven exists, and so does Allah. Yet, trapped in your delusion, when the truth was clear to you, you chose willful ignorance, until your arrogance completely blinded you."

My brother adds, his voice ringing with finality, "Do you know where arrogance comes from?" He doesn't wait for an answer. "From your Mutated Shame. You have it, too. So does your father. You are both the same."

"Father ..." the Voice sputters. The threads trail back, clumping on one another, unable to re-enter Sama.

My brother continues, "There was something your father and you ... overlooked. That is why you have failed. Why you will keep failing to destroy us, the believers, even if you tried with all the forces in the world."

"What?" the Voice rasps.

"That Allah is on the side of good. Whoever He guides cannot be misguided. You only have power over the ungrateful, and the defining trait of the believers is their gratitude."

I reach into the Arched Chest and retrieve the letters to my son. I smile, though the muscles around my mouth feel stiff, the skin papery. My hands tremble slightly as I place them in my dress. I will return these letters to Yahya when I see him. The thought, once a vibrant promise, now carries a faint, hollow echo, a whisper of doubt. I notice the delicate skin on the back of my hand, the faint blue veins tracing a fragile map. The letters I wrote to him were once a symbol of hope. Now they feel like a weight, a tangible reminder of the years that have slipped away, of the time I may not have left.

As for … the Voice. It is in its raw form now. An awful-looking, little thing. No wonder it hides in the dark.

I slam down the lid of the Arched Chest, the creature inside. With its release from Sama's body, the feather pen rolls from her fingers, coming to a stop as it *taps* against the silver-eyed mask.

"Destroy them both," I say to the Hollows, my voice sharp.

"We do not kill," they answer, their voices a single, echoing thought.

"You do not kill life. This pen and this mask steal life. Destroy them both," I command.

With one strike, both mask and pen shatter into pieces.

ME

I wanted this. I wanted to be in the Arched Chest.

Fools!

I recite the words, the ancient verse from the Book, my key to Heaven, repeating them in the confined space.

ADAMAH

Sama's breathing is heavy. Noor is next to us. I take a deep breath. My ribs rattle with the effort.

Noor scratches at her chest as Elias joins us. They both have that same awkward, high forehead. Now that I see them side by side—

A small, hesitant voice cuts through my thoughts. "Can't feel my legs," Sama whispers.

"You're going to be fine," I reply quickly, avoiding her gaze.

When our eyes finally meet, she gives me *that* look. The look that says she knows I'm not telling the whole truth. I wipe at the tears that keep leaking down my face, trying to compose myself.

Her gaze shifts to Elias and then to me. "Seems we all had parts we needed from each other. The man who hurt you, AmaNoor's—" she pauses, a flicker of pain crossing her face. "Had knowledge, but no worship or sincerity."

Her eyes find mine. "You had sincerity, but no knowledge or worship." Then, she lowers her gaze. "And I ... I had worship with no knowledge."

"Mama," Noor whispers, taking Sama's hand. A piece of Noor's dress has come loose from her bony neck. For the first time, I see what she has been scratching. A thin, dark line snakes out from beneath the fabric.

Sama squeezes Noor's hand, pulling her head down to her chest. "What I did to you," she murmurs, her voice thick with regret. "Can you forgive me?"

"Of course, Mama," Noor replies, her voice muffled against Sama's clothing.

"It seems forgetting is in our nature, Elias," Sama says, her voice laced with a bitter irony. "When you arrived, I . . . I forgot who you were. That's why I hid Noor from you. I thought it had always been like this. My child and I, living together, in the Golden Dome. When you read a verse from the Book, 'Verily in the remembrance of Allah do hearts find peace.'¹ I started to remember . . . things."

Her breathing is shallow. "I told you Adamah became our queen, a battle that happened. Still, there were so many gaps. Like the part about the baby in the bloody blanket. My mind wouldn't let me see what happened, what my role was in it. When you left the Golden Dome, you left as a blind man. It was after you were gone that my memories flooded back. I saw the children . . . their bodies . . ."

"Mama," Noor says. "Don't say anything, just rest."

Sama shakes her head, cupping Noor's head in her hand, pressing a kiss to her forehead. "I'm so sorry," she whispers.

Noor is already crying, scratching the wound on her chest. She says again, in a plea almost, "Don't say anything, Mama."

Sama looks at Noor. "What I said down there, in the Deep . . . about not being your mother—"

"You *are* my Mama . . . it hurts," she whispers. "My chest hurts, Mama."

"I know. It's open, that's why." Sama whispers back, her voice thick with emotion. "That day, I made the biggest mistake of my life. I have tried to make up for it all these years, but I couldn't. I didn't know how to love you. I just hurt you even more."

Elias reaches out a hand, hovering over Noor's shaking back, then hesitates, drawing it back to himself.

Sama tries to touch Noor's face, but her weakened fingers falter, falling back to her side. "That day, I had already . . . stabbed you, straight through the heart. When I turned, I saw Yahya with purple flowers. He took you from your mother's arms and left. I didn't see where, because I was kneeling over the dead body of my daughter by then. When I woke up after, in the Golden Dome, there was a baby there, with a hole through her chest, a wound scabbed over. I had forgotten everything before that. I thought you were mine. Until Elias came."

"Is that why you never gave me a name?" Noor asks.

Sama nods. "Even when I thought you were mine, a part of me knew the truth. Every time I would try to think of a name for you, my mind would go foggy. I just couldn't do it."

"But you took care of me," Noor says.

"I did. An obligation to make up for my wrongs. But a name … I didn't deserve to give you that," Sama continues. "I need to tell you why I stood on the roof that night."

"It doesn't matter," Noor says softly, her voice filled with love. "You chose to live."

"You need to know," Sama says between coughs.

My brother's eyes meet mine. A silent communication passes between us. I blink: *She's your daughter.*

He nods, wiping his eyes and face, and blinks back: *Purple is the color of the dead who look alive.*

Of course, he's talking about the dream he had when he was younger. I am reminded of the nature of the Hollows—vines, from the Vine Tree of purple blooms, which is what the Hollows' blood is made of: purple gas, which can heal.

Now, I know who Noor's mother and father are, the dots of recognition from all the time I have been with her connect. Her clumsy walk, her one eyebrow. The way she had a dreamy look at times, the way she cried. The snorted, high shrieked laugh. Her forehead.

Sama says, "You needed a mother—"

"Don't speak, Mama, you'll hurt yourself," Noor says, her voice breaking.

"I needed a daughter." A tear rolls down Sama's cheek, landing on the carpet, a small dot darker than the rest. "I thought I could put my love for my Sumayya into you, but it hurt even more, and I hurt you because of it." Sama's eyes are flickering. "Your mother was a …" She takes a soft breath, "A great woman." Her voice fades into a whisper, "No better father than Elias …"

Despite her fragility, Sama still squeezes my hand lightly. She takes a deep breath and says, "Is there hope for me?"

I try to speak, but the words won't come out.

"It is the end that matters more than the beginning," my brother says, a sobering echo of a recent conversation I had with the Ram.

Noor cups Sama's face in one hand, taking my hand in the other. She turns to Elias. "Can you ... can you help her?"

He nods. "Say, 'There is no god worthy of worship except Allah, and Muhammad (peace be upon him) was His final messenger.'"

Sama's eyelids flicker, her breath shallow. She repeats the words and then exhales. Her body goes limp. Her chest stills. One last look at her face. She is smiling.

"Peace be with you, sister in faith," I say softly. "I will see you soon."

A thunderous roar echoes through the air, vibrating through the ground beneath us. A stifled shriek of laughter, chilling and triumphant, escapes from the Arched Chest. Elias, Noor, and I exchange uneasy glances.

"The Queen of the orbees," I say, my voice tight.

Noor's eyes widen. "Is she angry because the Voice killed her orbees?"

"Killed them?" I ask, my brow creased. "When? How?"

"In the Deep," Noor replies, her voice trembling slightly.

Though I can no longer feel or sense the Queen——as if a channel has been severed——I have no doubt she can still sense *me*. And her orbees. What would she do if she discovered her daughters were gone? That their new 'queen' allowed it to happen?

I look to Elias, who is already moving towards the door. "Stay with Noor," I say, my voice firm. "I need to do this myself."

"I'm staying with you," he replies, his voice resolute, stepping through the doorway into the hall.

"I have an army," I say, gesturing towards the Hollows, their metallic forms still reflecting the sliver of moonlight. "The Great Wall is gone. You can go straight through to the desert. Go as far away as you can from here until I make things right. Take Yahya. He's waiting for me there."

"I'm staying with *you*," Elias repeats, his tone leaving no room for argument.

"What about your daughter?" I retort. "Who's going to keep her safe?"

"I can fight too," Noor says sheepishly.

"No fighting," I say, my voice firm.

"We can fight in different ways," Noor says.

"The greatest fight is the fight inside," Elias agrees.

Elias and Noor exchange a brief, almost hesitant glance. A quiet moment of shared understanding between a father and daughter.

"When I was in the Apex—" Elias begins.

"The Apex?" Noor and I ask in unison.

"The mask. A different kind of reality. It shows you everything you want, using it against you. There were many … figures there. I believe they were the voices of the Cast. Every time I relived whatever heaven on Earth they gave me, I began to remember more. I recited verses from the Book, and by the third time, the voices stood in prayer with me. All except one. Yahya's voice. The others left with someone."

He looks momentarily lost in thought. He catches himself and continues. "If there is only Yahya's voice that stayed, then the rest of the Queen's power is her evolution—how she has *had* to adapt to her situation."

"Like the Deep adapted to the dark?" I ask.

"Yes, our eyes became different after just a few generations. Maybe …" Elias sighs, a weight settling on his shoulders.

"What would a mother do for her child?" I ask, my gaze fixed on him.

He raises his eyebrows, looking at me with a somber expression. "She would destroy the world and all that is in it."

"Or she would keep her safe," Noor interjects, her voice soft.

"And if that child was hurt by someone?" I press.

"I don't know that one," she replies, her brow furrowed. "I never got hurt."

Elias looks at her sadly, a flicker of pain in his eyes.

Her eyes flicker, too. She looks away. "Mama's lesson was that she needed knowledge. What's mine?"

Elias puts a hand on her arm. "To be a child."

"I don't know what that means." She looks at his hand on her arm and then up at him. "What do I call you?"

A thunderous roar echoes through the air, shaking the very foundations of the ground beneath our feet. We exchange a nervous glance, Elias, Noor, and I. This would be lovely if we weren't facing the wrath of an enraged, grief-stricken beast—Queen.

"I have to stop her," I say to them both, my voice shaky. It is getting harder to speak. To breathe.

"We'll come with you!" Noor insists.

"It *must* be me," I say. "The last thing she remembers is her orbees making *me* their queen. And the nature of her kind is that there can be only *one* queen."

"I have an idea," Noor begins. We both turn to her. My neck cracks slightly under the sudden tension. "Do you want to see it?"

I stare at Noor, trying to suppress a smile. "Yes."

She walks ahead, her figure a stark contrast to my labored movements. Turning back, she gives a curt nod to follow. I push my body forward, each step a painful negotiation with my weary limbs as I pass through the hallway.

Elias holds his arm out for me. When I clutch it, I find it a solid, reassuring anchor, a stark contrast to my frail limbs.

"What's happening to you?" he asks me quietly.

As we pass through the hallway and leave the door of the Golden Dome, I look to the Hollows who follow behind us. "One cannot thrive without another suffering. This is a law of nature."

Elias nods. "You speak of competition. In things that perish, it is true. Balance must at times be sought through the diminishing of one so that another can flourish. But it is not true in the case of good deeds. There is no scarcity in the everlasting."

I know why he is saying this. Why he speaks of Heaven. Of not perishing. Of perishing. I study his face and attempt to catch his eye so I can offer some lightness to his heavy words.

He doesn't smile, his gaze fixed on the path ahead, a furrow deepening between his brows. I can feel it in the rigid set of his arm, the almost imperceptible tremor that belies his stoic facade—a deep, quiet sadness. It's the sadness of watching time steal what you cannot reclaim. The grief of seeing a loved one fade.

But in that moment, despite the weight of his sorrow, I feel a warmth spread through me. A precious, fleeting moment of connection, a shared understanding that transcends words. He was quick to forgive, just like his daughter, a trait I have always admired, even envied. He holds my arm, not with pity, but with a gentle, unwavering strength, a silent promise to support me through this. And in that simple gesture, I find a fleeting sense of peace, a quiet joy in the shared moment, a love that time cannot diminish. I suppose there is no scarcity in love either.

He looks down at me as we walk slowly. "I need to tell you something. It's about the place I visited before I was imprisoned. I returned to it after I awoke from my deep sleep after the prison."

"The one AmaNoor sent you to, so you could remember what you forgot?"

He nods. "I found our parents there."

I stop walking. "Our parents?"

"Baba told me to tell you something. He said, 'Should have believed you. Forgive me. Good deeds are the currency for Heaven, but the key is sincerity.'"

A gasp from the Arched Chest, mirroring my own.

I hold onto my brother's arm more tightly. "Are they alive?"

He looks to his wiggling toes and shakes his head. "They were the ones who took the Book far away from the Deep. That's where the vines and the purple flowers came from."

Still so many questions. Why did they take the Book away? How did they send the vines and the purple flowers? Did they ever plan on coming back? I am finding it hard to stand. My legs feel weak. I sit at the top of the steps.

Despite all my questions, strangely, it is as if a cycle has been completed. As if the final piece of what I have been searching for inside has been revealed. I need to know one more thing. "Did they die well?"

"The best of deaths." Elias sits with me.

Martyrs. My parents died as martyrs. I nod. "I hope to see them."

My brother turns and sniffs. "Tell them when you do, tell them, I love them."

I stand. We both stand. I take a deep breath. Feels clearer now. Everything feels a little clearer. The familiar marble steps sprawl before us, followed by the shimmering ones of the Silver Path.

Another roar fades, its lingering echo causing me to turn towards its source. The Hollows spill through the doorway behind us, surrounding us in a silent, reflective wall.

As they do so, Elias turns to me again. "Listen, Adamah." His gaze is intense. "I might not be able to tell you this later, but there are three questions you must know the answer to when you face the angels of the grave."

I gulp. Even he can see how close death is to me. "Tell me."

"The first, who is your Lord?"

"Allah." My voice doesn't waver.

"What is your religion?"

"The way of peace through submitting to Allah."

"The final question is, who is your prophet?"

I repeat the words Elias told Sama in her final seconds: "There is no God in truth except Allah... and Muhammed——"

"Peace be upon him."

"Peace be upon him," I repeat. "Is His final messenger."

He lets out a long breath. "Now, you're ready."

A chill goes through me. One of finality. Of inevitability. *Am I ready?*

"My idea," Noor's voice chimes in. We turn to Noor, who has been focused on Jinnah, her gaze almost casual, as if she were sightseeing. After a few drawn-out minutes, my brother looks at me, a question in his eyes.

"What is your idea, Noor?" I ask.

She meets my gaze. "Oh," she says, her tone light, "save the Queen."

"Noor," Elias begins, his voice laced with caution.

Noor continues, "But to do that, we need to understand her."

"We do," I say softly. "She's angry and wants revenge."

"She still has her wings," Noor interrupts, her thoughts already racing ahead.

"Her wings?" I ask, confused.

"Yes, that's what the buzzing sound is. Why does she still have her wings?"

A good question. The answer is glaringly obvious. I remember the Voice's words about flying to Heaven. "That's what the Voice wanted to use to get to Heaven," I say, realization dawning.

Silence emanates from within the Arched Chest. Well, not quite silence. I lean closer, hearing a constant muttering, a melodic cadence. Not the threads, but ...

"The Queen isn't bad," Noor says, her voice filled with conviction. "She's just really confused. And sad. And a lot of mixed feelings." She turns to me. "Like you had when you first came. Maybe, if we remind her of who she is ..."

Elias turns to her. "There's another part here, Noor. About why the Voice needs the Queen of the orbees to get to Heaven, when it could simply fly there, itself."

I nod slowly. "The orbees are—were—firstly, healers."

Noor continues, "Like the knife, we can use it to build or break, which means—"

"The most powerful healers can also be used to hurt. Their power can make them the most dangerous," I finish.

"Yes," Elias says, with a look I recognize. He knows something. He turns to the Voice in the Arched Chest. "It's true, isn't it? You did try to create an army. You cannot kill an angel."

"I can do anything!" the Voice croaks, the sound barely perceptible through the chest.

The Queen's roar intensifies, my ears ringing with the force of it. "Then her nature is clear," I say, my voice grim. "She is a weapon. She must be stopped."

"Don't kill her," Noor pleads, her voice trembling. "She isn't the bad one. She's just got layers on her, which won't let her be free … she's *good*."

I pause, a shiver running through me at the unsettling degree to which I understand the Queen. I shake it off, focusing on the task at hand. "She might be good," I concede, "but she's dangerous, and only I can stop her."

Elias steps forward, his voice gentle but firm. "Let us help you."

I gulp; the unfamiliar sensation of accepting help makes my throat tighten. I'm not used to this. The idea of not facing this alone … it brings both an ache for a life of mostly loneliness, and a lightness in my chest. At the same time, my eyelids feel heavier, the weariness of this entire body pressing down on me. I am a contradiction.

I nod as I take a deep breath. It still feels shallow. Yes, it *is* getting harder to breathe. "The attachment of the voices to her body made her like this. Rageful. Their nature is fire. Some of it is still on her. It runs through her blood, keeping her rage alive. What is stronger than fire?"

"Water," Elias replies without hesitation.

Noor gasps, her eyes widening. "If the water stops the fire, the Queen might be free enough to remember who she is."

I nod. "The Zam is special; we can use that."

I watch the Hollows. Their eyes are closed, awaiting my orders. They can help. They are made from both vines and metal. They can absorb the water of the Zam. There's enough of them to put out a fire much bigger than the one in Shahwah.

I turn to the Hollows and relay the instructions. Immediately, they prepare to move forward.

I direct my focus to two of the Hollows closest to me. "Guard Elias and Noor."

They bow and nod their head in acknowledgment.

Noor strides ahead with Elias into Jinnah, followed by lines after lines of the Hollows. I wait until the last ones pass the border before stepping forward into Jinnah.

When I do, something pulls me back, an invisible force. I try again, but I'm met with the same resistance.

It's the Arched Chest. A feeble laugh echoes out.

"Wait!" I call to Noor and Elias, but the stomping of the Hollows and roaring of the Queen drown out my voice. I try to enter once more, but this time, I'm thrown back, landing heavily on my back.

I lie here, staring up at the smokeless sky, the stars shimmering with an intensity I've never witnessed before. Alone again. Now that the adrenaline of Noor and Elias is gone, the full weight of my exhaustion crashes down on me. An odd time to succumb to sleep, yet the urge is overwhelming.

"There is only one way you can pass through Jinnah with me," the Voice says in a harsh whisper.

I continue to watch the stars.

Its tone is laced with amusement. "There is a trapdoor under the platform in the carpeted room. It leads to—"

"The Deep," I finish, my voice flat.

I could call back the Hollows with a mere thought.

No.

There are some things that we need people to help us through. Like when my brother taught me how to defend myself as a girl. Like when he mastered his emotions, so he could advise me on how to redeem myself. Like when he and Noor refused to leave my side when I faced the Voice, and now, as I am about to face the Queen of the orbees. I needed Ruqaya to help me give birth to Yahya. Sama, to listen to me as I cried to her through the night, when the guilt of luring the elders out became too strong. When the creeping hate of my body became overwhelming because of what that man did to me.

But this next part: facing the Deep and crossing my darkest place, must be done alone.

A flicker: I am not alone; I have the Voice with me.

A tremble: I have never been more alone than when I was with the Voice.

A realization: I have never been alone. I am *not* alone. *I have Allah.*

With that final thought, slowly, I push myself up, my joints screaming in protest. I climb the steps, each one a monumental effort against my brittle bones. My joints fight me, an ache with a familiar, now chronic pain. I reach the carpeted room.

I fumble with the latch of the trapdoor, the metal hot and unforgiving against my frail fingers, whose roughness does not allow my skin to burn. The trapdoor finally gives way, groaning in protest. I peer into the darkness. It smells *old*. Does old have a smell? Like dust, mixed with aged smoke and stagnant air.

My descent is a jarring jolt, a painful reminder of my body's decline. My weakening frame protests with every step, the stone beneath my feet unforgiving. I walk through the tunnel, expecting the darkness of the Deep. Instead, an unexpected brilliance. Light. How could there be such vibrant light down here?

A wave of dizziness washes over me, a physical manifestation of the dissonance between my failing body and the bright light. I pause, leaning heavily against a rough wall of the tunnel.

Once I am steady, I continue walking. I reach the Main Hall. Orbees! Hundreds of them, flitting and darting, bouncing off the walls. The room grows brighter, blindingly so, and it takes a moment for my eyes to adjust. I finally tear my gaze away from the swirling mass of orbees.

Then, I see them.

The nine.

A couple have fallen from their positions, but the others remain frozen in postures of prayer and supplication, their open palms turned upwards, some with eyes closed, as if time itself has frozen them in an eternal act of worship.

I manage to crawl towards AmaNoor, who is near the altar, facing the direction of the East. Her legs are folded beneath her, head slightly bowed, her hands outstretched, palms open to the unseen.

I sit opposite her, the ground warm and damp beneath me. I knew she didn't know what her husband did. I knew when she found out, she told the other elders. She always spoke the truth about what he had done to me.

But she also hid the truth of what he had done to her.

As a girl, I had seen the bruises on her face, a constant, silent reminder of the violence she had endured. Yet, I couldn't see the whole picture when she returned to us from the prison with Elias and Yahya. After Elias awoke, he left again— now I know to the place where our parents left to.

When he left, Yahya disappeared too. I assumed Elias took my son, but I was wrong. I became blinded by my rage—no, my Mutated Shame. I needed someone to blame, and AmaNoor was a reminder of the man who had caused me so much pain. She became my target. She and all those who followed her, like the parents of the children of the Deep. Like Ruqaya.

"I'm so sorry," I whisper.

I hold out my hands, hovering above her, afraid to disturb the stillness, the peace that has settled over her. I don't want to break her out of the position she died in. An honor to be preserved like this, in submission to our Lord.

A part of me, a surprising part, envies that. To be rid of the trials and tribulations of this world, to end like this. A fleeting thought crosses my mind. *Can the Hollows heal her? Can the orbees heal all the martyrs?*

No. No one can bring the dead back to life.

No one except Allah.

An orbee lands softly on my shoulder, its presence a gentle weight. I sense its nature. It is like a plant. Like a kind of jellyfish, too. It dies and then comes back to life. It regenerates. A sign that one day my body will do the same after it has turned to dust.

The roar is closer now, a deafening crescendo. I must keep going. If I don't, Noor and Elias will face the Queen alone. I won't allow that to happen. Yet, I want to stay here, to sit with AmaNoor. She was the one who believed in me. She fought for me. I see that now.

With a monumental effort, I push myself up.

"I'm sorry," I whisper again, my gaze sweeping across the faces of the martyrs of the Deep. "Peace be upon you all, brothers and sisters in faith."

The orbees, like tiny guides, illuminate my path as I pass the chambers. I pause outside of Yahya's room and smile softly.

Reaching the bubbling pond, I look up. The glimmering hole above, the one that leads to the Surface, is widening, growing larger with each passing moment. It's illuminated by the fiery light from above, a light that dances and reflects off the water's surface, transforming the pond to look like a river of molten lava.

I force myself through the narrow tunnel and into the shallow pond. White spiders crawl over me, their delicate legs brushing against my skin. I let them. I sense they won't hurt me. They have not used their venom since they accidentally killed Amir's parents, all those years ago. Since then, they became afraid of hurting anyone, choosing to remain hidden in the pond, afraid of the power of their poison.

I've climbed this ladder so many times, I tell myself I can do it even in this state, even with my failing body.

But I know I can't.

Not now.

Not alone.

I need help. I turn to my weary vines, which grip the Arched Chest.

I take the first step up, my arm feeling as though the bones that hold its shape are splintering. I pull myself up another step, then another. Each movement is agony. My hips crack, popping out of place. I falter, falling back into the water.

I can't climb this. I can't get up.

My vines flail around me, mirroring my exhaustion. "Do you have the strength?" I ask them, my voice barely a whisper. They respond with a gentle hug, a silent reassurance.

Then, they give me a push. Not enough to lift me entirely, but enough. Enough to make me *want* to push myself up. Another push. One from me. One from them. More pushes. Step by step, I rise, a combined effort of my own weakening limbs and the vines' silent, unwavering assistance.

When I finally reach the top of the hole, something warm and pulsating engulfs me. I'm lifted, carried by the orbees, surging through the opening.

Noor and Elias's eyes widen as they see me emerge, a shower of glowing balls of light erupting from behind me. Yahya is next to Elias, standing behind him like he used to as a young boy. Noor catches as many of the swirling orbees as she can, her face buried in their soft, buzzing bodies.

The Hollows stand silently, organized in metallic rows, their mouths closed and cheeks full, the water of the Zam brimming from their ears and noses.

A thunderous roar erupts, a shockwave that sends the orbees into a chaotic frenzy. They scatter, throwing me to the ground, the impact cracking my weak bones. The pain is destabilizing.

Another primal scream of rage and grief thrusts me back to the stark reality of the situation.

I turn, my gaze unwavering, to face the Queen.

PART 30
The Stars

ADAMAH

Askinless worm. Her body writhes, a grotesque dance of exposed muscle and bone, the swirling mass of smoke-colored mini-tornadoes obscuring her true form, making her seem … obsolete. No longer in her orbee form, she is faceless. Only five protruding orbs glow with an eerie light from the tip of her monstrous form.

The ground beneath her crumbles, collapsing into the fiery pit from which she rises. She expands, growing wider and taller, reaching beyond the skeletal remains of the once colossal building in Shahwah, a building now reduced to melted metal and dust that lines the edges of the pit, mixing with the Dark Fall, which hardens the metal with its coldness.

Through those five orbs, she stares at me, a laser-focused gaze that pierces through me. I am unable to look away, drawn to her.

Even with my fractured limbs, the pain fades away. *Everything* fades away as I edge towards her. I am vaguely aware that I edge dangerously close to the precipice of the pit. She lowers her head, closing the distance, until I am no longer looking up, but straight into the abyss of her gaze.

"Your children live," I say, my voice trembling slightly.

The Queen roars, her voice a cacophony of distorted sounds. I don't know what she is saying.

"They are confused," I whisper.

Her orbs lock onto my eyes, and a wave of disorientation washes over me. I take a step closer, and the rock beneath my feet crumbles into the pit of fire.

I can't look away from those eyes.

Two hands grab me, pulling me back from the edge. Yahya. I blink, unable to fully shake off the daze.

Yahya moves me out of the way, and Elias turns to me and shouts above the roars, "The Hollows won't listen to me."

I nod, still slightly disoriented. Turning to the Hollows, I manage, "Follow Elias."

They bow and nod, their metallic forms shifting to him in response.

I collapse to the ground. My limbs feel heavy, unresponsive. Even my vines are limp, devoid of any strength. It is as if the stare of the Queen, the emotional impact of everything that has happened since the Cast died, Sama dying, learning of my parents' death, and facing AmaNoor in hers, has plunged me forward into my final moments of life.

"Are you ready?" I hear Elias's voice, faint and distant, as if through a thick fog.

"Ready," the Hollows reply in chorus.

"Front line, throw!" Elias shouts.

The first line of the Hollows ejects a torrent of water from their metallic mouths, like a powerful hose. The water strikes the Queen, and she thrashes wildly, her huge form convulsing. I can feel her orb eyes on me. I try to raise my hands to cover my ears, desperate to block out the sounds of her pain, but I can't. My hands feel like bricks. I don't want to fight her. I don't want to hurt her. I don't want her to be in pain. I don't want this.

"Second line, throw!" Elias commands.

Yahya is sitting beside me, his lips moving, whispering something. I can't make out the words; everything feels distorted.

I look up, my vision blurring. I can't see Yahya's face.

"Is it working?" I manage to ask, my voice weak.

The slurping sound of the vines, the rhythmic intake of water, abruptly ceases.

"The Zam isn't working!" Noor shouts.

There was a time my vines could shatter through the Queen's leaves, where they could shatter the Voice's threads. Now, I cannot even meet the gaze of the Queen. She is too powerful.

A realization dawns on me. Strength won't stop the Queen. So, what will? Though I cannot move my body, my legs fully numb, I can still think clearly. She *is* like me. Her love for her children has triggered her rage, and now she can't see clearly.

No. Strength won't stop her.

It didn't stop me, not when the Pale Tree blocked my way forward and I bashed into it. All it did was make me fall. Nor did trying to provoke Noor into fighting back through my jabs. Force will only make us want to fight harder. Both times with the Pale Tree and Noor, I was not fighting them; I was fighting myself.

I lift my gaze to the vast, star-studded expanse above, exposed, even with the smoke. The orbees, once a coordinated force, now flail and dart erratically, their movements frantic and desperate. Their light is flickering and wavering against the backdrop of the looming night.

Their frantic dance is a silent, desperate plea, a reflection of the chaos that threatens to consume us all. They are no longer a unified force, but individual sparks of light, lost and afraid.

I look at my boy's face, clearer now, and smile. I finally understand what the Queen needs.

"Stop!" I whisper. I can only whisper now.

Yahya raises his head and shouts, "Stop!"

Everything stops. The Hollows, Elias, and Noor. They stare at me expectantly. I look at Noor and whisper, "She needs to remember."

Yahya repeats my words.

Elias rushes over. "Why are you—"

I glance at Noor, who stands beside Yahya, both watching the Queen, unaffected by her gaze, unknowing of the turmoil that consumes me, steps away.

I nod, attempting to speak, but my vocal cords don't work anymore. Not even to whisper. I blink at Elias: *It's almost time.*

He lets out a small, sharp gasp. He opens his mouth to speak, but I shake my head, silencing him.

"How do we make her remember?" Noor asks, breaking the tense silence, oblivious to the silent exchange between my brother and me.

I blink: *Light*.

The orbees flutter around Noor. Her words come back to me from when she ran inside Thanae through the open door of the Great Wall.

Hold on to the light, so you don't fall asleep.

I blink to Elias: *The Queen needs the light, so she can fight the darkness inside her. To remind her of who she is.*

The numbness spreads through me, creeping upwards from my legs to my belly. I can no longer feel anything below my waist. It reaches my chest. With the last vestiges of feeling in my hands, I weakly clutch at my throat, gasping for air. Only shallow, ragged breaths escape my lips. My head is light, my vision blurring, my eyelids heavy. Yet, strangely, there is no pain. Not yet. Only a creeping emptiness.

Noor looks down, realizing the weakness in me. She holds my face in her hands, placing her forehead next to mine. She is shivering from the cold of the Dark Fall. Her tears fall on my cheeks, making the cold dust wet against my face.

I try to wipe her face, but my hand won't move.

A child this young should be laughing, not crying. But the children of Thanae stopped laughing in abundance long ago. Our laughter died when Earth's second shield shattered from the blasts unleashed by the self-proclaimed 'Chosen' that fell from the sky, diminishing our land to rubble.

How could our children laugh when instead of playing games, they were carrying pebbles to fight giants? What choice did we have when the 'Chosen' offered us a new home, in the same land they tried to take from us? One where we would bury ourselves beneath them at their request, just so we could live. What choice did my ancestors have when the world watched and those in power did *nothing*?

The worst betrayal of all for my people was when those who claimed to be of the same faith remained silent as the bodies of our children, the ones who stopped laughing, piled up. When the bodies of their parents joined them.

I remember my Mama and Baba's last message to me before they left. They told me they had to find the light. That we had to wake up. Then my Mama sang the song of our nation, a song I thought Elias taught me, but now I remember it was her: *I will stay here until the pain goes away, I will live here, so the rhythm one day will change.*

My fleeting body reveals a truth: just as the greatest fight is internal, so too is the greatest fight within the very people of our faith. The Chosen and other external enemies won't be the cause of our nation's demise.

Our dark fall will be from within us.

Cowards. Hypocrites. The ones I could not stand the sight of amongst us, so I wiped them out.

I regret it. I regret it all. I wish I could have reminded them, reminded myself of the light of this faith—the Truth—so we didn't fall asleep again.

And again.

And again.

I turn my attention back to Noor. Elias was right. She should just be a child. But this is not the world we live in. Has it ever been?

When she looks at me, I blink: *The orbees know you. The Queen is not threatened by you. Return her children to her.*

Noor wipes her face; her eyes filled with a resolute determination, and she stands.

When I look ahead, my vision, though fading, is momentarily clearer. Noor stands on the precipice of Shahwah's fiery pit, her small figure silhouetted against the fierce glow. She raises one arm, the orbees hovering above her, and whispers something to them. They are frantic, confused, and their lights flicker erratically. She continues to whisper, her voice soft but insistent, and one by one, in a steady line, they begin to circle the Queen.

For a moment, the Queen stills, her monstrous form frozen. Then, she roars, a sound different from before. Not a roar of fury, but of a heart-wrenching sadness.

The orbees, one by one, float towards the Queen's body, absorbed into the grey layers of smoke that swirl around her. They dissolve into her, each one a tiny act of surrender, of homecoming. With each absorption, a thin layer sheds from the Queen's skin, a shedding that continues until she grows smaller and smaller, her monstrous form diminishing.

Almost all the orbees have been absorbed into the Queen, but a disturbing transformation is taking place. The layers on her body are rebuilding, thickening, and she is ballooning in size, growing larger than before. She screams, a raw, piercing sound of agony, her pain sending shivers down my spine as she battles the forces within her.

"Fight the pain," Noor says through gritted teeth, her face streaked with tears.

Elias gently touches her arm, and she collapses into his embrace. "You can't fight the pain, Noor," he says softly, "you have to feel it."

Noor looks up at him. "That's my lesson, isn't it?"

"That's everyone's lesson," Elias replies, his voice filled with a gentle wisdom. "Do you remember what I taught you in prison? About language?"

She nods, her eyes wide and attentive. She says, "You can only use it if you allow yourself to understand it."

I don't know what they are talking about. What has language got to do with anything? She looks down at her hands, which are shaking uncontrollably, and at her chest, which is heaving with rapid breaths. "I can't do it alone."

"You're not alone, Noor." Elias grips her hand and holds it in his.

A small dot gleams through her dress, marking the wound on her chest. A similar dot appears in the palm of her hand. The small lines of light come from the scars that crisscross her skin. They join to form a larger shape. The container of this gleam is her arm.

She has it. She has the ability of light. It's entwined within her flesh, wrapped around her body, spreading outwards. It outlines her lungs, her heart, until it reaches her other hand, a shimmering, luminous cocoon.

Once it reaches her chest, the light surges through her entire body, racing through her veins like a torrent of starlight. Even through her clothing, I can see the light emanating from her skin. Her eyes are closed, her mouth clenched, her entire body trembling with the intensity of the light within.

My brother stands beside her, his light a beacon in the growing darkness. Yahya rises to join them. With all my strength, I try to grab him, managing to barely stroke his arm.

The Queen stops thrashing, her monstrous form shrinking as the layers of darkness peel away, ascending into the sky, taking the rest of the blackness of the smoke with them. The stars, previously partly revealed, are now shining in all their glory.

Noor's body begins to convulse, her breaths coming in short, ragged gasps. But she clenches her hands more tightly, her forehead creased with the intensity of her focus and the discomfort that accompanies this newfound power.

She is even closer to the edge of the pit now, a single, crumbling rock the only thing preventing her from plunging into the fiery depths below.

Yahya turns to me and says gently, "Mama, you have to let me go."

I let go of him, even though I was barely touching him, and he lunges after Noor and Elias, just seconds before they fall into the pit and drags them to safety, both lying next to me, Elias's eyes flutter open, but Noor's remain closed.

Yahya looks over them and fumbles with something purple in his pocket, breaking it and scattering it over Noor's and Elias's mouths.

When he finishes, he comes over to me to do the same. He scatters the purple flowers over my mouth, which are scentless and tasteless. Nothing happens. He tries again. Nothing. He becomes more forceful. I use my remaining strength to shake my head.

"I have to fix this," he mumbles, as he prepares to distribute the flowers differently, trying to crush them in his big hands.

I catch his eye and blink: *I am not broken. There is no cure for death, Yahya.*

He blinks and looks away. I wait for him to return my gaze. When he does, I blink: *Purple is the color of the dead who look alive*, echoing my brother's words from a dream he had long before he even knew what the purple flowers were.

The same purple flowers that were used to create the gas within the Hollows. The same purple flowers that healed Noor's chest, despite the hole through her heart.

Back in the Golden Dome, when the Voice tried to tell me Yahya had followed my legacy of murder, Elias reminded me of his dream of the purple flowers.

Now, I raise my eyes to Yahya and blink: *You tricked the Voice into thinking you had killed the children. When I saw you here again, you kept saying 'safe'. You were counting them, weren't you?*

Yahya nods and says, "I knew if you saw what I could become, you would see that killing was not good. I had to make sure you believed it, because the Voice would too. That was the only way I could convince it to let me stay, so I could wait for you. Take care of you."

I try to nod, but I can't.

"There is one more v-v-voice which holds the Queen," he continues. He stutters when he is scared. And I can't help him. His eyes flit to the Queen. "*My* voice. I need to use my light to take it away from her, Mama. No one else can do it but me."

The roar of the Queen shatters the moment, tearing us apart. Yahya winces in pain at the loud noise and then, grits his teeth, breathing heavily, gently removing my hand as he steps back, towards the Queen. His fingers are flicking as he pulls away from me.

I need to get him away from the fire.

But I can't.

I can't.

Yahya turns to me and says, "I have to, Mama."

I blink, pushing tears out of my eyes: *I just got you back.*

"My s-silence gives power to my voice," he says.

I blink: *I don't want to lose you again.*

"You will never lose me, Mama. You never have. I'm fighting," he says, looking down. "I'm fighting, Mama." He glances at Noor, whose eyes are fluttering open and closed. "She showed me how."

My weak fingers try to grip his hands. I don't want to let my son go. I blink: *Yahya means life.*

My body slumps, and the letters fall out of my dress. My vines meekly offer them to him. A tear rolls down my cheek as he takes them and puts them in a pocket near his chest.

"I used to fear death," he says. "Now I fear a life with no meaning." His lips brush against my hand, sending a fresh wave of tears from my eyes. I know how hard it is for him to express his emotions, and this simple gesture feels like he has opened a part of himself that he has kept hidden for so long.

When he looks at me, I blink: *Then live*.

"Let me go, Mama," he says softly. "I fell, now I need to——"

Rise. He needs to rise. Like the Black Assad did. This is the way. Though my body has let him go——it does not have the strength to hold on——I let him go in another way.

As he rises, parts of his life flash before me. Now I am not reliving those memories, I am witnessing them.

I thought there was something wrong with him when he was born. It was his cry. High. Often.

Then, it was the way he would watch the fire burning. He would sit cross-legged for hours, looking at the flames as if memorizing each ember, after which he would look at his hands. Then, there was the way he would not look me in the eye. Months went by until finally, he met my gaze.

His behavior made the others move away from him. Elias stayed and became closer to him, sitting with him and talking about his inventions whilst teaching him the Tap.

Soon, Yahya began to communicate more, but in a way that was different from the Deep.

He had taken the Tap and used it for something else.

One day, something had changed in the Deep. A new light illuminated the cavern, casting strange, dancing shadows on the walls. It wasn't the fire. This light was from Yahya's body. An ability.

A gift.

He was sitting there, his eyes closed, his hands glowing with that soft, ethereal light. He had made a map of the Deep, which was projected above his head, each tunnel and chamber clearly defined, through shadows he had moved around to create it.

He was two years old.

Then, Yahya noticed the picture of a butterfly on my wall. He would fixate on it. I told him about it, how this creature was from the Surface. How the Surface could fit all of us in it and how wide and beautiful it was, even though I had never been.

Soon after, he started to speak the language of the elders, a language of words. Some of us could still use our voices, but most were mute. A self-imposed mutism, born from the abandonment of our mothers and fathers. In my case, it was from the guilt of being the cause of that abandonment.

Those of us who *could* speak spoke in a specific way. In a drastic way. Saying words like *ecstatic* instead of *happy*, *shocked* instead of *surprised*, *terrified* instead of *scared*, *depressed* instead of *sad*, *loath* instead of *dislike*, *enraged* instead of *angry*.

We went to extremes in everything.

Some became focused on rebuking everyone else. Rigid. Rule-driven.

Others became focused on 'love' and nothing but 'love'. Overly loose. Overly permissible.

When the Voice became evident, we were ready for whatever extreme path it displayed to us.

But how did Yahya know the language of the elders so clearly when their children didn't? It was a language of less extremes. More balance. I followed him one day. I found he had rebuilt the ladder to the Surface—the ladder I had kicked off after I showed the elders the place beyond it. The ladder Yahya built was sturdier.

He had been going through the Ghar to listen to the conversations of the Surface.

I climbed the ladder, avoiding the spiders, which I now realize where avoiding me after they had killed Amir's parents, and put a lock on the door of Ghar, so he couldn't leave anymore.

He distracted himself with other things. He built. Small things at first. A lamp, to hold the torch of fire, which kept it burning for longer. He was eight years old.

As he grew older, his creations—like him—became more complex. He invented a system of pulleys and levers to make it easier to transport heavy objects through the winding tunnels. He designed a device that could purify the cave's water, which for a long time was just for show in the Main Hall. His invention made the water safe to drink. Useful. He also created a network of lights, powered by his energy. These lights lit up the entire Deep.

But something changed with him. As more children were born into the world, he became increasingly withdrawn from me and would have more outbursts, ones where he would break all his inventions. During this time, the only person he would speak to was Elias. Yahya told him the voices were too loud and something bad was going to happen.

Then, Yahya disappeared.

I searched for him and found the lock above the ladder broken. As I began to leave the Deep to go after him, Elias stopped me. He said he would do it. That it wasn't safe up there. Not for me. He said to practice my fighting while I waited. To take care of his wife.

I told him I was strong enough. He told me to listen. That if the Surface found the Two Nation Treaty broken, they would have grounds to crush us in the Deep, reducing our underworld to rubble. The risk was too high. If he got caught, he could take care of himself. He knew the loopholes of the treaty. Said Mama and Baba told him. He wouldn't tell me what those loopholes were. Now I know there were none. My brother just wanted to keep me safe.

So, I stayed and waited.

And waited.

For one month. Then, two. Nothing. On the second day of the third month—I remember the day because Ruqaya had been counting the days of her pregnancy—there was a knock at my door. Someone had left a box, the same one I had received soon after the elders left. It had disappeared for years, but there it was again, delivered to me. I didn't think much of it at first, but I liked its simplicity.

I wasn't used to gifts, so I kept it next to my bed. Then came the Voice. I think it was always there, but I had never paid attention to it. Until it became too loud to ignore. It taught me how to read and write, didn't it? Why am I not so sure anymore? Then again, who else could have taught me that? It's not important. I used the skill to write letters to Yahya. I put all the letters in the box—the Arched Chest.

After writing another letter to Yahya, I had had enough. I was sick of waiting. I made a deal with the men that I would bring down what they admired—an 'angel'—they agreed.

I took the knife. And the Voice. I climbed up the ladder and reopened Ghar.

A lot happened after.

I got my son.

I lost him.

Now, I have him back.

Yahya turns towards the Queen and raises his arms. The light within my boy is more powerful than any who had come after him. No one knows why. Perhaps it is because he was the *first* to unlock the ability. Perhaps, there is something special about being the first.

Yet, for the first time, I wish he didn't have it. Then, he would be with me, safe. A flicker of truth: I am not safe myself, not from death.

A small light emerges from his chest as he stands before the pit of fire, traveling down his arm to his fingers. The threads of his cloak let light beam from them. His body is getting smaller. His face and hands, peeling.

He endures the pain. His light grows brighter. I try to run to him, but I can't. My body won't let me. It is shriveling. Shrinking. Fighting the sobs so I can see clearly, I keep my eyes fixed on my son.

The Queen is shrinking too, finally exploding with a blinding flash, throwing layers of debris upward. It crashes above the sky, clearing the final bit of smoke to reveal a rising sun.

The sky is clear.

It is dawn.

Yahya did it.

She is free.

A flutter rises from the pit. The Queen. Her majestic figure emerges, a creature of immense size—50 of the orbees clumped together—her smooth, elongated stinger glints in the rising sun. She hovers above Yahya, her wings creating a gentle breeze, before landing delicately on his face.

She then darts towards me, her body vanishing in my ear. A tingling sensation. She says: *I am sorry.*

With a final, resounding buzz, the Queen flies away, joining her children, who are now free from her form. Hundreds surge around her, and they fly up the hill to Jinnah.

I try to rise, but a sharp crack echoes through my thin legs, a bone snapping under the strain. I try again, another bone breaks, and I wince against the pain, my vision blurring.

I can't tap. I can't speak. But as always, my brother, who seems to be there just when I need him, comes to my side. I blink to him: *Take me to my boy.*

He lifts me, my body now completely limp, my legs broken. He gently places me beside Yahya, leaning me over him.

His body is frail and shrunken, a stark contrast to its former fullness. The smoke and fire have ravaged the skin on the rest of his body, leaving it scarred and blistered. Yet, where the Queen had hovered over his face, the skin is smooth and flawless, a testament to her lingering power. Even his thick eyelashes have grown back.

As I lean over him, a single tear rolls down my cheek, landing softly on his closed eyelid. As if sensing my presence, his eyes flutter open, revealing a look of wonder and confusion. In his hand, he clutches the crown, its jewels now consumed by fire, revealing its true, ancient form. A plain, rounded, golden ornament. No spikes, no adornment. Just pure.

Yahya looks up, his eyes rolling back. I haven't seen him smile very often, but he smiles now, deepening the lines around his eyes, which crinkle.

"I did it, Mama!" he whispers.

I blink to him: *My brave boy. It won't hurt anymore, I promise.*

A heavy silence falls over us, and I fight back tears, determined to be strong for him. Determined to keep looking at his face.

He mumbles something else, the testimony of one God. None other than the one God. His gaze is fixed on something behind me, and he smiles. A final whisper, "Yes! Yes."

His body goes limp, mine does too.

On top of his.

I have lost the will to live.

My heart stutters, a sharp pain radiating through my chest. My vision flickers, the edges darkening. My lungs struggle for air, shallow, burning breaths. The taste of copper fills my mouth.

Dizziness and disorientation wash over me, the world spinning. My skin begins to crack, a dry, brittle sound. Nausea and stomach convulsions. Everything convulses.

A cloud descends, but through it flashes. Memories, broken shards. A face. His face. Who is he? It's *him*. A whisper of a name, sweet and aching, on the tip of my dissolving tongue as my skin gives way to bone. But the name, what is his name?

Clip clop.

Clip clop.

I smile.

ELIAS

The Hollows are on the ground, a curious blend of metallic sobs and serene smiles, echoing the strange tranquility in Adamah's expression. I pull Adamah and Yahya close.

"Choose to live Adamah," I say, my voice firm but gentle.

She looks at me. Her eyes are accepting. She blinks: *I have. Many times. I've chased life, and now it has brought me to death. I'm ready.*

I nod, suppressing the emotional surge. "How does death look?"

She blinks: *Kind.*

Her feet, folded under her, begin to disintegrate, returning to the dark material that blankets the ground, mixing with the black icy dust that falls from the air. Her hands tremble slightly, a subtle acknowledgment of the change. She turns to me and blinks: *What's happening to me?*

"Your body is returning to the Earth."

She blinks: *And the thing which gives my body life?*

"To its Creator," I answer.

She smiles and blinks: *Home. I'm going home.*

She looks at her son, then at the crown, now resting beside him, and then at Noor. I know what she wants.

I look over towards my daughter, Noor. She sleeps soundly, her toes twitching, a soft murmur escaping her lips. I rest Adamah's body on the ground with Yahya beside her.

I lift Noor gently, carrying her to Adamah, placing her in front of us both, so her feet face where the Great Wall used to be.

Adamah watches peacefully as I raise the crown and place it upon Noor's head.

Adamah smiles, a serene expression, and begins to crumble, her hands turning to dust. She stops smiling and looks ahead, past Noor, to the desert. A small gasp. She blinks: *The wall is gone!* Her eyes shift around her, resting on the Hollows. *I'm here.*

I ask her, "What do you need?"

She blinks: *Prostration.*

I place her body in the posture of prostration, towards the East. Her head touches the ground, and she closes her eyes.

I force the lump in my throat to go down.

The rest of her physical form dissolves into dust, filling the air around us before settling on the ground.

The Hollows' forms dissolve, the metallic shells giving way to a surge of vines. The vines snake and thread their way towards the fiery pit, the metal remnants forming a protective boundary around the flames, blocking it as the vines melt a hardened cover on top of it.

"To Allah we belong and to Him, we return," I whisper in the language of my ancestors.

ME

You are gone. I am unbound. I survived the first few recitations of that verse. Then, another voice joined me.

I was released from the Arched Chest. It is, after all, a fundamental misunderstanding of my nature to believe I could be so simply confined by human hands.

The Voice that came to me … Mother. Her recitation, ancient, primal, a linguistic echo of the very genesis of things. The Book. She recited the Book.

I drift above the Scholar … Elias. I address him. "Do my kind change?"

A question, perhaps, pointless. I already know the answer. The other voices of the now-deceased Cast are a shimmering chorus around Mother and her path, which is the same as Adamah's and her brothers.

Elias remains unresponsive. I amplify my vocalization, a subtle shift in the resonant frequency. He turns, as if sensing a disturbance in the quantum foam. I whisper, a near-silent vibration.

He pivots, his gaze settling on my direction.

"Create your kingdom of believers. But stay away from my kind. Fire and clay will never mix," he states. His voice is a low, resonant hum.

Is that a promise?

Or a threat?

Or a truth?

He buries his head where his sister's body once lay and sobs into the earth.

What? Did you—the reader of my story—expect some grand, theatrical display of justice at the end? Some reckoning for all the pain I've caused? I implore you, dear reader, to be honest with yourself.

The end of my story has not yet arrived.

If it did and I *had* chosen to remain upon this path, my end would be Hell. But if the *end* is—in your narrow vision—a simple worldly closure for your itching need for justice, then I pity you. There is no true and full justice in this world. There rarely is for the proud tyrant.

Justice comes in the next world, even *I* am aware of that. Why else did I try to rewrite The Book of Decree?

That ... truth of justice, an impending doom for the oppressor, a liberation for the oppressed, is more terrifying than any earthly punishment.

I hold myself together, preventing a final, shattering collapse. I know now, with chilling certainty, that I cannot force my way into Heaven. Nor can I deceive my way in. *No ruined spirit will enter Heaven.*

I know the one thing I have control over is my book of records. One which leaves me with a sobering thought. I have two choices. Two paths. One which leads me to a blazing fire more violent and more painful than my own. Another, to a garden where everything I have ever wanted becomes real. To matter. To belong.

Both paths are of everlasting life. Both paths are places where death does not live.

Mother. She leads, and we, the voices, dissolve into the desert's haze. Yahya's voice, a silent observer, remains, lingering there above his dead assignment, looking slightly frazzled as to what to do next, now that he is free.

I pause above the graves of the Cast. I gather the letters Adamah wrote for her son and sigh. The Hollows are all gone. And what of Father's message? I never did receive it, did I? Did he invite me back? Did he apologize? Do I care?

I turn back towards Yahya's voice, with a sneer. *I do care.* I hope ... I hope he will relay my movements to Father.

My story has not ended. Not yet.

NOOR

The first thing I notice is how colorful the sky is, like a big painting. The smoke—the smoke is gone! Someone is crying behind me, and I turn my eyes upward, whilst still lying down—I am too tired to get up fully.

I can't see who is crying. A golden hat blocks me.

Still, I get myself to sit up. Stretching my toes now, that's a bit easier. Before I can turn back, a loud noise makes me jump. A kind of … song.

I look to where the noise is coming from. Just ahead, where the Great Wall used to be. Whoever is singing is a blur. That's how far away they are.

But then, everything becomes a little clearer. People. A group of people, with small creatures next to them. Ones which walk on four legs and have colorful fur with round ears. Like open leaves. Dogs. I've seen a dog before. Only for a little while before it left Thanae again. It had a snout. And it was smaller than the Black Assad. *Much* smaller.

There are also other creatures. These are *much* bigger. They look like Lashes and Smiley. I gulp away something in my throat. With a shaky breath, I turn back to the creatures. They have no bumps on their backs and smaller feet.

Now, the people are closer. They walk on the Silver Path. Some of the people ride the interesting creatures. I like their colors: white, black, and brown. I never thought of riding Lashes and—I gulp again—Smiley.

It looks fun.

I push myself up so I can stand. The song fills the air again. I know what it is. Elias sang it in prison before he did his prayer. I thought it was good that he still prayed even though his chains stopped him from moving much. I know, now, that the sound is the Call to Prayer.

I look up towards the sky, the colors are more even now, with a few bits of pink and orange scribbling through the blue. Hmm, they're late—but better late than never, I suppose.

I look at the people walking beside the riders of the creatures. They wear cloaks, the same brown color as the orbee tree trunks. Altogether, including the riders … seventeen, eighteen, nineteen … twenty. Twenty people.

The Call to Prayer echoes through the air again.

"Come to prayer!" It is a deep voice, a man's voice.

The voice is gentle, which is why I'm not afraid.

"Come to success!" he adds. He sounds nice.

The person reciting the call lights up, the light shining through the threads of his cloak. Others do the same.

They look like stars.

The figures become clearer as they come closer. One of the riders climbs off a creature and walks in front of the others.

This rider is wearing a dress that goes past their knees. They also tie the bottom of the dress around their ankles, like my friend Adamah. Where *is* Adamah?

The rider comes closer before I have a chance to turn around. Something about the way they walk draws me in. I think, how a person walks says a lot about them. This rider is not scared. They are gentle in their steps, as if they are careful not to hurt the ground.

I feel a pang shoot through my chest. I don't know why or what it is, but with it comes some tears. I blink them away before they fall, so I can see better.

As the rider comes closer, I breathe more quickly. They take a step forward, and I take a step back. The golden hat brushes against my ankles. I don't look at the rider, but I know they look at me. I want to run away.

Slowly, I look. When I do, I can't look away.

Deep black eyes. Long eyelashes. One eyebrow.

Like me.

She removes the veil from her face. A kind, roundish face. There are lines like squiggles around her mouth instead of her forehead. There are more around her eyes.

I stare at her. She is just a few steps away from me. I can't move. Wait, I can. My legs are already moving. They are shaking. A lot. Like her hands. She brings those hands to her chest, so they stop shaking a little bit.

She walks those last few steps, slowly. She is even closer to me. Now, she is in front of me. So close. I look up to her. I touch the lines around her mouth.

She takes my hands and brings them to her lips, closing her eyes, which are filled with tears. She kisses my fingers, something that feels strange and— I can't think of the right word. Why can't I think of the right word?

The Call to Prayer has ended, leaving the air feeling a little empty, except for the Dark Fall. Even the coldness of that feels far away, right now. The crying behind me has stopped, too.

"I have lots and lots of friends!" I say. "I used to have camels, but they're gone now. But I still have the orbees, a-and there's a place up there called Hadeeya!"

She looks me in my eyes, her eyes are all sparkly, and she smiles. "Can you show me?"

I nod.

But then, my legs go all wobbly, and I start to fall. She catches me. Her arms are strong and warm, and she holds me up. I let my eyes do the thing they've been wanting to do since I first saw her.

I cry. She holds me as I cry into her. Safe, that's the word I couldn't think of before. I feel safe.

Two more arms wrap around me. Elias. I peek up to see him putting his big forehead on hers.

He whispers, "Zawjati."

Then we all look up at the falling dust. It falls in heavier drifts now, blanketing everything. Even the sun. It makes us all shiver, as we huddle close together.

ENDNOTES

[1] Quran, 13:28

[2] Quran, 4:28

[3] Quran, 67:5

[4] Quran, 112:1

[5] Quran, 112:2

[6] Quran, 112:3

[7] Quran, 112:4

[8] Quran, 103:1

[9] Quran, 103:2

[10] Quran, 103:3

[11] Quran, 17:105

[12] Hadith 6, 40 Hadith Qudsi

[13] Quran, 12:92

[14] Quran, 24:35

[15] Quran, 1:1-7

[16] Quran, 7:23

[17] Quran, 114:1-6

[18] Quran, 55:33

[19] Quran, 51:56

[20] Quran, 2:164

[21] Quran, 2: 255

[22] Quran, 18:57

Acknowledgements

This book was a six-year journey written amidst two pregnancies, a house move, and earning both my Islamic and Social Work degrees during the challenges of COVID-19. Despite facing procrastination and perfectionism, perseverance saw me through.

I am eternally grateful to my incredible husband for his consistent support, time, and the intellectual exchange that sustained my momentum. My daughters, my greatest muses, with their inherent hope, anchored me to the story's purpose. Their beautiful spirit is channeled into the character of "the Girl." I love you all.

The legacy of my parents infuses this narrative: my mother's resilient spirit shaped my main character, and my father's passion ignited my love for storytelling. I also thank my sister for first planting the vital seed for this book.

My heartfelt gratitude extends to my dedicated team at Strange Inc., especially my editors, Rumki Chowdhury, for her unwavering support, and Khadijah Hayley, whose insightful feedback was my compass. Thank you to Vivien Ries and Cassandra Kokenos, the gifted illustrators, and to Smashed Gird Studios for the stunning cover art. I also want to thank Abdul Moiz for his wonderful work on the internal design.

Above all, I thank Allah (SWT) for the inspiration, for the beautiful religion of Islam, and for deepening my connection to it as I wrote this journey to redemption.

I stand in solidarity with those enduring hardship in countries like Palestine, Kashmir, Sudan, Syria, and beyond. This book is dedicated to the strength and spirit of the children in these regions who navigate profound trials every day.

Finally, I acknowledge a significant source of inspiration—one that fueled a profound need to tell the story of those who confront darkness and face individuals like "the Voice." Their influence, though disturbing was undeniable in shaping that character.

About the Publisher

Strange Inc. is a New York-based nonprofit publishing house dedicated to empowering the authentic voices of Muslim women. Born from a passion to uplift the creativity and diversity within the Muslim community, Strange Inc. champions narratives often misrepresented or silenced in media and politics. Guided by the Quran and the Sunnah, they operate with a commitment to truthfulness and excellence, collaborating with Muslim creatives worldwide to foster positive change through faith-based art. Since refocusing their mission in 2022, they've published notable works and cultivated a supportive community for Muslim women writers, striving to ensure their stories of faith, integrity, community, and culture are heard loud and clear. Find out more about Strange Inc.: www.strangeincorporated.org.

About the Author

 Aishah Alam is a New York-based author from Leeds, England. She is a certified Integrative Somatic Practitioner specializing in childhood trauma, and she uses her background in social work and Islamic studies to write compelling stories that explore spiritual and human experiences. Aishah is also the founder of Strange Inc., a nonprofit publishing house that supports Muslim women writers. Her previous works include nonfiction and a children's book. She lives in New York with her husband and two children. You can find out more at **www.aishahalam.com**.